ASSAPH MEHR

MURDER IN ABSENTIA

PURPLE TOGA PUBLICATIONS

Book cover design and layout by, Ellie Bockert Augsburger of Creative Digital Studios. www.CreativeDigitalStudios.com

Cover design features:
Tempio di Segesta: © mickyso / Dollar Photo Club
Statue Humaine: © Jean-Marie MAILLET / Dollar Photo Club
Griffin #01, fantasy series, with clipping path: © Ralph Kraft / Dollar Photo Club

This novel is a work of fiction. Names and characters are the product of the author's imagination and any resemblance to actual persons, living or dead, is entirely coincidental — with the notable exception of a few long dead Greek and Roman artists and philosophers.

Published by Purple Toga Publications, Sydney, Australia.
ISBN 978-0-9944493-1-3
5th printing

National Library of Australia Cataloguing-in-Publication entry : (paperback)
Creator: Mehr, Assaph, author.
Title: Murder In Absentia / Assaph Mehr.
ISBN: 9780994449313 (paperback)
Series: Mehr, Assaph. Felix the Fox ; 1.
Subjects: Detective and mystery stories.
Fantasy fiction.
Dewey Number: A823.4

FOREWORD

This book is born of love of both fantasy and ancient Rome, with a hardboiled detective thrown in.

I have always been fascinated by ancient history and, in particular, Rome, from the time I was in primary school and first got my hands on *Asterix*. This was exacerbated when my parents took me on a trip to Italy — I whinged horribly when they dragged me to "yet another church with baby angels on the ceiling", yet was happy to skip all day around ancient ruins. Life took a few twists and turns, but a few years ago I randomly picked a copy of Lindsay Davis' Marcus Didius Falco novels in a used book fair. I fell in love with Rome all over again, this time from the viewpoint of a cynical adult.

The backdrop for this novel is the city of Egretia. It is a fantasy setting as I did not wish to be constrained to a particular period in Roman history, with its associated people and troubles. Instead, the setting borrows heavily from a thousand years of Roman republic and empire eras as well as other exotic places of the period, such as Alexandria. I have appropriated many Latin terms, using and abusing them for this fantasy world. Most, I hope, can be understood from the text, but a glossary and some notes at the end should help elucidate.

Lastly, I want to offer my thanks to the people who encouraged and helped me with this book. First and foremost my wife and inspiration, Julia. My friends and family who acted as editors — Ramit Mehr and her husband, Eric Klein, and my friends Alex Abrate, Boaz Karni and Lipakshi and Rakesh Das. This novel would not have been as good without you.

I hope you enjoy reading this novel as much as I did writing it.

Assaph Mehr
May 2015
Sydney, Australia

MAPS

High-resolution maps — as well as an expanded glossary, short stories and more — can be found at **www.egretia.com**.

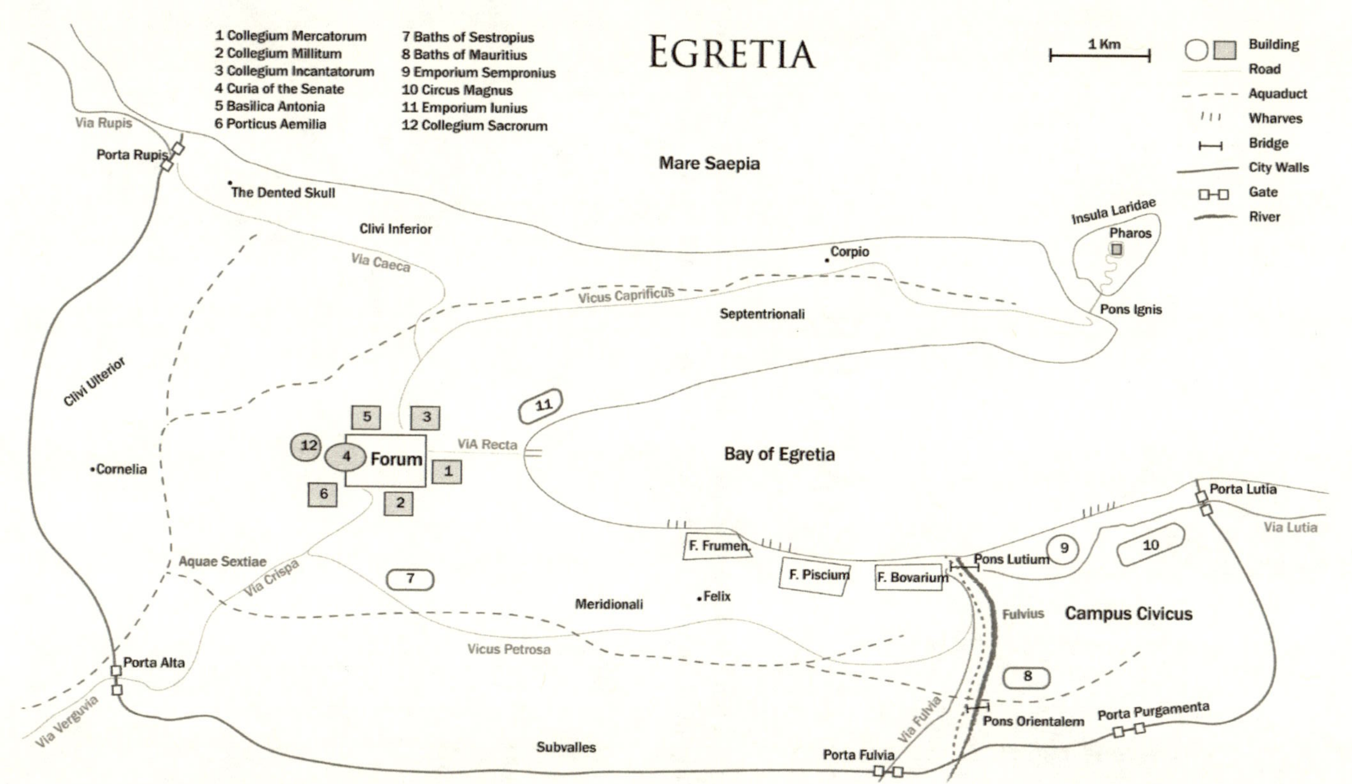

EGRETIA
1 Km

1 Collegium Mercatorum
2 Collegium Militium
3 Collegium Incantatorum
4 Curia of the Senate
5 Basilica Antonia
6 Porticus Aemilia
7 Baths of Sestropius
8 Baths of Mauritius
9 Emporium Sempronius
10 Circus Magnus
11 Emporium Iunius
12 Collegium Sacrorum

Building
Road
Aqueduct
Wharves
Bridge
City Walls
Gate
River

Mare Saepia
Via Rupis
Porta Rupis
The Dented Skull
Clivi Inferior
Via Caeca
Corpio
Insula Laridae
Pharos
Pons Ignis
Vicus Caprificus
Septentrionali
Clivi Ulterior
Cornelia
Aquae Sextiae
Via Crupta
Forum
ViA Recta
11
Bay of Egretia
Porta Lutia
Via Lutia
F. Frumen.
F. Piscium
F. Bovarium
Pons Lutium
9
10
Fulvius
Campus Civicus
8
Meridionali
Felix
Vicus Petrosa
Porta Alta
Via Verguvia
Subvalles
Pons Orientalem
Porta Fulvia
Porta Purgamenta

EGRETIA - COUNTRYSIDE

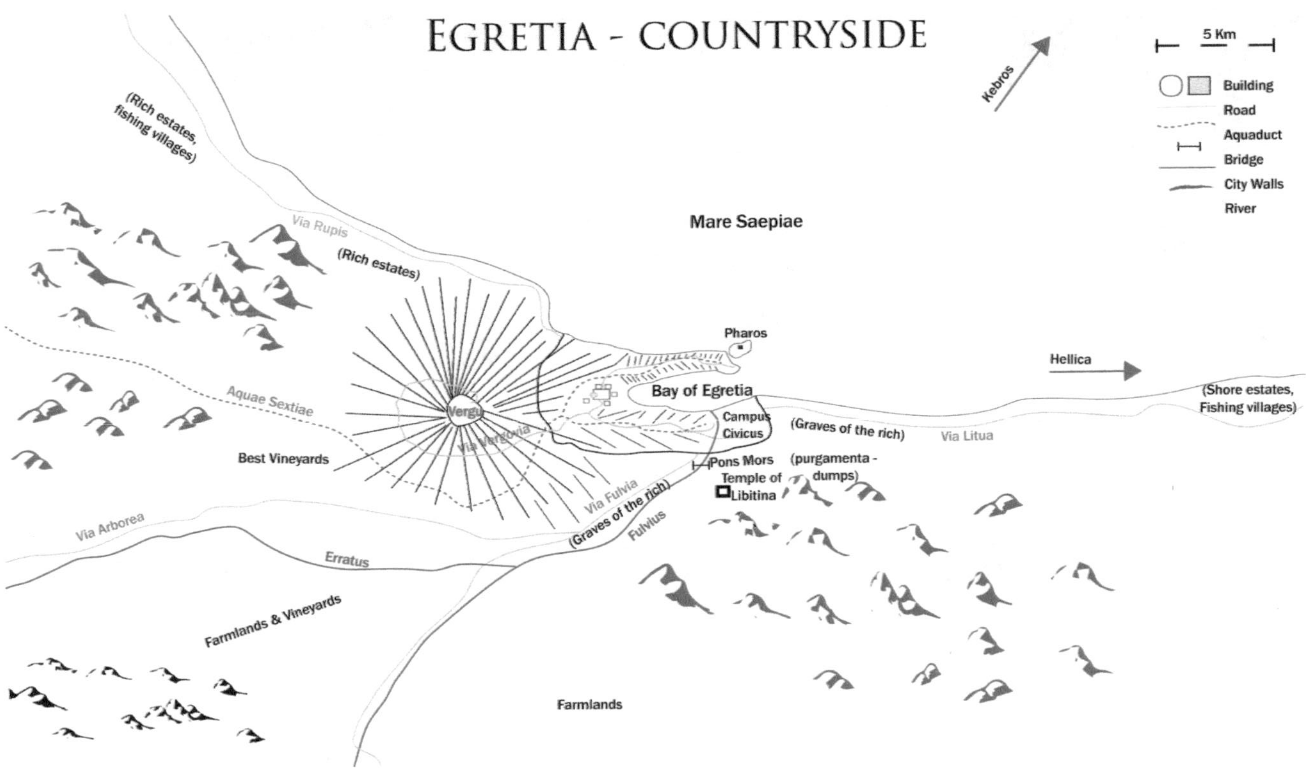

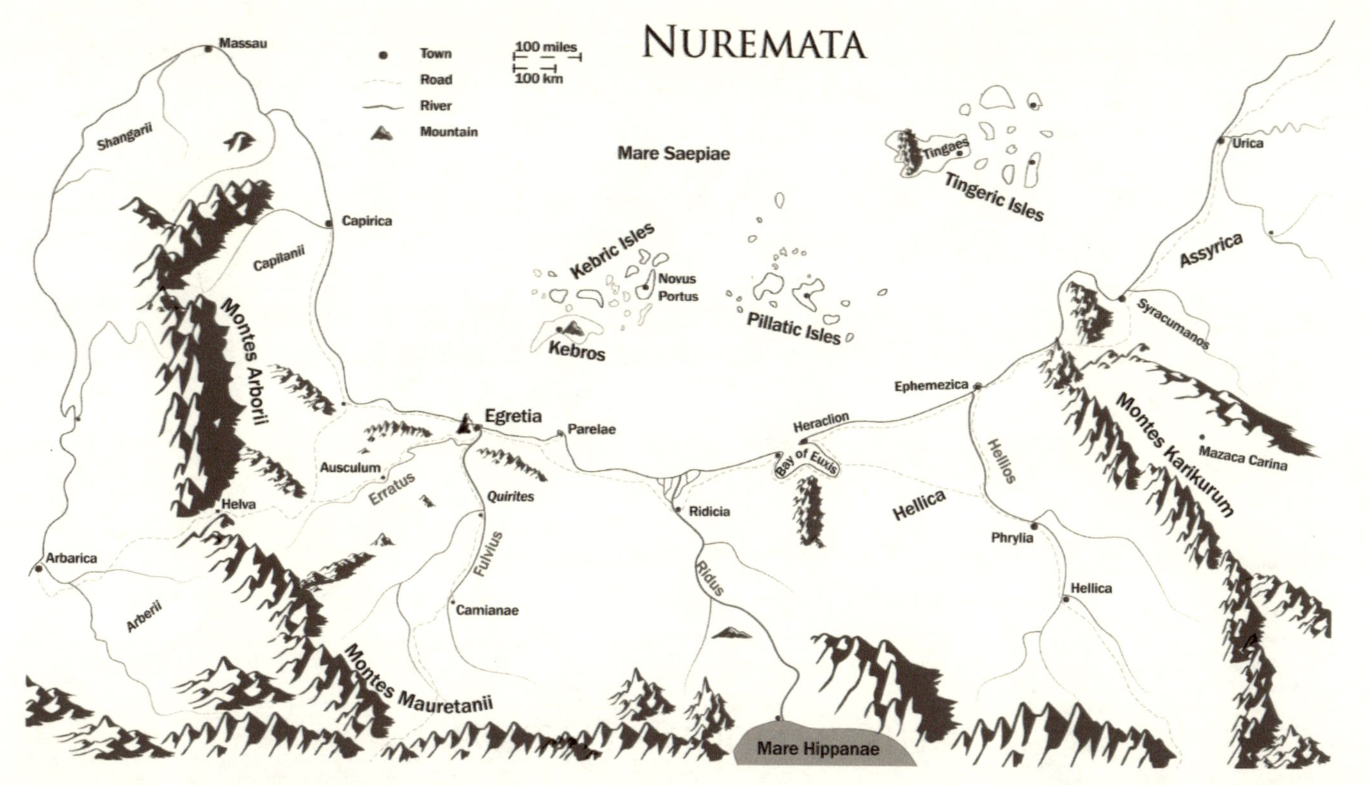

NUREMATA
Town
Road
River
Mountain
100 miles
100 km
Massau
Shangarii
Montes Arborii
Capirica
Capilanii
Ausculum
Erratus
Helva
Arbarica
Arberii
Egretia
Parelae
Quirites
Fulvius
Camianae
Montes Mauretanii
Mare Saepiae
Kebric Isles
Novus Portus
Kebros
Pillatic Isles
Tingaes
Tingeric Isles
Ridicia
Ridus
Heraclion
Bay of Euxis
Hellica
Ephemezica
Hellios
Phrylia
Hellica
Mare Hippanae
Urica
Assyrica
Syracumanos
Mazaca Carina
Montes Karikurum

SCROLL I - CAESO

CHAPTER I

Walking through the dense wood I could hardly see the ground, for the faint moonlight did not penetrate the canopy of trees and a thick white mist was curling around my legs, obscuring roots. I tripped and fell, got up, walked on. Vague glimpses in rare breaks amidst branches offered me faint stars that were not enough to show me direction. Before me, around me, behind me, between the trees, all I saw was the fog. I kept walking, avoiding branches and roots, drawn inexorably towards my unwanted destination.

The clearing.

I slowed as I walked out from between the trees, taking careful steps across the moonlit grass. At the clearing's edges, out of the corner of my eye I saw what I thought was moonlight reflecting in eyes, the sheen of purple-black fur, but whenever I turned I saw only grey-white mist and leaves.

I edged to the middle of the clearing. The grass looked like brittle shards of silver in this light.

In front of me loomed a well. I knew that was where my destination lay, the reason for my being here.

I walked over to it. I placed my hands on the stones of its sill and turned my head to look up to the stars. I stared at them and they blinked back at me coldly.

I steeled myself to face the well. Face what was inside it. That was why I was drawn here. To make me confront the thing down its depths.

I didn't want to, but I had to. I circled the well, so that I would not obstruct the moonlight, let it shine on its contents.

I turned my gaze down and saw the armless, legless body floating in the well, face down. As I was looking at it, it bobbed and flipped around and I could see the bloated and decomposed flesh, the scars marring the marble breast, its face deformed, the stare in its vacant right eye, the maggots eating away the left eye-socket and through the cheek, and even through all the ravages and the filtered moonlight I recognised her…

I am certain the neighbours heard my scream as I sat up in bed.

"Dascha!" I cried, "Dascha, you old crone, where are you when I need you?"

No use. Deaf as a dead donkey when she sleeps, that one. I should have sold her years ago, however no one would pay me for that useless old bat. Besides, she was the last living reminder I had of my parents.

I got up in search of water to wash my face. Not being one to insist on social graces, I stumbled naked out of my sleeping cubicle and into the peristyle garden. I shoved my head under the cool fountain waters. Head cleared of cobwebs, I looked up and saw the rampant faun grinning madly at me as it peed fresh water down on me. That statue at the top of the fountain was the work of a nameless artist, and rightly so. The upper body of a man, the legs of a goat, a mad look in his eyes, set above a leering grin. The right hand holding high a lyre, the left clutching at a member that would make Priapus envious. My father's impeccably horrendous taste in interior decor.

Day had dawned. Dascha must have gone down to the markets for fresh bread and produce for the day. I went to the kitchen, raided it for some old crusts and went to my study. I looked at my desk and saw the open scroll by Nikander, cataloguing and establishing a taxonomy of venomous monsters, with a plate with leftovers of last night's chicken in fish sauce on one side and an empty wine goblet on the other holding it open. Those must have been responsible for my night terrors and I was in no mood to pursue them further, even in the daylight.

I decided instead to immerse myself in the memoirs of Plautus. His life, according to him, was even more farcical than his plays. Nothing high-brow about him, all foreign kings and concubines, indigestion and inebriation.

* * *

Dascha ambled into my study, bringing me out of my reverie. "A visitor, *domine*," she announced with her croaky voice. "Of the paying kind."

It was mid-morning by then, the sounds of the city in full swing around me. Dascha must have returned from her shopping and busied herself with the sundries of household maintenance while I had been reading. Most people have a door slave, a large burly type to intimidate potential visitors and deter the less savoury element of society from making a forced entry. I had Dascha. This has proved sufficient on three counts — first, I had no money to pay for a proper door slave. Second, with Dascha giving her one-eye-squinting stare, naught but the most stout of heart would do anything except mumble and move away. Third, in my line of business a crone is akin to good credentials. Even a fake crone.

"Well, show him into my study, and then come help me into my toga," I said.

When I walked back into my study, dressed appropriately to do business, I saw before me a fidgety young man. He looked apprehensively over his shoulder, as Dascha was eyeing him with a slight mad drool.

"Dascha, bring us some wine and cold water," I dismissed her. I walked around my desk and sat in my backless chair, indicating to my guest to do the same in the client's chair in front.

"My *dominus* would like to hire your services," he began as soon as he sat down. "The matter is private and urgent, and my master will be willing to pay for your time. If you would come with me, I will take you to him right now."

I looked him over. Dressed in a plain tunic made of good fabric, with a circular embroidery outlining a fish and an *amphora* on the left side of his chest. Healthy looking. Soft hands. A scribe or secretary, wearing his master's insignia.

"So what does one of our esteemed *rhones* want from me?" He didn't register any surprise, so my guess must have been correct.

"I have only been asked to fetch you, Felix the Fox. *Dominus* did not authorise me to discuss details; however, the matter is important. My master will pay well."

'He can afford to,' I thought, 'being one of the fifteen *rhones* elected this year to administer Egretia.'

Dascha appeared in the doorway carrying a tray with a silver jug of wine and a jug of cold water. She set it on my desk, and I offered my visitor the refreshments.

"Well watered, if you please," he replied, resignedly.

"There are some things we need to discuss before I will accept your master's summons. Let's start with your name and your master's name."

"My name is Typheus, and I serve his most excellent Marcus Quinctius Corpio, *Rhonus Piscium*."

"And what does the Rhone of Fish need from me? Surely he has access to all the resources of the Collegium Mercatorum, and, one would hazard, to those of the other collegia as well."

"That, as I explained, you will have to hear from my master's lips alone."

"What can you tell me, then, to satisfy my curiosity and assure me I will not be wasting my time?" Not that I had better plans for the day, but I could smell good money coming my way.

"Really, the matter is of utmost importance to my dominus. It is personal and does not concern his position of Rhone of Fish. It is also urgent." He looked like he hadn't gotten much sleep the night before. "Please come," he pleaded.

"Very well, I will go with you if you agree to my terms." I quoted him double my usual rate and added "plus expenses." He acknowledged it without a blink.

"Let's go," I said, finishing my wine and wishing I had tripled my rates.

* * *

We took the alley down from my house to the Road of Unsavoury Smells, or as it is more commonly known, the Street of Cheese Makers. My house, you see, lies on the Meridionali, the Southern of the two arms of Vergu that make the Bay of Egretia. Not the more fashionable Septentrionali, the Northern arm, or the ludicrously rich slopes of Vergu itself, but still high enough from the docks and meat markets on the bay shores to be considered decent.

Typheus walked ahead in a brisk pace, taking me further down the hill and angling towards the Forum at the head of the bay. He walked confidently through the warren of alleys that lead down to the water, rather than going the long way by the Vicus Petrosa, the main road that runs along the ridge of the Meridionali behind my house.

We reached the shores of the bay and walked along the embankment, with its wharves and storehouses, towards the Forum Egretium.

"So tell me, Typheus, what kind of man is your master?"

"A good man, quicker of mind than of temper. And right now, a very distraught man, one whom I would gladly see served well."

"And the place we are going to?"

"His *domus*."

Not the talkative type. Or maybe just loyal, which is why he was entrusted with the errand of fetching me.

When we reached the head of the bay with its official navy wharves, instead of heading towards the Forum we turned right and continued to walk next to the water, passing between the wharves and the Collegium Mercatorum. We were heading towards the Septentrionali, rather than up the slopes of Mons Vergu. Most *rhones*, even the lesser *rhones* like Corpio, would be rich enough to own houses on the high slopes, above the Forum. Some, however, preferred not to remain too close to their colleagues, or to keep close to the business districts, or even just to remain in their quiet ancestral houses.

We went past the Emporium Iunius and climbed up the Septentrionali, joining the Vicus Caprificus to walk along the ridge of the hill that runs throughout the Northern arm of the bay. The neighbourhood changed gradually as we ascended, from wharves and silos and porticos of merchants and artisans, to mansions of increasing size. The further up we went, the longer the distances between side alleys and doorways, and the fewer the features on the walls facing the street.

This being early in the month of *Avrilis* right after the spring equinox, and the day still young, I did not mind the walk. It gave me both plenty of fresh air and a chance to think about what business might a *rhone* have for such as me.

I tried again.

"How is the Rhone's health these days?"

"His excellency is a man in his prime and in excellent health."

"And his business?" I added, "This past winter has been mild, no storms to speak of."

"His business is prosperous, as always. The new-season cuttle-fish are now in the market, the people are happy, and his year in public office is off to a good start."

"A personal matter, then."

"A most personal one, indeed."

"His wife…?"

"My mistress has been dead these past seven years," he said with a stony face. "Please, let us just get to my master, and he will explain the matter to your satisfaction."

I gave up and resolved to enjoy the walk and the view.

* * *

We reached Corpio's *domus*. It was located past the crest of Septentrionali on the cliffs side, away from the noise and smells of the markets around the lower shores of the bay. On a clear day like today, from the houses at the very top of the hill one can see the whole city — the bay with the Port of Egretia and its wharves, surrounded by rising slopes of red tiles on the other side and going up the mountain; to the north one can see the wide blue sea. Almost as importantly, from up here one cannot see the squalor and misery of lower Egretia, or smell the cramped humanity with its life of markets, cooking and refuse that lie beyond the crest of the Meridionali away from the bay.

Corpio's mansion presented an unassuming facade to the street. A blank wall, painted in muted russet colours. A large oaken door with brass knobs and lashes was set deep in the wall, flanked by tall cypresses on both sides. A tile painted with the family crest of fish and *amphora* was set into the wall next to the door. Typheus knocked politely, and a small slit opened up and closed a second later. The heavy door swung inwards.

"Please wait here," said Typheus, "as I go and announce you to my master."

I remained as told in the vestibule. Through the open doorway, I could see a large atrium flanked with columns, with corridors and doorways running further in. The natural light filtered through the open roof and shimmered on the shallow pool filled with goldfish and embedded with mosaics depicting sea life. The columns around were painted turquoise, and the reflected light dancing upon them gave a feeling of an underwater grotto. 'This must be his ancient family home,' I decided, as the effect was too refined to be anything less.

Typheus returned. "Follow me, please," he said, and led me through the house to his master's study, gestured me inside and then followed me in and closed the door.

Though I knew of him, as I followed the forum gossip about all our elected *rhones*, this was the first time I had encountered Corpio in person. It pays to keep abreast of the movers and shakers, though I find it best to stay out of their way or risk getting crushed in their politics.

Corpio was in his early fifties, a large and healthy man, getting soft around the middle. Long nose, high cheekbones, the bronzed skin of his face and arms showing signs of much wind and sunlight, as did his sun-bleached blond hair. His eyes were bluish-green, now shot with red as if he had been rubbing them. He must have spent much time in his youth on ships out at sea, but since gone soft from spending more of his days on land for his public career.

"Come in and sit down, please," He indicated a chair in front of his desk, into which I lowered myself. "I have knowledge of your reputation, Felix, and more importantly I have knowledge of your discreetness. Both are of the utmost importance to me at this time. Do we have an understanding?"

I nodded my assent. It was my experience that when men who have risen high in society open like this, the details will come only on their terms.

"This is a personal matter, one where I have need of your special skills. It does not concern the other *rhones*, nor the Senate. Whatever you may find, you are to report to me and only me."

I merely nodded again.

"This matter concerns my youngest son, Caeso." There was a catch in his voice as he said his son's name. He stared at me and blinked several times. I remained silent, letting him collect himself. "My son is dead. He was found last night in most unusual circumstances, which I require you to investigate.

"My son… my youngest son Caeso… he was not like his elder brother Marcus, never found his sea legs and was never interested in our family's business and traditions. And yet he was his late mother's little darling. I tried to bring him up to be a man as befitting his heritage, bought him the best tutors and exposed him early to our life. Unfortunately, he hadn't showed any interest in that. Always more interested in wines and poets, never anything respectable. Nothing kept his attention for more than a season, and yet he was gregarious, full of life and vigour, out and about with his friends.

"Late last year something changed. He became morose, secluding himself for days on end. At first I thought this to be just another phase, as all his affairs of the heart were quick to pass, but soon his studies were affected. I arranged for him to travel to my brother on Kebros. I thought perhaps a bit of travel and sea air will improve his health. My brother Publius Quinctius promised to look after him and get his mind off from what was troubling him. He has a big country estate as well as many businesses there, and we hoped to entice young Caeso out of his doldrums. I sent my friend's son, Gnaeus Drusus, with him.

"At first this seemed to have worked. My brother had written to me that life amongst the isles seemed to have done Caeso well, even if he was not interested in learning about the family business. They came back at the end of the shipping season, and resumed their studies.

"However, over winter his health seemed to deteriorate. He became pale and thin, wasting away. I called for the most renowned *magisteri carneum*, the best physicians money could buy, but he refused to see them and claimed that he needed no medicine.

"I then decided to send him on a sea voyage again, this time for an extended period. However, when I informed him of my decision yesterday, he became distraught. He absolutely refused. At first he argued that he simply could not be away from Egretia, that I was sending him into exile, ostracising him and might as well just execute him. When I persisted, he became hysterical, frantic. He started to abuse me in the most offensive language. I had my steward confine him to his room. We could hear him railing and wailing for a while, and then he seemed to calm down."

He stopped and took a deep breath, steeling himself. "My steward was closing the house at midnight as usual. Being fond of Caeso, he went into his rooms to check on him. Caeso was not in his room, but my steward thought he merely sneaked out to find food. He searched for him, and was about to call me when he saw Caeso come back from the street. He saw him proceed to his room, and was satisfied that my son had regained his senses. However, in the morning when he went to check on Caeso, he found him in his bed, dead, and upon his face a horrible grimace. His face… You will soon see that about him which made me question the circumstances of his death. If for no other reason than to please the shade of his mother my late wife, I would like to know how — and why — he died last night."

* * *

We walked together, Corpio himself leading us with Typheus following behind me. We crossed the atrium, went through a short passage and entered a large open garden. We were headed towards the living and sleeping quarters, located at the back of the mansion. As we drew close, I glimpsed a loggia facing the ocean, with magnificent open vistas visible between the columns.

"No one knows yet," continued Corpio as we walked, "besides the three of us and my steward. We kept the door locked and ordered the staff away. After the initial shock, Typheus recalled stories about you and your… expertise in these matters."

We stopped before a closed room, and even from this side my skin tingled and I could smell that tell-tale odour. The door was guarded by a short, bald man with a harried look, which Corpio introduced as his steward. He nodded at the man, who unlatched the door and opened it. "See for yourself," said Corpio. "We left everything as we found it."

I stepped into the room. The shutters were still closed, and morning light filtered through the cracks, its angled rays providing faint illumination. I could see a figure lying on a sumptuous sleeping couch and smell the voided bowels.

I stepped closer. Caeso was on his back, body straight, kept taught and rigid by rigor mortis, his arms by his side and his backside lifted clear off the mattress. He appeared as if frozen in the middle of a spasm of pain. I looked at his face and the impression was made stronger. His eyes screwed shut, nostrils flared, mouth in a rictus with bared, clenched teeth. One could almost hear his teeth grinding in death.

I have seen people die, some with terrifying spasms of pain. I have seen men die and their bodies left to freeze in a fixed position in rigor mortis. Yet never have I seen someone die and their body freeze in the middle of such a spasm.

Under the smells of sweat, urine and faeces was that acrid-sweet scent which meant I had a serious paying job ahead of me. I walked to the window and opened the shutters. I heard a stifled cry behind me. I turned back to examine the body. Caeso was about eighteen years of age, a handsome fellow. Shoulder length, honey-coloured hair. Smooth skin, strong chin and cheekbones, long nose. A picture of health, were it not for the obviously painful death.

I approached the bed and ran my finger lightly along Caeso's forearm. I could feel the goose-bumps of his flesh, and the tingling that ran up my own skin became almost palpable. I knelt down beside him and with my hand tried to gently pry open his eyes. The muscles of his face were screwed tight, and refused to be moved. I tried the same with his mouth, but got no further. His teeth were clenched so tightly they showed hairline cracks.

I drew back his light sleeping blanket and exposed his body. I heard the sharply drawn breaths behind me, and had trouble myself not to react. Caeso was a young man, with good physique. He was lying in front of us, naked, with body held rigid and backside raised off the mattress. But that was not what caused the gasps. On his chest above his heart was a livid, red-purple tattoo with the outline of a seven-point star. From it, spokes radiated along his ribs, enveloping his torso and keeping clear of his abdomen. I leaned closer and could see faint traces in blue that worked their way around the red lines, all of which extended down his sides and on to his pelvis and genitals, spiralling around his manhood.

The acrid-sweet smell, the tingling touch, the tattoo — it was enough to confirm the general cause of death, but I needed more information and this was the only opportunity I would have to gather it. I drew my knife from inside my tunic and looked back at Corpio. "May I?"

He stared blankly at me.

"I need to… extract some samples. I will open his mouth and his eyes as I need to look into them. This will not be pretty, but I will not disfigure him. I have to ascertain certain things to be able to investigate his death."

He turned even whiter than before, covered his mouth with a kerchief and nodded faintly.

"I may be able to reset his features," I added to try and ease his pain. "You should be able to hold him on the customary bier without much sign of the way he died."

I turned back to the corpse. The easiest way would be to break his jaw, however, I had just promised his father to keep him presentable for a proper funeral. From my dagger's sheath I pulled out a couple of very small and very thin blades that were stored in special pockets in the side of the hard leather. I ran my finger along his jaws towards his ears, feeling the bunched muscles. At the point below the ear where the muscles terminated and attached to the bone, I placed one of the small blades at a sharp upwards angle and stuck it gently with the hilt of my dagger. It slid in and I could feel the ligaments rolling under the skin. His face acquired a lop-sided expression, half relaxed and half in rictus, like a person who suffered a stroke and went mad. I repeated this on the other side, and his whole jaw became relaxed.

I unscrewed the back of my dagger's pommel and extracted a tightly-wrapped parcel. I carefully unrolled it and took out a thin, sharp sliver of light-coloured wood from amongst the contents. I pricked my finger with it and then chewed on its bloodied end.

I braced myself against what I knew was coming, and moved so that my back would hide the corpse's head from his father. I put my hands on his jaw with my thumbs pressing on his chin and forced his mouth open. I pulled the sliver of wood from between my teeth and poked it as deep as I could down the throat, bloodied end first. A noxious cloud of foul-smelling, thin black vapour escaped his teeth. I shut my eyes and held my breath, leaning back to avoid getting it in my face. I heard retching and retreating feet behind me. There was no mistaking the boiling, bubbling, melting sounds and the foetid smell of putrefied flesh as the wooden chip blackened when touching his oesophagus. I hastily moved closer to the window and saw that Corpio was leaning weakly in the doorway, Typheus was on his knees in the garden, and the steward was gone. Corpio was doing better than I expected, I must say.

Caeso's jaw now slack, I retrieved my thin blades and set to work on his eyes. These would be harder to relax without leaving more visible marks. We always look to people's eyes to connect with them, to feel their humanity. A person's eyes tell you so much about them, without a word crossing the gulf between the two of you. We fall in love with a look. Poets far better than I have scribbled many a verse on the subject.

But what awaited me behind Caeso's eyelids when I finally lifted them up was decidedly not human. At first all I could see was a yellowish ball. When I coaxed his eyes around to face the front, there was no trace of original irises, just a red hexagon lined in black. I let them roll back inward and let the eyelids to snap shut. Better that way.

One last thing remained. I placed myself so the watchers would not see my next actions, as what I was about to do was *nefas*, sacrilege. I moved next to the corpse's torso, and carefully cut the skin down from his solar plexus along the line of the ribs, trying hard not to cut across any of the red and blue markings on his chest. I did the same on the other side, and ended up with a bloody red wedge on his abdomen pointing up at his sternum. I inserted the tip of my dagger under the skin at the top of the triangle and lifted it gently, then rolled the skin back to expose his inner organs. I set to work separating the layers of flesh and muscles. I reached inside, gingerly pushing my forearm half way to my elbow under his ribs, making my way down through moist innards and up past his lungs before I felt the calcified mass where his heart should have been. I withdrew it, yanking and cutting gently with the knife where it still connected to flesh and veins. I could feel its hard facets as I grasped it tightly. At last I stood up and held out my hand, the light from the window reflecting in the blood covering my arm. In my hand was what had been Caeso's heart and was now a large heart-shaped ruby.

"It would pay for a lavish funeral if you could sell this," I said, "but I doubt you would find a buyer. This is most definitely the product of necromancy."

CHAPTER II

I walked lazily down the hill, thinking of my next move. As I was nearing the harbour, I became aware of the time by the pangs of hunger. I stopped at a roadside stall and bought a squid-on-a-stick, roasted with garlic and spices. Our city may be named after the regal birds that grace our shores, but our people march on squid.

Back in Corpio's study, after he had recovered sufficiently to walk there without aid, we shared a pitcher of unwatered wine, just the two of us. "But why?" he kept mumbling, "My beautiful boy, who would do such a thing?"

"You know as well as I do that necromancy is illegal in Egretia, and indeed everywhere else across Nuremata," I said. "This predates the founding of our city. To my knowledge, the Collegium Incantatorum has managed to enforce this quite well, both internally and whenever we encountered it among the barbarians."

"Of course, of course. This just makes it all much more perplexing. Caeso had never shown any interest in the *incantatores*…. Naturally, I had him enrolled in the Collegium Mercatorum, as our family has been for ages. He was not a star student and I didn't hold high hopes for him, but he had never shown an interest in the other collegia…." Corpio was rambling, gulping his unwatered wine at a rapid pace. I let him continue, grunting my sympathy to keep him going. "I tried to push him in the right direction, naturally, as any concerned father would. He never objected, though I could see his heart wasn't in it. He was far more interested in attending plays and parties, even the street mimes interested him more…. No head for numbers, that one, and never got used to the sea. His late mother and I indulged him, being our youngest, and once she passed away…. Perhaps I was not as close to him as I thought I was, as I should have been. What is a father to do? If he would have voiced an interest in the other collegia and presented a good argument I would have let him go; I have my Marcus to continue with the family business when I am gone…"

"Tell me about his friends," I asked.

"He attended the college with the son of my good friend Gnaeus Drusus Scaevola. Drusus *filius* still lives with his parents, not far from here. Caeso and he had known each other since they were little, as our families have always been close. Drusus is not even a year younger than Caeso…. But that doesn't matter any more, does it?" His eyes filled with tears.

I remained silent as he dabbed at his eyes and sipped more wine. He took a deep breath before continuing. "Drusus will be able to tell you about his social and college life. He has been in the college for two years now, so was not such a freshmen that my Caeso would shun him. Drusus always looked up to him, you know.

"Besides Drusus, I have heard him mention Gnaeus Porcius and Gaius Lutatius. I met them both briefly in the Forum once, but I do not really know them or their families all that well. Respectable, albeit not in our circles. I am sure, though, that they had visited Caeso in this house. I am often away sailing, both due to my business and to my duties as the Rhone of Fish, as you can imagine. Caeso was a good boy, still young. I only let him wear his manly toga the year before last. I held him back till the last moment, hoping to keep him a boy for as long as I could…. But a boy he still was, and had entertained his friends with my best wine when I was gone. My steward will be able to tell you more, and Typheus, too, perhaps.

"He would have had other… acquaintances… amongst the mimes and performers he liked so much, although of course I am not acquainted with any of them. Caeso was intelligent enough to know not to sully the ancient family name of the Quinctii Corpiones with too overt a relationship. A young man of our class may cavort and fornicate with the street trash as much as he likes, but never treat them as equals." I could hear the steel in his voice, see the flint in his eyes. Distraught though he may have been at the death of his son, he still came from an ancient family of senatorial status, and had risen to be elected a *rhone*.

Deeming Corpio's constitution sufficiently restored, I began to approach the less savoury events leading to his son's death. "How much do you know of Caeso's last few days? I ask, because while not much is known about the actual workings of necromancy, sufficient information has filtered through the ages. The tale of Servilius Ahala from the days before our people founded Egretia is still taught to our aspiring *incantatores* as a tale of caution. Necromancy was a dark offshoot of the *magia vita* by our reckoning. In all our encounters with its manifestations, it was an elaborate process with lengthy ceremonies, many participants and arcane requirements. It was not something one dabbled in, and the signs are taught to our young *incantatores* so that should a necromancer arise again our whole state would unite against him."

I looked into Corpio's eyes. "So please forgive me. I really need to know everything odd about your son, whom had he met and where he had been in his last days."

"I was here, busy with the *Contio* of *Rhones*. With the winter now over, shipping has resumed. While I haven't gone for any extended length of time this year, I did have quite a bit to oversee of both my private enterprise and in my official capacity. When I was home, though, Caeso was always alone. He had been neglecting his studies, and had been looking ill, as I mentioned, though by the end I had given up on the physicians. Not because I do not trust them, but because they agitated him even more and he would refuse to come out of his room and meet with them. I will instruct Typheus and my steward to answer your questions. You can have the run of the house, though I would remind you to remain discreet."

I sat up in my seat, gathering my toga. "One last question, Rhone, if you please. Why me? Surely you suspected the nature of his death. Why not contact the *rhones* of the Collegium Incantatorum?"

"I thought that would be obvious. At the end of this year I will have to step down from the office of *rhone*, but that is not the end of my public career. I am in good standing to be granted concessions to open sea routes around the Cape Massau. Surely you are aware of this through the forum gossip? A scandal such as this would spell the end of my political career, and the total collapse of my business. All of my family's business, including my brother's, would collapse, as no one would trust us ever again. The name of the Quinctii Corpiones will be forever blackened, and the work I have done on the treaties from Massau to Urica would collapse.

"I will not risk this! I will not have one of the *mentulae* in the Collegium Incantatorum hold this over my head, or even just blabber drunkenly to his mistress, only for the name of Egretia itself to be tarnished amongst all the nations around the Mare Saepiae!"

He forced himself to recompose. He sat back in his chair and folded his hands in his lap, took a deep breath. "Your reputation precedes you, Felix the Fox. While some of your sordid history is known to me, so have you managed to rise from it on the back of your integrity and confidentiality. What I need now from you is absolute discreetness. I wish to know the circumstances of my son's death, yes, but I do not wish to see my world collapse around me. Caeso was young and, as we clearly know, foolish. Yet I do not believe that in his heart he was rotten. Find out for me who did this to him, find him and deal with him and keep my name out of it, and I will see that you are well recompensed."

* * *

I finished my squid and almost wiped my hands on the hem of my toga. Dascha would cluck her tongue at me, should I return it with fish sauce stains. After my mother's passing she had taken it upon herself to care for my appearance, and her values and aesthetics were just as conservative. I kept walking down to the harbour, stopping to wash my hands and take a drink from a public fountain.

When I finally made my way down to the waterline of the bay, I turned left to the east, instead of right towards the Forum and the direction from which we had come in the morning. This way would lead me to the mouth of the bay and the small island of the Pharos lighthouse. The view and the clear air, I hoped, would bring me fresh ideas as well.

I walked on the promenade that runs along the inner shore of the Septentrionali. The sea traffic on this side of the bay mostly revolves around private jetties and moorings. Most commercial wharves are on the south side, on the Campus Civicus and along the base of the Meridionali where the great markets are. I walked past private yachts, ranging from small, fast sailing boats to gargantuan pleasure barges powered by tiers of rowing slaves.

The alleys going up the hill disappeared between the blank walls of the mansions of the rich, with the occasional fig-tree-lined avenue offering public open spaces and routes back to the Vicus Caprificus that runs along the ridge of the hill.

Interviewing Typheus and the steward at Corpio's invitation had not provided me with further details. They had both corroborated Corpio's account of the events, confirmed that Caeso's friends Porcius and Lutatius had not been as close with Caeso as Drusus, though they had visited him recently nonetheless. Neither Typheus nor the steward had had any insight into Caeso's activities with his friends. He did not seem to have confided in them, which was not unusual, and he had kept his activities outside of the house to himself. Being a student at the Collegium Mercatorum and still a young man, he had not been accompanied on a regular basis by any slaves.

After the interviews, I had searched Caeso's rooms. I had turned over his mattress and looked under it, went through his chest of clothes, looked under his bed, tapped the walls for hidden compartments, went over the desk at his small study, read all the tags of the scrolls in the pigeon holes of his library and opened a few randomly to check their veracity, tore into his mattress, tapped his table again for secret compartments.

Nothing.

Not even the hidden cache of pornographic poetry one would expect from a youth of his age.

I had asked the steward where else Caeso could have hidden prized possessions around the house. With Typheus and the steward under instruction from Corpio to assist me in any way possible, the three of us went over the whole mansion in as much detail as the time allowed. We had asked questions of those in the household who might have seen Caeso about, making it appear like a simple enquiry. We'd tried to look nonchalant as we poked around in unusual, out of the way places where Caeso might have stashed private possessions, but I'd had no doubt that gossip would circulate that night amongst the slaves about the stranger who had even used a mirror to shine a lamp down into the latrines.

And still, nothing.

* * *

I reached the tip of the Septentrionali, where the Bay of Egretia opens to the Mare Saepiae. As I walked around the bend, the Pons Ignis came into my view — the viaduct bridge that leads to Insula Laridae, the tiny island on which the Pharos stands. Going further north around the tip was not possible beyond this point; the northern side of the Septentrionali, the side facing the open sea, was all sheer cliffs. The mansions of the rich at the top enjoyed both spectacular views and natural protection from intrusion, at least from that side.

The massive blocks of stone that make the five arches of the bridge had been laid centuries ago. When our nomadic people had finally decided to settle around the bay, they had established a fishing village at its innermost point. As trade grew, so did the village. The erection of the Pharos is considered one of the three marking points in the establishment of our great city.

I crossed the Pons Ignis and climbed laboriously on the steep path up the hill to the foot of the Pharos. Both the location and the features of the hill made it the ideal place for a lighthouse. Our people had maintained a bonfire there for ages, well before the lighthouse.

As our port had grown, so had our knowledge. It was the incantator Iunius Brutus who had summoned forth the Pharos over four hundred years ago, and announced to the world the rising of our city and our collegia. He had used his mastery of the six elements to raise up a square pediment upon which stood a slender tower of solid marble, and to bind a permanent flame at its head. His skill had been so refined, that on the spire of stone he erected were scenes in bas-relief spiralling up to the top, depicting some of the important events in our city. From our humble beginnings as nomads, to our victories over the Volsci and Gabii who had inhabited this region before us, to the original Curia of the Senate, to Curtius' famous sacrifice in the Forum, to the eruption of Vergu that had nearly destroyed the city, and to the image of himself raising the self-same spire at the top.

At the very top, on a capital styled with acanthus leaves, Iunius Brutus had crafted a white marble statue of a magnificent egret with the plume of feathers on its head looking almost too delicate to be made of stone, and in its beak it held the eternal flame. In the four hundred years since, despite wars and natural disasters, this flame has never gone out. It was said that he had been rooted to the spot for seven days and seven nights as he had chanted and directed the mystical energies that had brought forth the Pharos, and that when the ritual had been completed and finally he had moved, a thin layer of marble dust had covered him.

I climbed the pediment at the base of the towering structure. The square podium of the Pharos was about thirty feet high, with stairs running along its side to a wide platform on which people could stand and watch ships on the horizon. The spire jutting out in its centre was a solid block of hard marble a hundred feet high, and none but the terminally insane would attempt to scale it and reach the fire of the egret at the top.

I searched along the depicted scenes until I located the mythical scene depicting Servilius Ahala striking down Athanasios the necromancer. What inspiration could this ancient hero give me now?

I sat down with my feet dangling and my face to the open sea. I gazed out and could see sail-ships and rowboats, fishermen and pleasure craft. The sun was at my left, the water dazzling, and a light breeze pushed a few wispy white clouds high above.

A perfect day, and yet my mind was occupied with dark thoughts. I was contemplating approaching Drusus first as the most promising lead, but I wanted to think before I did. The problem I was facing was that this assignment was much stranger than what I was used to. Not only that, it was much stranger than anyone I know of would have dealt with. The subject of necromancy does not come up often. Even to bring the topic up would cause most people to dismiss me as crazy at best, or report me to the *rhones* of the Collegium Incantatorum as a dangerous lunatic at worst.

This was definitely not my usual line of business. Purloined jewellery, missing persons, cheating spouses were what paid for my bread and fish sauce. The occasional debunking of charlatans, confirmation of ancient scrolls, and even, rarely, a real magical ring were what would one day fill my memoirs. But necromancy? Definitely out of my way. If I should live to see the end of this, it would make the shining pinnacle of light in my memoirs. Who knew, perhaps I could even sell them!

A big if, considering surviving anything to do with necromancy was no mean feat.

I needed some insight, a few discreet levers I could test when talking to witnesses. A way to delicately broach the subject of Caeso's mysterious death, test and see reactions without bringing the authorities breathing hard down my neck for dealing with forbidden arts. I needed a refresher on necromancy, a review of the current schemers, any recent events that might involve illegal sorcery and trading in contraband.

In short, I needed to meet with Araxus.

Araxus the Mad, as he was known.

CHAPTER III

Last I'd heard, Araxus had been living in the slums out on the Campus Civicus amongst the disowned slaves, the lost foreigners, the mad and destitute and other nonentities. Since this was directly on the opposite side of the bay from me, my options were to swim, walk the long way around the bay, or try to catch a ride across the bay with a hired boat.

I crossed the Pons Ignis back to the mainland and walked along the promenade, scanning for passing ships. This being the more afflu-ent side, a few enterprising people were always lurking nearby to carry the rich to destinations around the harbour. Wearing a respectable toga I had no trouble in hailing one to me. I chose one captained by a man who did not look like he might slit my throat and dump my body in the bay, and haggled him to the price of two bronze sestertii. More for the practice than the money, as the cost would be added to Corpio's bill.

My seaman had four slaves to row us towards the Campus Civicus. We zipped past larger ships, making our way across the bus-tling harbour traffic. His rowboat had space for several people and the crew were used to heavier loads — rich people rarely travel without a retinue. We aimed at the public wharves, busy at this time with ships loading and unloading goods of all kinds. We imported the fish and squid sauce our people loved so much, shipped from the Kebros archipelago in large carinate clay vessels stamped with seals of quality, ranging from the exquisite to rotgut. We also imported grains, livestock, fresh catch, and bales of cloth from all around the shores of the Mare Saepiae. Our main export consisted of wines from vineyards on the rich volcanic soil on the other side of Vergu, if one didn't count the navy ships transporting soldiers and patrolling our shores as an export. Pleasure craft and messengers carrying official dispatches accounted for the rest of the traffic. Our harbour was the pumping heart of our empire and on a clear spring day such as this my driver had his hands full in guiding the small boat amidst all the traffic.

We reached the Campus Civicus and moored at one of the public wharves. I got off, and the boat quickly pushed back out to scan for customers from the water, rather than remain in berth and pay the harbour master his fees.

I walked past the great silos and warehouses and the basilicae with their merchant offices, avoiding the constant traffic of slaves and wagons carrying loads, yelling foremen and hurrying clerks. An ox-drawn cart was blocking my way, delivering farm chickens to the market. I went behind it and stepped in a steaming turd left on the pavement by one of the oxen. "*Merda! Fellator asini!*" I called after the driver. He turned round and gave me an evil eye, raising his whip. I hastened around the corner. Discretion and all that — it really wasn't the time to hang about.

I walked behind the busy port and towards the Circus Magnus. In all the cities I have been to, the areas of public entertainment are always bordered by the establishments catering to the common patron — taverns to get them drunk first, and then brothels and gambling houses to relieve them of their money in their inebriation. I stopped at a few and got myself well-watered drinks of cheap wine; I took time to chat with the whores standing in doorways advertising their wares and special tricks in the most obvious of ways; I distributed a few copper *quadrans* to street urchins. Eventually, I found those who had seen a mad hermit with the features of Araxus. I followed their leads to the refuse heaps outside of the Campus Civicus.

* * *

Araxus and I had been friends in our youth. We had started at the Collegium Incantatorum together, embarking down a promising path of a life steeped in magic and adventure. But then Fortuna had dealt me the first of many blows.

My father's business had collapsed. He had been a trader of antiques, fine arts, exotic jewellery — and the occasional enchanted item. His business had been strong enough to keep us well supplied, if not carry us into riches. He'd had agents scouring remote kingdoms and had been a fixture at auctions, always ignoring the slaves and furniture and browsing for the unique items of interest. He'd kept a warehouse to store curiosities of all flavours and for all tastes. His patrons had known him and trusted his reputation in acquiring oddments.

I had not followed him into his business. Instead, I had been the first of my family to attend the Collegium Incantatorum. My parents had been so proud the day I had passed the entry exams; my father had gone around buying drinks and declaring to anyone who would listen that one day his boy would make it to the Curia of Senate.

His fall had been sudden and swift. Brought on by natural disasters, and then aided by his rivals who had kicked him further on his way down. Within a month he had lost shipments and caravans, his bankers had refused to extend his loans, and irate creditors had been knocking on our door day and night.

In the end my father could bear it no more, and had taken his life with his sword. My mother had never recovered and had spent her remaining short years crying herself to sleep every night.

My family's fortune gone, I could no longer continue my studies at the Collegium. I had been lucky to keep our house, though I had had to sell almost everything except Dascha.

Throughout this, Araxus had been my unbending support. I had many times escaped the pressures of my own home to his. After I'd finally left the Collegium, he had tried to keep me abreast of his learning, sneaking me an occasional scroll. When all others had turned their back on me, he had been my one true friend.

I had rebuilt my life, or rather built a new life. I'd tried the legions briefly, but quickly realised that soldiering was not for me. By chance, I had run a few errands for the firm of *Gordius et Falconius* and found that while I had neither the training to be an *incantator* nor the money for a merchant business, I had the nose for both. I had learnt much from these esteemed men, and then forged my own path as a fox; though often a ferret would have been a more accurate name. I'd even managed to find love.

And then Araxus had had his accident. His mind was gone, and no one could restore it. I still am not sure what he had been attempting, when he'd blown up his rooms and half a wing of his father's house.

I'd never forgotten his kindness to me, though, and strove to repay in kind now that the tables were turned. I had done my best, at first to find a cure and later to keep him from harming himself.

And then had come that sordid affair with Helena, and I could never forgive him. I had not seen him since.

* * *

The stench was incredible. Our great city has a sewage system, the underground *cloaca* that runs from the top of the highest neighbourhoods on the slopes of Vergu and throughout the two arms. The sewers are flushed with water from the *Aqua Sextiae* and carry the human refuse out to sea; usually excreta, though the occasional body is not unknown. Anything that cannot be carried by water has been dumped by slaves for centuries in the dales of the hills behind the Campus Civicus. Laws prohibiting the dumping of refuse in the streets had some effect, and taxes fuelling gangs of slaves to cart street trash to the city dump had more. From broken furniture to dead babies, if it was unwanted, it ended up here.

I coughed and held a linen kerchief to my face. I scanned the mounds of rubbish for moving figures and saw a sad few walking about. I wandered around, looking for those who had made their habitat there, trying to see faces that were trying to hide from my gaze, examining profiles without getting too close to their owners.

Eventually, I saw his figure. Stooped and thin, a man my age who had once been tall and slender, now walking leaning on a makeshift crutch, more like a pole of rough wood. Hair hanging in ragged greasy strands all around his face, a scraggly beard, a dirty and torn tunic that might once have been fine. As I approached he lifted his head and stared at me, and I knew it was he.

In his youth, Araxus had been handsome. Slender, with a face like an old Hellican statue by Praxiteles — high cheekbones, a firm chin, long nose, wide forehead and rings of strawberry-blond hair neatly framing his visage. And in the midst of it all a pair of laughing eyes and a welcoming smile that made him adored by all.

The face in front of me had lost all that charm. Gaunt, dirty, weather-beaten, looking much older than his thirty-four years. Un-shaven and sickly. But his eyes, oh his eyes! These showed the sign of the curse he had brought upon himself more than anything else about him. His green right eye was looking at me with animal-like cunning intelligence; his black left eye was constantly wandering around, inde-pendent of the other, and when it turned to me I shivered.

I approached slowly. I took the kerchief down from my face, hoping for a sign of recognition. "Araxus…" I began, and saw recogni-tion hit as his right eye widened.

"No! Do not look at me!" He started, turned and ambled away from me, fast despite his uneven gait and bent back.

"Araxus, I need to speak to you!" I hurried after him, trying not to slip on the rotting garbage. "Araxus! You owe me this!"

But he kept running away.

"Araxus! Do not make me say her name!"

That stopped him as if hit by a mallet. He stood with his back towards me, rocking gently. I stopped a few paces behind him. Slowly, he turned. Both of his eyes focused into mine, and I felt a cold chill.

"Some debts cannot be repaid," he stated, "and some things cannot be forgotten. No matter how hard we try."

"That is true, Araxus, the facts remain as they were, as do your past transgressions. But for whatever small and insufficient comfort, you now have the chance to repay a little of this back, before Dis claims you for all eternity."

We stared at each other a moment more, and then he sagged.

His left eye finally resumed its incessant wandering and I felt my own body relax as its gaze was no longer transfixing my soul.

* * *

We walked back amongst the busy alleys of the entertainment quarter of the Campus Civicus. I wanted to talk to Araxus in quiet, so I found a tavern that wasn't bustling with customers. I ordered us some wine and olives. The proprietor looked askance at Araxus, so I put a full silver *denarius* on the counter and ensured us a flow of cheap wine and a quiet corner table.

I looked sidelong at Araxus. I hoped I was not wasting my time. By the looks of him he had not kept in touch with any of his old life, or much of any public life in Egretia, for that matter. But then, the invisible people on the outskirts of our society often hear and know and realise far more than we give them credit for.

"After all these years, I still cannot forgive you," I said, "and this doesn't change anything. But right now I need some information." A slave girl came to our table and set up two wooden cups before us, filling them with wine. I sipped mine and wished I hadn't, it was so sour. When she walked away I resumed. "Have you heard anything of late to do with your old interests?"

"Perhaps," he said, and when I gave him an unimpressed look he continued, "I hear a lot of things, mostly rubbish and superstitious gossip. I no longer move in the official circles of power, as you can well imagine. However, other channels circulate their own stories, and ring true more than others. What brings you back to those subjects? Why turn your gaze on something you walked away from?"

"I did not turn my back on it, as you very well know! I had no choice in the matter. I turned my back on *you* after… Well, let us not go there. This would have been recent. A cabal, most likely. With activities carried on in darkness, and nothing to alert the authorities. Those are my guesses; I know not for certain."

His right eye wandered to look at the passing slave girl, and his black left eye gazed into me. When the girl got out of earshot, his mad eyes switched back. "Whatever you are after, it cannot end well. Walk away now. Leave these accursed dealings to those who seek them, before you join me and mine."

"I thank you for this advice," I said coolly, "but I have a better record of keeping my affairs in order than you. Now, can you tell me anything of use?"

"Do you know what your supposed cabal was attempting to do?"

I gazed at him for a long moment. "The Rite of Pelegrinus."

He choked. His right eye looked at me with incredulity and his left was roving madly, trying to see all directions at once and even turning back into his skull, exposing a yellow orb shot with red veins. "No one — no one! — is that stupid. Any *matris futuor* apprentice of an *incantator* will have had this drilled into their brain, and the *rhones* of the Council at the Collegium Incantatorum will disabuse anyone who even dreams of starting down that road, like a centurion a green recruit missing his mommy!"

"And yet someone did. He failed, of course, but I saw the *stigmas* and even held the heart of ruby in my hand."

"Who was he?"

"The son of a merchant. He shall remain nameless."

Araxus sipped his wine, lost in thought. He chewed on the tip of his unkempt beard. I flagged the passing slave girl, gave her a *sestertius* and asked her for stuffed pastries, feeling the rancid wine churning in my stomach. Araxus continued to stare into space, mumbling occasionally to himself. The girl returned and left two pastries on a plate in front of us. It was surprisingly good for an establishment of this kind, a sturdy dough filled with chopped herbs and garlic and some slivers of meat of unidentified origins. Drizzled with fish sauce to complete the flavour.

Araxus wolfed down his pastry. "Tell me what you remember of the rite," I asked.

"A nasty business. We don't know much, as the whole *terminalis* branch of the *magia vita* has been outlawed for centuries and never properly studied. The heart of ruby is a definite sign, nothing else quite like it. Requires a cabal, certainly. From the one scroll about it I have read, all those many years ago at college, it will involve long preparations. Chants, consecrations, potions, ceremonies. I still cannot believe one would be able to hide such a thing. I don't know for certain what the ceremony entails, at least it was never in the accessible parts of the library. What I read was a treatise of the effects and signs. There might be more detailed references to the requirements, the ingredients and formulae hidden somewhere in the locked rooms. I don't imagine you could get access again…?"

"Not a chance." I replied. "My client would not have access or enough influence to get it, and anyway prefers to bury the matter discreetly and without any undue attention from the *incantatores*. Now, if I were to ask around and look for cabal members, do you know of any signs I should watch out for?"

"From memory, such rites involve many *stigmas*. It would depend largely on how the ceremony was completed, though I would hazard that other members might also require tattoos of power to channel the energies. Smaller than those of the chosen one, of course. All these *stigmas* require preparations and special inks. I could ask around…" Araxus began with a suggestive tone.

"You do that, but quietly. No names or details, listen more than you talk. And tell me as soon as anything even remotely relevant turns up." I got up and left a few coins on the table. Araxus would need them if he was to go around, and Corpio would hardly notice them on the expense account.

On the way back home after leaving Araxus, I stopped at the Baths of Mauritius just next to the Pons Orientalem. I paid extra and hired a slave to scrub and massage me after a long dip in the cold and hot plunges. I needed to get the smell and memory of Araxus and this day off me.

CHAPTER IV

I set out the next day to seek out more information, to cast a net and see what catch it might bring. The meeting with Araxus had not provided me with anything concrete, but could yet bear fruit in the future. However, there were other sources I could tap that might prove fruitful.

I put on my toga again, my only toga, and started to visit all of my father's old contacts. At least the honest ones, not those vultures who had danced in glee at his downfall. I went from portico to basilica, tracking men I'd once known. These were all men who traded in artwork — from marble statues and scrolls of poetry to Assyrican fine silks and Arbarican gold jewellery. They were men who understood the value of things beyond mere ordinary goods and knew a lot about mysterious origins and exotic materials that might be used in illicit enchantments. Well, knew enough to make convincing stories for their buyers, who sometimes knew far more and sometimes far less. These were all well-respected citizens, owning offices and warehouses filled with exquisite items for the connoisseurs.

I shared many stuffed dates, honeyed almond cakes and sweet sesame biscuits, and far too many cups of watered wine. I asked non-specific questions and got non-specific answers. The result was that the word was out that I was in the market for a certain kind of information, and was willing to pay handsomely. Now to wait until greed got the better of discretion for those who were traders and hagglers at heart.

In the afternoon I came back to my home, feet aching from the walking, stomach aching from the sweets and head aching from the wine. I wriggled out of my toga in the atrium and went to bed in my loincloth, stopping only for a refreshing drink of cool water delivered by the mad faun's engorged member.

I collapsed on my bed and slept the sleep of the drunk, tired from walking and from bad dreams the night before.

* * *

I woke up after sunset, which suited me fine. Time to do more canvassing, this time amongst people who wake up with the night.

Dascha prepared a dinner of farina porridge with bits of bacon and some fried eggs and bread. Her cooking skills may not have been much, but she knew what I would need without my asking. I ate the meal reclining on a couch in the square garden at the back of my house, with the ever-present leering faun for company. It was done in bronze, and the paintwork was worn and chipped. I had sold the rest of my father's artwork collection, though somehow I have grown sentimental about this one — or so I told myself rather than face the fact that no one would buy it.

I put on an old but still-decent tunic, strapped my dagger under the sleeve of my forearm and put a money pouch with small coins on my belt, with the real pouch hidden deep within my tunic's pockets.

I set out on foot from my house, heading south back above the ridge of the Meridionali and down the other side. All the establishments I planned to visit would be local, either in the Subvales, along the waterline or in the Campus Civicus. The Subvales, the far side of the Meridionali away from the water and facing inland, is mostly built up with tenements, housing the poor, foreigners and freedmen — the Egretian stews. Along the shores of the bay are the great markets — the Forum Bovarium, Forum Frumentarium and Forum Piscarium — and in between them are the silos, warehouses and pens to hold the products that will be sold the next day. These areas become devoid of respectable citizens when the sun sets, and another crowd of dock workers and labourers takes over.

Considering the establishments I was planning to visit and the streets I would be walking tonight, I made my way as quickly as I could to a disreputable tavern called the Pickled Eel at the base of the hill, near the Porta Fulvia. I located the scrawled sign of an *amphora* with eels peeking out on the side of a narrow alley off an odd-shaped public square. I walked up the alley for a few paces and ducked into a low doorway. This being night, my eyes were already accustomed to the dark, yet the perpetually dim-lighted interior still gave me pause. I walked in, looking at the back tables as I went, but could not see the person I was after.

I went to the bar at the back corner, bought a drink for myself and asked the proprietor, "Is Crassitius in tonight?"

"Busy at the back," he said with a leer, "though I'd say he should be finished soon."

I settled myself to wait at a free table.

I sipped my wine once, and decided to leave it. I had a long night ahead, and did not wish to start it off with heartburn.

A few minutes later my friend Crassitius walked in from a back passage, buckling a belt. A short and plump girl followed him, and he patted her backside as she passed. I hailed him over.

"Felix! By Servilius' shrivelled scrotum, if it isn't Felix the Fox!" He clapped me on the shoulder.

"Marcus Crassitius," I smiled with a wince. "Still keeping fit, I see."

He laughed. "Yes, indeed. In my business one can hardly avoid it. What has it been now, two years since I saw you last? You bastard used to come here more often. What's the matter, suddenly too good for your old pals?"

We talked for a while, trading insults and news. When he ordered his third cup of wine and was beginning to reminisce about our short army tenure together, I thought we had exchanged enough pleasantries.

"Do you still hold that stable of ex-gladiators? I need to hire one for tonight."

His smile never wavered, but his eyes narrowed and all signs of inebriation vanished at the smell of business. "Yes, yes I do. I have some waiting nearby, as one never knows when a customer requires arms broken or ladies entertained. What are you after tonight?"

"Something large. Suitably intimidating, to avoid trouble."

"I have just the thing. A huge Arbari, all red moustaches and rippling arms, trained as a *cestus* and decent with the *gladius* as well. For how long?"

"Just for the night." We haggled just a bit and agreed on the fees and insurance costs in case I returned damaged goods. Crassitius insisted he was giving me mates' rates, but it still seemed a bit steep. Still, in order to claim my expenses from Corpio I needed to come back alive from this night.

Crassitius sent a slave boy to fetch the gladiator, whose name, I learnt, was Borax. He was not exaggerating. A hulking Arbari, bending his head under the low ceiling, complete with big drooping red moustaches done in plaits and long red hair, plaited as well. Wearing only leather breeches, a cloak and a permanent scowl, he was bare-chested and covered in blue woad tattoos. He looked like he could lift a boar one-handed, and probably fit one in his stomach in a single meal. The costs of feeding him must have accounted for the significant sum of money I'd paid to hire him.

I set out with Borax on my trail to visit all the seedy establishments where Egretia's night life takes place. As with my father's respectable contacts, I wandered from one establishment to the next. I visited bars, gambling dens and whorehouses, tracking down people who often wished their whereabouts not to be publicly known. These were also men who specialised in moving items of value, though usually without their previous owner's permission. I asked about rumours, oddments, trading in contraband and suspicious activity. I asked about rich youths out of place, and characters asking the wrong kind of questions.

Unlike with the more respectable people of the morning, when I cast my lines at night I had to put more bait on the hooks. Good deeds are seldom their own reward with that crowd, so I also spread a few coins. I had to be careful, far more careful, for these people were both more and less discreet than the professional traders. More discreet, because they knew the value of contraband and secrets and the dangers of dealing with them. Less discreet exactly because they knew full well the price attached. I needed it to be known that I was in the market for unsavoury information, and yet not expose my client.

And just like in the morning, I walked for mile after mile, talked endlessly about non-specific things and got non-specific answers. The food was worse, though, and the wine wretched. At least the presence of Borax's garlicky breath behind me kept me safe.

I returned to my home in the small hours of the night. Not a fruitful day, but that is the inglorious nature of my business and I did not expect immediate returns. My nets cast, if any information about this unfortunate affair was available, in whatever social stratum, it would make its way to me.

* * *

I woke up late on the following morning and decided it was time to meet Gnaeus Drusus. I chose to forgo a formal toga, and instead wore my best tunic, the one in light blue with a golden trim of Hellican key design along the hem. I needed to balance my appearance and project a respectable yet approachable image to the young aristocratic friend of Caeso.

I made my way to the Forum Egretium through the perpetually busy streets near the harbour. I went to the Collegium Mercatorum, where Gnaeus Drusus *filius* would spend his days in apprenticeship to a master trader, learning anything from geography to accounting to foreign languages. There were the shop keepers, tavern keepers and small business holders — and then there were the privileged youths of the rich families, attending the Collegium Mercatorum and learning how to run trading empires.

I located the door-slave. Not a burly guardian, rather a scrawny-necked, balding little man with his nose up the air, who made it clear that even though he was a slave, he was still better than anyone not on his lists. I enquired after young master Drusus, and had to grease his palm with a full *denarius* to learn that he was indeed inside. Another silver *denarius* went to buy a promise that he would deliver a message to Drusus to meet me at a corner tavern.

On the way to my selected vantage point, I stopped at the fountain of Iuno Moneta that stands before the college and refreshed myself. I caught one of the running street urchins, gave him a *quadrans* and waved at the door-slave, who nodded slightly. A fall-back, in case the young master would be too busy for the likes of me; he would point him out to the boy, who would alert me discreetly.

I settled myself at a small table in a seat with a clear view of the Collegium, and made ready to wait.

I did not need to wait for long. Right around midday, the cadets and personnel of the Collegium started to pour out of the huge building with its impressive colonnade front. All were in a rush, keen for a break in their busy day. Eventually, the door-slave whispered something in the ear of the boy I had hired, who promptly ran to me and pointed to a young man walking alone. "This is the man you are waiting for, *domine*. The short one with the dark hair."

I rose and approached Drusus as he came closer. "Gnaeus Drusus, allow me to introduce myself. I am Spurius Vulpius Felix, known as Felix the Fox. I would be most delighted if you would let me to treat you to some wine and refreshments."

We sat and I waved for the slave girl to bring us good wine and a light lunch. The crowds normally around the Forum Egretium were of a better class than the ones I had seen last night, and consequently the vintage was significantly more palatable. The girl laid out a set of plates in front of us, with pickled quail eggs, tiny fish battered and fried whole, olives, bread, and bits of goat meat and carrots in a cumin sauce.

"To what do I owe this pleasure?" he asked as he popped a pickled egg into his mouth.

"I am sorry to be the bearer of bad news, Gnaeus Drusus, for I have the unpleasant task of informing you of the death of your friend Caeso Quinctius three nights ago."

He blanched.

"He was found dead in his bed. His father, as you can imagine, is quite distraught."

"What happened to him? He was well the week before when I saw him last."

"We are not entirely certain." That was not a lie. "As a matter of course, his father the *rhone* asked me to look into his death, to ease his own conscience. You said Caeso appeared healthy, however I understand from Corpio that his health had been deteriorating of late?"

"Maybe not in peak form of late, though not about to keel over. But you're right and his health had been deteriorating throughout the winter."

"His father mentioned that you went with him to Kebros last autumn. Would you tell me all about it?" I asked.

"Last year he fell in love with a street mime, and was acting all forlorn, losing appetite and sleep, because of course he could not tell his father. So Quinctius Corpio had either guessed or completely misunderstood, and decided to send us both on voyage to get Caeso's mind off the subject. We went on a trip to Kebros late in the shipping season. His father made all the arrangements with his brother on the island, and asked me to accompany Caeso to keep an eye on him and try to lift his spirits up."

"Do you remember the girl's name?"

"Who said it was a girl?" he leered. "But no, I do not. Never met her. To hear him moon about her was quite enough."

"Did the trip cheer him up?"

"Well, at first he was dejected, as you could expect. Like a brat whose favourite toy was taken, he kept pouting throughout the whole voyage. I tried to console him, pointing out that while there was no future with a street trash mime, he could still bed her — or any number of similar *moechae* — any time he wants. Why couldn't he just make his father happy and marry a nice girl and keep the mime as a mistress like the rest of us?"

"Having seen young people in love, I will assume that did not impress him."

"Not in the least. Caeso wandered around the island listlessly.

His uncle had even arranged for a suitable young girl of wedding age to be present during a few of the dinners, though he showed little interest. Not that I blame him, she was a bit of a shrew — too well educated for my tastes. Any which way, after a while on the island Caeso was improving. All that fresh air, walking, riding and sailing. Got a bit of appetite back. We took a few boat trips to the smaller islands. I got bored after a while and he continued alone. He started to come to dinners all aflush and excited, with a healthy appetite. He seemed to be back to his usual excitable self. He even made some advances on Aemilia — the girl I mentioned — but then we had to return to Egretia before the shipping closed for the winter."

"So what happened that his health deteriorated again when you returned to Egretia?"

"I am really not sure. We sailed back in November, right at the closing of the sailing season. I was eager to return by then; I had enough of that wretched island and could not imagine being stuck there for the winter. When we arrived in town, Caeso went searching for that *moecha* of his, but could not find her. Her troupe had gone for the winter. This dampened his spirits — he must have been hoping for some tryst with her at Saturnalia," Drusus winked.

"What was her name, that mystery woman?"

"Sorry, I don't remember. I'm sure he mentioned it, but she was a nobody, really. I think he might have just gotten some fever, the poor fool, as I have not seen him around the Collegium much recently."

"Do you know of any of his activities during the *intercalaris*? Or of anyone I might ask who would know? His father would be most appreciative."

"Not really, I had not seen much of him lately, as I said, and to my knowledge neither did the rest of our little circle. He started to miss attending the Collegium more and more, though of course the teachers cut him some slack because of his father the *rhone*. If you ask me, he just got an embarrassing venereal disease from the street trash mime, and didn't want his father to find out."

We chatted a while longer, but I learnt nothing more. Soon after Drusus left, and I finished the lunch alone. In my line of business, one learns to eat when one can, especially when it can be charged to an expense account.

CHAPTER V

I spent some more time that afternoon chasing others of Caeso's old college mates, and by late afternoon managed to track down Lutatius and Porcius. Lutatius was a lanky youth, of light reddish hair and pimply face. His friend Porcius was slightly taller and heavier, with chestnut hair and a straggly beard in what I presumed was a failed attempt to hide his even more numerous pimples.

At first it seemed they did not have anything to add to Drusus' story. They had all seen Caeso become withdrawn and unhealthy over the winter *intercalaris*, had all lost touch with him recently as he'd shifted from his usual haunts. None had followed him to his new pursuits, and none could offer me new insights or leads.

However, when Porcius said that Caeso and Drusus were thick as thieves, my interest picked up. "Have you seen them much together recently?" I asked.

"Oh, yes," said Lutatius. "They were always going around, their heads together. Not just in the college, mind you, but after hours as well."

"I did hear them mention a club they frequented," said Porcius, "A place up on the Clivi Inferior by the name of The Dented Skull. It's an upmarket tavern, masquerading as a den of debauchery for the entertainment of the rich who want some excitement without the actual risk. He mentioned a name, now what was it? Something foreign,

Hellican, I think."

"No, I'm certain it was Assyrican," responded Lutatius. "Zymaxis. That was it"

"That's right! You are correct, Gaius Lutatius," said Porcius. "Definitely Zymaxis."

"Have you ever visited that tavern?" I asked.

They both shook their heads. "Not our kind of place," said Porcius. "Too up-market," added Lutatius with a sigh.

"Did you notice anything odd about Caeso's behaviour throughout winter?"

They looked at each other. "Well, his health was deteriorating, that was certain," said Lutatius. "It started last autumn, I think. It got worse as time went by, though. He became gaunt, lost colour. Dark circles around his eyes. Withdrawn. Started to miss out on studies. We visited him a few times, but could not lift his spirits."

"I don't know what wasting disease it was," said Porcius, "though I do know his father hired the best *magisteri carneum* in Egretia and even they couldn't cure it. In fact, Caeso refused to see them, though we tried as well to convince him that it is for his own good."

"If you ask me," said Lutatius, "it wasn't a fever at all. He was heartbroken."

"You and him were always such saps," said Porcius.

"A romantic heart is not a sap!"

"Why do you think he was heartbroken?" I asked before they could continue their debate.

"He told me once of a girl he met," said Lutatius. "Her name was Mahatixa, a Mitzrana from the other side of the Montes Mauretanii. Exotic, lithe and very attractive. I haven't seen much of her, though I remember Caeso did have good taste in women, even if he didn't have the sense to choose those of his own class."

Porcius grunted in agreement to this.

Lutatius continued, "I think I saw her troupe on the streets maybe a month ago, just before the new year. They put up the usual mime tent and move it often, flying a pennant with the image of a sphinx. They perform next to the docks and the Circus Magnus, in the Campus Civicus."

Nothing more in my conversation with Porcius and Lutatius seemed relevant, as the two friends kept interrupting each other on tangential philosophical flights. I thanked them and requested that they inform me should they remember anything else of note. I paid for our wine, and thus had a feeling that they would come calling if something did rattle their memories.

A more interesting question raised, was the significance of the differences between Porcius' and Lutatius' version of events and that of Drusus. Did Drusus really not know of his friend's involvement in the matters leading to his death, or was he aware but trying to mislead me? Was he himself involved, perhaps, and now trying to downplay it? Or were the two men I met today just prone to overstating innocuous events? Given Drusus' — and more importantly, his family's — background, I would need more evidence before I could confront him.

* * *

I decided to go in search of Mahatixa before tackling the Dented Skull. While I had no doubt I could handle the Clivi Inferior at night, it being a reasonably quiet neighbourhood for the most part, I wanted to see first if I could learn anything about the mysterious woman who had captured Caeso's heart.

I stopped at home briefly to change and then started to poke about at the docks. This being *Avrilis,* twilight came early, and I did not wish to get caught out on the Campus Civicus in full darkness. I walked for a while amongst the hurrying people finishing their work for the day and making their way home. Fortuna must have smiled on me that night for I saw a crowd gathered just next to the silos of the Forum Piscarium, and in its midst a mime troupe tent flying a flag with the sign of the sphinx.

I approached and stood at the back, watching the show. It was a crude affair, and so was the crowd. These were not the people to appreciate a fine Hellican drama, with intricacies of hubris and inescapable fate. This show involved stock characters and a farcical plot — a scatterbrained old master, a young vixen wife, her neighbour-come-lover, and the ubiquitous slaves that see everything and snigger behind their masters' backs. Plenty of hiding behind curtains and baring of breasts to the catcalls of the crowds. They were good at what they were doing, though, better than most such troupes.

There were about seven people I could distinguish despite the masks, playing the various roles. Two were women, both young. No self-respecting Egretian troupe would put women on the stage, but this was neither Egretian nor particularly respectable. There would be a few other people involved, no doubt, though no more than ten.

Between one skit and the next, while resetting the stage, the troupe put out more entertainment so as not to lose the crowd. It involved the usual children performing acrobatics and playing flutes, and a big hulking brute who lifted them all together above his head. I could not be certain, of course, but I felt reasonably sure that the dark-skinned beauty dancing the Dance of Seven Scarves would be Mahatixa. Her body glistened in the last rays of daylight, shimmering on her clear, dark skin as the scarves snaked their way around her contours, wafting behind her as she danced and somersaulted, eventually floating to the ground like leaves in autumn. Not a single man in the crowd looked elsewhere while she was dancing, though the more worldly ones clutched their money pouches even while their jaws slacked open. She disappeared into the tent with the last scarf lingering behind her, floating in the breeze. A collective sound between a sigh and a groan escaped from the lips of every man amongst the audience, as the rest of the troupe emerged quickly and started on the next skit.

I waited until the show was over and the crowds dispersed. The actors and dancers went around with bowls, collecting donations for their performance. I moved closer to the girl, and as she neared me I said her name as if I knew her. She looked up at me, and I smiled at her. I offered a full *sestertius* for her bowl, and said, "This is for the lovely show." As she smiled at me I produced a silver *denarius* and held it between thumb and forefinger. "And this," I added, "is yours if I can just talk to you about Caeso Quinctius."

She looked doubtful for a moment. "Pretty girls going alone with strangers makes a good story," she replied, "one that seldom ends well for the girl."

"My name is Felix, called Felix the Fox by some. And you are Mahatixa, the marvellous Mitzrana dancer who stole Caeso's heart. So there — no longer strangers." I smiled. "But to reassure you, why don't you ask that brute of a strongman you have with your troupe to accompany us? I will gladly buy him a cup of wine too, if he will just sit at the next table and let us talk."

That seemed to have reassured her that I meant no harm. "Wait here," she told me.

* * *

She went back to her troupe and helped with the final packing. A few moments later she returned, dressed sensibly in a pleated dress and cloak, and accompanied by the hulk, whose name, I learnt, was Harkhuf.

We walked to the closest tavern I could spot and settled ourselves at a side table with Harkhuf at the table behind Mahatixa. I ordered wine for us and beer for the brute. His scowl disappeared as the buxom serving maid placed the tankard before him, and I was certain he would not bother us.

"I heard about you through some mutual friends of Caeso Quinctius, Gaius Lutatius and Gnaeus Porcius," I started, waiting to judge her reaction to news of his death. "Have you seen Caeso recently?"

"Not since we came back. We got here just a few weeks ago in time for the festival of *Anna Perenna*, after having spent the winter in Hellica. How is dear Caeso doing?"

My pause caused her to knit her perfectly arched brows. "I am sorry to be the one to tell you — Caeso passed away. He was found dead in his bed on the morning of the day before yesterday."

She shuddered and drew her cloak tight around her shoulders.

"Did he fall to some illness over the winter?"

"He was unwell, yes, though his family knows not what affliction it was." I looked at her eyes as I said that, and could see no guile. Her reactions seemed genuinely surprised, sad to hear about Caeso's death.

"And what is your role in this?" she asked. "You are paying for this interview, so you are not here to bring me this news out of the kindness of your heart. Your eyes have a keen look in them, and you do not strike me as a spendthrift. A hired ferret then, hired by Caeso's father. Something odd about his death, then! Surely you cannot suspect me; I have not been in Egretia this whole winter!"

I smiled, despite myself. The girl was intelligent and not afraid to show it. "No, no, please do not be alarmed. You are correct that I was hired by Corpio *pater*. I found out about you from his friends, Porcius and Lutatius. I am only trying to piece together Caeso's life, to ease his distraught father's mind. I heard from Drusus, as well, that he was much in love with you. Would you tell me about your involvement with him?"

"Oh, it was just a summer fling," she started. "We were performing one day last spring at the other side of town, for a more respectable crowd. We tried to see if we could earn more money that way, rather than the *quadrans* and *semis* we get from the dock workers. We even put on not a mime show but selected scenes from proper dramas. Still, we needed to draw crowds for that and when I did my dance of seven scarves the *vigiles* decided to chase us away. I guess some old stuck-up sourpuss passing on the street had taken offence. Caeso must have been in the crowd, for he followed us here. At first he seemed to me just like any other moon-struck puppy that follows me. He was quite insistent, however, and quite charming, and quite good looking…

"I refused him, of course. But he came back with flowers, jewellery and other gifts almost every day. He seemed so naive, a boy really, and I just found it so charming…. So I let him buy me dinner one night. And then another night. And we talked. And went on walks. I am my own person, you know. Not a slave of the troupe. So long as I was around during performances to draw the crowds and help with the tent, Djaty, our leader, does not mind."

I stirred the dregs of wine in my cup with my finger, and waved the servant maid to fetch more wine. Behind Mahatixa I could see Harkhuf down yet another tankard of ale, and shamelessly pinch the maid's buttocks as she passed by. The maid was young, voluptuous and flirty, and yet had nothing over the woman sitting in front of me. I traced my wet finger on the table leaving behind doodles in wine, and looked at her sparkling black eyes as she was telling the story.

"And so it went on through the summer and into autumn. We spent time away from both our lives. We took many walks; he liked the island of the Pharos — close yet far, we found seclusion there. He could not present me at any formal events, of course, his family would never allow it. But we saw his friends for informal dinners with other people our age. I met Lutatius and Porcius and liked them, and we met Drusus, though I liked him less. Too judgemental, too proud of his family's history to appreciate the likes of us. Caeso and I went to sideshows and games together. Private poetry parties. Taverns of a more relaxed nature. There is quite a lot going on at night in Egretia, and one just needs to know where to look and who to ask.

"He tried to make promises he could not keep, about marrying me one day. I did my best to disabuse him of this notion. His family would not allow it, he could never join our life, and I would never agree to be cooped up inside like some Egretian matron. He would not listen, though. He kept talking about how one day he would make it all work, and damn the social order.

"Well, I tried to get him to cool down, though unsuccessfully. Thankfully, his father sent him away to Kebros, and Caeso went. Cursing and pouting, but went nonetheless, bent to his father's will.

"My troupe moved to Hellica for the winter part of our circuit. We visited Heraclion, Ephemezica and Phrylia. We went back out in spring and took a ship here. I wondered if he would show up again, as I haven't seen him these past few weeks. And now you come to tell me that he is dead..." She shivered again.

"You must be distraught." I placed my right hand on top of Mahatixa's left on the table, covering her hand in a gesture of sympathy. She must have been used to this kind of affections from men, and hardly even glanced down. She must have been used to flirting for a living, too, as she did not draw her hand away, and I will not compliment myself that she had any other interest in me.

"Tell me," I decided to move the conversation, "you are Mitzrani, am I correct?" She nodded, and I continued. "Your people have a great interest in the afterlife. They even preserve the corpses of the dead, for the life after life. Did Caeso ever show an interest in the subject?"

"Not really," she said. "He was very much a young socialite. Dreamt big, but lacked the determination to achieve anything beyond a mediocre career as a merchant in his father's business."

I kept my hand covering hers and brought it gently towards me, looking at her eyes. As her hands reached the doodles of wine dregs I drew on the table, I could feel a slight warmth from them, saw them glimmer and shimmer in the corner of my eye, and I smelled the tinge of fresh air after rain.

"Come, now," I said, "there's no need to lie. We both know that he was interested in such matters, and that he shared this with you." She sat back and tried to withdraw her hand. I held on to her wrist firmly, but without squeezing too hard. "Please, let us be civil. If you will just look behind you at Harkhuf, you will see that my generosity with the beer has left him quite inebriated. If you try and shout to the other patrons, well…"

I extended my right index finger and touched the faintly glowing wine doodle on one side, and then drew it across her wrist, and touched the pattern on the other side. I withdrew my hand. She tried to snatch her hand back, but found it bound to the table with the shimmering tracery holding her wrist tight.

"I am just a citizen sitting across from a foreign woman. You, on the other hand, will not be able to remove your hand from this table while you tell me lies." I looked into her eyes and saw tears of frustration tinged with fear. "Please, do not be afraid. I will not harm you; I just need to know what you have omitted from your story."

She tried in vain to pull her hand away. She looked back at Harkhuf, who was talking to himself with an unintelligible slur. She sat back then, straightened up, and looked at me squarely.

"I did not lie," she said fiercely. "What I said was the truth."

I saw the tracery brighten just a little. "You have omitted something."

"Yes. I did. I guess… I guess I did not like the direction Caeso was taking last year, and tried to distance myself from him. I got scared, you see. He did see me after he got back, a few days before we left Egretia. One night he took me to this little tavern, out on the

Clivi Inferior. At first I thought we would just be meeting some of his friends there, the neighbourhood is quite sedate with plenty of houses for the affluent merchants. However, when we got there he went right to the back, beyond the tables and the dancing girls. He led me down to the basement, and we did meet some other people already there. The room was dense with smoke, lit only by bad oil lamps. I thought I saw Drusus there, but I was not sure.

"We sat at a table to one side, and Caeso did not talk. Just told me to wait and watch. After a while a hidden lyre player started, playing something atrocious and discordant. Some red light shone through the smoke, and in walked this short bald man, wearing strange robes and kohl around his eyes. He talked about eternal life, about riches and power, about upsetting the natural order and taking what was rightfully theirs.

"Frankly, I thought he was a nut case and a fake. He tried to pass himself as a Mitzrani, but to me it was obvious he was not. None who believe in our old ways would ever talk like that. Caeso was mesmerised, however, drinking in his every word. He kept talking about passing tests of loyalty, and how only the worthy will be elevated, become privy to this power when they finally attain it. Eventually, I could not take it any more and left. Caeso wanted to stay, and we argued, and eventually I walked home by myself.

"After that I cooled things with him, or at least I tried to. He was still obsessed with me, only now I could see it for what it was, an obsession. He would not apologise for letting me walk back at night by myself, only tried to persuade me to come there again, to see the 'bright future', as he called it. I tried to shake him off; I wanted none of that. Luckily, we left Egretia to Hellica right after that incident, and I have not seen him since."

I looked down at the table. The tracery was faint, pulsating slowly and calmly. She was telling me the truth.

"And who was that man? Do you know his name or anything about him?"

"I don't know much more about him. I only saw him that once, and refused to go there again. Caeso later told me his name was Zymaxis."

* * *

I walked home slowly, deep in thought. Mahatixa had told me all she knew, of that I could be certain. After I had finished questioning her, I'd felt uncharacteristically guilty of mistreating her, so had offered to help carry Harkhuf back to their lodging. Never leave a pretty woman spitting at your back, as my father used to say.

At first she had refused and wanted nothing more to do with me, and in an effort to patch things up I had told her I believed her tale about Zymaxis, hinting without revealing the mystery of Caeso's death. I'd assured her that I would be going after him. That, and a generous pay for the interview, had seemed to mellow her opinion of me a little, though I wish I could believe my own words with the same confidence.

I had offered her again to help carry Harkhuf, but Mahatixa had given him a disgusted look, kicked the chair from under him, and exclaimed "let the big ox sleep here on the floor! He deserves whatever happens to him, such a lousy guard he turned out." She had emphasised this with an extra kick to his thigh.

I had still ended up walking her to her troupe's lodging. I had dragged the heavy frame of Harkhuf after her, and disgusted as she had been with him, she'd come back to help me. These troupes stick together like family, knowing full well no one else will. The shared exertion had mellowed her attitudes towards me even more, and I had managed to part with her without getting spit upon.

As I walked back from the inn I considered all the questions this day had raised. Who was the mysterious Zymaxis? Were his powers real, or was Mahatixa's assessment that he was a fake correct? If he was responsible for the necromantic spell that killed Caeso, how did he manage to avoid detection by the *magisters* of the Collegium Incantatorum? What should I do about confronting him? To what extent was Drusus involved or innocent in this matter?

I would have to tread carefully. I could cast my cantrips in a stinking tavern on a foreign woman of low standing, but I could never do so on someone of Drusus' standing, or even Porcius and Lutatius. If any of them were involved, it would require an official court, something Corpio was particularly keen to avoid. And as for Zymaxis, I would have to ascertain his identity and status. If he was indeed performing necromancy inside the boundaries of our city, he might have very powerful patrons.

CHAPTER VI

I slept badly that night, plagued by dreams of the body in the well again. I gave up on sleep before dawn and decided to see if I could still catch the night crowd of Egretia as they dispersed to their homes, before the day people took over the city. I dressed and armed myself, raided the kitchen for some unappetising cold leftovers of cod in coriander and caraway sauce, and left before first light.

I walked up the maze of alleys leading from my house to the Vicus Petrosa at the top of the Meridionali and continued briskly along that main road to the Forum Egretium. Near the Baths of Sestropius the road angles down the hill towards the Forum, the living heart of our city, and offers a spectacular view of the open space ringed by impressive public buildings. Despite the hour there was plenty of traffic through the streets — straggling wagons hurrying to get back out of the city before the daylight curfew, slaves starting their day before their masters, *vigiles* doing the last rounds.

I crossed the Forum and headed up the Vicus Caprificus, and turned left at the Via Caeca. To continue right would have put me on the Septentrionali, where Corpio and many other rich and powerful had their city mansions. I was heading towards the Clivi Inferior, the lower slopes of Mons Vergu. It is a respectable quarter of smaller houses and low tenement buildings. An area populated not by the upper crust, yet by people still rich enough to own a good house close to the cliffs and fresh sea breezes.

The Dented Skull was located somewhere near the sea cliffs not far from the Porta Rupis. At least, that was the description I got from Mahatixa. Wandering through the winding streets and asking around, I eventually managed to locate the dented legionary helmet hanging by its top loop over a door in a side alley off a round public square. It was well after sunup by then, though still at a time when taverns are rarely busy.

The tavern itself was situated on the ground floor of a four-storey *insula*, with a different entry than the common areas and the upper floors. I went inside, sat at a table near the wall and ordered a breakfast of bread and eggs from a sleepy-looking girl. I looked around the place. Two drunk patrons snoring in a corner. A tired whore, getting ready to leave. A middle-aged couple, finishing their lovers' tryst. As my eyes adjusted to the dark interior, I saw more of the decor. This was a respectable neighbourhood of successful merchants, retired generals, *quaestors* and clerks of the various colleges. People with a good income and a decent lifestyle, believers in old ways and values. And yet the place was decorated like a dock-side tavern, dimly lit, crude images on the walls, rough, long tables. However, as I looked closer I saw the images on the walls were crude in subject but not in execution. The tables were rough, but the benches padded. The place was masquerading as a low-brow haunt in order to give some illicit excitement to the otherwise drab surrounds.

I also noted the doorway in the back and caught a glimpse of stairwells going up and down.

The girl returned a few minutes later with my fare and a cup of well-watered wine. She was blond, barely eighteen, a slim figure in a low-cut tunic that barely covered her buttocks and must have helped distract paying customers. I put my arm around her waist and drew her to me. "Tell me, honey, do they have back rooms around here?"

She looked me up and down. I was just barely old enough to be her father, but she was probably used to amorous advances of men old enough to be her grandfathers. It did not take her long to evaluate me. I have a classic Egretian look, with the bumpy nose and curly dark hair.

Clean shaven, of average height and medium build. Nondescript. I try to keep myself fit. I have been called handsome by my mother, but by few others.

The decent tunic I was wearing and the jingling of my purse must have had more effect than my looks. She glanced quickly around, and, satisfied that none of the other customers would notice her absence, said "Sure, why not? Come."

I went with her towards the back. Once past the doors to the kitchens, I turned to the stairs leading down. She pulled my arm, saying "No, my room is upstairs," and started on the way up.

"I have heard some tales of fantastic deeds done in basements of taverns around here. I was hoping you would show me." I winked at her.

"The room downstairs is strictly for private functions. Mine is upstairs."

"Are the 'functions' as wild as the stories go?"

"Some, yes," she answered, "but last night's orgy has finished already."

The upper floor consisted of a short, dark hall with small cubicles opening from it, sheets of cloth hanging over the doorways for privacy. Her sleeping cubicle was cramped, most of the space taken up with her bed. A tiny shuttered window high up on the wall let in some light and air, and a little picture done on a wooden slate was the only decoration. Her cot was simple, and a chest of clothes acted as a table as well. She turned to me, pushed the sleeveless tunic off her shoulders and let it fall to the floor, standing completely naked in front of me. Slim of figure, fair of skin, with small breasts and pink nipples, her body was unspoiled by the ravages of time, yet her eyes looked old beyond her years. "Two *denarii*, and anything kinky will cost you extra," she said, as if in agreement with that last thought.

When we were done we lay side by side, heaving and sweating. After a while, she turned on her side, facing me. "If you're interested in the orgies, there will be a young boys' orgy tomorrow night, if that is your thing." She traced the scars on my chest with her forefinger. "And if not, I am sure I could find the time for you…"

"And tonight? What kind of party goes on tonight?"

Her face darkened. "Not tonight. The nights before the *Nones* of the months are reserved. I do not like the people that come."

I put my arm around her shoulders. "What do they do that is so bad?"

"Nothing sexual, if that is what you mean. They hold meetings in a darkened room and their leader, that horrible little man, leads them in frenzied chanting. He pays my master well enough, so my master doesn't lose on food and wine. But I do not like them, not at all."

Before I could ask any further questions we heard a shout from downstairs, "Didia! Didia, where are you? Come here and finish your cleaning!"

The girl, Didia, jumped out of bed and started to dress hurriedly. "My *dominus*! I must go down. Please stay here a minute and do not tell him. Instead of giving him his commission I can put it towards buying my freedom."

She hurried out. I got up, dressed, and left three silver *denarii* on her little chest. I picked up a strand of her blond hair from the bed and rolled it safely in my kerchief.

I went down the stairs softly. When I reached the ground floor I looked about, heard the noises in the kitchen and the tables at the front. I continued quietly down the stairs to the cellar.

The room under the tavern was dark, with only a single candle left sputtering in a corner. From what I could see, it had no windows or other exits. A few couches and small tables were arranged haphazardly around, cheap pillows strewn about. There was a low dais in one corner away from the door. Sconces on the walls held extinguished lamps. Little alcoves with draperies offered intimate seclusion from the main room. The frescoes on the walls depicted various scenes of debauchery, from lesbian orgies to fauns raping nymphs. The place smelled of spilled wine, smoke, sweat, and semen.

I heard stamping feet upstairs and ducked from the small landing into the room. There was not enough light to search properly, and if I ventured inside I would risk bumping into the furniture. I bent down and gathered some dust from the floor, adding it to the kerchief.

I waited patiently for a minute more, then climbed upstairs when I could not hear anyone walking around. I sneaked past the kitchen and into the main room. Didia was busy cleaning the tables, but I could see no one else. I winked at her as I walked out.

* * *

From the Dented Skull I made my way back home. Unlike this morning I walked along the waterline and bought a live chicken at the Forum Bovarium. I needed fresh blood, even though I was certain it would only tell me what I already knew. The earth of the floor of the house, hair from its denizens, blood of a sacrifice, wrapped in white cloth, thrown in the fire. Look at how it burns, and see if any residual *magia* was there to permeate the place.

I had the blood of a sacrifice (the chicken, soon to be dinner), dust from the floor (of the actual room), and a hair of a denizen (Didia, who lived above). Close enough. It would tell me what the lack of tingling on my skin and nose had already told me, that the room under the Dented Skull saw nothing more untoward than a little buggery.

So where did the Rite of Pelegrinus take place? And what did Zymaxis do in the Dented Skull, if not hold ceremonies with a cabal?

The stuff I do is small fry, things just above what any piddling charmer can do, not worthy of a decent *incantator*'s time. But a necromantic ceremony like the one performed on Caeso requires a lot of raw power to be channelled correctly, and would shine like a beacon for anyone with the true sight. It would cause ripples and echoes that would be felt far away and stay around for a long time.

And yet someone had managed to pull just such a necromantic ceremony without raising an alarm. That an alarm would be raised, I was certain, for our *quaestors* of the Collegium Incantatorum keep a close watch on dangerous activities. That I would hear of an alarm being raised I was also certain, for such a thing could not be kept a secret. The rumours would percolate through the city faster than bad fish sauce through an old lady.

I was planning on returning to the Dented Skull that night to check out the mysterious Zymaxis. Planning ahead is always prudent, so I stopped at the Pickled Eel on the way and arranged with Crassitius to have the services of Borax again for the night.

By the time I got home it was almost midday. I was planning on catching up on sleep, but that was not to be. As I walked in, I was informed by Dascha that Quintus Sosius had sent me a message saying he might have some information for me. I turned about and left again.

Quintus Sosius was a trader specialising in rare manuscripts. One of my father's fellow cronies, they competed in an amicable manner, almost as often combining resources to collaborate on specific deals. When my father's business collapsed, he had been one of those who were truly sorry to see it happen. He had even tried to help me afterwards, and although appreciative, I had not been seeking the life of a merchant and had struck out on my own.

His main offices were in the Basilica Antonia, as a measure of his success. He also owned scribe shops, producing copies of scrolls to be sold separately. He dealt with anything and everything, from ancient comedies by Aristophanes to the occult writing of the Assyricans, from verified original manuscripts to high-quality copies made for discerning customers.

When I reached his offices I was shown in by his secretary with no delay. Sosius was a man in his sixties, still with impeccably-styled white hair, with a slight build, a small paunch, and green eyes as keen as you would ever see. He rose from his desk and greeted me warmly. "Spurius Vulpius! Come in, come in, have a seat! Wine?"

"Please, Quintus Sosius, no one calls me Spurius Vulpius these days. Just Felix will do." Sosius clapped his hands once, and an obsequious servant rushed in with a silver tray carrying a pitcher of wine and a pitcher of cold water. "Well watered, if you please," I asked, remembering the breakfast I'd never gotten to eat.

"Please do not insult my Verguvian wine. This is from my private estate on the Erratus," he said and continued to pour a generous amount of wine into our cups and only a splash of water. He handed me a cup and we sipped together. He was right to brag; the wine was excellent. I said so.

"Thank you, but I did not ask you here to discuss my wines. I have some news of that matter you asked me about. I received a letter from one of my agents in Hellica regarding an old library being offered for sale. This is an old collection which I always hoped to acquire one day. It seems like the master has finally passed away, and his children are more concerned with converting it to cash.

"This library, if my sources are correct, has a section with an interesting collection of manuscripts of the various branches of *magia*. Most are probably known here, some are completely foreign, and some — so I am told — have been banned. While I cannot confirm this with absolute certainty, the rumour is that it does contain a few ancient scrolls on the *magia vita terminalis*.

"Whether the information is correct or will prove germane to your investigation I cannot promise you. However, I can offer you this. The sum being asked for the whole collection is a staggering ten talents of silver. It is not a sum I am willing to pay without close inspection of the contents, however, the library is located in Ephemezica and I am loathe to travel there now. Instead, I will give you a letter of introduction making you my agent. You can peruse the scrolls and find out their true worth, and, of course, find out any information you deem relevant to your case in the process. You will have the authority to bargain on my behalf, either for the whole collection or for part of it, for a price you see fit. I trust your judgement — your dear old father raised you well. I could even pay you a modest commission. My agent there will be able to arrange for the actual payment and shipment if required. What say you?"

It did not take me long to decide, as I saw no downside. I planned on confronting Zymaxis tonight. If he was a true necromancer and responsible for Caeso's death, I would have this matter resolved and be free to undertake the errand. If I lived through confronting Zymaxis and solved the case, the travel away and extra income would be appreciated. However, if this line of investigation did not pan out for some reason, this library might still turn out to benefit my investigations if it would help me find elusive information about necromantic rites. And, of course, the commission would be welcome just as much.

"Your offer is most kind, Quintus Sosius, and I would be happy to take advantage of it. However, I may not be able to leave for a few days, as I am still investigating leads here."

"Excellent, excellent. I would rather have you there to evaluate the collection. This reminds me of the old days with your father, how we used to manoeuvre together and get the best of both buyers and sellers…. At any rate I will have my scribe issue you the official letters, and send them over to your house by tonight."

When I got home there was another messenger waiting for me. Typheus was standing in the atrium, examining the faded mosaics of the pool. "My master would like to know if you have made any progress on the matter. Marcus Quinctius wishes to proceed with the funeral as quickly as possible. He was loathe to call the embalmers, for fear of rumours spreading. The body lies in state in our atrium, attired according to custom, but since no embalmers have been to it… The funeral needs to happen very soon. My master was worried about the cremation, though, in case there were some… residual effects."

"I understand his concern. Nobody likes an exploding body on the pyre. I will give you the name of someone who can assist Quinctius Corpio discreetly in this matter. He is a foreigner, of course, but can be trusted. He has knowledge about tattoos of power, and if any residue remains in Caeso's body he will defuse it. Come to think of it, I will see him later and give him directions to your master's house. There is also an embalmer I know, one with looser connections to the official guild of embalmers than traditional Egretian ones. A man of great talent and discretion.

"As for the investigation, I have made some progress with leads which I am following, and will report back as soon as I have something concrete. Corpio must surely understand the delicacy of this issue." A thought struck me, and I decided to try it. "The knowledge of these arts comes from afar. Here in Egretia it has been locked or burned for centuries. However, I have information from a trusted source about a trove in Ephemezica that will likely contain information on the… on what Caeso was involved in. I was wondering, could Corpio arrange a passage for me on one of his ships? Unless I can find all the sources of the power used on the young master here in Egretia, I will need to go soon, both there and to Kebros where Caeso spent last autumn."

Typheus left a short while later. I gave him directions and instructions on how to engage my acquaintances Brewyn the tattooist and Akhirabus the embalmer. In return he promised to speak with his master and give me a reply soon about passage on one of the *rhone*'s ships.

Finally, I got to sleep.

CHAPTER VII

I woke up at dusk. Two neatly-folded papyrus squares were waiting for me in my study, sealed with wax impressed with Quintus Sosius' ring. One was addressed to his agent in Ephemezica and the other to the owner of the library. Just as I was finishing Dascha's chicken and beans, I heard her open the door and speak softly. Borax was here and it was time to go.

We made our way to The Dented Skull. The place was half empty, the daylight crowd having gone by now and the night people not yet arrived. I selected a table near a wall, with clear view of the rest of the dining hall and the passage to the back.

I waved down a passing girl and asked for wine. When she got back with two cups and two pitchers, I had her pour more water than wine. "Tell me," I asked, "where is Didia tonight?"

"Helping in the kitchen. She will come out later, when the place fills up."

"Would you be kind enough to tell her Uncle Felix is here?" I produced a bronze *quadrans* and held it to the girl.

She took it, nodded and left.

We sipped the wine as we waited. True to my expectation from the clientele, this was a decent vintage, spiced lightly with honey and thyme. The owner knew his customers would not settle for less.

We didn't have to wait long. Didia passed by bearing a tray

loaded with small plates of pickles and distributed them among the guests. On her way back to the kitchen she stopped at our table and laid a plate of olives down. "Couldn't stay away?" she winked at me.

"Not from your blue eyes. Tell me, though, has Zymaxis arrived yet? I was rather hoping to speak to him."

She frowned. "He's bad, that one, thoroughly bad. But that is your business. No, he is not here. He usually arrives later, though they seclude themselves downstairs well before midnight, when their chanting begins." She shuddered.

I took out a *sestertius* and left it on the table. "Please point him out to me, when he comes."

She took the coin, hoisted her tray and left without another word. Borax and I remained at our table, sipping slowly and keeping an eye on the back stairway.

After a short while, when it looked like no one was coming or going to the downstairs room, I got up, stretched, scratched myself, and told Borax, "I am going to look for the latrines, will be right back."

I went to the rear of the house. As I was walking past the kitchen, a large man wearing a dark blue tunic came out and headed towards the main room. He looked me up and down and said "This is the private section. If you're looking for the latrines, it's out the front door, around the corner to the right and twenty paces down the alley."

I had to make a quick decision. Since he appeared like he might be the proprietor, I lowered my voice and said, "Actually, my good man, I have heard your fine establishment holds the most excellent private parties. I was hoping to see if I can get an invitation." I jingled the purse inside my tunic.

His face relaxed and registered interest now, but he replied, "Tonight is booked up. Private party. Come tomorrow — it's pretty boys' night; or three days hence we have an open banquet when I am sure we could find you something you will like."

I put my head closer to his. "I have heard about special parties, not your usual orgies. I was told that the *Nones* are the nights to come."

His face became inscrutable. "I do not know who you are. If you give me your name and stay in the main room, I will let… the organiser know that you are interested. He will either contact you or not. But you must not come here again without invitation. Now return to the tavern and wait there."

I went back to my table and sat down with Borax. Crassitius had given me a true professional, not your usual drunken ex-gladiator, for I saw his wine cup was still untouched. And suddenly I felt this would be handy tonight.

We sat in our corner table for what seemed like an hour. We kept sipping very slowly from the spiced wine, nibbling on olives, pickled onions and radishes. The place filled up with what I presumed were the usual clientele. A mix of respectable men on the way back from their day of labour, and cheap human entertainment starting their night's work.

One by one I saw men going to the rear of the house, nod to the proprietor on the way, and head down the stairs. I counted seven, all men. They all seemed affluent by the cut of their tunics and hair, the youngest in his late twenties, the oldest about fifty. Occasionally, I caught Didia's eye, but she always shook her head slightly and moved on.

Sometime during our third cup of watered wine, I saw a man come in and walk straight to the back room. He was short, completely bald, tanned skin, of lithe and graceful build. In his late thirties or early forties, I estimated. He wore a dark green tunic, embroidered with gold thread in a classic pattern of squares around the edges. On his waist was a leather belt, beautifully tooled and with shining brass buckle and studs. Even before Didia gave me an urgent look, I knew this must be Zymaxis.

As the man walked to the back stairwell, the proprietor (whose name I never learnt) poked his head out and went after him. I saw them standing at the top of the stairs going down, heads together conferring in whispers. The proprietor nodded in my direction, and Zymaxis turned his gaze on me. Our eyes locked and held together for a long moment.

Without averting his gaze, Zymaxis cut off the other man with a wave of his hand and walked to my table. "I understand that you have been asking about me," he said, without introduction.

I held his gaze for a moment before answering. His eyes were pale green, accentuated by his tunic. His voice was clear and resonant, his accent cultured. He gave me the impression of an intelligent and charismatic man. "I believe I have," I answered.

"Leave your slave here and come." He turned around and walked to the back of the tavern. I got up and followed.

Before we went down the stairs he ducked into an empty private dining room, located close to the kitchen. He faced me and said, "We can speak a bit more openly here. Now, who are you and what have you heard about me?"

"My name is Felix, sometimes called Felix the Fox. I have heard of you from a friend of a friend of a friend. I have heard rumours of ancient rites and found it most intriguing."

"And why should I be interested in you?"

"I make my way in the world in the service of others, although that was not always so. I used to study in the Collegium Incantatorum, until my family's fortune was lost and I was expelled in shame. I am still keenly interested in such matters, though, and have always been drawn to the real powers that flow throughout our world. I make my living as a fox, a diviner of occult matters and items for others. However, if what I heard was correct, you have a better vision of both power and future."

He gave me a calculating look for a long moment. "Interesting. What you might be referring to sounds highly illegal to me. What is to stop me from reporting you?"

"If what I have heard is true, you will be avoiding the officials just as much as me. If what I have heard is *not* true, they would hardly care for either you or me. But if what I have heard is, indeed, true, then you are looking for men like me." That last bit was a guess, of course, but if he was running an underground cabal he would no doubt find my story intriguing enough to be considered.

He thought a moment further, and I could see on his face when he made his decision. "You are direct, I will give you that. And I ap-preciate directness. Come," and he walked out of the room and turned down the stairs.

***

The room under the tavern looked quite different than it had that morning. Lamps were lit in the sconces, giving me a better view of the lurid frescoes. All the couches and tables were pushed against the walls. Two tripod tables were set aside from the others, close to the doorway. One had only a simple black cloth on it. The other had some items but I could not discern what they were, for they were covered with a similar black cloth. And, very noticeably, in the centre of the room hung a single rose from the ceiling — the whole affair was done *sub rosa*, in secret. Yet my skin did not tingle and I could sense no enchantments present.

The seven men I had seen before going down were waiting here. None were sitting, all standing talking amongst themselves. The conversation stopped as soon as we stepped in, and all eyes turned on me.

"Friends," said Zymaxis as he walked to the gathered men, "this is Felix. He has put himself forward as a candidate for our little group."

As Zymaxis was talking, I took a better look at the other men present. The man to my left seemed like a merchant. In his mid-thirties, wearing a very fine, red tunic richly embroidered with gold thread under a pristine white toga. Fashionably barbered reddish hair, soft hands. He wore a larger than usual iron citizen's ring, showing an ornate seal.

The next man to him was taller and slimmer, standing erect. In his early forties, fit, with close-cropped dark hair, greying at the temples. An inscrutable look was on his face as he studied me. I imagined him to be a military man. With his gold senator's ring, he must have been high-ranking.

To his left again stood a man with wind-weathered face and arms. Short, tanned, wiry muscles, legs slightly apart. Wearing a grey tunic of a style favoured by sailors. Clearly a seaman, though I was not sure if navy or of the merchant fleet. He projected self-assurance and I imagined him to be a captain.

Somewhat behind Zymaxis stood a mousy little man, with thin brown hair and blue eyes. I estimated him to be in his early forties as well. I could see some scars up on his arms, though they were mostly covered by his well-tailored tunic and toga. His manner was very passive, and even though he rarely looked directly into my eyes, I saw them sparkle with intelligence. He wore an iron ring and a *pileus* — the small conical felt cap of manumitted slaves.

The next man in the circle was the youngest, in his late twenties. A trained *incantator*, that much was obvious from the trappings of his belt and the wide saffron-coloured stripe on the right side of his tunic. He wore his hair longer and sported a thin jawline beard that was currently fashionable with the young rich boys of our city. His citizen's ring was of gold, indicating he was from a family of senatorial rank. I tagged him as a recalcitrant son of a senator.

The last but one man was the only one not wearing a citizen's ring besides Zymaxis. He was in his mid-thirties, dark of skin and fair of eyes and hair. A long, straight nose. Classic Hellican look, even without the Hellican pleated chiton he was wearing. He looked at me with open curiosity.

The last man, immediately to my right, was another *incantator*. He wore an iron ring and a good but slightly faded tunic, and was the oldest and the shabbiest of them all. In his early fifties, with straggling hair covering his balding pate from one side to the other, and greasy stains on his tunic. He gave me an unkind look, and my reaction to him was similar.

With varied backgrounds, all were men of middle years, successful, and — I was feeling certain — hungry for more.

"As is common with us," Zymaxis continued, "there will be no introductions as of yet. Only should Felix be chosen for initiation will he be welcome into our circle.

"You all have been initiated; you all are dedicated to our cause. You are all exasperated at the stifling choke-hold the collegia maintain over our city. This arcane ruling by the archaic collegia is preventing honest citizens from pursuing knowledge, success, power! We, men of action, men of the morrow, are looking to shed the yoke placed upon us and rise once more. Egretia is being held back from its true potential, and it is up to us to free it from its shackles and lead it to a bright future, taking its rightful place as the leader of nations — with us at its head!"

Zymaxis paused and drew a deep breath. "And as you all have pledged and proven your dedication and loyalty to our cause, so now must Felix." He turned his gaze on me, and so did the others. "You are now required to prove both your merit and dedication. As with all other initiates, you need to complete a task to show your value. Considering your self-proclaimed expertise of being a fox, sniffing items of enchantment, I would task you to provide our group with an object of significant value. Not mere riches, but an item of learning, of purpose. You must ascertain and procure something that is declared contraband by our collegia, an item that can be used in the pursuit of knowledge by educated people, that can further us in our cause. What such a thing shall be, I will leave to you. My only advice is that you should think carefully. It must not be a trinket or a trivial enchantment that can be bought on the black market by any common criminal, but something to impress the future directors of Egretia's greatness.

"Once you have procured such an object you will return here and present it to us. If we accept your offering, we will ask you to swear your allegiance to our cause. You will take a sacred and binding blood oath together with all of us. This oath cannot be broken save by death, and will mark you as one of us. From that moment on you will devote all your life, possessions and skills to our group and our cause."

All eyes were focused on me at that moment. Zymaxis had a zealot's glow on his face, the soldier and captain inscrutable as before. The boy and the foreigner seemed interested in my reaction, the freedman similarly but with sidelong looks. The merchant to my left and the ageing *incantator* to my right both had unkind looks in their eyes, not openly hostile but disapproving and unsympathetic.

"Now, then," said Zymaxis, "will you accept those terms?"

The task, while I had no definite idea at that time what I could use to gain their trust, did not concern me much. I have been in the business of ferreting information and small items of power for long enough, and have learnt enough from my father's dealership in antiquated and enchanted paraphernalia, to know how to approach traders in illicit contraband.

The blood oath did worry me, though. These things can be binding, and who knew what else would Zymaxis add to it? I could end up completely in his thrall. Such oaths can be mutual to ensure people remain true to each other, but the more sinister of these binding charms affect the bound profoundly, with complete subjugation of their will. The other members did not seem to suffer any of those effects, though that could just mean a more subtle enchantment. Could I risk such an oath?

In the end, of course, I did not have much choice. With all their eyes upon me I accepted their terms with as much enthusiasm as I could muster. Reactions were congruent with their previous dispositions, from smiling acceptance, to guarded nods, to barely masked disapproval.

"You have chosen wisely," Zymaxis told me with a smile. "I am confident that you will complete the tasks and pass our tests. However, now we must ask you to leave us. Until such time as you have been initiated into our circle you may not attend our meetings. Ah, here is our good host, Titus Septimius! Right on time."

I looked behind and saw the proprietor walk in carrying a large silver tray bearing two pitchers. Rather uncommonly, both pitchers contained wine, and not wine and water. Behind him walked in Didia, carrying cups, bread, and shallow bowls of olive oil.

Septimius nodded to Zymaxis, placed the tray on the clear table and left the room with Didia. He gave me a curious sidelong glance as he walked past me, but made no comments.

"One last thing before you leave us on your quest, Felix." Zymaxis went to the two tables at the side of the group. He uncovered the objects hidden so far by the black cloth. I saw three little lidded jars, like the *pyxidae* women use to store their cosmetics. He opened one of them and took out a pinch of what looked like ground herbs, which he dropped into one of the cups. He poured wine on top of the herbs, and some into another cup. He picked up both cups and gently sloshed the spiced wine as he walked back towards me. "This is not yet time for your blood oath, of course, but you would understand that we must still carry our meetings in secret while the oppressive collegia remain in control. I am certain that you will prove yourself dedicated to our cause, however as a simple precaution I would ask you to drink from this cup before you leave us."

He extended the cup with the spiced wine towards me, and I took it from his hands. He raised his own cup. "To free knowledge and a better Egretia!" he exclaimed and drank deeply. All eyes were on me.

"To free knowledge and a better Egretia!" I repeated and drank from my cup.

* * *

Borax must have been quite concerned at the look on my face, for after I climbed back to the main room I hastily made my way straight out of the tavern. He followed me outside and saw me pushing my fingers down my throat, retching and vomiting repeatedly on the corner, until nothing was left in my stomach.

I walked shakily to the nearest crossroads, and rinsed my mouth with water from the public fountain. Only then did I respond to Borax's concerns about my health.

We went back to the Dented Skull and sat at our previous table. I wanted to think about the events that have just transpired, but I also wanted to remain close to where the cabal met. By now the place was quite busy, with patrons drinking, eating, and socialising; with whores scouting for customers and thieves scouting for victims. As we sat down, I fished out of my tunic the small pouch I always carry with me and took out a few herbs of my own. I chewed on them slowly and washed down their bitter taste with wine.

Zymaxis must be a *veneficitor*, an *incantator* that specialises in the *veneficium* branch of enchantment, concerned with herbs and poisons. If he was using concoctions and potions to achieve his ends, it would explain why I could not feel any magic taking place here. Any extra enchantment required to bring out the potency of his admixtures, could have been performed well in advance and in another place. I could only hope that my immediate expulsion of the treated wine together with the antidote herbs I was chewing would eliminate any effect Zymaxis intended.

I didn't want to stay here long, however. When Didia next

walked by I drew her close and pretended to request her favours again. From the corner of my eye I saw the proprietor shrug and nod upstairs at her.

Once in her room, I held her hands from taking off her tunic and looked into her grey eyes. "Lovely as the idea is, right now I need to ask you something. I will pay you just the same. I saw you bring the wine to Zymaxis' gathering. Have you noticed the three little boxes, the *pyxidae* he keeps on the table next to the wine?"

She nodded and I continued. "I came in the room together with him, but the boxes were already there. Does he keep them here?"

"My master keeps the *pyxidae* locked for him in a special trunk, and Zymaxis is the only one allowed to open them. He comes and refills them at times, usually on the day before their meetings."

"Do you have access to them? Could you get me a sample of their contents?"

"No! My *dominus* would beat me! He keeps the chest locked in his room, and even if I could open it, if my master caught me poking in his room he would have me whipped!" She was shaking.

"No, we wouldn't want that." I hugged her and waited until she calmed down.

"I will have to think up another way to get them, then. My employer is most interested in their contents, and would be quite generous." I hummed for a bit. "Say, do you ever help set up or clean the room after their little gatherings?"

"The master sets it up in the evenings. He has specific directions from Zymaxis, and sometimes they have… other things there," she shuddered again. "Sometimes, though, if *dominus* is too busy or just too tired when they are done, he will send me down there to clean up before he puts the boxes and paraphernalia away. This is how I know he locks them."

"Well, now, that suggests a plan. I could tire out your master with songs and drinks. If he sends you down to clean after tonight, will you be able to steal a small quantity of the contents of each of the *pyxidae*? Even a pinch would be enough. My employer would be most grateful, and reward accordingly for all your risks."

In the end the promise of monies that would make a significant contribution to her freedom fund made the most impression. I also promised her ten *denarii* for every name of the cabal she overheard. I left her five silver *denarii* as a down payment for the herb samples and the names.

With the money on the table and my hands around her shoulders, we ended up in bed again.

Back at the main room, Borax was patiently waiting for me at our table. Rather than risk drawing attention to myself by staying there, we settled our account and left. Out on the street I outlined my plan to Borax. He wasn't a natural actor, but the role suited him well enough.

We started to wander the streets of the Clivi Inferior, like two old chums gone carousing. Whenever we passed others on the street we discussed, loudly, the merits of the wine and whores at The Dented Skull. We marvelled at that randy old goat who was marrying the sweet teenager tomorrow, and was so happy he was buying drinks for everyone present there. We told each other of the serving maids at the Dented Skull, their relative merits and measurements. We even sat for a drink at a few other taverns, drank the wine, complained bitterly on how lacklustre it was compared to the one served at the Dented Skull, and declared loudly that we were making our way back to that Elysian place of sweet wine and kindly prostitutes. Finding celebrants was not hard that night, as this was the first day of the *Megalenses Ludi* and a great number of people were out and about looking for thrills.

By the time we circled our way back to the Dented Skull, it was packed. New customers were eagerly ordering wines and food, giving the local ladies a brisk night, running into old friends and colleagues, and generally making merry. The proprietor must have been surprised at the sudden turnout, though he was too busy to really care once the money started flowing in.

Borax and I waited mostly outside, near the public fountain at the square up the alley. Only occasionally did we go to take a look. As the night progressed, so did the revelry. Whenever things seemed in danger of calming down, we found a way to get a round of drinks to all the patrons without drawing attention. I had not seen Zymaxis or any of the other members of his cabal leave the tavern, but with the crowds that were there I might have missed them. Of Didia I barely saw more than a glance, as she was kept busy with the night's activities.

It was well past midnight when affairs started to calm down. The patrons were getting tired and the whores were getting frayed. By two hours before the dawn the Dented Skull was mostly deserted. When I peeked inside there was no sign of Septimius or Didia, and only one of the other maids remained, cleaning up the place.

I waited patiently with Borax in the alley outside the Dented Skull. A while later Didia came out, emptying a bucket into the gutters, looking haggard. A square of folded linen and a small pouch full of coins quickly exchanged hands without a word, and Didia went back inside. There was nothing left for Borax and me but to head back home.

CHAPTER VIII

Iawoke late and spent what little remained of the following day analysing the samples Didia had gotten for me from Zymaxis' *pyxidae*. I had no way of telling which one he had put in my drink, so I was interested in all three samples to see what else he might have used. My knowledge of herbs, poisons and potions was limited to practical titbits, and I could not hope to match a trained *veneficitor*. I ran all the tests I could think of on the tiny samples Didia had gone to the risk of getting for me. I detected no poisons, only mild hallucinogenics, which relieved me somewhat. I also did not detect any enchantment, however, *veneficium* doesn't necessarily involve a raw power called into the potion. Besides, as much as I hate to admit it, it could just as easily have been too subtle for my meagre skills.

I needed to find more information, and wanted to carefully consider my options first. While I had met with Zymaxis and his cabal I had still known very little about them, and in fact hadn't even known any of the names of the other members. Asking around after a military man with an unknown rank or affiliation of an unnamed senatorial family, or of an ageing, failing *incantator* of unspecified speciality and with bad manners would not get me anywhere. The answers I was likely to get would be "aren't all of them like that?"

And what if these men heard I was asking after them, and decided they did not like this turn of events? Of course, some of them might be asking after me regardless; if I didn't try to find out about them I would be facing an unknown cabal, completely in the dark if they took exception to me and chose to strike. I was beginning to feel paranoid and washed my face in the fountain to cool my head.

That left asking around after Zymaxis himself. The name was foreign, vaguely Assyrican, though he spoke perfect *Quirite* with hardly an accent. I had learnt about him from Caeso's friends and from Mahatixa, and both times only in relation to The Dented Skull. I had not seen him or any of the other members of the cabal leave last night, so I had not been able to follow any of them. And so again, a dearth of leads. The proprietor of the Dented Skull was in Zymaxis' employ, and my feeling was that he would not talk to me — and would alert him in detail later. I also felt that I had extracted all the information I could out of Didia.

So I had to consider other options available to me, in addition to fishing out about the men of the cabal. For my task, I was told their next meeting there would be on the night eight days before the *Kalends* of *Maius*, the free night between the festivals of the *Parilia* and the *Vinalia*, sixteen days from today. The one after that again on the *Nones* of *Maius*. They might meet at other times, or they might not, but those were the days I was told to show up to impress them with my solution to their puzzle.

I paced around the unkempt peristyle garden in my old and empty house, mocked by the grinning faun and his enormous phallus.

Still, a man such as Zymaxis, a man with charisma, with an agenda, a man who managed to recruit — and possibly kill — from all walks of Egretian life, a man like that must surely leave tracks. I left my house determined to sniff them out.

* * *

I started with my friend Akhirabus, herbalist and specialist embalmer. His shop was located near to the Porta Fulvia on the street of the embalmers. When walking down that street between all the shops of those whose business is the end of life, one is accosted by many fragrances. Funeral wreaths, fresh flowers to lay about corpses, unguents and balsams for the preparation of dead bodies — all very aromatic, to mask the unsavoury smells accompanying death.

When I entered the shop of Akhirabus my nose was blatantly assaulted, like a green recruit facing his first enemy cavalry charge. It was not so much that the smells were strong or clashing — although there was plenty of that, too — but just the sheer variety of them was overwhelming. With every small draught, with every step, with every turn of the head, new heady smells and perfumes clamoured for my attention. Akhirabus was not a mere embalmer, he was a master herbalist as well, and his shop was stocked with amazingly varied supplies from all over the known world.

Happily, I found Akhirabus on the premises, and he greeted me warmly as I entered. "Thank you for the commission, my friend. The money was good, but more than that — the interest! I have not had so much fun with corpses for a long time. In my business, human innards start to all look the same after a while. But this! An intriguing puzzle. You Egretians do not like tattooing yourself, and place so many restrictions on the *magia vita* as you call it, so I rarely get such interesting corpses to prepare." His jet-black eyes were twinkling, set in an old and wrinkled face, brown leathery skin covering his head without a single hair to be seen. "Your friend with the funny name — 'Brew-in' — and I worked together on the young man's remains. He is a professional, too, it was a pleasure see him remove the tattoos."

"What can you make of it? Have you seen the likes of this before?"

"Seen? Oh no, not seen. But heard. A long time ago in the old country. It reminds me of tales by my old teacher, tales of ancient rituals transforming the *ib*, the heart. None of them have been practised for aeons, and I fear the knowledge might be lost. For good reason, too. You saw what happened to the poor boy, his whole *ka* was torn horribly from his body," said Akhirabus.

"It reminded me of something I had read about before, in the libraries of the Collegium. It was named the Rite of Pelegrinus."

"Pelegrinus, Amon-Ib-Khat — names change, the essence does not. How did the child become involved?"

"That is what I am trying to find out. I was hoping you could help me." I said.

"I am afraid my knowledge of these matters is flawed, and I am most ashamed that I cannot offer you more than you already know." He shook his head in genuine sadness as he spoke this.

"Would you make a guess as to what was required?" I asked. "Even with flawed knowledge, your opinion is still better than anybody else's."

"You flatter me," Akhirabus said. "For what it's worth, I would advise that you should not limit yourself to the specific ritual you mentioned. Search for the essence. The peak of a mountain can be reached by many paths. The mountain is still the same, but the view on the way up may be different."

I asked Akhirabus for help with the spice mixtures I'd gotten at the Dented Skull as well. Herbalism being his passion, he was delighted at yet another puzzle, although he was not able to tell me anything I did not already know. "If you leave them with me," he told me, "I will be able to examine them with more care later. These things take time, you understand. The samples are small, and I will need to carefully consider each test, use them most sparingly with the utmost care. If you come back in a few days, I will tell you what I find."

* * *

This was the *Nones* of *Avrilis*, the fifth day of the month named after *Fortuna Virilis*, and the city was on holiday due to the *Megalenses Ludi*. Virilis is the aspect of Fortuna dedicated to hiding the imperfections of women from men. Only fitting that the games dedicated to the Great Mother would be held then. These games were not like the usual circus games with chariot races and wrestling bouts; after the opening ceremonies of discordant chanting by self-flagellating eunuchs, most of the celebrations consisted of theatre plays. Everywhere people were attending theatres, from formal Egretian masked dramas and comedies to the most debased street mimes with bare breasts and bottoms. A cultural melting pot at its best, as the Great Mother is not an Egretian presence.

In this atmosphere, I decided to spend the rest of the daytime on locating Mahatixa's troupe and querying her in further details about Zymaxis.

Easier said than done. I spent hours walking streets full of happy revellers, chasing rumours of a foreign troupe with the sign of the sphinx. Mahatixa's troupe remained elusive. Whomever I asked, from tavern owners to sailors to passing citizens in the street, had either never heard of them or swore on his mother's shade that they had just been spotted on the other side of the city from where I was. There was no shortage of mime troupes in Egretia during the festivals of the *Megalenses Ludi*, many apparently even with dancing dark-skinned beauties, though the one I was after was nowhere to be found. After walking for miles around the city and visiting neighbourhoods from the fancy to the slums, when it was getting late at night I gave up.

In between chasing the entertainers, I attempted some discreet queries about Zymaxis. Most people were in a happy and festive mood, and I tried my best not to stand out like a diseased facial wart. I stopped at taverns where I knew seditious elements visited, I asked friends known to follow the town gossip, I bought wine and chatted, asking oblique questions and getting oblique answers. Nothing concrete, no rumours of an Assyrican, *veneficitor* or otherwise, dissatisfied with the current regime. I could not be too open with my questions, and thus did not get informative answers.

I ended up feeling like a dog chasing its tail, trying to talk to people I had already spoken to and get them to reveal things they probably did not know.

* * *

I trudged up the hill back to my home. I was tired from little sleep the night before and much walking today, and knew I had a lot more pounding of pavements to do over the following days. I opened my front door and stepped into the vestibule. Something did not feel right. I put my hand inside my tunic and clutched my dagger's hilt. I closed the door quietly behind me and walked into the house.

I stepped into the atrium and froze. Sitting on folding chairs and facing each other were Dascha and Araxus, staring and giving each other the evil eye, looking for all intents and purposes like two rival mangy cats hissing and spitting.

I relaxed. A little.

"He pushed right in, *domine!* He said he has a message for you, but if he's a messenger I am a young nymph." Dascha sniffed in indignation.

"Dascha, this is Araxus. He used to come here quite often. You should remember him."

She peered at him incredulously. "Araxus? But he looks as old as me, *domine.* That can't be your old friend, can it?" Araxus scratched his side under his filthy garment and chewed on the end of his unkempt beard. Dascha turned away in disgust. "I never knew what you saw in him, young *dominus.*"

"It's all right, Dascha, I can address this from now. You can go back to your duties."

She went away, shooting a last disgusted, spiteful look at Araxus over her shoulder.

"Dascha said you have a message for me. Did you find something?" I said, with vague hopes that my attempt at trusting him would not be frustrated.

He looked up at me with his green right eye, while his left black eye kept following Dascha. "It's the light, don't you see?"

I stared at him blankly. "What?"

"It's the light. The light! It must be the light. That's the only way, the light. Surely you see it?" he pleaded.

"What are you babbling about?"

I got nothing coherent out of him. Araxus kept babbling something about the light, how bright it was, how it distracted him, how he could not look at it, how surely I should be able to see how it was related. I couldn't. I had no time or patience for his mad ramblings; all he did was remind me of Helena. Some days he was lucid and sharp as he was in our youth. Some days his mind was gone, a dangerous raving lunatic. Eventually I ejected him none too kindly from my home. A bad ending to the day.

CHAPTER IX

I got up the following day, the day after the *Nones* of *Avrilis*, five days after starting the investigation, in a foul mood. Running into Araxus last night had resulted in sleep plagued by bad dreams again. Feet sore to match my head and heart, I set out early to try to chase leads.

The day did not disappoint my low expectations. I started by trying to locate Caeso's friends, to ask them again about Zymaxis or Mahatixa. Drusus, it appeared, had sailed off on an errand for his *magister* at the Collegium Mercatorum. Of Caeso's two other friends, Porcius and Lutatius, there was no sign. The door slave at the Collegium was as snooty as ever, and no bribe offered seemed to satisfy him. I had to hasten away with my tail between my legs when he called the guards.

Trying a different tack, on the way back from the Forum I stopped at another acquaintance, Brewyn the tattoo master. His shop, if one can call it that, was at the rear of another shop of sundries in the Subvales, where the large tenements and stews of Egretia were. His clientele was made up of other Pictonii, Arbarii and Capilanii — all the people we subjugated, who mark their skins in a very un-Egretian manner.

I walked into the outer shop, walked past the snoozing elderly man on his rickety chair, past the bags and shelves haphazardly loaded with miscellaneous sundries and supplies, nodded to the elderly wife at the counter who gave me a sour look, and passed through the curtain to the back room. Brewyn was sitting with his back to me, the blue woad tattoos on his neck and muscular arms peeking out from under his light tunic. A large man in his thirties, his dun-coloured hair showed no signs of receding.

He was working carefully on a man sitting in a chair in front of him. "Wait your turn," he said without turning.

I stood obediently at the door, leaning on the frame and watching him work. He was finishing a design on the man's face, an intricate spiralling maze of lines and dots. He had the lines traced in place, and was carefully pricking the skin with a sharp fish-bone needle. After each section, he daubed at the blood and then rubbed the blue ink into the wounds.

"There," Brewyn said as he straightened up. "Give it a few days, and rub the ointment daily. You'll be able to go back to your family in Capirica, and no one will be the wiser about the marks your *dominus* left on you here."

The man thanked him, picked up the small *pyxis* with unguents from Brewyn, paid generously, and left. Brewyn finally turned and lifted his eyes to me. "Oho! Felix the Fox! I thought you might come by. Here, have a seat," he indicated the client's chair.

"You liked the commission I sent your way, then?" I asked as I sat down and accepted a cup of wine.

"Indeed, indeed. A very peculiar case. Took me the most of the night to defuse the *stercus* that the young *mentula* had on him. What did that rich *cunnus* get into? I thought you Egretians despised tattoos."

"You know we do. I have been hired by his father to find out exactly what mess he got himself embroiled in. I was hoping you could tell me something about it."

"I could tell you it wasn't your regular corner-store *fellator* who gave him those. Those were power tattoos — *stigmas*. But you knew that, didn't you?" He looked into my eyes with a half-smile. "That is why you had him ask for me to work with the embalmer."

"I thought it would be prudent. Did you recognise the design, or the method?" I asked.

"No. The design was detailed enough to look… specific, though I have never seen a combination of lines and arrangements such as this. I tattoo people of all nations who pass through Egretia, or at least notice them on people more than most. And I thought I saw them all! However, that was not a style I have ever come across."

"And the method?"

"It was a reasonably clean hand, though not a professional. Definitely not a hand I recognised. I would say that whoever did this probably practised some on animal skin but does not tattoo for a living. I could see more hesitant lines at the edge of the pattern, growing bolder and surer as the work progressed."

"And the power, could you tell how it was done?"

"After it was completed, if you ask me. I have drawn a few power *stigmas* myself, albeit not this big. There are several ways of getting the *magia* into them, some from the beginning, some at the end. It depends on the method used and the effect desired. This one… this one was drawn first, and then juiced up with a lightning bolt. It was still crackling on the poor *stercus'* corpse. I had some fun getting rid of the residues, I shit you not."

I sipped my wine and gathered my thoughts. "What can you tell me that will help me track the ones who did this?"

"I don't know the hand or the style, but… the ink for those tattoos was not regular woad, nor any of the dyes I have encountered in my many years of tattooing. That much I am certain of. If you get me the recipe for the ink, perhaps I could help you track who might deal with those items, and who might have the skill to prepare it. There will not be many found in Egretia, and exotic materials could be traced by their suppliers."

I thanked him, stood up and promised to return when I discovered the recipe.

"Why don't you let me tattoo you, eh?" Brewyn asked me. "I can do you some nice design, under the toga. No one will ever know except the ladies you entertain. I can even put some power into them, so those ladies will be guaranteed entertainment," he said with an awful leer.

"*Mentulam caco,*" I declined.

***

After a hasty lunch of bread stuffed with overly spiced pork that did more to my indigestion than my hunger, I changed tack and again went after anyone who might have heard of Zymaxis' cabal. The members of his little group had come from all walks of life. An army officer, a naval officer, two *incantatores* — one young and one old — a merchant, a freed slave and a Hellican. Two from obvious senatorial-rank families, four of regular citizen status, and one non-citizen foreigner. All of them, however, seemed well-off, educated people. All with a grudge against society, if they subscribed to Zymaxis' rants.

I tried to put myself in Zymaxis' shoes. If I were starting an illegal cabal to stage a coup, where would I find such men for support? This was certainly not something I had previously ever thought to do. I tried to go by way of elimination. None of his recruits were low criminals, so I discarded those aspects of society. Neither did they seem to me exceedingly rich nor high ranking, as those tend to resist change, with more to lose than to gain from a social upheaval. I flattered myself that my lack of ideas was because I was an upright citizen who always supported the traditions of our republic, but the cynic inside my head laughed at me.

I had on the first day of my investigation sounded out old contacts for possible necromantic connections. This yielded one lead, the library in Ephemezica that Sosius had asked me to review, in the belief that it might contain ancient scrolls with knowledge of *magia vita terminalis*. Would approaching them again, now on the subject of social unrest, produce any different results? Or would it land me in trouble, asking so many dubious questions?

The other matter troubling me was that if I wanted to join the cabal, I had to fulfil their task. In between searching for information about the cabal members, I gave thought to what I could impress them with to gain acceptance. And here, too, a dearth of options: I did not have the time to really devote to it, and buying something outright would have been both too cost prohibitive and too obvious.

Thus, when I saw no other leads, I visited the Forum and gossiped with the old chinwaggers, trying to suss out any rumours of civil unrest and of the political bickering and manoeuvring within the Senate. Were there any factions more dissatisfied than usual? Were any names associated with shady dealings in *magia*? Were there any rumours of interesting items being discovered, procured or moved around? Did the descriptions of the men I had seen ring a bell, sound familiar?

Nothing, or at least nothing more promising than gossip so wildly speculative that even at my desperate state I could not credit it.

I found this oblique way of investigations, this constant misdirection, of trying to ask questions without truly ever reaching the heart of the matter, all very frustrating.

The funeral for Caeso was due the next morning. I decided that if I could not come up with any promising avenue for investigation by then, I would take Sosius up on his offer and visit the library in Ephemezica, and try to find information about the rite that Caeso had undergone. Even if all I found were ceremonies of a similar vein and not the specific rite, it might still provide me with insights into the requirements and preparations, which could turn into leads as I retraced his preparations. I would have something to give to Akhirabus and Brewyn, who could point me further in the right direction. And if I got lucky, I might even find a scroll of sufficient value and interest to be my entry pass to the cabal!

I also resolved to visit the island of Kebros, as Caeso had seemingly experienced something there that made him come back with renewed vigour. Understanding the steps he had taken on his way from the start would help me understand the end of his path, as well.

* * *

The next morning I got up early, broke fast with millet porridge sweetened with dates, put on my toga and went to pay my last respects to Caeso. A crowd was already gathered outside Corpio's mansion on the Septentrionali. I joined the queue of people waiting to go inside.

Caeso's body was displayed on the traditional bier in the atrium, feet facing the door, laid at an angle so that his face was visible to onlookers. He was dressed in a toga over a long tunic, hiding the tattoos or what remained of them. His face looked calm, a testament to the skill of Akhirabus, and in his mouth the traditional coin. The small scars my blade had left at the sides of his jaw were hardly visible, concealed with makeup. Around him were arranged many fragrant flowers and boughs, though they could not completely mask the reek. Akhirabus had done an excellent job, considering he'd gotten to him quite late.

I shuffled back out with the rest of the gathered people and waited for the funeral to start. Around mid-morning the procession finally embarked on its way. As Caeso came from a rich family of senatorial rank, he was given every custom and rite, even though he was still too young to have achieved much by himself.

First came the specially trained musicians hired for the day. They led the procession with deep brass trumpeting alerting all that a dead body was passing. After the musicians came the professional mourners. Women dressed in rags, crying, wailing, in tears, pulling their hair, vocalising the abject misery of a family who could not participate in such unrespectable behaviour.

After the mourners came the mimes. Special actors, they wore the wax masks of the notable ancestors of Caeso, acting and mimicking their behaviour in life. I have never met them of course, but from the discussion of the people around me the actors had an uncanny talent that reminded everybody of past members of this great family.

The body came next, borne by friends and relatives, lying in state on the same bier as before. A formal event, the two fasces-bearing *lictors* of his father preceded the bier, while Corpio walked alone behind it. Other close relatives and friends followed a few steps behind Corpio. I saw Typheus walking amongst them, as well, showing his respect to his master. I looked at Corpio, trying to discern his mood; however, since he was a professional politician it was hard to tell how much was genuine and how much was an act. He walked erect, his face sombre, his pace measured. Never smiling, looking ahead, the picture of the respectable, stoic Egretian.

The procession stopped for a short while in the Forum Egretium, and Corpio himself delivered the eulogy. Caeso being a young lad at the time of his death, there was not much to talk about besides his youth in itself — and his family. A true politician of the eternally scheming Senate, Corpio did weave his own ancestry's greatness into the eulogy, for the benefit of future voters.

After the eulogy came the arduous part of Egretian funerals. From the Forum the procession wound its way up the steep Via Verguvia. The road starts at the Forum and climbs the steep sides of Vergu. Once out of the Porta Alta, the road keeps climbing up the mountain. In ancient times, it was the custom of our people to climb all the way to the top and hold the funerals on a large ledge overlooking the mouth of the volcano. These days, thankfully, most funerals are held a short way out of the city gates, or there would be a lot more funerals when men and women keel over from exertion.

The procession reached its destination on a flat area overlooking the lush valley of the Fulvius and Erratus rivers. A pyre was already waiting, prepared in advance by the undertakers. The musicians, mourners and actors ceased their performance and stood respectfully to the side. The bearers laid the bier upon the ready pyre.

Corpio took up a torch from a waiting slave and held it aloft. He paused and looked at the body of his son, lying peacefully and awaiting passage to the next world. He mumbled the old traditional saying, the one hardly heard these days for the departed,

Tu non estis.
Fortassis ut oblatio carne vestras auxilium reperiat viam lemuri tuum ad Dis.

'You are no more. May the offering of your flesh help your shade find its way to *Dis*'.

I guess everyone becomes sentimental and superstitious at funerals.

He paused again, drew breath and cast the torch onto the pyre. The kindling caught and soon the air was full of swirling particles of ash, the flames dancing higher as they consumed the body of Caeso. Corpio stood for a long while, staring silently into the flames.

On the way down the mountain, I jostled my way gently through the crowd to walk next to Typheus. While the people made their way down, the funerary slaves remained behind and would later collect Caeso's ashes and place them in an urn. The urn would be placed in the family's collective tomb, probably along the Via Fulvia where most old families' tombs were. With the exception of close family and friends, the majority of the people on the mountain that day cared little for Caeso. Most were clients or associates of Corpio, there to show their support and to enjoy the feast and gladiatorial games that were to be held in honour of the deceased later in the day.

As we walked, I saw Typheus being the dutiful secretary, committing to memory the lists of people who came to pay their respects and those who just rejoined the procession back inside the city gates.

"My condolences," I offered.

"Thank you. My master is most grateful for your recommendation of Akhirabus and Brewyn. They were remarkably efficient in removing the… signs on the body and embalming it properly. This will be remembered when the time comes. Which naturally gives rise to the question of your progress? And please, do not be explicit while we are in public."

"I have found a potential group Caeso may have been involved with; however, I have not managed to confirm this yet. To break into their circle I will need more information. I think I mentioned a potential source in Ephemezica. I will also need to retrace the young master's trip to Kebros last year, as some unknown event during his visit there seemed to have set him on this path."

"If you have found a group here, why not hire a few gladiators and break some bones? Surely that would be more expedient."

I looked at him sidelong. He was not looking at me but at the people around us. With so much commotion from the walking crowd, our low voices afforded a modicum of privacy. "The men I saw there," I replied, "will be missed. This approach, while its time may come, is certain to raise much public outcry and bring about unwanted commotion and attention."

"I see. I will speak with my master when this is over. Please come tomorrow."

SCROLL II - KEBROS

CHAPTER X

I stood at the bow of the ship, breathing fresh air and letting the breeze ruffle my hair. We were well on our way to Ephemezica, and the captain had promised me that we would be landing tomorrow. A journey of seven hundred and fifty miles, hugging the coast of Nuremata, done in an incredible five days.

Corpio was indeed exceedingly grateful for my recommendation of Brewyn the tattoo master and Akhirabus the freelance embalmer. I had been expecting to hitch a ride in one of his trading boats, making short hops along the coast and hoping for favourable weather. Instead, when I came to pick up the letters of introduction, Corpio had provided me with official courier papers bearing his seal as Rhone of Fish.

Rather than hop on and off a series of boats travelling short distances, I was able to get on board of an official Egretian dispatch. These ships have their own dedicated *incantator elementorum*, who with their mastery of the six elements ensure calm seas and good winds. Our square sail was always bulging gently with the wind, the single banks of oars on each side never used, except in docking. Three days and two nights of a smooth, swift voyage, and we made port at Heraclion. We stayed there just the night, and on the next morning the ship left Heraclion for Ephemezica.

A regular transport boat could take three times this long and consider itself lucky, and going by horse would have taken me a month.

At least. With a very sore backside.

As it was, I got to enjoy the glorious feeling of speedy, uninterrupted sailing from Egretia to Ephemezica, under the Egretian official flag which reduced the appetites of pirates, even if their ships could hope to catch us.

"So how was your journey?"

"Swift and uneventful, Marcus Baebius, thank you. Quintus Sosius sends his warm regards."

"I see from his letter you are to assist me in negotiating a deal and procuring the library of Epphelipos."

I distinctly remembered Sosius had written to Baebius that he was to assist me, but I let it slide. "Sosius requested that I examine the library's more esoteric segments and assess their suitability to the market back at Egretia. I have some small expertise in those matters."

"Yes, well, that is only a paltry part of the collection."

"Do not worry, Marcus Baebius, our dear friend Quintus Sosius trusts your judgement. However, he has some particular clients with specific interests. I am here to evaluate the material in the library for this purpose. Sosius expects you to handle all the usual business arrangements, from payment to shipment back to Egretia, with the usual commission."

"Very well, very well. I will arrange with Epphelipos tomorrow for us to examine the library. I did not yet get a chance to go over it in detail, and only got a cursory glance. While the price is steep, I do believe there may be some hidden gems in it. The heirs seem to be aware of its general value, though not of specific items, which may be where we can make the real profit."

We spent the rest of the evening exchanging news. Baebius, Sosius' agent in Ephemezica, kept abreast of the latest tidings and gossip from the Forum but my speedy voyage offered him fresher news than he would have otherwise had. In return he was happy to share with me his knowledge of the local politics and events. He was quite amicable, after establishing that I was not there to take over his operation for Sosius.

I was a bit restless after five days on the ship, so I bid Baebius an early good night with the intention of touring the city. He had cautioned me about touring the streets of Ephemezica after dark without escort, and I did not want to get lost at night in a foreign city, so I planned on an early morning instead.

Ephemezica is an old port city. Sitting on a rocky promontory off the coast, it is connected to the mainland by a narrow strip of low-lying land. Fishermen and traders have been casting anchor in the small bays on each side from time immemorial. With the rise of the Hellican nations, Ephemezica became one of the most important ports of the Mare Saepiae. Trade routes from inland Phrylia and from the only overland route to Mitzrana met the traders sailing along the coast of Nuremata and out to the archipelagos of the Mare Saepiae. Goods were traded and exchanged, and made the city rich from taxes and levies. These days Egretia had eclipsed Ephemezica as the world's emporium, but the port was still busy and the town had an old-world charm to it.

In the morning I climbed to the top of the hill in the centre of town, passing increasingly richer mansions on the way to the temple district at the very top. I visited the shrines and sanctuaries of Ephemezica, with their strange human-like gods. I looked both out to sea and inland to the distant mountains ridges of the Montes Karikurum beyond the lush river valley of the Helios.

In the afternoon, after buying spit-roasted lamb rolled in flat-bread from a stall vendor, I went back down to the city and the port. The lamb was cooked in the traditional Hellican way, with too much thyme and not enough fish sauce to suit my Egretian tastes, and their wine had that characteristic pine-resin taste.

The area next to the harbours was as seedy as in any other port town around the world. Visiting sailors on shore leave and the businesses catering to them acquire an almost universal flavour. I took the chance as well to review the ships in the harbour for potential transport back, as I was not expecting to stay long in Ephemezica. Either we bought the library and I was able to acquire some of its knowledge, or not. There was no reason for me to linger here any longer than necessary, and many reasons why I should proceed to Kebros to continue my investigation of Caeso's life and death.

* * *

The next day we met Epphelipos in his study. The room was in disarray, as was the rest of the house. From what Baebius told me, Epphelipos had inherited the mansion recently and was renovating. His wife did not care for the hundreds of scrolls, and instead wanted to knock down a few walls and turn that part of the mansion into private baths.

Epphelipos may not have been a great lover of literature, but was enough of a merchant to recognise the potential value of the library and demand a high price for the scrolls.

I sipped from the excellent Hellican wine he served us, and considered the man before me. Of medium height, aged about fifty, I believed, heavyset with fleshy jowls. The shrewd gleam in his eyes foretold these would be hard negotiations.

"As the letter from my colleague Quintus Sosius indicates, he heard about your library for sale from dear Marcus Baebius here. Quintus Sosius is a well-known and respected trader in ancient scrolls in Egretia. He has many customers of discerning and specific tastes. Marcus Baebius has been his agent for many years here in Ephemezica, and I have been sent to ensure that the contents of the collection for sale match Quintus Sosius' current interests."

"Yes, yes, his letter was most detailed. I have reviewed the library myself, and I am quite certain you will find it to his satisfaction. The selection, the age, the quality of preservation and the rarity of material, all make this an exceeding collection. I am confident your esteemed selves will no doubt recognise this, and report back to dear Quintus Sosius for a most satisfactory conclusion."

"This news would make Quintus Sosius extremely happy. I would be deeply thrilled to send him a detailed note. After I have had the chance to examine the scrolls, of course."

With the preliminary haggling done, Epphelipos escorted us

to the library. It was housed in a room the size of a formal *triclinium*. The walls were covered with pigeon-hole shelves, all crammed with scrolls, with little tags hanging off them denoting contents. *Capsae* were standing on the floor, sometimes lidded and stacked, overflowing with scrolls. A few round tripod tables were propped around the room, covered with more scrolls. This was one of the largest collections I had seen outside the collegia libraries, certainly one of the largest private collections in the world.

I tried to keep my face expressionless, thinking of the haggling to come. "Tell me, Epphelipos, is there a catalogue to this madness? Or I fear it will take me days to ascertain whether it contains what Quintus Sosius requires."

"Indeed it has, though I fear the shelving may not match. The previous owner has been most careful — a work of passion, as you can see! — with keeping the index updated. However, we had to move the library due to the renovations, and I fear not everything made it exactly back to the same place. Perhaps if you told me what you were after…?"

"Oh, I am sure I will be able to find it," I said with confidence, "if it's here." I did not want to let Epphelipos know what I was interested in even vaguely, and besides — I had promised Quintus Sosius that I would review the library as a whole. "If you would be so kind as to have a slave open the windows for as much natural light as possible, and perhaps a cup or two of wine, Marcus Baebius and I will set ourselves to review the catalogue and state of the scrolls."

It took us the rest of that day and all of the next to audit the material offered for sale. We divided the material between us, Baebius concentrating on the more mundane scrolls of plays, letters and scientific treatises, and I focusing on the arcane and military works.

I located a few promising scrolls, sufficiently odd and foreign, which might contain further information about *magia vita terminalis*. I could not review them in detail, as deciphering them would have taken far too long, though from the glances I could get of them they seemed like the genuine article. By late afternoon Baebius and I conferred, and arrived at a sum of eight talents of silver as a fair price for the collection.

Back in Epphelipos' study we sat down for the serious haggling. Faces were pulled, teeth sucked, aspersions were cast, doubts raised, the wishes of his wife were hinted at, the good name of Sosius and his standing with his customers alluded to, other potential buyers mentioned, and their financial solvency dismissed.

In the end Baebius and I managed to press Epphelipos down to seven and a half talents of silver and a marble fountain in the shape of a nymph that Baebius was willing to part with in order to please Epphelipos' wife. We drank together for acceptance, and put our seals in wax on three copies for the bill of sale. Baebius would organise tomorrow for slaves to come, pack everything and ship the collection to Sosius.

* * *

Once Baebius had taken hold of the collection, I sorted through it and extracted the few scrolls I thought most promising. The rest would be shipped to Sosius in Egretia, but these I wanted with me in order to review in detail. I had already earmarked a few when I had reviewed the collection before the sale, so I could dedicate a full day to sorting through the rest of the library's catalogue and locating those scrolls I wished to take with me. I was faced with another sea voyage and planned to do my reading on the way to Kebros.

When I went in search of a ship to take me to Kebros or back to Egretia, however, I found that I had missed the official dispatch. My courier passport would still allow me to get board on most vessels, however the journey would take longer. I decided to stop at Heraclion and from there see if I could get on another ship directly to the Kebric isles, instead of going all the way back to Egretia first.

There were plenty of cargo ships sailing my way, but I was trying to find a faster vessel. Eventually I found a speedy-looking Hellican merchantman on its way to Heraclion, and paid for board. The captain was an enthusiastic little fellow by the name of Philomenos, keen on entertaining an Egretian and assuring me that winds were favourable and his load light. He traded along the Hellican and Assyrican coast and wanted to extend his routes to Egretia. He insisted on talking to me in broken *Quirite*, a small price to pay for his otherwise well-catered hospitality. My diplomatic passport had impressed him, though he still charged me a nominal fee. "A trader is a trader in the blood," he said.

During our four-day trip back down the coast I set myself to decipher the scrolls I had taken with me. I had packed them as closely as I could in a travellers' *capsa*, enhancing my diplomatic image. Deciphering them would take me some time, though. The scrolls I had selected were from a variety of sources, Hellican, Assyrican, Mitzrani. Each had its own script, often mixed, and with various dialects. I will not pretend to be fluent with these languages, though I did remember the basics from my aborted training as an *incantator*. The one thing all of them had in common? The vagueness, obliqueness and infuriating use of superlatives. I skipped sections, trying to find the heart of each and determine which one was the most promising.

On the night before we made land in Heraclion I found what I was looking for. This one was ancient, written on parchment rather than papyrus paper. It was faded in places, and crumbling about the edges, which required extreme care. Its ink appeared like old, dried blood.

It was written in a variety of languages, primarily Hellican and with a bit of Mitzrani hieroglyphs and even Assyrican cuneiform characters. Surprisingly, there were even passages in *Quirite*, the language of Egretia and its people. It did not mention the rite by name, only hinted that it was known by many names across different lands. Something about the description caught my eyes, though, and when I found the symbols for 'star' and 'tattoo' together, I knew I had the right thing. I sat there for a long while, deciphering the ancient dialect strewn with foreign glyphs. It took a constant effort of will to move word by word, symbol by symbol, racking my brain to recall old lessons from my youth.

According to the scroll, the purpose of the rite was a combination of *magia vita* and *magia elementorum*, a merging of life and elemental forces.

And thus, should the ceremony be performed correctly in all its details, the unguents prepared to exacting measurements without deviation, the chants pronounced precisely and with perfect harmony of the steps of all the cabal, then would the sacred Rite as given by that paragon of stellar sciences be completed successfully.

And the chosen one will have their heart changed unto a precious stone, but will not die. Their shade will be trapped within the stone forever after, their breath shall not cease and their flesh shall never rot.

And the chosen one shall become an adept. The mystical forces shall flow through him, and bend to his command. His flesh will become impervious to harm, his mind stay clear of distractions, his heart forever pure. The earth shall tremble at his stride, and the animals and all manner of living things shall bend to his will.

The scroll continued elaborating in the same vein, how the chosen one was promised dominion over both living and elemental forces, granted an everlasting life of power to control the elements and animated things. The details were sketchy, with a lot of excited superlatives and euphemisms as is common in such texts. Still, I imagined that one would trade a significant part of their humanity for such immortality and power.

To perform the rite requires a cabal of eleven. It takes five days and three nights to complete, although preparations must be done well in advance — gathering materials, manufacturing inks, mixing herbs and compounds and collecting samples of the chosen one's blood in special vessels as prescribed.

It begins on the first night with chanting, the complex verbal formulae detailed in the scroll. The words were ancient, some I did not even recognise, and when spoken aloud their syllables and sounds would be grating. All eleven must chant differing parts, creating dissonant disharmonies.

On the next day, the chosen one washes and anoints himself with special infused oils during the day, and keeps a lone vigil at night.

On the second night, the chosen one is tattooed in the star

pattern. It begins with different chants than the previous night. At midnight, the chosen one must strip down completely and lie naked on the floor, arms and legs splayed wide. The cabal then begins the process of the tattooing. The scroll gave exact recipes for the two inks to be used, the shape and composition of the needles, the order in which each line had to be pricked into the chosen one's skin, which member of the cabal drew which line while which of the others sung which verse.

At sunrise the process must be completed. The chosen one is wrapped in clean white linen, and given the day, the night and the following day to rest and for the bleeding to stop.

On the third night of ceremonies the power is invoked. It begins with the chosen one again lying on their back, arms and legs splayed wide. The ten other members of the cabal position themselves in pairs at each extremity and the head, and begin to chant. They then move, rotate and change locations around the chosen one in complex patterns, all the while keeping up their discordant chanting.

Beginning at midnight, they draw sharp knives and start to prick the chosen one in specified places. They use the blood they draw as they move about to draw patterns around and over his body, as their chanting increases in tempo.

With frenzied chanting, the last stroke of the blood pattern must be performed with the first ray of the sun over the horizon, and the ceremony is thus complete.

This rite would require a lot of the raw power of life to complete. Channelling such power is hard, even for the best of *incantatores*. The words uttered, the patterns danced, the ritualistic blood drawing all take a significant amount of concentration and will for an *incantator* to accomplish correctly. With the precise instructions from inks and ointments to chants and movements, the adepts must be well rehearsed in advance. This was the reason for the elaborate preparations and the time it took to complete. A single mistake, and the power drawn down into the target would surge and wreak havoc on the whole cabal, and probably beyond. I wondered if that is what happened to Caeso.

I also could not see how such a ceremony could be performed

in Egretia without alerting every *incantator* for miles. Even the pre-liminary chanting of the first day would set vibrations, and by the fifth night their heads would be ringing. And if anything, why Caeso? What would make a young merchant cadet the chosen one, rather than the more natural candidate in the leader of the cabal?

CHAPTER XI

We arrived at Heraclion in mid-morning. This was the last stop for Philomenos, my jolly captain friend, who planned on unloading his cargo of Assyrican silk and loading up on Egretian salt and wine before sailing back up the coast. We said our farewells, and Philomenos promised to visit me in Egretia as soon as he could follow up on some business opportunities there.

As the time was early I decided to first stay in the harbour and look for passage to Kebros. I walked along the piers and wharves, searching for a fast-looking ship on which I could use my courier's passport or pay for board.

I was in luck. I located an oddly shaped ship flying the Corpio family crest. The captain, a grizzled sea dog by the name of Titus Margaritus, was at first very gruff, and almost ordered his sailors to throw me off the boat — and not on the port side — when I dared to climb the gangplank uninvited. But as soon as I waved at him my letter bearing Corpio's seal, his demeanour changed.

"Welcome, welcome! Please come aboard, I will give you the master's own cabin. Please forgive our little jest before, no harm done, no harm meant."

"Of course, think nothing of it. I am sure Corpio would appreciate you protecting his property so zealously."

"That we are, indeed. Do not worry, your travel with us shall be safe, and as quick as can be we shall set you down in Kebros."

It turned out that Margaritus was operating one of Corpio's pearl diving operations. He would go out to secret locations amongst the isles, and his divers would swim to the depths and seek out the queen of gems. Considering the complexity of the operation, the risk of piracy and the expected gains, Corpio had even installed an *incantator* as part of the crew. The only reason the ship was in Heraclion was that the *incantator* had suffered indigestion from a bad oyster, and a storm had blown them off course. Margaritus decided to make for the nearest port, restock and then go out again.

I had been to Heraclion in the past, and so at first thought to continue reading the scrolls. The stuffy inn I found lodging in, however, was not conducive to serious study. I soon decided to go on a walk of the city, revisit its temples and climb the hill overlooking the bay.

For those who have not visited Heraclion before, the town is situated on the slopes of a steep hill on the eastern side of the mouth of the Bay of Euxis. The town prides itself on the beauty of the white walls and red-tiled roofs of its houses, kept clean by city ordinance. The bay has long been the source of the best oysters and shellfish known to man. The booming fishing industry together with the intersection of trade routes from Egretia to Hellica has made Heraclion a busy port.

Standing at the top of the Acroheraclios in the middle of the city, I looked out over the bay with its many small boats on the water and the estates of the rich lining its shores. I could see large barges plying the waters in chains, acting as ferries between Heraclion and the village on the western side of the bay. Taking the overland route around the bay meant a several days' journey of over two hundred miles, while crossing on the ferry was a tenth of that distance and could be covered in a few short hours by the heavy barges.

Around two centuries ago, when trade between Egretia and Hellica had first boomed, these ferries began to be powered by *incantatores*. Conflicting operators who charged their *incantatores* to raise great winds and waves had soon left the entry to the bay a mess of turbulent waters that were a danger to all sea craft. A particularly nasty collision that had caused the death of a minor potentate from Mazaca Carina had been followed by a loud public outcry, and rules had been set — and enforced — by both sides of the bay. These days the use of *magia elementorum* to speed up boats around the bay was strictly illegal, with heavy fines imposed on offenders.

Having enjoyed the sea air and the stretching of my legs, I returned to my inn at sundown. My luck from this morning seemed to have held, as the rather dilapidated room I slept in was surprisingly free of fleas and bedbugs.

* * *

We set sail early the next morning, ten days before the *Kalends* of *Maius*. After the customary sacrifice and prayers to Neptunus for a safe voyage, the captain set course to the Pillatic Isles where we would stop for the pearl divers. We would then continue amongst the small isle chains of the Mare Saepiae to Kebros. On first consideration this might have appeared like a detour, however, the presence of an *incantator*, now recovered and feeling much better, meant that it would still be faster than taking a regular ship to Parelae, or even going all the way to Egretia to find a good ship to Kebros. And, of course, I was not guaranteed to find anything that didn't rely on sails or slaves, which would have been much slower.

From Heraclion to the Pillatic Isles is a distance of some two hundred miles. The *incantator*, whose name I learnt was Aulus Didius Rufus, was a young man, red haired and freckled, and quite eager to practice his arts. He was very keen to talk, a naturally curious and energetic fellow, cooped up on a ship for days on end, with naught but a grizzled captain and the crew to talk with. Over the two days it took us to get to our destination — the captain kept the exact location a secret — we shared meals and discussed worldly affairs. I had to keep a close watch on my words and the scrolls I had brought with me. I could not risk Didius Rufus or the captain finding out about the nature of my business for Corpio. Necromancy is a dangerous taboo, and I did not wish to swim back to Egretia.

In between, I continued to study the scrolls I took with me. I doubted very much I would be able to keep the scroll describing the Rite of Pelegrinus or any of the others when I reached Egretia. While some knowledge about such rites existed in the vaults of the Collegium Incantatorum, most copies with detailed instructions like those I'd found in Ephemezica had long since been destroyed. The scrolls were the property of Sosius, and if they managed to survive discovery they would be his to dispose of. I knew him well enough not to think he would surrender the ones containing forbidden subjects to the Collegium of his own free will, and I suspected he would try to sell them for an exorbitant price. I took the precious time I had with these scrolls to study as much as I could.

For the uninitiated, it is worth noting that our Collegium Incantatorum was established almost five hundred years ago, some decades after our people made Egretia our permanent settlement. The uniqueness of the Collegium Incantatorum, and indeed of the other collegia, lies in a level-headed approach to organisation and knowledge. We *Quirites* always had a practical bent. Other nations had kings to rule them and court intrigues and power struggles; their accumulated knowledge was closely guarded. Our people developed the system whereby the collegia were open to anyone — or anyone with money, at least. In the beginning the major collegia were administrative or-ganisations, controlling the smaller associations and sodalities. Over time they also accumulated knowledge and became the sources of the best trained men in their respective fields. Quick to capitalise on it, the collegia established a *cursus honorum* of their own, to match the course of offices for those in public careers.

Men who had proven themselves by generating wealth and social distinction could apply for a cadetship within the Collegium of their choice. With the years, it became obvious that training early in life was more beneficial, and more often those whose families had managed to amass wealth were enrolled in the collegia to learn their trades as soon as they formally became adults.

That, of course, had quickly become a self-perpetuating oligar-chy. Nominally, our city was a *res publica* — a thing of the people, a republic — but everyone with eyes in their head knew that the rich mattered more. The strength of the collegia was just another way for the rich to retain their power. Even so, the effectiveness and relative openness of our teaching methods has given us highly trained soldiers, merchants and enchanters. Not every footslogger of a legionary or small shop owner was a graduate, of course. The cadets of the collegia came from the rich, and with their training and family connections had become a most effective ruling class. These days it became the favourite path for those seeking public office, and one who did not graduate and generate a name for himself faced slim odds of joining the Senate.

But I digress. Our methods were not the only methods. Other people had armies, merchants and enchanters, yet with different governments, different weapons and military training regimes, different ships and naval tactics. And just as much, not everyone had subscribed to our taxonomy of the five branches and six elements of enchantments. Other philosophies prescribed a different division of the natural world.

All of which had made my reading of the scrolls a laborious process. While I never finished my studies and apprenticeship at the Collegium, the basic lessons in the history, terminology, hieroglyphics and foreign philosophies of enchantment are a part of the curriculum one has to complete before moving to the practicalities. Our Egretian standard training gave us huge benefits in the preservation and dissemination of knowledge, though with so many foreign sources we students had to learn the alien ways of thinking. Still, that had been a decade and a half ago.

After embarking with Philomenos from Ephemezica I sat with the scrolls and read and read and read until my eyes felt like bleeding and my head exploding. I hoped that the knowledge I was gaining would prove beneficial, even beyond my current investigation.

* * *

On the third day we reached the Pillatic archipelago. Between islands not much more than the spires of rocks jutting out of the waves like fingers of submerged giants, I had the chance to witness the retrieval of pearls. First the divers, three Shangarii and two Capilanii, assembled at the rear of the boat. I now understood the odd shape of the ship, with its square, untapered stern. This served as the diving platform for them, and with rope ladders they could easily climb back in.

The divers were nude, each carrying only a pouch tied to his left wrist with a string, and a curiously shaped thick dagger tied to his right. Aulus Didius walked amongst them, drawing a pattern dedicated to Neptunus on each with a special pigment and letting each drink a draft of something foul-smelling from a wineskin. The divers seemed familiar with the process, and kept chattering between themselves as Didius Rufus was performing his enchantments.

When Rufus finished, Margaritus gave a sign and the five walked to the low rail at the end of the ship, climbed on it, and one by one jumped with effortless grace into the waves. As we watched the water swallow their lithe bodies, Margaritus produced a small pouch of salted and baked sunflower kernels, and began to expertly split them between his teeth to get at the seed inside, spitting the empty husks into the water.

As we stood there, he and Rufus explained the process to me. The divers would swim down to the base of the rocks, where the oysters who produce the pearls like to make their home. They would search around until they found one, and then pry its hard lips apart with the steel dagger. Some of the oysters could get quite large, enough to snap off a finger of a careless diver.

As Margaritus was talking we saw occasionally the head of one of the divers pop to the surface, take a few deep breaths while floating on his back, and then dive down again.

The pearl producing oysters are a rare kind. Of those oysters that do, not all produced them all the time, as a pearl took years to form. Of the pearls that did form, most were not smooth but had wrinkles, like small uneven rocks. A large, smooth and round pearl with a perfect creamy sheen was a rare thing indeed, and would fetch a commensurate price.

After a long while, the divers started coming back to the ship. The enchantment and brew that Didius Rufus had placed on them was wearing off, and they could no longer hold their breaths quite as long or swim down quite so well. They all climbed wearily up to the boat, looking tired and disappointed as no pearls had been found.

Margaritus put away his little bag of seeds and cursed his crew into activity. We set sail to another region of the isles. The locations of the best diving grounds for pearls were a closely guarded secret. I had no doubt the only reason I was allowed to stay on deck, or be aboard at all for that matter, was the diplomatic courier's letter with Corpio's own seal.

This time the crew sailed the ship by natural wind alone, and mostly used oars to assist and navigate carefully between the isles, the jutting rocks, and the sandy shoals. This served the dual purpose of allowing for very delicate navigation and of letting Rufus rest after performing the enchantments on the divers before he would need to repeat them. While we nibbled on hard bread and dried fish, the divers had only drunk fresh water, and elected not to eat anything between dives.

By now we had also attracted a flock of seagulls screeching around us, waiting for scraps. We reached another spot, this time in a sheltered cove off a rocky island covered with grasses and low, scrubby bushes. We cast anchor and the same ritual happened again — the divers had the pattern around their necks renewed by Rufus and took another draft of the concoction in his wineskin. Then one by one they climbed the rail and jumped in a gleaming arc into the water.

This time they had more success. Within minutes one of the divers resurfaced and waved and hooted excitedly. He swam back to the boat, climbed aboard and extracted a pearl from the pouch on his left wrist. The pearl was a thing of beauty. Not a perfect sphere, but a large, smooth rock with dimples, it had a clear and creamy colour to it that glistened in the sunlight. Didius Rufus was visibly excited, and even the gruff and grizzled Margaritus was impressed. Such a pearl would easily fetch a talent of silver just by itself.

As the day progressed the divers came back with more pearls. The excitement of the captain grew in proportion to the small mound of shiny orbs in the palm of his hand. When late in the afternoon a diver returned with a mid-sized, perfectly round black pearl that was worth more than the ship and all its crew, he was so excited he even offered me to have a go at Aulus Didius' charms and join the divers to see for myself the underwater wonders. While this would no doubt have been an experience of a lifetime, I respectfully declined. I knew how to swim, of course, from my short career in the legions, and I had witnessed the efficacy of Rufus' charms. But as exciting as the idea was, the idea of willingly holding my breath and submerging into the deep realm of Neptunus was an uncomfortable one. And in the back of my mind the memories of another drowned body kept nagging, and even the fresh sea air and lustrous pearls could not completely dispel them.

That night there was a big celebration on board the ship, for the haul was superbly profitable. Aulus retired early, exhausted from the strain of incantations, while Margaritus, drunk with the success of the day as well as wine, was singing loudly. The captain had planned on staying longer at the rich pearl grounds, however, I managed to make him promise me that the day after tomorrow we would set sail directly for Kebros. Everyone slept well that night, after a generous meal accompanied by good wine.

And that is why no alarm was raised until the pirates were almost upon us.

CHAPTER XII

Iwoke up to urgent yells from heavy slumber. Not bothering with clothes, I grabbed my dagger and ran outside to the deck. A ship larger than ours was heading straight at us under power of oars. Their crew were silent, no drums to keep pace and no shouts. That they were pirates was evident from the vessel itself. A fast and decked *bireme*, its prow was painted with large blue eyes, slightly slanted to give a menacing look as they stared at us. Its sail was folded and the mast down, the pirates were ready for battle and boarding. A row of men stood at the railing, armed and ready with ropes and planks.

The pirate ship was perhaps three hundred paces from us, and by their angle and equipment I knew that they did not intend to ram us, but rather angle next to us and board us. Piracy does not make profit by sinking treasures — these come from the robbery of goods, selling the crew to slavery and holding any notable passengers for ransom.

Our crew was frantic, everybody suddenly awake after last night's celebrations. Margaritus was yelling orders, the sailors were hoisting the anchor and going to the oars. Aulus Didius looked particularly dishevelled, not yet recovered from yesterday's enchantments, and seemed unable to focus on the events storming around him.

With two hundred paces between our ships and us barely moving, it was becoming obvious that they would gain on us and that we would have to fight if we wanted to escape capture. Margaritus had broken out the weapon stores, and the crew and divers each grabbed a tall oval shield and a short *gladius*, and braced on the side facing the pirate ship. I picked up a shield and grabbed the handle inside the shield's boss with my left hand, though I elected to remain armed only with my trusty dagger.

Margaritus yelled at the remaining crew to put up the sail with the hope that Didius Rufus could conjure sufficient winds, as the oarsmen armed themselves instead to prepare for boarding. I stared out across the dark waters watching the moonlit vessel closing in on us rapidly. At this distance I could make out the individual faces of the pirates and the murderous intent written on them. I wondered what mess I had gotten myself into and whether I would live to see the morning.

With fifty paces to go, the pirates banked oars, grabbed ready bows and let a volley go. All of us in the front lines raised our shields and managed to absorb most of the volley. Only two of our men were hit, though from the quick look I cast in their direction the wounds seemed slight. Our ship did not have a means to return fire — it was not a navy vessel, and was designed for the specific operation of the divers. It relied on speed generated by its resident *incantator*, who unfortunately seemed in a state of battle shock like a green recruit. The lack of a proper night guard could only be blamed on Margaritus.

Thirty paces to go, and another volley of arrows. This time one man fell down when an arrow that ricocheted from a shield lodged itself in his neck. The deck became slick with the blood spurting from his wound. Margaritus was shaking Didius Rufus by his shoulders, yelling in his face to get the wind up.

Ten paces, and the pirates cast ropes with hooks onto our rails, dragging us closer. We dislodged the hooks and struck at the ropes, but within the space of a deep breath the pirate ship bumped into ours, shaking the deck under our feet. The two ships screeched like racing chariots colliding.

The pirates were upon us. With wild cries they jumped from their ship onto our deck, swinging swords, axes, hooks and clubs. I braced my shield, and as the pirate who targeted me tried to land his curved sword in a neat arc from above straight on my head I took a step back, causing him to miss his mark and forcing him to stumble as he landed, and immediately with my full weight behind the shield I jumped and slammed into him, forcing him backwards and the boss of the shield knocking the wind from his lungs, yet still with his back against the ship's rail he tried to raise his sword to protect himself, but I knocked it aside with my shield and plunged my knife deep into his chest. His eyes widened and a gurgling, rattling sound came from his throat as he lost balance and fell overboard, splashing into the waters in the space between our ships.

What followed was a mad free-for-all battle. The pirates were ferocious, the deck was slick with blood and the air was heavy with the din of fighting, the shouts of enemies colliding and the cries of the wounded and the dying.

The battle seemed to stall for a while, for although the pirates were more numerous, Corpio's men were better armed and trained. Normally, the pirates would have tried to board and capture the ship, relying on their terrifying reputation and surprise attacks for a minimal struggle. They probably did not expect an organised resistance like ours. However, once committed, they could not stop.

As we parried and stabbed, clashed our shields against their swords and ebbed and flowed around on the deck, I saw Aulus Didius finally getting ready. He was standing at the back of the ship next to the far rail, some ten paces from where I was busy with another pirate. His head was bowed as he raised his arms wide to the sides, palms open as if about to hug a loved one. His tunic was buffeted by a breeze we did not yet feel and his red hair started to drift up around his head, giving him a fiery halo. I could feel the crackling in the air and on my skin from where I was standing.

He looked up, and his eyes were blazing white. He stood so for a moment, almost oblivious to the melee around him, then suddenly clapped his hands forcefully in front. An upswell of water burst between our two ships, tilting them, rocking them, pushing them away from each other.

I saw a pirate step in a pool of blood as the ship lurched, skid and trip over a dead body and fall screaming into the sea. Rufus swayed as well, but steadied himself on the railing at the last minute. A moment later and the battle resumed. Three of our crew were lying on the deck, and four of the enemy. How many others had fallen overboard I did not know.

From the corner of my eye I saw Didius Rufus straighten up and begin to gather the elemental energies about him again. I wasn't the only who saw it and understood, and two of the pirates were trying hard to disengage themselves and go after Rufus.

I slammed the lower edge of my shield on the foot of the pirate in front of me, and as he drew back I stabbed low into his guts, and again at his head as he collapsed, slicing open his face from his jaw to his hair and turning his scream into an incoherent burbling. I turned before another could jump in the gap, and started towards Aulus Didius. The two pirates had managed to disengage themselves, and one of ours lay dead at their feet as they drew upon Rufus. I was still too far away, and so, without thinking, I reversed my hold on my dagger and threw it at the back on the closest one. It sank in between his shoulder blades, and he fell to his knees with his hands trying frantically to reach behind him even as his life was ebbing away.

Now weaponless, I put my shoulder to my shield and ran screaming into the other pirate just as he was swinging his sword to strike Rufus. I hit him with the shield and all my weight behind it, and the force of the impact sent him reeling away. Before he could regain his balance I lifted my shield and jammed its boss into his midsection and followed with a knee to his chin as he bent double. This caused him to jerk back up, and with another jab of my shield at his chest I managed to push him overboard.

"The wind, man, get the wind!" I shouted at Aulus Didius, who resumed his incantation. I retrieved my dagger from the back of the corpse at Rufus' feet and turned around to face the remaining battle. I could see Margaritus off to one side, dispatching another pirate though he had a nasty gash on his thigh. Our crew was still holding, their discipline prevailing over that of the pirates. Behind me I could feel the enchantment that Rufus was weaving, and above me the sail began to bulge with wind. The tides of battle turned; a few pirates lost heart and jumped into the waters to swim back to their ship. The others saw and followed, and those who did not do so quickly enough were overcome and killed without mercy.

***

"You have been in the legions," stated Margaritus without a shred of doubt in his voice.

"Briefly," I replied. "What made you think so?"

"The way you fought, using the shield. That was as classical infantry training as I ever did see." We were busy administering to the wounded and the dead. I was bandaging Margaritus' leg as we were speaking.

"True. Perhaps my centurion would finally admit that I was not completely useless — though I doubt it." I smiled wanly. "And your crew as well, Titus Margaritus, I should think. These are not slaves cowering in fear, but trained marines that could hold their own in our finest navy ship."

Margaritus smiled proudly, then grimaced with pain. "That they are. The Corpio family invested a lot in this operation, and I recruit and keep my crew well trained."

"Whatever your training," said Aulus Didius, "I was glad that you were there today. I have not yet thanked you for saving my life, and will do so properly as soon as we are ashore."

I pointed up at the bulging sail, "You saved this ship and everyone aboard it. We owe you our lives just as much."

Twelve out of a crew of thirty-four were lost, including two of the divers. Of the dead, three must have gone overboard, for we never recovered their bodies. We disposed of the corpses of the pirates unceremoniously by heaving them over the rails for the gulls to feast on. The bodies of our own crew, which I now understood to have been all free men and not slaves, we kept to be cremated with the proper rites once we made land at Kebros.

I had sustained a cut on my right arm, one that I had hardly noticed during the battle and now stung like hades. Aulus Didius bandaged and treated it himself, after which we went amongst the crew treating wounds as well as we could. My pouch contained only enough herbal and medicinal supplies for personal use and the ship was not stocked for dealing with a full battle. Still, Aulus Didius and I stretched them as much as possible, and treated the worst of the crew injuries to the best of our abilities. I did use minor enchantments to aid the healing, stop the blood flow and reduce infections, not something I would normally do with a member of the Collegium Incantatorum standing next to me. While not exactly illegal, it would be frowned upon — but I felt none of this mattered in the circumstances. Aulus Didius himself, although trained primarily in the *magia elementorum*, had by necessity picked up applications of the *magia vita* as well. Both because this was required for his enchantment of the divers, and also because as a lone *incantator* on the ship he had to pick up bits and pieces of everything that was useful.

As we worked I taught him some of the tricks I had learnt over the years to aid in the healing of wounds — nothing more than home-brew poultices and old wives' enchantments, charms to aid the natural healing rather than those of a fully trained *magister carneum* who could regrow lost limbs.

In his grateful state of mind, once realising that I had the basic knowledge of incantations, Aulus Didius taught me his charm for the divers. I suspected it to be a trade secret, one that he probably had only learnt from his employer's *incantatores* and under oath to use it only for his master's business. I swore to him I would not teach it to anyone else. I doubted very much I could perform it correctly, as it did require skill and practice I did not possess.

And thus, with a third of the crew dead and most of the rest wounded but not beaten, we made our way in haste towards Kebros.

CHAPTER XIII

Aulus Didius kept our square sail full of wind for two days without rest, and we could all see the toll this exertion took on him. As we neared Kebros from the east the wind changed in our favour and Aulus slacked his hold on the winds, letting the remaining crew navigate with natural winds and oars while he collapsed and slept. While I could not assist Rufus in his task, I did my best tending to the wounded amongst the crew, and, thankfully, we had no more mischief on our voyage.

We arrived in Kebros in the evening of the sixth day before the *Kalends* of *Maius*. We saw Mons Krodus first, with the sandy shore on the northern side and the eastern of the two rocky bays on the South. We sailed past the jutting bulk of the mountain with its sheer cliffs dropping to the sea and entered the larger bay, and the town of Kebros came into view.

Originally a tiny fishing village, it was now a sprawling little settlement along the shore and on the hills beyond it. With the conquest of the archipelago by Egretia three hundred years ago, the Kebric Isles had become the base for large commercial fishing and fish sauce manufacture. It had everything from wharves and docks for the ships to clay quarries and factories to make the *amphorae* and vessels for the *garum*.

The original inhabitants of the archipelago were by now

absorbed into the new life of business, although without Egretian citizenship there was a distinct class difference.

And once the rich had started to investigate the isles for commercial reasons, their natural beauty had attracted them further. First a few villas for those whose business centred on the island, then little summer retreats, followed by country estates. From small villas to large mansions, some of our elite had even laid claim to whole islands for themselves. And with the rich had come their staff, and the suppliers and special merchants, until by now the town was a busy centre of commerce with picturesque houses on the hills beyond.

* * *

By the time we had docked and Margaritus had dealt with the port-master, the stars were out. Margaritus promised to take me in the morning himself to Publius Quinctius Corpio, Marcus Corpio's younger brother, and swear on my help against the pirates. While I had the letter of introduction, any extra help in gaining trust was always welcome. We spent the night on the ship once more, gazing at the twinkling lights of the city reflected in the dark waters of the bay.

In the morning Margaritus hired a mule-drawn cart to take us to Publius Corpio's mansion, five miles out of town. We rode along the shore road going west, passing several estates. We reached a side road marked with a pylon bearing the Quinctii Corpiones family crest of fish and *amphora*, turned and climbed up the hill on a tree-lined gravel path.

The door slave recognised Margaritus and showed us inside without delay. He led us to a second-storey loggia where the master of the house had set up his desk. As we stepped onto the open space I saw the whole hillside estate and the bay beyond spread out before me. The view was absolutely stunning, from the well-manicured ground to the immaculately placed shrubs, trees, flowers, paths and ponds to the shimmering waters of the bay beyond, dotted with the white sails of craft plying the sea lanes.

It took me a moment to notice the man sitting at a beautifully carved wooden desk at the other end of the loggia. As we strode forward I recognised the family resemblance. The same long nose and high cheekbones, the same blue-green eyes and sun-bleached hair. He was younger and trimmer than his brother, though, probably keeping more active with the family business on Kebros. I remembered his face from Caeso's funeral, walking with the family behind the grieving Corpio, but I doubted he would recognise me.

Publius stood up. "Titus Margaritus! I trust your latest expedition went well?"

"We had a very good catch, though it came at a price." Margaritus produced a closely tied pouch from his tunic, undid the strings and poured forth the handful of pearls on the table. The little gems gleamed in the morning light from the open balcony, with the black pearl sitting majestically in their midst.

Publius Corpio's eyes gleamed in unison with the captain's.

"And the price?" He lifted his gaze off the small fortune lying casually on his desk.

"Pirates. We were attacked at night. Twelve dead, including Arubio and Bretix, my best divers."

"Pirates? Where was this? When was this?"

"Two nights ago, a bit further out from the Pillatic Isles. We repelled them, of course, though it cost us dearly and they escaped with their ship. This is the point I should give my thanks to Felix here, as he fought with us bravely and proved valuable in preserving our lives and property."

Publius shifted his gaze to me, openly scrutinising me. "Do I know you? Your face seems familiar."

"We have never met," I replied. "I bear a letter from your brother; this is how I got to be on Margaritus' ship." I took out the letter of introduction that Corpio had furnished me and handed it over to Publius' outstretched hand.

Publius examined the wax seal and then broke it, unfolded the letter and read carefully. "I see," he said at length. "Well, Margaritus. That is most unfortunate, although these diving grounds you discovered would certainly make up for the loss of lives." His gaze darted to the pearls at his desk. "Make sure you leave exact descriptions of the pirate's ship and location with my clerk. I will have them sent to the Collegium Militum and see if I can get some navy patrols in the area. Do not expect a swift response, though, so recruit and train your crew anew."

After the captain left, Publius Corpio turned back to me. "I should thank you, too. Margaritus is not one to give praise lightly. I am surprised he allowed you on his boat at all."

"Yes, I noticed his jealous guarding of your property," I said with a faint smile. "Your brother's seal on that letter was the only thing that saved me from a dip in the port of Heraclion."

"I read Marcus' letter. That boy was as useless as a harness on a hamster, if you ask me. Oh, I know it is bad luck to speak ill of the dead, and him being family, but since he was a child he was spoiled by my brother and his wife. So you are here to investigate his death, then?"

"With your permission, I would like to talk with the people in your employ who knew him, and learn about his activities and travels last autumn."

"I'm sure you will soon see my point regarding him," Publius said with certainty. "For the entire month he was here he showed little interest or thanks. A more out-of-place member of our family I have never seen. He had no interest in business or in shipping, activities our family has been fostering for generations. My brother is not the first *rhone* from amongst the Corpio branch of the Quincti, nor will he be the last."

"I understand Marcus Quinctius sent Caeso here for you to distract him, to see if you could find a business undertaking he would like?"

"That's correct. I took him around our shipyards and *garum* factories, but his head was always elsewhere. Pining after a street mime, would you believe it?! We had hoped to betroth him to my wife's niece, a lovely girl from a family as old as ours. However, even with that, he showed no interest and rebuked the family's mandate. After a while I gave up, and he was just left alone to wander around the isles."

"Yet I am told that upon his return he seemed enthusiastic about a new endeavour?"

"That I do not recall. Aemilia, the niece I mentioned, is here again with her mother." Was that a shudder I saw? "You could speak with her about Caeso as well. I will also instruct my steward to assist you — he organised the travel arrangements for the young men and would be able to tell you where they went."

We chatted for a while longer, though I learnt nothing more. Publius offered me a stay at his villa and the use of his private sailboat and stables should I need to travel around the Kebric Isles in my investigations. I did get the impression, though, that he was not expecting me to remain there for long.

As I was getting ready to leave he said, "I am going soon to visit my *garum* factories, to deal with the emergency of the day. Would you like to join me? I do not know what insight this will offer you about Caeso's demise, however, he did spend some time there and you might see something I did not. My opinion on my nephew aside, this whole affair has devastated my brother."

* * *

We left Publius Corpio's mansion on a light dray driven by Corpio himself. We were heading to the hills on the other side of the town, where his factories were located. On the way, he asked me to recount the whole encounter with the pirates, quizzing me for as many details as I could remember. Piracy had always been a problem in the Mare Saepiae, and since he was in the shipping business, it was acutely relevant to him. If he ever wanted to pursue a public career like his brother, then dealing with the piracy issue would make a good platform.

We reached the factories via another road marked with the Quinctii Corpiones crest. The most immediate sensation when nearing them was the smell. The pungent, inescapable odour of fermenting fish. It hit us well before we heard the clamour of the workers or saw the row of low, long buildings. Publius directed me to a stone bench in the shade of some trees and promised to return shortly. As I sat there looking at the busy workers, I could sympathise with Caeso. Fish sauce may rule the Egretian cuisine, but the methods of its manufacture were not for the faint of heart.

Publius returned accompanied by another man. The man was in his sixties with wispy grey hairs floating at the base of his skull and withered skin, but he still appeared fit and sharp-eyed.

"This is Gaius Corfidius," Publius introduced the man. "He's my foreman in charge of this factory, and spent time with Caeso last year, teaching him about the technicalities of the business. I have instructed him to assist you." They sat next to me on the benches.

"Tell me, Gaius Corfidius, what was your impression of Caeso Quinctius?"

"A youth. His heart was taken with the things that occupy young men's hearts, of which fish sauce is not one."

"How much time did he spend here?"

"Not much. Not enough, or too much, depending on whom you ask."

We continued in this way for a while. Gaius Corfidius, despite his oblique, non-committal way of speaking, did eventually describe enough of Caeso's visit for me to get the picture. The boy was resigned to be there against his will, had made half-hearted attempts to understand the business in the first few days, and then mostly avoided coming to the factory, preferring to take trips elsewhere.

Publius let Gaius Corfidius do most of the talking, and interjected only occasionally. Servants brought us wine, water and a light lunch — olives, bread and some of the best *garum* I have ever tasted in my life. I complimented Corpio profusely about it, and in return was offered a tour of the facilities.

Fish sauce comes in three grades, as Corfidius explained to me. The highest quality is called *garum* and is made from cuttlefish alone; real garum is relatively rare, as what is sold under that name often contains some fish. The next grade is *liquamen*, which is made just from fish, usually small and oily ones like mackerels, sardines, anchovies and mullets. When the cuttlefish and fish come in, they are taken to the first of the three buildings, sorted and cleaned. The lowest grade — the one I had been buying when I could afford nothing else — is made from the mixed leftover entrails of the fish and squid and is called *muria.*

"Sorting the fish, even of the same type, into batches of differing quality is an important part of the process," Corfidius expounded. "A good nose is required to understand the qualities of the catch, its freshness, and its willingness to accept flavours." Sometimes they created special batches, with carefully selected mixtures of both fish and squid, and spice mixes more exotic than the usual recipes.

Next, the fish were layered in vast clay pots, and each layer covered with salt, herbs and spices. "The salt we import directly from the salt marshes at the delta of the Ridus. The grade of salt, the level to which it has been refined, matches the level of the fish. The mixture of herbs and spices is, of course, a family secret. None but the master knows."

"We buy our spices in bulk," added Publius, "and not everything gets used. This is to prevent our competitors from figuring out our recipes."

The mixture is then sealed with corks and wax, and left in the sun to ferment for between one and three months. "A fine nose is the most important tool. The batches have to be opened every ten days, mixed gently and tasted. The fish have to ferment and liquefy to the right consistency, and the aromas from the herbs and spices have to be in harmony. Here, let me demonstrate."

We walked out of the fish preparation building and into the open hillside. Corfidius stepped to the vats standing in the bright morning sun, inspected their seals for dates and called for an assistant to open one of them. "This is the second mixing of this one," he explained as the assistant carefully cut the wax seal with a knife and lifted the wooden lid.

My eyes began to water and my knees nearly buckled. Corfidius kept talking as he took a very large wooden paddle, almost a small oar, and gently tossed the half-liquefied contents, but I could barely breathe. He sniffed, dipped his finger and licked it with closed eyes. I closed my eyes so I would not gag. The assistant then placed the wooden lid back and sealed around the edges with wax. Corfidius took off a bracelet from his arm and rolled it around the edge to imprint on the wax. He then personally signed and dated a corner.

"This one should be mixed one more time and that will be that. The taste is maturing properly, and now the *garum* needs to separate from the *allec*." *Allec*, as was explained to me, was the residue left behind by the liquid fish sauce. It was a by-product, though it was sold as a condiment in its own right. Many a boy in our city grew up snacking on a slice of bread smeared with the sticky, salty spread.

The next building was where the clay *amphorae* were made. Here, too, special care was made. The right type of clay was quarried on the other side of the Mons Krodus and brought here to be shaped and fired in kilns. The types of wax and resins used to seal the inside affected the flavour of the finished product as well. I had never been aware of the complexities that went into creating our people's favourite condiment, and my respect for the experts who made it grew the more I learnt about it.

From the big clay vessels that were used to ferment the *garum*, *liquamen* and *muria*, the sauces were strained and packed in *amphorae* ready for shipping. The *allec* was packed in differently marked vessels, and everything was loaded on ships sailing back to Egretia and other ports for trading all over the known world.

* * *

When we left the *garum* factory Corpio took a back road towards the northern hills. I looked on in interest as we rode along, passing from the busy precinct of the factory with its many employees and delivery carts to a rural landscape of vines and fields.

"There is one more stop on the way back," said Corpio. "Considering the circumstances of my nephew's death — and your suspicions — there is another person you should meet."

We turned off the back road onto a narrow farm track. It led us past picturesque groves of trees and open meadows covered with grasses and shrubs. As we rode around a bend in the track I saw before us another low, long building. "This is our family's honey farm," explained Publius Corpio. "We have an exclusive method of extracting honey that gives it a very refined taste. We do not produce a lot, and what we do fetches the highest prices from the most discerning customers in Egretia."

We dismounted, and a slave came out of the building to take the horses and cart. "My ancestor of seven generations ago developed a unique way to collect the honey. You know how it's normally done?"

"The beehives are placed next to flowering fields, the type of flowers affecting the final taste," I said. "At the end of the summer, some brave man builds a fire of green leaves close to the hives, and the smoke puts the bees to sleep."

"But this is not how we do it here," said a man emerging from the building with a smile. He was young, perhaps in his mid-twenties, with clear skin, dark hair and blue eyes.

"Allow me to introduce Gaius Opimius Agrippa," said Publius. "Gaius Opimius, this is Felix. He is here to enquire after my late nephew, Caeso. I do believe that Caeso spent some time with you when he was here."

"Oh yes, nice lad. I was very sorry to hear of his death."

"Tell me, Gaius Opimius, why was Caeso interested in honey collection? I understand from his uncle that he was otherwise disinterested in the family's business."

"May I talk freely?" asked Opimius, glancing at Corpio. Publius Corpio nodded and Opimius turned back to me. "The reason is the same as why our honey is so special. I am a trained *incantator*, you see." He smiled at me, and I gave myself a mental kick — I should have paid more attention and picked up on it. "Instead of using smoke, which alters the complex aroma and taste of the final product, Marcus Quinctius Apiarius developed a unique method of putting the bees to sleep and extracting the sweet nectar. In this way the honey does not absorb the smoke, and comes out with an extraordinarily enticing taste and the clearest amber colour."

"Somehow, I don't think Caeso was interested in the honey," I said. "He approached you once he learnt you were an *incantator*?"

"That he did. He was very interested, though he tried to pretend it was purely professional. He asked a lot about my studies at the Collegium, but I'm afraid I had to disappoint him. It was not as glorious as one may think. I mean, look at me," Opimius said with a smile, "I am a glorified beekeeper. I like this life tremendously, yet it is hardly what might catch the imagination of an excitable young man."

"Did he leave it at that? Disappointed?"

"Well… I told him to visit a friend of mine back in Egretia. I gave him a short letter of introduction as well." He looked apologetically at Publius Corpio. "My friend, Gaius Famnius, graduated the same year I did. He joined his father in the family's business; they trade overland in exotic stone and glass products from Mitzrana, Assyrica and even further away. Gaius Famnius would have been able to show him things more exciting than bees."

We spoke a bit more, about Caeso and about bees. Opimius let me try some of the new year's honey, and with the first drop of it on my tongue I understood how the Corpio family could have grown rich on it alone. I learnt little more about Caeso from Opimius. The new lead to follow back in Egretia was a sore compensation for having tasted honey so refined it put all others to shame, yet I could never afford to buy.

On the way back I thanked Publius Corpio for the tour. He took real pride in his operations, and the secret *garum* recipe and honey extraction charm that have been in his family for generations and were the keys to their initial success and rise to power. To a man like him, Caeso's rejection of the family's business was unthinkable, a betrayal. He could not comprehend how any member of his family was not as excited about it as he.

CHAPTER XIV

When we returned to the mansion I took advantage of my host's hospitality and treated myself to a long soak in their baths. I moved from the cold plunge to the warm plunge and then to the hot, and then back and forth again a few more times. The cut on my arm from the pirate attack was a livid red and would leave a scar, but it had closed and did not seem infected. I still had to keep my arm out of the water, which dampened the pleasure a bit.

After the plunges, a slave scraped me thoroughly with a *strigil* and then rubbed me down with some of the master's oils and unguents, helping me shed the aches of long days in cramped travel on ships. Our people have been seafarers for centuries, though sometimes I think the extent of our empire is limited to how far we can sail before we need to stop for a good bath.

I asked the steward if I could borrow a toga for the dinner that night — I had not brought mine as there is no point in travelling with an unwieldy garment that requires competent help to get into — but happily, the steward informed me that dinners at the Corpio estate were informal affairs. Thus I was saved from donning that unwieldy garment for the walk to dinner, only to take it off before reclining.

* * *

True to the steward's observation, when I reached the *triclinium* I saw the women reclining together with the men, rather than sitting on chairs facing them, and all were wearing comfortable tunics. This was no doubt the smaller *triclinium* of the mansion, used for more intimate family dinners rather than the entertainment of large parties. Everything about it, though, was exquisitely done — from the floor mosaics with motifs of various foods to the wall paintings depicting sea and country life to the three couches made from polished wood with ivory and gold leaf insets.

There were four people already present when I arrived. Publius Corpio and his wife Cornelia on the centre couch were saying good night to their daughter. The girl looked to me about twelve and was still wearing the long-sleeved tunic of children. Publius Quinctius had introduced her as his "darling Quinctia", but she darted quickly from the room as soon as I walked in. Cornelia herself was a good-looking woman, in her mid-thirties, with dark auburn hair held up with pearl-studded pins. Her smile seemed genuine to me, no doubt well trained, as the Cornelii have always been consummate politicians.

Corpio indicated the couch to his right, "This is my son, Marcus. He will wear his manly toga later this year, so we are allowing him to accompany us with adult company. Please join him." Young Marcus shared the family looks, with blond hair, green eyes and high cheekbones. He was three years younger than Caeso. I took a mental note to talk to him later in private; he might know something about his cousin that the adults would not.

As I reclined on the couch and had my sandals taken off by a slave, more people came into the room. I raised my gaze and laid eyes on two strikingly beautiful women. The first was aged around forty, very dark hair pinned up exposing a delicately white neck that led down to a voluptuous figure. She wore a saffron coloured tunic that hung loose yet managed to complement her curves most enticingly as she walked. Her skin shone with health and vigour, and her bright smile was like distant snow on a mountain peak.

The second was almost certainly her daughter, the same dark hair, milky skin. Her figure was not as full and mature, rather younger and firmer. I estimated her to be around nineteen years of age, and her piercing grey eyes gazed out with a twinkle, suggesting a curious nature. She wore a simpler blue tunic and let her hair cascade down, held back by a simple diadem of green cloth. I got the feeling that one day she would eclipse her mother in beauty.

"Come, darlings, sit by me," said Cornelia. "Felix, may I introduce my elder sister Cornelia *maior* and her daughter Aemilia." Both women turned their eyes to me, examining me with varied and mixed interests I could not quite fathom. "Felix is a friend of my husband's brother and will be staying with us as well for a few days."

I could scarcely believe that they were sisters. Where Cornelia *minor* the wife of Publius Corpio was a nice-but-average-looking woman, her older sister Cornelia *maior* was remarkable. Wearing less elaborate hair and makeup, with darker hair yet lighter skin, she would forever steal the thunder of any gathering.

"Now that we are all here we can finally eat!" exclaimed Publius Corpio and clapped his hands. Servants hurried in, placing glass goblets in front of us and pouring us *mulsum* and water, though I noticed the women and young Marcus were given only a splash of wine with their water. The servants then came back bearing large silver trays which they placed on the low tables in front of us. The first courses were simple, albeit expertly cooked; although admittedly after eating ship-fare and tavern-food for days almost anything would have been delicious.

As we nibbled on boiled gull eggs speared with olives on toothpicks, followed by sautéed artichokes, peppered black fungi in cream, and finally sea urchin roe in egg sauce, I tried hard not to stare at the two women reclining in front of me. Holding in my mind the image of Caeso's dead body frozen in mid convulsion, I spoke with young Marcus Corpio. Still not formally a man, he had been raised in the Corpio family heading towards a mercantile career. He seemed eager to don the manly toga in autumn and start his education in the Collegium Mercatorum — but what boy would not be excited about stories of piracy?

As I recounted to him my adventures of three nights ago, my sole intention was to gain his interest so I could question him later regarding Caeso. However, I soon found myself in the centre of a room full of people listening eagerly to my every word.

Suddenly the focus of attention, I stammered. "I hope I have not offended the women with my uncouth stories of pirates."

"Not at all," said Cornelia *maior*, looking at me with a twinkling smile.

"Sounds like you saved the day," said Aemilia rather flatly.

"Our family has been in the shipping business for generations," added Corpio, "and the ties with Cornelii by marriage just as long. We are all used to the hazards of the sea, as well as its bounty."

The servants cleared the dishes of the first course, and brought on the main courses. These consisted of roasted gulls stuffed with pine nuts, a salad of fresh herbs and sharp cheese, boiled ham with honey and sage, and fried baby octopus in spices.

The conversation resumed, though thankfully on subjects other than me. The two Cornelias were chattering away; Young Marcus was keenly interested in his father's dealing — the fishing and *garum* manufacture, the pearl diving and other enterprises, the long-distance trading. Aemilia, surprisingly, was quite animated about those subjects, expressing original opinions. She seemed very knowledgeable, as well, on matters ranging from geography and foreign cultures to trade goods and routes to business practises of finance and manufacture. I found it surprising, as not many women of her class and age would receive this level of tuition nor feel so free to express it. Voicing her opinion seemed tolerated and even accepted by her family as well, another uncommon arrangement.

The last dishes of the main courses were cleared, and the servants came to tempt us with desserts. These included dates stuffed with almond paste, honeyed sesame cakes drenched in wine and thin pastries with poppy-seed filling. The conversation moved to family matters. Cornelia *maior* and Aemilia, I learnt, had made it their habit to come visit Cornelia *minor* and Publius Corpio often; to "escape from the pace and interminable gossiping of Egretia" as they put it. I gathered both mother and daughter enjoyed the freer environments of the Corpio island mansion.

Cornelia had been widowed these past six years, her husband Tiberius Aemilius Mamercus having passed away suddenly at the early age of forty-nine. Her eldest son, bearing the same name as his father, had joined the Collegium Militum and was currently on campaign against the Tigumani, who had been recently encroaching on our province of Arbarica Inferior.

I was not used to women reclining together with men, and the view it offered me of Cornelia's curves as she talked was most distracting. I also found her daughter enticing, with her large grey eyes and youthful vigour, yet at the same time her gaze was sobering with its clear and level directness. And yet, as my gaze kept wandering uncontrollably back to Cornelia *maior*, I found her looking keenly back at me just as much, eyes atwinkle.

Inevitably, the subject of my business on the island had come about. Not being sure how much the extended family knew of the circumstances of Caeso's death, I looked to Publius Corpio. By now he had stopped watering his wine, and his face was flushed. "Oh, he's here to poke at what that young *pedere* had gotten himself into," he said, and caused some consternation to his wife with his uncouth language. "Well, he was, woman," continued Corpio over Cornelia *minor*'s attempts to shush him. "No appreciation of the family. That's how he got himself into whatever shady dealing ended up killing him in this way."

"I think it's time we retired," interjected Cornelia *maior* tactfully, and rose from the couch. Aemilia obediently followed. As they left the room, both gave me curious looks — the daughter, a mix of curiosity and interest, the mother, a completely different mix of interest and something quite else.

I decided it was the wine which made me read things that were not there. I shook my head and rose, as well. "I thank you kindly for your superb hospitality, Publius Corpio and Cornelia. I think I shall retire, too, as I have a busy day tomorrow."

* * *

As I left the dining room and tried to find my way to my sleeping cubicle, Marcus Corpio followed me. "They won't tell me how cousin Caeso died," he said. "He was here last autumn, you know. Is that why you are here?"

"Perhaps," I replied. "Do you know anything about his whereabouts while he visited?"

"Oh, I know some places he went to, all right. I could take you there if you wished."

"That will be most appreciated. Could you tell me where he travelled?" I asked.

"I could, but I'd rather go with you," he said with an excited look. "I bet you would find the… places… really interesting!"

"I don't want to put you at any risk. What would your father say?"

"He doesn't have to know. I told cousin Caeso and his friend Gnaeus Drusus, but they went without me. Took them too long to find her as well; served them right."

"'Her'?"

"I've said as much as I'm going to say. Will you take me with you?"

"You strike a hard bargain. I need more details, though, before I will even consider going behind your father's back. Why don't you tell me as much as you are willing, and I will decide then? I give you my word that if your story sounds plausible I shall share my investigation with you."

He thought for a moment. "Fair enough. Come with me; we can talk in the library."

He led me through an open colonnade bordering the peristyle garden, and ducked into a large room. "This should be far enough from everyone else," he said in a low voice, "however, we should still keep quiet." The room was dark as we did not have a light with us. I could not see Marcus' face clearly, only the gleam in his eyes. "Is it true that cousin Caeso got turned to stone by a medusa?" he asked.

"What? No, he did not encounter a medusa. What made you think that?"

"I heard my father and uncle talking after the funeral," he said. "I thought I heard them say something about how he turned to stone, but they stopped talking when they saw me. So how did he die?"

"That is what I am trying to find out. Why don't you tell me what he did on his visit last autumn?"

"He came with that friend of his, Gnaeus Drusus. My uncle sent them here because Caeso was doing poorly at his studies and wanted to marry a street mime. At least he said he wanted to marry her — she must have been really good in bed," he guffawed.

"When you grow up you'll find that it's the ones that you don't bed that prey on your mind the most," I said, hoping I sounded more like an older brother than a father. "And what did Caeso Quinctius and Gnaeus Drusus do while they were here?"

"At first my father took them around to the *garum* factories and docks. I went with them, as *pater* is preparing me to join his business. Drusus was alright, his family is in trade as well, but Caeso just wasn't into it. My father tried other things too, even introducing him to Margaritus, hoping he might get excited about the pearl business; Caeso was being a stubborn ass about all of it. Eventually, father gave up, told him to just go take a cruise around the islands and get out of his way."

"And is that when you started to send them to those 'interesting' places?"

"Yes. It's somewhere on one of the small, remote islands."

"And what, or should I ask who, is on that island?" I asked.

"First tell me why you need to investigate my cousin's death," he said with a grin.

"He died in extreme pain. He got involved with the wrong people, and they convinced him to participate in something very bad. He died alone and in intense agony, the look upon the face of his corpse was indeed like one who has seen the medusa." I hoped to scare him, and by the sound of his swallowing, I thought I might have managed. "You should be careful which friends you chose in life. Now, what was so special about the place you sent Caeso and Drusus to?"

"I sent them to see the *lamia*! Oh please, I hope that this is not what caused his death!"

"*Lamia*? You mean there is a *lamia* somewhere on these islands?"

"Well, that's what the legend says. It was something our nurse used to threaten us children, and stories we'd tell to frighten each other. Then one day I took a sailboat to one of the outer islands, and I saw a blind hag there, and I could swear that she had the lower body of a snake. I jumped back in my boat and rowed and sailed away as fast as I could. It was just my imagination, I told myself later. But what if she was a real *lamia*? And what if dear Caeso found her, and she was the one responsible for his death?"

"*Lamiae* are not known for their patience, nor for their intelligence." I recalled my tuition and the writings of Nikander. "If it was indeed a *lamia*, and I doubt one would live on these isles without notice, she would have attacked Caeso immediately. No, I think it was something else. What did they tell you when they got back?"

"Oh, nothing. Just made fun of me, saying I am still a child, afraid of nursery monsters, that there was only an old lady there."

"Still, we will go and take a look. Did you send your cousin and his friend Drusus anywhere else?"

"Caeso and Drusus went on a few more cruises without me, probably visited Novus Portus. They climbed the Mons Krodus, too, one day, right before they left to go back to Egretia."

"And did they tell you anything out of the ordinary or behave differently, anything at all that caught your attention, when they got back from those places?"

"Novus Portus they visited first, after my father let Caeso do as he wanted. Drusus was more excited, probably because of the whores. I think they both went to the *lamia*'s place, even though by then Drusus was losing interest in sailing. Caeso did come back excited, though he wouldn't tell me anything. He was nicer after he came back, in a good mood. They climbed the Krodus a few short days after. I don't know if they found anything there; we had no chance to speak before they returned to Egretia."

I thanked Marcus for the information. I didn't wish to waste time hunting around the small islands, so I made a deal with him to sail together to the mysterious *lamia*'s island the next day so long as his father gave permission. "You will just be showing me where Caeso went. I will promise him that I will keep you out of trouble — though I think your father will be more concerned with keeping you away from whorehouses than any *lamia*."

CHAPTER XV

We left before dawn the next day. Young Marcus turned out to be a decent sailor, and we were accompanied by one of his father's slaves to help. Marcus introduced him as Ariarathenes, and he seemed used to the young master's trips. For people who lived primarily in the Kebric archipelago, sailing was a part of life. Every child learnt to swim and sail almost as soon as they could walk.

We sailed west out of the bay of Kebros as the sky was just beginning to pink behind the massive dark shape of Mons Krodus. We rounded the western cape of Kebros, and Marcus kept us on the outer edge of the archipelago. From his description I understood that the island on which he had seen the *lamia*, as he still insisted on calling her, was on the furthest northern reaches.

We barely spoke as we sailed, Ariarathenes and Marcus so used to sailing together that they hardly needed to talk. I helped where I could, but spent much time merely sightseeing as we passed many islands on the way. Some were green with trees and shrubs, dotted with farms and villas; some were barely more than rocks jutting out of the sea, covered in wind-swept hardy grass and fit only for seagulls. Boat traffic increased between the isles of the archipelago as the day wore on, and we tried to stay away from the bulk of it.

We anchored in a cosy cove for a short rest and early lunch, and Marcus assured me that we were near, with perhaps an hour's sailing left to the *lamia*'s island. Publius Corpio's kitchen slaves had packed provisions for us for the day. Sitting on the deck, eating our lunch amidst the pastoral islands, watching the blue skies with scudding white clouds, the clear waters teeming with fish, the sailboats dotting the horizons with their striped square sails — I found it hard to consider that we might be facing a dangerous monster on our next stop.

Sometime in the seventh hour of the day we reached an island standing alone some distance away from the rest of the archipelago. It was of medium size, a big hill in its centre supporting a large copse of trees, and a brook running down through verdant meadows to the rocky beach. I saw no signs of human habitation on it. Mere separation could not explain why the people of the archipelago would shun a bountiful island like this.

We anchored close to the beach and rowed a light dinghy ashore, Ariarathenes staying with the boat. Marcus led me up the hill towards the copse of trees. "I saw her on this side of the island," he said in a low voice, "and I think she lives in a cave of sorts amongst the trees."

We continued to clamber up the hill in silence. We reached the tree line and stopped for a moment to catch our breath in their shadow. As we stood staring into the gloomy dark shadows amongst the dense foliage, the folly of my actions suddenly caught up with me. Taking my employer's nephew, still a child, without escort, without proper preparation, armed only with my dagger, to meet an unknown entity, who may or may not have been a flesh-eating *lamia*…

Not the time to dwell on such matters. I loosened my dagger in its scabbard, and we started into the woods. We wandered under the branches at the edge looking for a path in. As we rounded a jutting boulder, I saw some sheep roaming freely in a green meadow. No one was in sight, and even the sheep were eerily quiet. Marcus touched my arms and pointed silently to a narrow path between the trees, leading into the grove. We turned in and followed it slowly.

We walked amidst gnarled trees and dense shrubs. A few paces in and we could no longer hear the waves of the sea, every sound becoming muffled, ominous. After a few minutes of walking as silently as we could, jumping with racing hearts at each snapped twig, we reached a sunny clearing. A low hut stood next to a pool fed by a spring at the side of a large rock formation. The hut was old, with wattle and daub walls and a thatched roof. A shuttered window was next to the rickety door, and both were closed. A thin wisp of smoke was coming out of the chimney.

We stepped into the clearing. "Hello?" I said loudly.

No answer.

We approached the small hut. "Hello?" I said again, louder.

"No need to shout; here you have no clout" said a hoarse voice right behind me.

* * *

We turned and saw a wizened old woman, old beyond belief. Her face was deeply lined with age and exposure to the elements. She was short and thin, though not bent. Dressed in a rough woollen tunic, much patched and frayed, but kept clean.

She looked at us with sparkling dark eyes, smiling faintly. "I had no visitors all this winter, yet I knew in spring you would come hither."

This is no *lamia* before me, I realised; the whole setting was too pastoral. I relaxed a little. I had met many charlatans and several mad hermits in my life, so I baited her with, "You knew we would come?"

"Oh, yes, this young man I have seen before, and last autumn his cousin came ashore. And you, a lucky fox, standing there like a slow ox, on a journey to find the truth of what happened to the poor youth."

I heard Marcus swallowing next to me and shut my own open mouth with a snap. That was far too precise to be mere charlatan patter. I deemed it prudent to proceed politely and carefully.

"Please forgive us for the intrusion on your island. Could you tell us about the cousin's visit?"

"The young man was seeking thrills, and attempted something lacking in skills. He came to me to find an answer, though he didn't know it would end in disaster. His actions caused himself the blight, for he did them well under the light."

"Could you tell us the questions he asked you, and what answers you gave him?" I asked.

"Those things I cannot do, they belong to him, not you."

I was talking to a sibyl, of that much I was certain. The trouble with their prophecies is that, while accurate, they are usually completely useless to us mortals until after the fact. How could I make the best of this?

"Would you help me find out who killed him?" The direct approach.

"That I can do with glee, but first you must drink my tea. However, you must beware of things neither here nor there. You seek now to find a missing spell, always careful when you look down a well." The image of the bloated body floating in the well rose unbidden in my mind, and I shuddered involuntarily under the sibyl's piercing gaze. I had no doubt that this was what she meant.

"Come, now, do not fear, there is a reason why you're here. We shall drink some tea, so that hidden things you might see." She walked past me into her hut. Marcus and I looked at each other for a moment, then followed her inside.

As we waited for our eyes to adjust to the gloom of the hut, our noses were subjected to a dense and complex aroma. From wood-fire smoke to dry meats to floral bouquets. It was not unpleasant, rather sweet and earthy. The interior of her hut was made up of one room. A simple cot in one corner, a hearth with a black pot on the embers in another. A rickety table and stools in the middle, a mid-sized chest against the wall, both covered with rough fabric and supporting household items — cups and dishes, a bronze mirror and a few closed boxes. Various dried sausages and bunched herbs were hanging from the rafters.

The sibyl handed me a pot, saying "Be a dear and take this thing, bring me water from the spring."

I took the pot and went outside. As I knelt on the moss-covered stones next to the small pool, I felt my skin tingle. I looked into the pool, but ripples made by the dripping spring-waters obscured its depths. As I dipped the pot into the water the feeling intensified. This was an old place, a place where the power of an ancient *numen* lived. Our people once revered the *numina* of nature, and many of us still do. Our months, our holidays are named for them. But then the *incan-*

tatores had asserted that this was just energy that could be harnessed, that new philosophies could free men from superstition. Regardless, the old folk wisdom knew better, and in places like this one could not argue with it.

I muttered an old formula of thanks to the nymph in the spring, feeling foolish as I said it and knowing full well my old college buddies would have laughed at me for saying it. Now, having been expelled from the Collegium and having travelled the world, I had seen more things than I could comfortably explain. I wondered how long there had been sibyls here, caring for the *numen* of the spring and living in its power.

Back inside, the sibyl took the pot from me, added crushed herbs and put it on the fire. "Now we wait until the tea is ready, which we'll know when the aroma is quite heady."

While we waited, the sibyl pottered around, clearing the table and setting three cups. She dipped bay leaves in honey and placed one in each cup. "We shall do this one at a time, or otherwise it might confuse my rhyme. First the young one, whose dreams are fun, then the fox should learn to trust, and this old sibyl's tea entrust."

"You don't have to do this," I said to Marcus. "We hardly know anything about this woman. You yourself thought she was a *lamia*. This is an unnecessary risk."

"It's a sibyl, Felix," he said, rolling his eyes. "I know my legends and lore. I may have been a frightened boy when I thought she was a *lamia*, but now I am almost a man. I will not miss a chance to receive my own prophecy."

The sibyl held the pot with a folded towel and took it off the fire, poured the steaming brew into the cup before Marcus and placed it back on the hearth. "Breathe the steam, drink and dream."

Marcus did as instructed, holding the cup gently, blowing on the liquid and inhaling the steam. He took a first careful sip, his face brightened, and he sipped some more. "Whatever is in here," he said, "is actually quite ni—"

His face and hands froze. His eyes glazed. Without changing expression, he very carefully put his cup down. I caught it and guided it gently to the table, so he wouldn't spill the hot brew on himself.

"The mind of the young, free of distraction, his dreams will grant him much satisfaction," said the sibyl.

"And mine?" I look at her sidelong.

"That you will see when you drink my tea," she said with a cryptic smile.

"Tell me," I asked, "when the young man's cousin was here last year, was he alone?"

"He came here with a friend, and both drank my special blend."

"And you will not tell me anything else about it, will you?"

She just smiled and continued to dust around her hut.

A few minutes later Marcus began to stir. He drew a deep breath and the colour and animation returned to his face.

"Did you learn anything?" I asked.

His face reddened. "I… I think so. Can't quite make sense of it, though."

"That is normal with sibyls' prophecies," I shot the sibyl a side-long look.

"The boy's prophecy is his alone, to heed its message or bemoan."

"I saw myself as an old man, sitting in my family's house, dressed richly with very fine things all around me," Marcus continued.

"That sounds like a good future." I said.

"It's just that, you see, I felt this great dissatisfaction. Disillusioned, thoroughly miserable, a life wasted." I waited for him to continue. "I am not sure what led me there. What choices will I make in life to lead down such a path, and how might I avoid making the wrong ones? I need to think about it."

"And now you," said the sibyl, "sit and drink my brew."

She poured another measure of the tea into the cup in front of me. I raised it carefully and breathed on the steaming surface. The aroma reminded me of the scent of spring flowers wafting over crisp snow. I took a careful sip. I could taste the honey, the flowers and other things besides which I could not quite place. It was earthy, rich, comforting in a way. I took another sip.

* * *

I was following Caeso up a narrow mountain path. I could clearly see the town and the bay far below us, the clear horizon of blue skies meeting with blue seas. We were climbing the Mons Krodus — Caeso together with Gnaeus Drusus, and me keeping well behind. The path soon reached the woods on the slopes and Caeso and Drusus disappeared from my sight.

I followed them between the trees. As I walked deeper into the forest the light dimmed until I could hardly see the ground for the faint light did not penetrate the thick canopy. A thick white mist rose and was curled on the ground, obscuring roots. I tripped and fell, got up, walked on. Vague glimpses in rare breaks amidst the branches offered me slivers of moonlight and faint stars that were not enough to show me direction. Before me, around me, behind me, between the trees all I saw was the fog. I lost track of the people I was following and just kept walking, avoiding branches and roots, drawn inexorably towards my destination.

The clearing.

I slowed as I walked out from between the trees, taking careful steps across the moonlit grass. In the edges of the clearing out of the corner of my eye I saw what I thought was moonlight reflecting in eyes, the sheen of purple-black fur, though whenever I turned I saw only grey-white mist and leaves.

I edged to the middle of the clearing. The grass looked like brittle shards of silver in this light.

In front of me loomed the well. I knew that was where my destination lay, the reason for my being here.

I walked over to it. I placed my hands on the stones of its sill and turned my head to look up to the stars. I stared at them and they blinked back at me coldly.

I steeled myself to face the well. Face what was inside it. That was why I was drawn here. To make me confront the thing down its depths.

I didn't want to, but I had to.

I dropped my gaze, and opposite me stood Araxus, looking straight back at me with both eyes.

Which was odd, because he was a raving lunatic who should be far away from here by now.

I cast my eyes into the well, and saw the body floating in it, face down.

Whole, and dressed in a tunic.

As I was looking at it, it bobbed and flipped around and by the filtered moonlight I recognised her...

But it wasn't Helena.

It was Aemilia, Caeso's cousin whom I'd just met the night before.

And the well, too, was not the same but filled with a liquid fire instead of water. And the ground was trembling, shaking, rising and falling away beneath my feet. Aemilia opened her eyes and cried to me, reaching to me with her arms, and I reached out to grasp her hand but the very earth was crumbling, and we were falling together into the liquid fire of the well that suddenly loomed so vast and Araxus tapped my shoulder with his staff and I opened my eyes and looked on the concerned face of young Marcus, his hand on my shoulder.

"Are you alright?" he asked "You started to shake and cried out in pain."

We were inside the sibyl's hut, and my mouth was dry, my mind full of cobwebs.

I nodded and rose shakily to my feet, stumbled outside. I stepped to the clear pool, knelt and splashed my face with its cold, clean waters.

CHAPTER XVI

I woke up late the next morning, having returned that night well after dark. The sibyl had left me with nothing that would further my investigations of Caeso's death. I was reasonably certain that he had visited her and had a vision, though of what it showed him and where it led him I was not any wiser. My own vision, hope as I did that it would shine a light, had been merely a strange mixture of the demons which tormented me and a face that had been fresh on my mind. How it could possibly relate to Caeso, or to anything meaningful, I could not see.

That left me with the more mundane methods of investigation, namely walking and talking.

I talked with Publius Corpio's steward and a few of the slaves who had cared for Caeso while he had stayed here. None added any more information to what I already knew, but that was half-expected. Caeso had stayed mostly by himself after Publius had released him. They confirmed he had been a love struck little brat from the moment he had come until the last few days of his stay. He had come back from sailing one day, suddenly full of purpose. I felt it safe to assume that this was due to his visit to the sibyl, not the brothels Drusus had dragged him to. After that day the only other meaningful event was the climbing of the Mons Krodus, something I arranged to do the next day.

I even tried hunting around in the small town of Kebros that afternoon as well, trying the taverns, gambling houses and brothels that are ever-present in port cities. None could remember a boy matching Caeso's description, or rather I heard a lot of stories of such boys but none matched what I knew of him. It was a half-hearted attempt, just to ease my mind.

I made it back to the Corpio mansion in time for a bath and dinner.

I took my towel with me as I moved from the warm to the hot plunge. I did not see him at first, for the foggy mist over the bath waters was thick and the light was dim, but as I sank my body gingerly into the water, I heard Publius say, "How went your sailing with my boy yesterday?"

"He was quite eager to show me around the isles," I said, and added "Your man Ariarathenes was with us, though young Marcus seems quite adept at handling the ship."

"He has been accompanying me for a few years now, Marcus, and has a career in shipping ahead of him. He won't be doing much sailing for himself, but he will need to understand what it takes if he is to run a business."

"Very wise of you," I said, feeling the heat go from my skin deep into my muscles, relaxing me as I submerged my body deeper under the water.

"Did you learn anything that would shed light on my nephew's demise? Or did you just revisit all the brothels around the town?" he asked.

"I learnt something, yes. Your son took me to a remote island, to which he previously had directed Caeso. There is an old woman living there, a sibyl. Did you hear about her?"

"I have heard some of the sailors and townspeople talk, although it sounded more superstition that reality. They leave that island alone, I believe, though sometimes they go there and leave offerings when times are hard. Does she have anything to do with my nephew?"

"He saw her, on his last week here. Had a prophecy or a vision. Though I could not find out the details, I believe the climb on Mons

Krodus he took next was related. You may recall his mood changing on those days. Did he mention anything back then?"

"Not much. At the time I thought he simply found a new diversion for his amorous attentions, something to take his mind off that street mime." Publius groaned and shifted in the water. "I think it's time we came out for dinner, pleasant as this may be. My steward has instructions to assist you, but please inform me as you progress. I hope we can get a swift answer to this business and put it behind us."

I got the message.

Dinner was another family affair, just like the previous day. The menu, which was probably normal fare for the Quinctii Corpiones and the Cornelii, was a cut above what I was used to. I enjoyed it with relish, particularly the fresh oysters and the pipis in wine sauce. These were farmed among the islands, and are an expensive delicacy in Egretia.

Publius did not bring up the subject of my investigation or of our travel the day before, and young Marcus was pensive and talked little. The same could not be said about Cornelia and Aemilia.

"So tell me, dear Felix, how was your trip around the isles with my nephew? Encounter any interesting views?" asked Cornelia *maior*.

"Quite lovely," I replied. "Young Marcus Quinctius here is a fine sailor."

"I am sure you must have had an adventure. Please do not be shy and tell of all the details!" she pressed me.

I looked at Marcus, who was chewing contemplatively on a piece of sticky honey cake. "Marcus has most helpfully provided me with some aid in uncovering clues to Caeso's whereabouts during his visit here. He has shown me around the islands, places that had an impact on Caeso. We have even visited a sibyl." I paused to take a bite of cake myself, and wash it down with some wine. "There is indeed a true sibyl on a remote island of this archipelago. I am surprised she has not proven more popular with the visitors to these isles. She confirmed to me that Caeso had visited her, and had drunk her potions. Of course, while no one can say for certain what vision Caeso saw, I did choose to partake in her brews as well." More cake, more wine.

What was I thinking, boasting like that? Quite unlike my usual self. I can only lay the blame at Cornelia's low-cut gown, the lines of her full breasts peeking out of her tunic directly in front of me. "Sibyls' visions are never clear, yet it is an important step in Caeso's fateful path. And speaking of paths, I think the time is rather late, and I do hope to get an early start tomorrow climbing Mount Krodus. If you will excuse me, I would thank you kindly for your hospitality and bid you good night."

"I don't know if I believe it," said Aemilia, quite openly. "A real sibyl? Potions? Prophetic vision?"

"I think it's time for all of us to go to bed," interjected Cornelia the younger.

I rose to my feet, stretched and said, "The visions were real indeed, though their contents mixed with private memories. I will now bid you good night."

"Oh, tomorrow our augurs predict rain," said Cornelia *minor*. "It will be quite miserable up there. Why don't you go the next day?"

"But the day after is the conclusion of the *Ludi Florae*," responded her sister. "I know! Why don't you join us, Felix? The town is holding gladiatorial games, and I am told that this year there will be a special surprise. You shouldn't be working on the holy day, it's *nefas*. After all, the Floralia is dedicated to pleasure." She looked at me with eyelids half obscuring a mischievous twinkle, and a licentious smile on her lips that warmed my blood.

"Yes, what a lovely idea!" agreed Cornelia *minor*, while the look on her husband's and niece's faces may have suggested otherwise.

"That is most kind of you," I said. "Nonetheless, I think I will climb the Mons Krodus tomorrow, rain or not. The death of Caeso haunts me, and I wish to get to the bottom of this."

The others were getting up as well, saying their goodnights. I walked out of the *triclinium*; Aemilia followed me ahead of her mother. "A real sibyl? Why has no one ever heard about her? And what visions could she had given you, that you refuse to tell us?"

I looked at her and saw her as I had in my vision — pale, falling, receding, reaching out to me.

"Young lady, there are more things on this earth than your tutor of philosophies may have told you about. Not everything that the common people know makes it to the scrolls and sheltered discourse of the highborn. And as for my integrity," — pale, falling, eyes pleading — "I suggest you do not question it again, not without evidence."

I turned and left her without another word.

* * *

I started early again on the following day, after a bad night plagued by dreams. The same dream as always, this time with Aemilia's infuriating face instead of Helena's. An hour before dawn I was already on a horse, riding along the shore road towards the dark mass of Mons Krodus.

I passed the sleepy town just beginning to wake up, and started on the track that led into the forested slopes. The sky was a pale blue by the time I reached the line of trees. From my already high vantage point I could see dark clouds out to sea, a storm coming.

Once I was amongst the trees the world became dark again, a place of shadows and muffled sounds. I walked my horse slowly over the broken path, not to risk her falling and breaking a leg. I had to duck often to avoid branches, and still got scratches and slaps from leafy protrusions. Once I yelped in pain as with a careless movement I bumped my sore right shoulder against a stout branch, right over the wound from the fight with the pirates. All this exercise was slowing down my healing, even with the special ointments and muttered spells I put on each night.

By about mid-morning I reached an open clearing. The sky to the north and east was bright and clear. The peak above me looming darkly, lit from behind as it were, and just beyond the western slopes I could see the dark storm clouds approaching.

I opened my bag and ate some bread and an apple, giving half to the tired horse. I looked at the path going up the hill, and it was obvious that I could not continue far on horseback, the path dwindling to a narrow track over broken rocks, sharp turns, gullies. I hobbled the horse and left her to roam the clearing, free to munch on the spring grasses.

I started the climb up the last part. At first the trees closed over the track, their sagging boughs forcing me to duck and stoop, the loose rocks necessitating careful treading. A few trees had fallen across the way, some looking as if they had lain there for a few years. Winter storms and rains had washed stones and debris over the track. I crossed narrow streams, with icy cold water freezing my toes in my sandals.

After a while the trees began to dwindle. Those that remained were further apart, gnarled and twisted from the wind. This high up the air was getting chilly, and even the *Maius* sun could not warm me much against the constant breeze. I was sweating from exertion, but as soon as I stopped walking the wind chilled me to the bone.

At long last after mid-day I neared the summit. The path was almost invisible between the scrub and low, hardy bushes. Lichen-covered boulders necessitated a twisting route and careful steps. I finally clambered on top of a particularly large rock and reached the plateau at the summit. A small flat area, about a *stadia* in length and half that in width, lay before me. Broken rocks, moss and lichen, low shrubs and a biting, whipping wind. I looked out, half the sky behind me clear and blue, the half in front of me dark grey with tumultuous clouds.

Our people have a name for the presence that resides in bare hilltops under the vast open sky. Today, at the top of Mons Krodus, under a sky half calm and half in turmoil, I had no doubt this presence was real. This presence was a *numen*, a power of sky and thunder and lightning that made its presence known in the most elemental way. Though it is the patron god of our city, its reality is doubted amongst the educated elite, in their libraries and marble halls. Out here, I knew and felt what our people had known and felt for millennia before. The presence they called Iovis Pater.

The wind whipped my hair and tunic about, telling me I needed to hurry or risk getting soaked. At the centre of the plateau I saw a large rock formation jutting out from the rubble, and walked towards it. As I circled around it, I came across an old altar of our people. Above a crack in a boulder some ancient people had carved crude lines, semi circles above two shallow indentations, lines angling down, a dark crack in the stone. Together with the scrub at the bottom, the image of a huge, bearded rock-face with its eyes half closed and mouth agape was eerie. Father Iovis of the skies, looking up beyond me at his approaching storm.

I squeezed into the low, narrow opening. My body obscured the dim light outside, and the cavity was pitch black. I felt the small hairs on my arms tingle, my whole skin becoming charged. There was power in this place, such raw power that even Caeso would have sensed it.

I groped in the darkness, felt a stone pedestal of sorts. On it lay something hard, made of rock, yet warm to the touch. I could not close my hand around it; it required two hands to lift up and carry outside. Once back in the light I stood examining at the thing in my hands. It was a curiously shaped stone, painted a faded red. I held it up and turned it around, and its shape became clear.

A heart.

A gigantic human heart, made of stone, painted red, inside the mouth-cave of a giant.

As I stood there gaping at it, perplexed as to its origin and purpose, the sky above me split open with a bright flash and a deafening peal of thunder, and together with the lightning and the thunder the stone heart in my hands *pulsed*.

I cried and dropped it to the ground, took a step back, tripped and fell on my backside. For a moment I just remained there, looking at it dumbly. And then came a second lightning bolt, striking the gravel in front of me, causing the stone heart to fly back inside the open mouth of the shrine, and the eyes to shine with light.

Pebbles of rocks thrown up by the lightning showered me, scraping me with their sharp edges. The clouds opened their contents above me, and in a moment I was drenched from the torrential rain. I scrambled back to the path, barely seeing ahead through the silvery curtains of water. I stumbled down the mountain, slipping and sliding over the wet rocks many times, bruising and scraping myself. When I got to my horse, luckily still in the clearing where I had left her, I rode her back down as fast as I dared.

CHAPTER XVII

In contrast to the misery of yesterday, the last day before the *Kalends* of *Maius* was blessed with clear skies and fresh-smelling air. Feeling still quite miserable and sore after yesterday, I let myself be persuaded by Cornelia *maior* to join them at the games.

The town of Kebros, having been an Egretian colony for centuries, had all the amenities of a civilised place. Their circus was a good-sized affair, well decorated with bronze and marble statues and able to seat comfortably some twenty thousand people. The concentration of businesses and residences around the town had made it a centre of provincial culture.

Leaving after breakfast, we travelled in a small convoy. We men were driven in one horse-drawn open cart, sitting erect in our togas, while the women were driven in a comfortably shaded oxcart. A train of slaves walked behind us. People from all over the island were making their way as well — on foot, riding horses and mules, or driving carts. The bay was dotted with many anchored ships, residents from other isles having made their way in advance.

We finally got there by late mid-morning, and having left the horses and carts with the slaves, walked towards the circus edifice. Publius Corpio was one of the more affluent residents of the isles; generations of his family have held magistracies both locally and in Egretia. The Quinctii Corpiones had therefore their own private section along the inner ring of seats. Other people around us found their gates, showed their imprinted clay seals to the ushers and climbed up to their allotted seats. We just leisurely strolled to a gated entrance and walked inside to a lavishly furnished vestibule. Tables were set along the wall, covered with red cloth with geometric green designs. On them lay silver trays laden with pastries and sweetmeats, and pitchers of wine and water stood next to waiting glasses. Slaves were running around, attending to everyone's needs.

As this was a public event, the women were dressed modestly in *stolas*. Cornelia *maior* was wearing a vermilion *stola* that did a wonderful job of hinting at her voluptuous curves, while her daughter wore an aquamarine one with an intricate floral design along the hem. In a room full of well-dressed women I still found the both of them standing out, although the looks they gave me — one twinkling, the other disapproving — made the mother a clear winner for me.

As we mingled and waited for the games to begin, drinking watered wine and eating honey cakes, I watched the people in the room. Publius Corpio was at ease, a born businessman and politician, talking to others of his class. His wife fulfilled her duties, walking with him when other wives were around and disappearing with them when the men turned their conversation to serious matters. Marcus kept close to his father, wearing a tunic of fine wool — a compromise between the long-sleeved tunic of childhood and the toga he would wear only later this year. Publius' associates seemed to recognise him, and his presence as they discussed important matters was understood as the son being groomed by his father. Cornelia *maior* and Aemilia walked amongst the guests as well, clearly a part of the elite's social life here.

At midday a slave came and announced that the opening ceremonies were about to start. The guests, the elite of the Kebric Isles, started to shuffle their way to the private booths along the inner ring of the circus. Somehow I found myself walking next to Cornelia *maior*, and when we were seated in Corpio's shaded box she was sitting beside me at the back row. I would have expected her to sit together with her sister, right in the front. Instead, in front of me was Publius, Marcus to his left, and Cornelia *minor* next to him with Aemilia at her left. The booth was large, enough to entertain several guests as well as the family.

I had stayed behind out of respect, though I cannot say I was dismayed when I found Cornelia the elder alongside me. The sailcloth shading granted a privacy of sorts, and Cornelia kept her gaze out to the sand and the crowd, which allowed me to study her profile surreptitiously.

I looked out to the circus as well. The inner ring, the one closest to the sands of the arena, was lined with booths like ours, shaded at the top and partitioned. To our right, about a quarter of the circle away, was the large box for the governor of the Kebric Isles. While I had not been introduced, I had recognised him from the foyer below. A thin, light-coloured man in his forties, named Aulus Paulinus, I believe.

Above the inner circle rose tiers of stone benches, now full of excited people. Between them I saw slaves walk around with trays of food and drink, no doubt paid for by the governor's *quaestors* hoping to win votes in coming years. Above hung large cloth sails, tied together on projecting beams and manipulated with ropes and pulleys to provide shade for the seats.

A fanfare sounded, and I lowered my gaze to the arena. Today was the conclusion of the *Ludi Florae*, the part most common people were interested in. Yesterday's celebrations had included the opening ceremonies, theatre plays and other observances and festivities. Today's were to include the concluding sacrifice, which the governor had elected to offer, somewhat unconventionally, as gladiatorial games.

In walked the governor's *lictors*, bearing fasces with axes, signifying the power of life and death about to be witnessed, their crimson leather sandals on the bright sand looking like pools of blood. Behind them came the trumpeters, followed by acrobats and clowns. After the entertainers followed the *rudis* bearing his referee staff and the palm fronds for the victors, and in his train walked the gladiators.

For the opening ceremony, the gladiators were dressed in fancy garb, ornate silver armour plates shining brightly with reflected sunlight. Their helmets sported plumes of ostrich feathers, long horse tails, and metal fish heads. On their belts hung thick knotted cords, showing their tally of previous wins. Seven gladiators walked in the parade, and I wondered if the special treat would be a one-against-two fight.

The procession circled around the arena, the *lictors* and entertainers disappearing back inside while the gladiators and *rudis* stopped in front of the governor's box. Aulus Paulinus rose and with a clear orator's voice delivered a short speech. An uninspired thing, he mercifully kept it short, touching on the importance of the Floralia to our people, how in spring life is celebrated with a touch of death, and ending by building up the excitement for the surprise main event.

The gladiators went back inside to change into combat armour, and the crowds settled in their seats with the program, to discuss the merits of each gladiator and place bets.

* * *

The first fight of the games was a classic match of a *myrmillo* against a *hoplomachus*. They walked on to the bright sands of the arena, saluted the governor and drew apart. The *summa rudis* — the senior referee — raised his staff and lowered it in a neat arc, and the match began.

The two men circled one another for a bit, the *hoplomachus* feinted with his spear a few times, finally throwing it when he thought the *myrmillo* was expecting another feint. The *myrmillo* caught it on his shield, deflected and advanced. The two men closed, clashed with shields, drew back. Exchanged more feints, stabs and clashes. They were obviously from the same school, and had trained with each other before. The *myrmillo* kept his larger shield in the way, effectively blocking the *hoplomachus'* shorter dagger from getting past it but at the same time not able to deliver meaningful blows with his *gladius*. The *hoplomachus* with his small round shield and dagger was more manoeuvrable, yet unable to push the *myrmillo* or get around him. He was fighting a retreating battle, letting the man with the heavier armour chase him.

Eventually the *hoplomachus'* tactic showed. When the *myrmillo* was backing him into the wall, he feinted right, threw his small shield against his opponent's head with all his strength, disengaged and ran quickly to pick up his spear. The *myrmillo* followed him, but his heavier shield and greaves kept him from catching up in time. The *hoplomachus* grabbed the fallen spear with both hands, clutching his knife along the shaft of the spear, and started hammering the *myrmillo* with both ends using it effectively as a staff as well as a pointed spear.

A crazy tactic, dropping a shield, yet vindicated as the *myrmillo* slowly retreated under the barrage of blows, tired now and unable to find an opening. The *hoplomachus* did not have long to wait. Taking a step back, he threw his knife at the *myrmillo*. No finesse to the throw, though none was needed. As the *myrmillo* lifted his shield to block the incoming knife, the *hoplomachus* took a step sideways and stabbed him in the ribs with the long spear held in his left hand. The *myrmillo* recoiled back, staggered and fell to his knees.

The crowd yelled with excitement at the sight of the first blood on the arena sands. I was excited as well, but for other reasons. As the *myrmillo* had fallen, Cornelia *maior* had clutched my arm. She was staring keenly at the men in the arena, as was indeed everyone else around us, and the gesture could have come as a purely unconscious action. At least until she added, "I do find the sight of men fighting oh so exciting, don't you?"

The *hoplomachus* resumed his battering of the kneeling *myrmillo*, and with a mighty kick pushed his opponent's shield out of the way and gave a harsh blow with the butt of his spear into the man's helmet, denting it in the process. The *myrmillo* fell on his back, unconscious.

The *rudis* placed his staff across the chest of the *hoplomachus* and stayed him from skewering the prone man. He stepped to the fallen *myrmillo* and prodded him with his staff. One of his junior assistants ran out to him carrying a hot poker. The *rudis* nodded, and the assistant held the bright red poker to the fallen man's thigh. As this happened close to our seats, I could smell the stench of seared human flesh rising from the arena.

The defeated man was truly unconscious. The *rudis* looked up at the governor, who as editor of the games gave the sign of life. The crowd cheered, though from scattered boos I think they would have preferred to see more blood. No doubt the *lanista* of the gladiator school had instructed them to aim for knocking each other out, and the governor had elected not to pay the compensation for a dead man.

Satisfied that the fight was concluded, the assistants dragged the body of the *myrmillo* by his heels out of the arena. The *hoplomachus* jogged around the ring for a victory lap and was awarded the palm frond of the victor.

Musicians and acrobats provided a short interlude while slaves raked the sands. The crowds attended to nature calls, got snacks from tray-bearing vendors, and reviewed the program for the next round of betting. Cornelia *maior* was talking to her sister, sitting well composed again.

The second fight was another classic match, this time between a *secutor* and a *retiarius*. They circled around on the sands. The *secutor*, wearing his heavy helmet with two round holes for eyes and his large shield, did his best to avoid being trapped by the *retiarius'* net. The *retiarius*, on the other hand, was free to move. He tried to outmanoeuvre his opponent, yet was unable to risk getting too close to the heavily armoured man, as he bore no shield and wore no armour except for one greave on his left arm.

Once, twice, thrice he cast his net but failed to snare his opponent, the net sliding on the *secutor's* smooth helmet, unable to entangle him.

At last the *secutor* managed to catch the net around his sword arm. In a smooth movement he simultaneously blocked the trident thrust with his shield and yanked hard on the net, making his opponent stumble. The *retiarius*, now armed only with his trident, faced a steel wall in the form a large shield advancing on him. His chances looked grim.

The *secutor* kept slashing with his short *gladius*, easily blocking the trident. Not giving up, the *retiarius* used his mobility to his advantage, wearing his opponent out.

At last a slower stroke of the sword gave him his chance. With deft precision, the *retiarius* managed to catch the *secutor's gladius* between the prongs of his trident and twist hard. It was not enough to rip the sword out from the man's hand, but it was enough to unbalance him — an advantage the *retiarius* was quick to capitalise on. He slammed his shoulder into the shield in front of him and sent the heavy *secutor* reeling back. A flurry of jabs with the trident, the *secutor* retreating but unable to get his balance, a high feint, a slash at the feet, a kick followed by a mighty stab around the shield.

A moment frozen in time, the *secutor* standing staring in horror at the trident sticking into his abdomen all the way to the fork, his arms hanging limply at his side. And then with a mighty cry and a heave the *retiarius* yanked his weapon out, the backwards-facing barbs of the prongs ripping skin and organs, and guts spilled steaming upon the sands from a belly now cut open.

As the *secutor* fell, the *retiarius* raised his trident above his head in a wordless cry of triumph. The crowd, finding this more to their liking, roared their approval of his victory. I saw the governor give a sign of death, combining mercy and crowd-pleasing. The *retiarius* put the dying *secutor* out of his misery, cutting his last scream short by driving his trident into his opponent's throat. The *secutor*'s hands and feet twitched and jerked as his life's blood gushed onto the sands, and then lay still.

The crowds were not the only ones pleased. At the sight of the human viscera spilled upon the sands, Cornelia *maior* hooked her arm in mine and held tightly. She now looked away from the ring and into my eyes, her face close enough for me to feel her warm breath. With a most excited twinkle in her eyes, she said, "Now that was a good fight, wouldn't you say? A good sacrifice to Flora for a bountiful spring, and very pleasing for us, too."

The last fight promised to be the most interesting. Two *dimachaeri* walked onto the arena, their twin curved swords held in their hands. They made their salutes and faced each other, the *rudis* gave the signal and they started their intricate dance.

Slow at first, feints and careful slashes. Then faster, harder, sparks flying from their short swords. They walked back and forth across the sands, circling, slashing, parrying, stabbing, diverting. A great concentration upon their faces — not having shields, only arm guards and light helmets, they had to rely on the sword in each hand to both attack and defend.

Their skill was superb. Whoever they were, however they had trained, they put on one of the best gladiator shows I have seen in long years of attending games. Evenly matched and at peak condition, their dance accelerated to an incredible speed, a constant blur of motion, the swords only visible as they locked and threw sparks.

Cornelia, the gladiator aficionado, was very much excited as well. Her eyes never left the combatants but her hand was resting on my thigh, gripping it tightly. Not a soul in the crowd would have seen it, as all eyes were on the show.

The fight lasted long moments. The gladiators, being men of flesh and blood, eventually started to tire out. One slowed down from his frantic pace, not much, just enough for his opponent to nick him on his ribs. The crowds voiced their appreciation of this first blood; Cornelia gasped and grasped my thigh quite firmly. And quite high up along the thigh, too.

The dance was now serious, lethal, yet no less graceful. Soon more cuts and nicks appeared on both their torsos, shoulders, legs; droplets of blood flew about, shimmering in the sun as the men spun and leaped about.

The suspense was intense, the whole crowd holding its breath, cheering, gasping as one. Until one misplaced step, one stumble and a dagger made its way deep into a shoulder. The pierced man cried out, sank to his knees and raised his other hand, index finger held up. The *summa rudis* interposed his staff between the two sweating, bleeding men.

The crowd was ecstatic. A few fists were raised, but far, far more hands clutching handkerchiefs were waved around. The governor scanned the crowd, and the mood was clear. Such talent was appreciated, and should not be wasted. He gave the sign, and the loser of the match was allowed to walk out of the arena with his life. The victor took his victory lap around the circus, and accepted his palm frond with a bow.

* * *

One last fight remained, the promised special event. After the ring was cleaned, the sand raked, the musicians and acrobats had done their pieces, the governor rose to his feet.

"Dear people of the Kebric Isles," his voice carried clearly. "You are now about to witness a very special event. Very few such spectacles as you will soon enjoy have ever been seen in the history of our great nation. Not even the city of Egretia will have such a wonderful event this year for the *Ludi Florae*, or indeed I imagine for any other games! You are undeniably lucky to be here, under the governorship of Aulus Paulinus!"

He sat back in his chair and waved his hand majestically at the arena. Then, instead of the doors opening to admit the *rudis* and the gladiators, something most peculiar happened. Slaves ran around the circus, drawing a strong net made of thick ropes across the inner ring of seats, hauling it up and tying it tightly to posts and projections. The result was a sandy arena enclosed fifteen feet above it by a huge net. Murmurs ran through the crowd as speculation mounted. Bets about what was coming were yelled and accepted amongst the spectators.

The *rudis* reappeared inside the governor's box. He raised his staff and banged it on the marble, and an excited hush descended on the crowd. First the doors on one end opened, and in strode the seventh gladiator, alone. He was wearing padded arm and leg greaves, a leather cuirass covering his chest and back, and a crested round helmet. He carried a spear and a whip, but no shield. This was no doubt a *bestiarius*, which left open the question of which beast he would be given to fight.

The *bestiarius* strode to the centre of the arena, spun around holding his spear upright, and ended facing the governor's box. He gave his salute, and turned to face the heavy gates at the other end. The *rudis* once again lifted his staff and banged it down upon the floor, the echoes of the noise bouncing inside the enclosed amphitheatre.

Slowly, the large double doors creaked open, revealing a dark, cavernous maw in the wall. At first nothing, and then, with a mighty screech that set my teeth on edge, came a golden blur of movement out of the doors and into the centre of the arena. People all around cowered and jumped back at the noise, and Cornelia huddled and clutched me. The thing crashed into the net and stretched it taut, and for a moment a baleful yellow eye above a sharp beak stared directly at me.

The thing was pushed back by the net, landed on the sands and shrieked in frustration again. We could now all make out what it was, and the crowds roared wordlessly. Before us stood a mighty gryphon, big as a horse, head held high and proud. The golden feathers of its fore-claws blended midway with the golden lion's fur of its back, right behind where the two magnificent wings sprouted from its shoulders. It gave a horrible shriek again, like a thousand birds of prey all at once, and rose into the air. It slashed the net with the claws on its front legs and tried to snap the ropes with its large hooked beak, but the net held against the assault.

From where Aulus Paulinus had got such a creature, and what it must have cost him, I did not know. Gryphons are creatures of high desert mountains, not the sea islands. To have managed to acquire the beast and import it in secrecy to the islands was no mean feat. His name would surely be remembered for years.

The *bestiarius* made the first move against the gryphon, sending his whip cracking against its hind legs. The gryphon landed on all fours and looked at him malevolently. The gladiator cracked his whip again, this time towards the beast's face in order to enrage it. The gryphon reared on its hind legs, wings outstretched, and bellowed its anger at the man facing it. It thumped down and flapped its wings forward, creating a dust storm to blind the *bestiarius*. The man moved sideways and made a stab at the creature of myth with his spear.

All this excitement reflected in Cornelia, too. She had her hand on my thigh in a way most inappropriate for a public event, and one that distracted me greatly from a fight the likes of which I had never hoped to witness.

For those few who are not familiar with our Egretian togas, bear in mind the following. The toga is made from a large swath of wool, an uneven rectangle with the corners rounded, more like a truncated oval, measuring fifteen feet by seven feet or thereabouts. To don a toga by oneself is an impossible feat. A slave is required to properly drape and fold and tuck the garment to achieve the correct effect.

Once togate, the left hand is practically immobilised holding the folds. The body must be kept perfectly erect while standing, walking or sitting. A swift movement and the thing comes undone. Because of the complexity and restrictions on movements men don only a short tunic underneath. Other than that, we Egretian men wear nothing else underneath the drapery, so that calls of nature can be attended to with ease.

And thus, sitting rigidly with back straight, left hand clenching at the folds of fabric at my chest lest they come undone, the crowds roaring around us, none noticed my gasp as Cornelia's hand expertly and deftly found its way past the *sinus* of my toga and down between my legs.

In the arena, meanwhile, man and beast were clashing. The man was tall and muscular, a fine specimen of manhood in its prime. Yet next to the gryphon he looked like a child. The creature shrieked and flapped and tore at him with its claws and wings, yet the man moved deftly about, darting around the circular walls of the arena. He cracked his whip to distract and enrage the beast, and stabbed his long spear whenever it got too close.

The man's skill was superb. He looked as if he had been training all his life for this fight. On a couple of occasions the gryphon managed to swat his spear away with his wings and get close enough to claw his guts out or tear at his face with its hooked beak — and yet each time the man managed to duck and roll, never losing his weapon and never sustaining more than small cuts.

The crowd by then was roaring, a noise so thick and uniform it felt like a wall of sound. Together with this excitement, I had my own mounting reasons to be flushed, thanks to the ministrations of Cornelia *maior*, whose skill was also quite superb.

At last the man managed to get his whip around the beast's neck. It tried to pull away, but the net prevented it from taking flight. The man advanced, his whip wrapped firmly around his left hand and his spear held tightly by his right arm against his side and levelled at the gryphon.

The gryphon reared again, flapped its wings, and in frustration lunged at the man, who was too tired to dodge again. He sank to one knee and brought the spear up. Its butt against the ground, its head guided by his hand, the man's aim was true. The beast did his work for him, impaling itself on the lance so far that it could reach the man with its dying breath to snap its beak at his face. Beast collapsed on top of man, raising a cloud of sand into the air, obscuring all.

The crowd hushed. As the dust dispersed, the body of the beast could be seen stretched on the sand, the spear sticking clear through it, its pale blood oozing on the sands, its head lying on one side with baleful yellow eyes open. And then the carcass moved, heaved to the side and from under it crawled the man, battered but alive.

The crowd went mad with shouts and I with it, for as the battle reached its climax, so did I.

And as I sat breathing hard, finally able to concentrate on the sight before me, there, with sudden inspiration, I saw, bleeding on the sands, my key into Zymaxis' little cabal.

CHAPTER XVIII

While the crowd delivered a standing ovation to the *bes-tiarius* and to Aulus Paulinus, and while the ceremonies for the end of the Floralia took place, my mind was racing. I did not have much time to do what I needed and to remain unnoticed. Luckily, Cornelia resumed her appearance of a proper matron, chatting with her sister and daughter as if nothing had happened between us. However, I was encumbered by a respectable toga, which is not the garment of choice for those skulking around; and, of course, I was unfamiliar with this particular circus and its layout.

So how could I go about locating the carcass of the gryphon, get access to it in a way that would not be traceable back to me, and manage to open it up and extract the precious internal organs to fulfil Zymaxis request for the arcane as my ticket into the cabal, and do it all swiftly and without getting even worse stains than I already had on my toga?

I was about to excuse myself to the latrines and begin the search, when Cornelia, her hands now respectably folded in her lap, spoke up. "That was just wonderful! What an extraordinary show! And we have all been invited to the post-game festivities, where I do believe Aulus Paulinus has promised a very special feast."

Publius Corpio, his face flushed with excitement from the spectacle, responded "We are all invited, indeed. I think now, from the comments he made before the show, that he is planning to serve us dishes of gryphon meat! That is surely the most exotic and spectacular menu anyone has served in recent memory."

"Aulus Paulinus is making such an effort this year," said Cornelia *minor*, "I believe he got quite a few of the *nobilitas* from Egretia to come here specifically for the event. He must be working already for the consular elections next year."

"Well, a fancy party is just what I need," said Cornelia *maior*, and linked her arm in mine in a way that made it clear that I was to be included in the invitation. Publius was in a generous mood and did not seem to mind, although Aemilia scoffed. I was sure I was not her mother's first plaything, and Aemilia seemed to have a stricter view of such affairs.

We descended to the exclusive vestibule of the circus and joined the queue of well-wishers congratulating the governor on games that would be remembered for years. As we got our turn, Cornelia introduced me to him as "a friend, a most interesting man of the world." Aulus Paulinus was a good-looking man in his prime, of medium height and build, with blond hair and clear blue eyes.

I congratulated the governor on the games, and added "This is quite a feat. No gryphons live anywhere close to here; the ship that brought and housed the magnificent specimen must have been a special vehicle, indeed."

"No expense is too big for my people," replied Aulus Paulinus with a smarmy smile.

"And to serve it for dinner as well! What a wonderful idea! Sending your cook for special training to Mazaca Carina in the Karikurum Mountains must have been a real inconvenience."

"Yes, yes… wait, what? Special training?" Aulus Paulinus peered at me with knotted brows.

"To handle the *fugum fellis*, of course. Any careless carving of the carcass, and the bile from that bladder will contaminate the meat. You will have such a mass run on the latrines by your guests," I added cheerfully, "the likes of which will certainly be remembered for a generation."

Paulinus swallowed, and sweat broke on his forehead. "And

this… this…"

"*Fugum fellis.*" I said helpfully. "Antoninus Liberalis talks about it extensively in his Metamorphoses."

"That. It exists in all gryphons?"

"I do believe so. A common bladder to all hybrid animals. Helps regulate their opposing humours, according to Liberalis."

"And it poisons their meat?" asked Aulus Paulinus, working through this difficult concept.

"Only if it is punctured and the bile spills out. If a careful cook knows his trade, the bladder can be removed quite harmlessly. Your guests will have a very delicious and memorable meal," I said. "Either way."

"And you are familiar with this bladder, yes? Perhaps you wouldn't mind having a talk with my cook. Just to double check." Presenting politicians with potentially unpopular moves is like presenting a slave with a cross — they rush at any alternative. "I would be most grateful if you would do me this favour; we don't want any undue risks to my lovely guests, after all."

And with that I was escorted quite hastily to my goal by one of the governor's aides, ensuring all doors were open to me.

* * *

The aide took me through back doors and underground corridors guarded by ex-gladiators and normally reserved for slaves. We got to the chamber where the gryphon was kept, and walked in. A team of slaves was working on the heavy carcass, hauling it on to a waiting cart. Luckily for me, the cook was not there but was overseeing the preparations for the feast at the governor's mansion. The aide spoke briefly with the foreman, and I was allowed to ride with the beast. I asked the aide to relate the message to his master and to my hosts that I would meet them at the villa.

I hoped my luck would hold, and that the cook would be as easy to impress with my fantastic knowledge as his master. For those of my readers who have never read Liberalis — and given his dry and uninspired style, I would not be surprised if that number was higher than those who have — he does indeed list the tales of the great monsters and creatures of our world. Liberalis has such a meticulous attention to details, from appearance to habitat, from habits to mating practises, and in such scrupulous punctiliousness, that many a student has been known to read him as a cure for insomnia. What he does not do, however, is mention any *fugum fellis* in relation to gryphons. Or in relation to any other animal, for that matter.

We rode along the road which leads from the circus around the edge of town and up to the hill where the governor's house perched. It was not a long ride, just long enough for my needs. As the driver sat in the front and kept the team of oxen going, and the slaves walked behind us, I quietly got to work. I pretended to examine the carcass, looking at the magnificent beast for signs of excessive damage.

First, I plucked the tail feathers of the gryphon. While the lower body is that of a lion, where the tail ends is a fan of feathers rather than a tuft of fur. I sat at the back end of the beast, and as unobtrusively as I could, lifted the tail and plucked a few of the unbroken long, golden feathers. I tucked these inside my toga. Not the most valuable part by far, yet sufficiently rare in case I could not get anything better for Zymaxis.

Next, I considered what else I might abscond with, without cutting open the beast and getting its blood all over me. I decided that the eyes would be the most appropriate, least likely to be missed in a feast and quite valuable if preserved properly. However, if I plucked them out now I would have no way to carry them discreetly. It would hardly be seemly if during the festivities planned for the night I reclined and they rolled out from toga to the middle of the room, or worse, I sat on them and made them burst inside my toga like ripe figs.

We reached the mansion, and the cart took a side track towards the back, where the kitchen received deliveries. I hopped off the cart just as the cook was coming out.

"You're late!" he shouted. "I still need to skin and roast the damn thing!" He took one look at the gryphon's carcass and started pulling his hair. "I'm ruined! There is no way that such a beast will be ready in time! It will take hours — days! — to cook! The master will roast and serve me!"

"Calm down, man." I spoke firmly. "Your master sent me here to help. I am here to assist you and ensure that all goes well for the feast tonight."

He looked at me suspiciously. "And who are you?"

"My name is Felix. I am a specialist in these matters. Aulus Paulinus requested that I attend the cleaning and cooking of the beast, so that the *fugum fellis* does not poison the meat."

"The what?" the man had a wild look about him.

"The *fugum fellis*, the poison bladder of the gryphon."

"You mean the thing's got poison inside it?" the cook shrieked. "Woe is me! Now all is lost for sure!"

"Calm down, calm down" I placed my hands upon his shoulders. "First, let us get the beast inside. Then we prepare it, and then roast it. By the time your master commands it served all will be well."

We ordered the slaves to drag the carcass inside. I took over giving the instructions for the handling of the gryphon, and the thankful cook, whose name I learnt was Gaius Nonius, started to take professional interest once he calmed down a bit.

First we had the carcass plucked of its feathers. "Just like a chicken," I instructed the girl called for the task when she gave us a dubious look. It took several of them to get it done. While they were working, we summoned a butcher to help skin the hindquarters where the lion's fur grew. I instructed the servants to be careful with both fur and feathers, and told the cook he could present them to the governor and his wife as ornaments and presents. The cook was happy at the idea, sure that it would buy him gratitude from his mistress.

As the assistants were working, I had a slave bring me a clay jar full of vinegar. "Now, the eyes," I told Nonius, "are absolutely noxious. Rather than spoil the effect of this magnificent roasted beast with the sight of the bulging, smoking, vile-smelling orbs, we shall remove them now." I had to borrow an apron and put my toga aside, but at least I could work without getting blood stains on me. With a thin, sharp knife I carefully cut out the white feathers around the eyes, and then using a bronze spoon I popped them out from the skull. I dropped them into the jar of vinegar and closed the lid. "I will dispose of these later," I told the cook, "just make sure no one accidentally tries to eat or serve this, or your master's guests will be viscerally sorry."

When all this was done, we cut open the belly of the beast. I poked a bit at the intestines and organs with a wooden spoon, pointed at a small intact bladder — the spleen, I think — and proclaimed "Aha! See there? That is the *fugum fellis*. You can see it is indeed intact, and we can rest assured that your master's guests are safe." I took the wobbly thing and dropped it with the eyes into the vinegar, and as an afterthought added the heart and a few other bits, declaring them unfit for human consumption. I then closed the jar and sealed it with wax from a candle. The rest of the organs and intestines were sorted and taken by the cook's assistants — the offal to be sautéed with onions, garlic and cumin for the master's closest guests, the intestines to become sausages for the rest.

From then on the cook took over. His men rubbed herbs and salts into the flesh of the half-lion-half-bird beast; a large, thick pole was brought, and its sharpened end was threaded from the beast's anus through its rib-cage and long neck, all the way out through its beak. A team of slaves mounted it over a hot fire and began turning it slowly.

"Now what?" asked Nonius. "How can we get this roasted in time?"

As someone who had marched, albeit briefly, with our legions and found himself crossing wild country on occasion, I at least knew the basics of cooking charms. I had also learnt some recipes for cooking game, together with a few other interesting poultices and potions, from a couple of old ladies who could not pay me in coin when I had returned their stolen silver mirror. "Now this is a trick I am willing to pass on to you," I said, "because I like you, Gaius Nonius. Have a servant bring us an *amphora* of wine, a cheap one will do." When the wine was brought together with some dried herbs I had requested, I proceeded to mix the herbs with the wine. While that would no doubt improve the taste, the real secret was in a small charm I cast as I mixed them. Nonius was a cook trained under the best tutors and kitchens, and thus had no clue about the proper casting of charms. Sometimes I think our people lost almost as much as they gained when the *magia* was formalised by the *incantatores*.

We worked as just the two of us in a side room with a closed door, and eventually he managed to repeat it correctly. I swore him to secrecy, a thing he had no trouble doing. By that time he had moved from lamenting his impending doom to looking at me like his saviour. I hoped his trust was justified, as it had been a few years since I had last performed this spell, and anyway, I had only ever used it on a rabbit and not something the size of a horse.

We poured the treated wine into a wineskin, and a boy was called to squirt it regularly on the roasting meat. The slaves kept turning the spit, the boy kept squirting and brushing, Nonius kept muttering the charm, and soon a wonderful smell filled the kitchens.

At that point I decided that it was safe to leave things. I washed myself as well as I could and had a boy help me re-drape the toga. I collected the jar with the eyes and organs and hid it in the cart we had come in, before going inside to the feast.

* * *

I made my way up to the mansion's interior gardens, where the governor had many couches arranged in close-fitting U shapes in the colonnades and around the garden paths. While I was looking for my host and his family, I was spotted by the same aide who had accompanied me at the circus. He came after me with an anxious expression.

"All is well," I reassured him. "The governor's cook is a fine fellow and has everything in hand."

He looked much relieved. "The master will be pleased. He won't forget it." I was sure the master would not remember my name by dawn. All of that mattered little, as I had my precious gift safely tucked away.

As I was looking for the Corpio family couches, I saw the *bestiarius* reclining on a couch in the governor's section, wearing only a skirt that showed off his well-muscled torso and with two midgets at his sides. The effect was to make him seem even larger than life, much for the entertainment of Aulus Paulinus' closest friends.

Corpio's couches were close to the governor's central location, about three sections away. That showed his relative importance in the Kebric society. The inner sections were taken by other magistrates and special guests from Egretia, and many more guests were seated further away than the Corpio family.

Publius, his wife Cornelia and their son Marcus lay on one couch, while Cornelia *maior* and Aemilia on another. The third couch in our little *triclinium* section was taken by a man I did not know and a woman, presumably his wife. The man was in his early thirties, thin and with a smiling face. By his attire I estimated him to be a local magistrate, in the beginning of his public career. The woman was a pretty flower in her early twenties, heavily pregnant.

"Felix!" cried Cornelia *maior* as she saw me coming, "Please join our couch. This is Titus Hortensius, the governor's treasury *quaestor*, and his wife Marcia. Titus Hortensius, this is Felix — an associate of my brother-in-law."

A slave came to take my toga, and as I sat down next to Cornelia he took my shoes off and washed my feet.

"You left us in such a hurry, I am anxious to hear all about it." She turned to Titus Hortensius. "Felix has special knowledge in matters arcane. Apparently, we are getting a most special dish tonight, and Felix had to ensure our esteemed Aulus Paulinus doesn't poison all the guests."

To the sounds of gasps, I muttered "Oh, it was nothing, really. There was never any real danger, the cook has things well in hand. No need to alarm anyone."

"Do not be modest; please tell us everything, so we may rest easy!" said Cornelia *maior*, and since apparently the matter had been discussed before I came, the others chimed in.

"Well, it is a little-known fact that gryphons, like other hybrid animals, have a small bladder of poisonous bile amidst their intestines. According to Antoninus Liberalis this is called the *fugum fellis*." I heard Aemilia snort in derision, but continued. "If punctured by a careless cook, the bile will spill and contaminate the meat, thus rendering the beast unfit for consumption. However, the poison is rarely lethal to adults. You need not worry, I supervised the cook removing the *fugum fellis* and can vouch for its intact state. The gryphon will be safe to eat and, I daresay, most delicious. Though now I fear I have ruined your surprise."

"I would have been more surprised indeed if anyone got anything worse than cramps from overeating," said Aemilia. And when everyone turned to look at her she added, "I read Antoninus Liberalis quite extensively, and — I daresay — there is no mention of any *fugum fellis* or any other poisonous bladders."

How had Gnaeus Drusus described her? A too-well-educated shrew. I could see his point. "Which edition have you read?" I asked.

"The original Hellican, of course," she said smugly.

"The one he dedicated to Aescliyanes, his king?"

"Of course. There is no other edition."

"In fact, there was," I said. "Aescliyanes was just a boy when Liberalis presented him with the work. It was hoped that the young king would become a patron of the sciences; however, since he was still of a tender age Liberalis edited out the more gruesome bits. The previous edition which he had dedicated to his mentor Democrithas, which contained further details, had unfortunately fallen out of circulation following the publication of the king's edition."

Aemilia looked sceptical, but that would at least keep her busy while she researched this non-existent edition. I changed the subject quickly. "Tell me, Titus Hortensius, is this your first child? You must be excited and delighted."

Conversation continued, mercifully away from me or the topic of monster cooking. Dish after dish was brought out, from fresh oysters to larks' tongues in aspic, from sea urchin roe in sauce to goat testicle skewers; dancers and acrobats, singers and lute players wandered around the rooms; wine was steadily provided by unobtrusive slaves.

Finally, when darkness had fallen and the first stars were out, Aulus Paulinus called for the main course. An expectant murmur passed through the guests, all conversation dying down and eyes cast in the direction of the kitchens. First, four muscular slaves walked in and erected two high tripods in the centre courtyard, in front of Aulus Paulinus. They then walked back inside, and after a few tense minutes returned carrying the huge carcass on its spit. The gathered guests erupted in cheers for the governor's largess and innovation.

The cook walked in after the beast, carrying his knives, and a train of slaves followed carrying plates. He proceeded to carve out bits of both the bird and animal parts and lay them on the plates. The first plate went to Aulus Paulinus who, after the briefest moment of apprehension, smiled and tasted the meats. He looked pleased, and raised a toast to his guests. I was certain some hapless slave had been force-fed this meat before it got to us though, just to make sure that the cook and I had indeed removed all traces of poison. Our turn came, as well, and a slave girl put down the plate with cuts of meat before us. While my little charmed wine had done the trick and the beast was well roasted, I have to say that the lion part was a bit gamy and the bird parts, while nice, tasted remarkably like chicken.

* * *

Two more things happened by the end of the night. First, Aulus Paulinus took me aside when he was doing a round of socialising. Gaius Nonius his cook had thanked him profusely for sending me along to help, vowing that the success of the dish could be attributed to my knowledge of cooking special creatures. Paulinus, properly impressed, was now also satisfied that this feast would etch him into the memory of future voters. I managed to deflect his queries about my business for the Corpio family and let him understand that my services were of a specialist nature and available for hire. I insisted that his sincere thanks were sufficient, and he vowed to remember me and my service to him. Someone at his level can be extremely valuable when cultivated as a contact in my debt.

The second was another fortuitous happenstance. Cornelia *maior* and Aemilia were planning to sail the next day, the *Kalends* of *Maius*, back to Egretia. Now that my investigations of Caeso's trail on the islands had been exhausted, Cornelia offered to let me accompany them on the voyage back. This was something I gladly accepted, despite some disdainful scoffs from Aemilia.

The next day, however, everybody woke up late and suffering the after-effects of last night's *convivium*, and departure was summarily postponed to the day after. We spent the day in relative quiet. With no further leads to follow in Kebros, I whiled away the time in Publius Corpio's library, reading more of the scrolls I had gotten in Ephemezica. Aemilia walked in a couple of times to borrow scrolls. I checked the ones she inspected, and they all had to do with natural histories, from Plinius to Ovidius. She would of course not find any references to a prior edition of Liberalis — there being no such edition — but she had a sharp mind and would likely pick up on things if I slipped. I was reminded of what my father had often said, that enemies should only be made on purpose. Then again, my father had lost his business and his life, putting his advice into question. Still, I resolved to mind what I said around her in the future.

By evening Cornelia and Aemilia's trunks were packed and sent to their ship. The simple dinner went quietly, and we all retired early expecting an early rise. I lay in my bed in the cubicle at the furthest end of the guest quarters, reading by candlelight, till I felt my eyelids drooping. I rolled the scroll and placed it on the side of my bed and was about to blow out the candle when my gaze was arrested.

In the doorway stood Cornelia *maior*, dressed in a gown made out of some sheer fabric. So sheer, that by the light of the torches behind her in the corridor I could see the lines of her shapely figure. She walked into the room slowly with a swaying gait, her hips moving in a most enticing manner. She closed the door behind her, approached my bed, and still I could not speak.

"You know, I found yesterday's games quite exciting," she said as she sat on the edge of the bed next to me, "and I know you did, too. I was quite impressed with your… performance, in fact. I thought perhaps another, private, performance might be in order."

I sat up and, still unable to speak, nodded in what I hoped was a suave and mysterious manner. She slowly unfastened the clasps of her gown and let it fall around her waist. I forced myself to look deep into her eyes and not stare at her pendulous breasts. I leaned forward to kiss her, but she pushed against my chest playfully and sent me sprawling on my back. She hovered above me and said, "Let's do it my way."

She blew out the candle.

I planned to spend the time during the cruise perusing the scrolls and formulating my next steps. I had to approach Zymaxis and gain the confidence of his cabal; I had to check up on Gaius Famnius and ascertain what information he had given to Caeso; and I wanted to chase down Drusus again and find out if omitting his own vision at the sibyl had been due to simple embarrassment or more sinister reasons.

None of that happened, of course. While the luxury ship possessed several cabins for its mistress and her guests, I saw little of my own sleeping quarters. Cornelia made it clear that once we reached Egretia she would have to resume a public life of respectability, and our paths would not cross again. She also made it clear, in many varied and engaging ways, that she planned to make the most of our trip.

SCROLL III - VERGU

CHAPTER XIX

We made port in Egretia late on the *Nones* of *Maius* after six days of sailing. Cornelia's ship was a sturdy thing, and while she did not employ an *incantator* her competent crew and the favourable winds got us back at a good pace. We sailed round the Pharos with its ever-shining light and entered the Bay of Egretia. We stood at the rails of the ship — Cornelia, Aemilia and myself — keeping quiet and gazing at the view of the city sprawled on the two arms descending from the high volcanic peak of Vergu. The sight, sounds and smells of Egretia always gave me pause after an absence, a welcome feeling of returning home.

I made my way to my *domus*, stopping on the way only to make a donation to Neptunus' temple as thanks for the safe voyage. At home I found Dascha continuing about her chores as if I had merely spent the night at some brothel. She sniffed at my clothes and took them away, informing me that a dinner of sea bass poached in wine and herbs would be ready soon. Thus I returned to my city and got my welcome.

This being the day of the *Nones*, I was too late to meet Zymaxis and his cabal; when I had met them last it had been on the night before the *Nones*, and I had been told to meet them at the same time this month. Still, I wanted to go there and see if the meeting had indeed taken place, if Didia had managed to find any names for me, and what else I could learn before confronting any members of the cabal. I stopped on the way at Crassitius' usual haunt, but unfortunately his gladiators were all spoken for this night — some high-society orgy. By the time I made it to the Dented Skull it was getting late.

I found Titus Septimius the proprietor, and took him aside. Zymaxis had left instructions with him that should I come he was to let me know the day of the next cabal meeting — which happened to be in five days. I learnt from him that indeed Zymaxis had been there the night before, and was not expected to come again before the coming session.

I settled into a bench at the back and waited. As I sipped my wine, I saw Didia come down from her room, adjusting her clothes and followed by a bald and sleazy man with a satisfied look on his face. She came over to my table and placed a small dish with olives in front of me. "Haven't seen you for a while," she said, and added with a wink, "Can I entertain you in any way?"

Not wishing to go where another man had just gone before, I declined, but I asked softly if she had managed to find out any of the cabal names. She nodded and said, "Not here; come with me."

We went up to her room again, and she turned to me. "I don't want my *dominus* to see how much you pay me. This way I can pretend I just got the usual rates. I heard three names. The first time was late, and not many customers were around. Most of the cabal had already left, only the tall one with the short hair stayed behind together with the fat creepy one, the one who always has stains on his clothes. I heard the fat man call the tall one Gaius Marcius as they walked out. The tall one was displeased, and told him not to mention his name again here. They did not see me, though, or did not care enough about me.

"The next time the fat creepy man was talking to the freedman. The freedman called him Quintus Fufidius. And they mentioned another name, Tiberius Pomponius, but I do not know who they referred to."

Three names. That was a good start.

I returned to my home late that dark night, doffed my clothes and ate a quiet dinner by myself. After dinner I sat in my study and read through the ceremony again; I prepared the heavily excerpted copies I planned to use the next day. By the time I finished, the hour was late, and I stumbled through the peristyle garden under the canopy of stars to my sleeping cubicle.

This was the first night I had spent in my own bed for some time, and the first one alone since setting sail from Kebros. I had been quite sorry when we had arrived at Egretia for the loss of the distraction Cornelia had afforded me. When my investigation into the death of Caeso resumed, so did my nightmares. What was it about this case, that dredged up these memories of my past? And why, after blissful nights with Cornelia, was the place of Helena in my dreams taken up by Aemilia?

* * *

I started the next day with visiting Corpio. I presented myself early at his *domus* and found a number of his other clients seeking their patron's favour. Typheus saw me, did a quick mental calculation and inserted me into the queue of clients at the right place for the importance of his master's business with me, without causing ruffled feathers amongst the more notable men.

I did not have to wait long before I was ushered by Typheus into Corpio's study. I suspect this probably had more to do with getting rid of my disreputable self quickly from his atrium than it did with my position in society.

I greeted Corpio and sat in the client's seat opposite him.

"Have you good news for me? Can we finally put this matter to rest?" he asked.

"Sadly, not yet," I said, "although I am here to report on some good progress." I gave Corpio an account of my travels to Ephemezica, of the scroll and the ceremony his son had gotten into. "With this information, we are now in a better position to track all those who were involved in his demise."

Next I gave an account of my visit to his brother, although here

I kept the report short and my speculations to myself. I felt it was not the time yet for half-formed ideas and tales of sibyls. I then got to the main reason for today's visit. "Do any of the following names mean anything to you?" I asked. "Gaius Marcius, a tall man of military bearing; Quintus Fufidius, a shabby-looking *incantator*; and a name without a face — Tiberius Pomponius?"

"Tiberius Pomponius sounds familiar..." Corpio glanced at Typheus.

The secretary cleared his throat and said, "A backbencher senator. A *novus homo*, the first of his family to be admitted to the Senate. Comes from a mercantile background. Voted with the majority so far, and did not distinguish himself in any way. I could find out his patron, if he has one."

"Do that," Said Corpio. "As for the other names, Quintus Fufidius does not sound familiar, which is not surprising. I deal with the *rhones* of the Collegium Incantatorum, and employ my own, of course, but I do not follow their circles. Nor is the family name Fufidia a prominent one. I will make some discreet enquiries amongst the *rhones* of the Collegium Incantatorum. And that last name again?"

"Gaius Marcius" I said.

"There are a few Gaiuses of the Marcia *gens*. Do you know the *cognomen*?"

"Unfortunately not."

"Well, the two most prominent ones with military careers are Marcius Paetus and Marcius Gaetanicus. The first was a *praetor* some years ago, now almost sixty."

I shook my head.

"The other has been a legate of Decius Corvinus in his campaign against the raiding of the Tigumani into our provinces. You might remember Corvinus' triumph of four years ago. My understanding, though, is that Gaetanicus studied in the Collegium Militum under the *fetiales*, so he's a diplomat now rather than a general." A spy, he meant. "And then there's Marcius Paullus, who was selected tribune of the soldiers last year, and posted with the legions garrisoned in Capricia. I shall make enquiries of all their recent whereabouts, and have this information sent to you." I heard Typheus scratch out notes on his wax tablets behind me.

I thanked Corpio and promised him another report soon.

I left Corpio's house and walked along the Vicus Caprificus. Through the avenues between the houses going down the hill I could see the Bay of Egretia, the clear water merrily reflecting the sunlight. Many small ships were moving about, driven by oars inside the harbour and docking at the many wharves along the shores. As the ships made their way out of the bay, I could just see them put up their square white sails as they rounded the ever-shining bright light of the Pharos and disappeared into the horizon.

* * *

I decided to restart my investigation in Egretia where I was sure to get information. It's always a good omen to start with tangible progress; it helps keep the spirit up when leads invariably dry up and the case keeps running into blank walls and closed doors. I walked across the Forum and all the way up the Meridionali, to the Subvales and Brewyn's tattoo parlour.

He wasn't in.

The old proprietor of the sundries shop, once I managed to explain to him in a loud enough voice what I wanted, just said, "Ah, him. He never wakes up before lunch. Lazy foreigner. Probably spent last night drinking that awful beer that his kind likes and now can't get his arse out of bed."

So much for good omens.

I trudged my way up the hill and back down towards the Forum. Gaius Famnius' family business was located in a small street not far from the Porticus Aemilia, on the posh western side of the Forum. I presented myself at the main offices and asked the clerk after the young master Gaius Famnius. At least here I was in luck. The clerk led me inside and left me to wait in a nicely appointed reception room. After a few minutes a young man entered, clad in a toga and with a thin saffron stripe along the right side of his tunic.

"Greetings," he said, "I was told you were looking for me."

"*Ave* Gaius Famnius. My name is Felix, sometimes called Felix the Fox. I bear greetings from your friend Gaius Opimius Agrippa."

His face brightened with a smile. "How is dear Agrippa doing? I have not seen him for these past few months."

"He is well indeed, happy at his residence on Kebros amongst his bees."

"He was always happiest dealing with the little creatures of this world. The city suffocates him on his winter visits." We sat down and Famnius clapped his hands and ordered a slave to bring wine and water. "Now, what can I do for a friend of my dear friend Gaius Opimius?" he asked me.

"I understand from him that a while ago he sent a young man to you. The young man came from a merchant family, yet his heart and mind were sparked by the *incantatores*. His name was Caeso Quinctius Corpio." I looked at his face closely as I said the name, but all I could see was a mild, not unpleasant surprise.

"Oh yes, an inquisitive young man, born to the wrong family. Like so many of us, he wished to follow a different path than that prescribed for him by birth and fate."

"Have you heard of his passing?" I asked.

"I have, I have. I was saddened to hear about it, he was so young and gregarious." That was the first I had heard anyone describe Caeso as gregarious. Perhaps the spark of interest had let him open up to Famnius. I chose my next words carefully.

"His father was quite distraught at his passing; it was very sudden. Purely out of love for his son, he asked me to enquire into the last few months of his life. Would you be able to tell me of his interests? What was he after, when you spoke with him?"

"He was quite interested in the *magia*, as you must have learnt from Gaius Opimius. Indeed, Opimius had sent him to me with a letter of introduction in which he described him as an eager student. I have always wanted to become a teacher at the Collegium, but my father and fate had decreed it not to be. I was happy to discuss with him the basic philosophies of incantation, and even let him borrow a few scrolls of elementary teachings. All introductory stuff, really, the things we *incantatores* all learn in our first term at the Collegium. He was a voracious reader, returning swiftly each time with more questions and an unquenchable thirst for knowledge. We grew quite close over those weeks, talking late into the night on many occasions.

"He was a natural, if you ask me. We could have gained a great *incantator*, if he was allowed to study properly. When I asked him if he would consider switching studies, he replied his father would not hear about it, that the family pride in the generations of leading the Collegium Mercatorum would not let him take another course."

As he spoke I looked at his face. An open and honest one, with clear green eyes set widely under unruly black curls. In my business one learns to distinguish between the truthful and the liars even without resorting to incantations, or one is soon dead. And in Gaius Famnius I sensed no shred of guile. "Tell me," I asked, "What else did he want to learn?"

"He had quite a wide interest, as I have said, always willing to learn. He was also very interested in the old *numina* of our people, looking for ancient myths about the places of power. We had a few discussions on these subjects, and I presented him with the modern philosophies of the nature of *magia* versus the superstitious beliefs of the common people. In that respect I fear he never really agreed with me. There was that unshakable belief in him, that the old powers still lingered amongst us, alive and sentient."

I thought about my own encounters with the sibyl and on top of Mons Krodus. I sided with Caeso on that one, although I stayed silent on the subject.

"Did he ever experiment with performing incantations and spells on his own?" I asked.

"He never told me, though I suspect he might have. I cautioned him against it. I told him it takes years to practice, learn how to draw the power. I explained to him the Collegium's view of unlicensed incantations within the city. He tried to argue that every washer woman and basket weaver, blacksmith or tailor have their own little chants and charms. How the crossroad colleges maintain the ancient *lares* alive in the city. I explained to the best of my ability that these people have no understanding, and thus no real power behind their blind mutterings. I cautioned that should he dabble in the real incantations, someone from a prominent family like him would not escape notice. I even gave him all the old cautionary tales to read, all the scary stories of old magic, of careless or malicious *incantatores* and their end. He seemed to reluctantly accept this restriction and limit himself to the theoretical understanding and pursuits, although as I've said I would not be surprised to learn he tried."

"Tell me, please, do you know if he went to any other sources? Have you referred him anywhere, or did he mention such?"

He looked uneasy for a moment. "Really, I do not know," he said.

"Come, now," I said, "This is to ease his father's aching heart. None of this will ever be made public, not by me nor by his family."

He looked apprehensive. "Was there anything about his death that makes you think it had to do with his pursuit of knowledge?" he asked.

A difficult question, though I had been expecting it. How much should I trust this young man? If I told him the truth, could I trust his apparent honesty or would he report me to the Collegium? That would be at cross purposes with the wishes of Corpio to keep the matter under wraps. Instead I said, "I believe he may have sought more knowledge and run into some bad company. Not everyone is as scrupulous as you. It is nothing definite, no charges I could bring forward. But he did end up in a miserable way. I intend to find more about the men he got involved with, and your knowledge will help see justice."

"Well..." he hesitated, and I kept my eyes locked on his. "I did sneak him into the library at the Collegium. Twice, in fact. The first was a late night, sometime in the middle of the *intercalaris*. We got together to discuss his most recent reading and stayed up very late, talking, drinking. I don't know how he convinced me to sneak him into the Collegium's library. It must have been the wine.... Anyhow, he took off his toga and put on a simple tunic, posing as my slave. I pretended to come do some research, as I often do for my father. By right the guard at the door should not have let us in, but we managed to keep a straight face and found ourselves inside, alone. At first he was in awe, wandering and looking at the vast number of scrolls. I don't know if you ever had cause to be there — the library in the Collegium Incantatorum is the most magnificent in the known world. Hall after hall, from floor to high ceiling, miles and miles of pigeon-hole shelves of scrolls, with everything from the banally mundane to the utterly arcane. I could see the look of wonder in his eyes, the excitement colouring his cheeks in the lamplight. He walked along like a boy in wonderland. I guess he still was.

"He was curious how we could ever find scrolls in there, so I showed him the master index and the way things work. He didn't have the *visus verum*, of course, so he couldn't fully see the index, could not use it properly. He looked through the parts he was able to perceive, and asked many questions about it. Now that I think of it, he was unusually observant, his questions altogether too… perceptive."

Famnius paused in his account of that fateful night, seeming to view events with a sudden new insight. I looked at the man sitting in front of me. Twenty-five, I thought, or twenty-six, not that much older than the boy he was speaking of. Not a man of guile by nature, so my instincts told me, yet growing up fast even as he spoke.

Famnius resumed, with knotted brows and a new understanding dawning in his eyes. "The next time was soon after. In our following discussions Caeso was most enthused about the visit to the library. He wanted to visit again. At first I refused, of course, saying that the risk was just too high. Eventually, he wore me down, and one night when we were quite drunk he got me to take him a second time." Famnius paused to draw breath.

"We went again with him posing as my slave. I bribed the night watchmen, pretending to have forgotten to complete a task for my father. When we got to the library… Caeso seemed to almost know what he was looking for. He looked at the index quickly and proceeded down the hall. At the time I thought he just could not see the lines of power and walked away, but now… now that I recall that night, I think he knew exactly what he was after. He started to run ahead, and I tried to follow but tripped. I lost him, and by the time I picked myself off the floor, nose bleeding, I could not see him. I went ahead, looking for him, whispering his name loudly, suddenly afraid. He reappeared then, all flushed and excited. I took him away from that place, and told him in no uncertain terms that he was a lunatic, a fool, a danger to himself and to others. I'm afraid our relationship chilled after that night. I saw him perhaps a couple of times more, though we did not speak as before." He paused again, disturbed by his own revelation.

When he resumed he spoke slowly and measured his words, his eyes not meeting mine, rather focused inward to witness once more the events of that night. "When he reappeared, that last time when we were in the library, he came from a side corridor. The rooms along that corridor house the scrolls of love potions, and beyond it lie the closed vaults, the ones housing the scrolls of *nefastum scientiam*. At the time I thought it was random, or that perhaps he managed to find his way to some minor love spell. After all, there is no way he could have gotten past the locks on the doors to the vaults. Now I am not so sure."

* * *

I sat in a small tavern, far enough from the Porticus Aemilia and the Famnius business that I could afford the wine I so desperately needed. Young Caeso, it seems, had had some instruction in the basics of incantation. That by itself should not have amounted to anything, however. To use the library's master index requires the *visus verum* — the true sight. It takes apprentices years to develop it. I myself studied in the Collegium for almost two years, and got sensitive enough to sense the flow of *magia* on my skin when close to it, yet never developed the *visus verum*. Indeed, one cannot graduate from the Collegium without it, and it is a part of the final test.

And then Caeso had been found wandering back from the direction of the vaults. Not many of my readers will have been inside the library of the Collegium Incantatorum. Those readers must understand the vastness of the library, the unlikelihood of just stumbling in that direction, tucked as it is in a lower hall far at the end. And the doors — oh the doors! — of the vaults. Thick doors, made each of layers of wood and bronze, held together both by iron rivets and sigils of power. All this to lock the *nefastum scientiam* — the scrolls of forbidden knowledge. Naught but the highest ranking amongst the *magisters* of the Collegium may enter. I have been very privileged, and was once there with my *magister* during my studies, helping him with a task I could not comprehend. The skin of my right arm was in goose-bumps and the hairs standing straight for a week, merely for brushing carelessly against some nameless scroll.

And yet… had Caeso managed to somehow use the index, pass the doors, find the scrolls kept there? It would give him knowledge which he was ill-equipped to use. Perhaps he had bartered it into Zymaxis's cabal. Perhaps he had even found the scroll that described the ritual of his own death…

But no. It was just not possible for an untrained son of a mer-chant to use the index of power within the library, to get past the doors, to steal a scroll unnoticed. Even if he had absconded with something, it was a lucky grab of a recipe for some love philtre. Surely that would still buy him the acceptance price of the cabal.

CHAPTER XX

I tried Brewyn again. It was well after lunch, so both he and his clientele were up and about by now. I walked in on him working on the back of a large Arbari, executing a traditional tribal design. I waited, and took the time to observe closely the techniques used. Brewyn kept the skin lightly stretched between the thumb and forefinger of his left hand, and with the little finger held a short brush dipped in ink. In his right hand he held a set of five short needles made of bone. He brushed the needles against the ink, and then pierced them a few times into the skin at an oblique angle. His hand was fast and sure, making a few repeated strokes before renewing the pigment on the needles.

Every few minutes he stopped to dab at the blood oozing slowly from the punctures and replenish the ink on the brush. As he did that I could see the man's face relax a little, only to become tightly drawn again as Brewyn resumed. It was obviously an uncomfortable experience, a moderate amount of pain to be tolerated proudly.

I wondered about the treatment that Caeso had undergone. How long would it have taken to complete the star design above his heart with the radiating lines along his ribs? How did he find the experience, endure the pain? From the description in the Ephemezican scroll, the whole pattern was to be done in a single night, started at midnight and finished by dawn. When Brewyn took a break, the man flexed his arms and back, grimacing in pain. How had Caeso managed to hide this from family and friends?

Brewyn finished, laid his tools down neatly and stretched. He dabbed at the blood carefully, cleaning the last of it. He picked up a *pyxis* and opened it, revealing a sweet-smelling unguent. He rubbed it gently with his fingertips into the man's back, covering the newly made lines and scars. I could see the man's face relax, the blood cease flowing from the wound, the skin grow less red and agitated.

As the man thanked, paid and left, I lifted the *pyxis* of the unguent to my nose. I could feel the skin of my fingers tingle lightly, a slight acrid burning in my nose as I sniffed. "What is this?" I asked Brewyn.

"The deluxe treatment," he replied with a grin, "for those who pay extra."

"Your own recipe, or a known one?"

"My own, which is sold at the shop outside as well. A successful business like mine requires significant knowledge. A number of people in Egretia can put ink under skin, and a few have a decent hand. Only some can manage pain. Fewer still can draw *stigmas* of power."

"Speaking of power *stigmas*, do you recall that business with the young man, a month or so ago?" I asked.

"The one with the blue star design? How could I forget? One does not come across such *stigmas* of power often."

"I found out the recipe for the ink, and the ceremony for drawing in the *magia*." I took out a wax tablet on which I had copied from the ancient scroll I had found in Ephemezica those parts of the Rite of Pelegrinus regarding the tattoo. "This is not the full thing, of course, just the relevant sections. I assume you can read *Quirite*?" I added as the thought struck me.

He gave me a pained look. "*Canicula*, please. Don't insult me. Do you think I could become a master tattooist if I could not? Do you think people would pay for an illiterate *mentula* who can't write to ink them? Would you like the name of your loved one misspelled, the letters mangled across your arse?"

I apologised hastily and handed him the waxed tablet. He examined it closely, working out the components, the preparations, the process, cursing and muttering under his breath all the time. At long last he lifted his eyes from the wax tablet. "This is truly esoteric stuff," he said. "Some of the power formulae are beyond my understanding, though I can see the general gist, the progression of it. The ink is special, the materials rare and the preparation is delicate. Placing the tattoo on the skin does not seem out of the ordinary. I'd say the one who wrote the procedure was complicating things, probably lacking understanding and being over-cautious. As with the young boy, this would awaken his *stigma* at the end, as a massive jolt of power. It would have been painful, much more than the inking."

"Is that a normal process?" I asked.

"Only for cruel bastards. There are many ways that a *stigma* could be awakened from a tattoo. It depends on the dye used, together with the method of inking, but most would allow you to gradually place the enchantment into the ink as you go, to do this slowly and carefully, shape the energies of *magia* to the desired effect. This…" he held up the tablet, his face showing professional disdain, "this has no finesse."

"And yet it is supposed to be a very powerful rite with some spectacular results," I said. "The recipient is reputed to end up with power over both life and elements, impervious to failings of the flesh, removed and elevated above mortal men. It has been performed successfully but once before, so far as I know, and that a very long time ago. I can't even be sure that this copy is the full and correct one."

"It doesn't matter," Brewyn said with conviction. "I can't tell you about the incantations and their effects; you'd have to ask one of the magic wand-wankers of your Collegium about that. But of power there is plenty here. See this?" he stabbed his finger at the wax, smudging the writing, "using ink from mountain orchids is pure extravagance, because any tattooist who knows anything would know that garden lilies are just as good. And mixing them all with bile from a ferret that had been poisoned by an asp? Whoever used that and lived? Sheer stupidity. And so are the chants. You may recognise more words of power than me, though I thought I knew all that were related to *stigmas*. And none are used till the very end! None!" He got quite worked up, and paused to draw a deep breath. "No, my friend, this is over-complicated and unnecessary. The cheap octopus ink they mention last, mixed with the spices, would be the real conduit. A drop of lily nectar would add all the refinement it needs. The words here and here," he pointed at the paragraph of chants towards the end, "will just draw the *magia* like a lightning into the *stigma*, burning all else in its path. A ceremony of raw power this may be, and its ultimate meaning I freely admit not to grasp, but as a professional master of my trade I can say with certainty that the inking is over-complicated. A simple lightning rod is all it is."

* * *

I left Brewyn with information on some of the importers and procurers of the more exotic ingredients, although he swore it would be a waste of my time. Also in his opinion, none of the known masters of the ink in Egretia had had anything to do with Caeso's tattooing. He maintained that the work had been done by the cabal, and the ink recipe almost immaterial to the amount of energy that coursed through it. Unfortunately, this didn't progress me much, as I had always been sure that the cabal had performed the ceremony themselves. It meant I still had to track down their suppliers for more conclusive proof.

Next on my list was Akhirabus. Before I had left for Ephemezica I had left him with the samples of herbs Didia had procured for me, those that Zymaxis used on me and, presumably, on the cabal. I was curious to know whether he had found anything that I could not.

I reached Akhirabus's shop by the eleventh hour of the day, late-afternoon. As much as I always expect it, the clashing, complementing, competing scents still overwhelmed my nose. I let my eyes adjust to the gloom inside and let my nose learn anew to block the assault.

"My friend of the puzzles!" he greeted me. "What new mystery brings you to my shop this fine day?"

"The same puzzle, but with new pieces." I showed him the wax tablet with another fragment of the Rite I had prepared, this one concentrating on the herbs and other ingredients, and on the preparations and anointment of the chosen one's body. He took the tablet from me and read through it slowly, eyebrows knitting and expanding repeatedly, muttering and exclaiming as he worked through it from obscurity to understanding.

When he was done, before he could speak I held out a second wax tablet. "These," I said, "are the symbols and names I am unfamiliar with." He took it from my hand eagerly, his face in deep concentration as he scanned it. I could see the succession of recall and comprehension on his face, until it suddenly darkened.

"Come," he said and turned, without lifting his eyes from the tablet. "Parennefer!" he shouted, still looking at the tablet, "Parennefer! Look after the shop and send us some wine up to my study."

We settled ourselves in the back room that Akhirabus had set up as his study. A slave girl soon brought us pitchers of fine Mitzrani wine and water. I poured us both drinks as Akhirabus was busy with the wax tablet I had given him, opening scroll after scroll from his collection and laying them on the table. At last he sat back in his chair and looked up, picked up his forgotten cup. He sipped his wine, organising his thoughts while I waited in silence. Finally he spoke.

"Most of these are trivial and I can give you the *Quirite* names, the explanations. But this symbol," he tapped his finger at one of the more complex ones I had copied from the ancient scroll, "this one had me perplexed. It is… a difficult one to interpret. Can you get me the original text? It must be viewed in context."

"I can," I said. "What is the name of that symbol? Can you shed some light on its possible meaning?"

"It is the ancient Mitzrani glyph for — how do I translate this? Your *Quirite* language is woefully inadequate — it is a symbol meaning that which can be counted both once and many. Or I should say, that which is counted many times but once. The indivisible unity of the multitude. The meaninglessness of numbers other than none." He stopped to smile at me. "Yes, your face wears the same expression as mine once did, and as I imagine my teacher's did when he was young. It is very old, older than many of our gods, although not all. From a time our people have viewed the world in a different light. It is called the *Aten*, and has many connotations. More recently, though, a mad pharaoh decreed that the *Aten* stands for the Sun, a supreme god above all other gods. He tried to do away with the established pantheon, and set the *Aten* as single god. A foolish man, his mummy long turned to dust."

"What might it mean, the presence of this glyph in the rite?"

"Ah, but I have not yet finished. This symbol is Mitzrani in origin, yet it has been borrowed. The Assyricans liked it, though I fear they misunderstood it. Being star-gazers, they transformed its meaning for the stars. For them it came to mean the futility of counting stars. The enormity of the multitude of stars in a singular heaven. Though they, too, in time neglected and forgot this."

"I still do not understand why this… concept… would appear in the rite."

"That I sadly cannot tell you, without first inspecting the context of the text in which it appears." Akhirabus said. "Bring me the scroll; let me see if the usage is Mitzrani or Assyrican, if it references natural or unnatural powers, philosophies or mathematics, and I will shed what light my poor understanding can."

"Thank you, my friend. And about the other ingredients listed in the ceremony?" I asked.

"Some are common, some rarer. I can see if I have sold any, although this was a while ago. I will give you a list of my competitors, for though I fear their stock is inferior, your unfortunate young man may have dealt with them."

"And the herb samples I left with you before I left? Have you found anything in them beyond spices for the wine?"

"I did but little," said the herbalist. "One, a mild soporific that will render the imbiber in a calm hypnotic state. Second, a weak hallucinogenic that will give dreams. Third, a hypnotic of a different nature, inducing trust. They contained herbs, fungi and some desiccated animal remains, and the *heka* — the *magia*, as you Quirites call it — the *heka* binding it was not above that of the common shopkeeper. I say these were produced by a competent herbalist to a discerning customer. They will not be advertised, only sold to those who know what to ask for. Their use would let the one administering control his guests, especially if he took an antidote before, and manipulate feelings and emotions."

We discussed the matter a bit further, and I convinced him —

though he insisted that it was unnecessary, that the mixtures were harmless — to give me a small batch of antidote to be taken, should I be made to drink again. He also gave me a short list of suppliers and other herbalists, who in his opinion were not abysmally incompetent and could procure the ingredients and produce such mixes.

Thus I was presented with two lists — one from Brewyn for ink traders, and one from Akhirabus for the ritual components and the herbs. I scanned the lists to see recurring names, and found three that could supply all. If Caeso was the naive sort of young man I thought he was, he would procure all from a single source. If not, well, more tramping around the town for me.

* * *

Having had a pleasant and productive day so far — three names for the cabal, a list of leads for ritual supplies — I decided to risk the ruination of my good mood and seek out Araxus.

The hour was getting late, but this being *Maius* I still had some time before darkness set in. I walked along the twisting alleys at the base of the Meridionali closest to the city walls, in between large and crumbling *insulae*. I reached the old walls, passed through the gates to the Pons Orientalem and crossed the bridge to the Campus Civicus. I wandered around the decrepit taverns and open cesspits, the unsavoury back alleys behind the places of base entertainment. I stayed inside the walls, however — it was not the time to wander outside, past the Porta Purgamenta into the real dumps.

I spread a few small coins amongst the street urchins, and soon enough found Araxus. The last I had seen him was when he came to my house before I left for Ephemezica, crazier than usual and babbling incomprehensibly. Today he was back to sanity, or as close to it as he could get; his speech made sense, his human eye focused on me and his black one thankfully turned elsewhere. I bought us some food and wine in as quiet a place as I could find.

The slave girl brought us plates of skewered meat and bread, wine and water, and left us alone. "Remember that business with the *magia vita terminalis* about a month ago?" I asked, never sure about him. "You promised to sniff around."

"How could I forget? Don't answer that. Yes, I did. Found stuff. At one point I was sure I solved it for you. Came to tell you, but you threw me out."

"You were raving," I said.

"I have my best inspirations then," he mused. I gave him such a dark look, he stopped short. "I'm sorry," he said, "I only meant —"

"I know exactly what you meant," I interrupted him coolly. "I never forget, not for a minute, and neither should you." I drew a deep breath and settled myself. "So what was the inspiration?"

"Buggered if I know now. Not all thoughts are seen clearly, when… when I am myself again." He sipped his wine. I could see that now, being himself as he called it, he was feeling the same pain as I did every night. Good. Part of me hoped he suffered. "Any which way," he resumed, "I did ask around. I didn't have a lot to go on — these rites are not exactly public knowledge. No tremors were felt, even amongst those sensitive to them. I cannot see a way for someone to concentrate such a power, manipulate and draw it, and not raise the hackles of anyone with the right sensibilities for miles around. Is it possible that it was done far away?"

"I haven't considered it," I said, "but it might be. How far must it be, for the ripples to die down before reaching Egretia?"

"Hard to tell. There are a lot of incantations being performed here, from the official ones by the Collegium to the shopkeepers and tradesmen with their inconsequential charms. Even the crossroad colleges, worshipping the old *lares* and *numina* as they are, contribute to the background noise of magic. The Rite of Pelegrinus, however, should have cut through that, still. I'd say at least ten miles for the ripples to disappear below the din, maybe fifteen for those truly sensitive."

"That sounds too far away," I said. "He would have had to travel, and even on a fast horse this distance means a couple of hours on the road. I know he spent his last days in the city, certainly his last few hours. He was at home that day, had an argument with his dad and was confined to his room, found dead in the early morning. I do not see how he would have escaped, travelled the distance, participated in the ceremony, ridden back still reeling from all the energies coursing through him, and gotten back in bed just in time to die."

"Perhaps this rushed execution would have tampered with the rite," suggested Araxus.

"My understanding of the rite is that it is supposed to take effect soon after completion. I cannot see him riding like the last survivor fleeing the annihilation of his legion, immediately following the hours of chanting required for the ceremony."

"Since when do you know so much about the process of the ritual?" Araxus asked me.

"I have been busy…" I got out the last wax tablet I had prepared. "Here, read this. I got this in Ephemezica, from a special collection that went on sale in bulk. I do not believe the owner knew the extent of the esoterica that was there, or he would not have been too keen to sell. I cannot vouch for the correctness of it, of course, but it appeared authentic."

Araxus took the tablet from me and started to work his way through it, his green eye and his black one reading different parts. On his tablet I had copied the most information, although I had still removed and simplified passages. I did not want this knowledge finding its way around. I still could not trust Araxus, could not tell when his mood would shift and his other aspect take over.

At last he raised his green eye to look at me, though his black eye kept roving about the lines of writing. "This is incomplete," he stated.

"True. It has enough of what I can track, and not enough on how to make final use of it."

He paused, but understood the implications. "Fair enough," he said. "There are also rumours about something big coming up on Vergu. Vultures seen circling the peak to the left, sheep becoming unsettled before being carried there for sacrifice, their entrails turning out green, that sort of *cack*. I shall track these rumours for you, as well as your shopping list. I shall ask the questions amongst the dregs of society, and should any of them have been sold without authority, you will know. That will still leave you with the bigger problem, though. It is one thing to collect and procure the ingredients, it is quite another to use them effectively. If you are certain the rite was performed here and not far away, you will need to explain how a cabal chanted its way through five nights of incantations without moving even a whisker on the most *cack*-faced of *incantatores*."

CHAPTER XXI

The next morning I set out to work my way around town again. I have worn out many a pair of sandals over the years in the piecing together of puzzles, and have learnt to accept it as part of the job. The Hellican philosophers maintain that the pursuit of knowledge is a higher purpose, that a man should need employ only his mind to reach the higher echelons of truth. My experience was that the truth is reached after much pounding of pavements and asking of uncomfortable questions. History will agree with me, no doubt, for while the Hellicans establish schools of thought, we Egretians are busy grasping the world from under them.

I started with the names that appeared in both Brewyn's and Akhirabus' lists of potential suppliers. The first owned a respectable-looking shop, in a quiet street not far from the Forum and the Collegium Incantatorum. He seemed a likely candidate, as location and respectability might draw in those members of the cabal I had seen.

I located the shop with relative ease and talked my way into a private audience with the proprietor — one Manius Acilius — pretending to be interested in his ability to import rare items. Once we settled down comfortably in his office sipping watered wine, pleasantries exchanged and the business at last at hand, I started to ask about some of the articles required for the Rite of Pelegrinus. Some, like

Assyrican kohl or the purest natron from the salt lakes of the Mitzrani deserts, raised no issues and he was quick to assure me of his quality stock. His interest piqued when I moved to more esoteric items, like shards of black star-stones or sand crystals fused by lightning. He was scratching his head when I got to the blood of a dog poisoned by a gorgon's snake.

"If you are unsure, dear Manius Acilius," I said, "I have heard good things about your colleague Quintus Mamilius. Perhaps I should go see him next."

"Oh, please, that charlatan sells only inferior quality. It is well known that his 'Mitzrani' natron comes from around the corner in the delta of the Ridus, and if you go so far as to ask for the blood of a dog poisoned by a gorgon's snake, you will be lucky to get the piss of a cat that died of rabies. No, if you are after quality and assured delivery, I am the only man in town who can deliver them to you."

"I am glad to hear this; it is indeed true that your reputation stands above all others in our city," I flattered him. "Tell me, though, and this is a delicate matter, those rarer objects — are they in much demand?"

"The only demand that matters is yours, my good patron. Just speak, and I shall endeavour to fulfil it."

"Well, and here is the delicacy of the business, I am in competition with some others who might wish to buy the same. Would you tell me, kind Manius Acilius, if such interest has arisen of late?"

"You are indeed a most esteemed customer, and I would gladly help, but surely you would appreciate your own privacy in such acquisitions? The name of Manius Acilius is synonymous with discretion."

In the end I offered to match the price of any authenticated bill of sale for such items he could show me. I could see in his eyes the irresistible attraction of the margins this afforded him, and I was certain that he would have sold me his mother for such profits.

If only he had anything to sell.

He insisted that none of the rare items had gone through his shop in recent months.

After leaving the shop of Manius Acilius, I naturally made my way to that of Quintus Mamilius, his bitter rival. The scene played out along similar lines, except that Mamilius was much more explicit in his profanities when referring to Acilius.

"That bastard son of a bitch and camel, 'dung-brains Acilius' as he is known amongst those in the business? You will never get anything out of him. *Cack* quality for the mundane stuff and empty promises for the rest! You will see, he will ask you for an advance, then say a storm sunk his ship and that he requires a second advance to procure the items again! That *irrumator* will lead you on and bleed you dry before you will see anything out of him."

But in the end he had nothing more to tell me, not for all the gold in the tomb of Croesus.

The next merchant I visited, the last to appear on both lists, was of a distinctly lower strata. His offices were shabbier, located nearer to the docks and the smell of fish. He would have loved to show up the two previous merchants of imported esoterica — and indeed, he managed to. He was also more direct.

"Mountain orchids and ferret's bile? Yes, I do recall something…" He looked at me expectantly.

I took out a pouch of silver coins from deep inside my tunic and measured a fair amount on the table.

"Yes, it's beginning to come back to me…" he paused.

I measured out more coins. A high sum, though nowhere near as what Acilius and Mamilius would have made me pay.

"It was a young boy, not even twenty," he said. "About two months ago or so. Yellow hair, worn long. He came and ordered most items you mentioned. Some I sold him, some he settled on alternatives, was not interested in delays. Paid in coin — real coin, not a banker's note. I prefer it that way anyway."

For an extra bribe, he got me an exact list out of his ledger of what had been bought. I compared it to my list. Most of the important ingredients according to both Brewyn and Akhirabus were covered, either directly or with decent substitution. The more esoteric ones, the ones they had scoffed at, were amiss or replaced. I would have to ask them to verify if the substitutions introduced side-effects, of course, although considering the nature of the Rite. neither Brewyn nor Akhirabus would be able to tell me for certain. My gut told me that these would do.

The more interesting question in my mind, as I was walking away from the shop towards the Forum Egretium, was 'Why was Caeso doing the shopping himself?'

I visited more of the traders down the list. A couple of them recalled a young man of Caeso's description — either remembered having sold something to him or just remembered his queries for truly exotic materials.

As I continued down the list of shops, I made another interesting discovery. It was in a dingy and smelly shop located at the ground level of a run-down *insula*. The whole neighbourhood was too close to the docks to be populated by anyone other than the poorest workers — longshoremen and whores. The inside of the shop was gloomy, barely lit through the closed shutters and one sputtering lamp. The floors were unswept and the place was a mess of haphazardly piled sacks and boxes. The smell of the place reminded me of Akhirabus' shop, although with a dank undertone. Despite the appearance, and while I am not an expert, the look of the herbs hanging from the ceiling and other supplies lying in open sacks seemed to be that of quality materials.

The proprietor was a dark-skinned, dark-haired fellow with an accent I could not quite place. I started with my usual enquiries after some of the herbs on my list, and then carried it to asking about how much he has been selling of them.

"You ask for special items. Special items have special demand, from special men," was the reply I got.

A show of silver loosened his tongue. He did not recall a youth of Caeso's description ever visiting, but he did remember a short, bald man of dark skin and a foreign visage, who regularly bought some base ingredients and certain prepared admixtures.

I had found Zymaxis' supplier.

I got confirmation of this from his reaction. He suddenly became cagey and insisted he did not discuss his customers' business. A contrast to his willingness to expound on such business before when I had showed him a purse of silver. When I tried to press the point he informed me that he must close the shop and escorted me hastily outside.

* * *

Next order of business was to start poking my nose in the affairs of the three names given to me by Didia. That Corpio would make enquiries at his level did not preclude my finding out other relevant information. Many avenues were open to me, and I planned to follow a simple one — find out who the men were, where they lived; observe their households; buy a miserable slave a drink. Our society is riddled with slaves, anonymous and invisible people we take for granted. But they are still people — they see, they hear, and with the right incentive, they tell.

I started with the Forum. That's where the worst gossips gather, and they were the ones I was seeking out. The process here was simplicity itself. Find a group discussing politics, or anything, really. Stand and nod. Then throw a name — "It's all well and true, my dear fellow, but what do you make of Gaius Marcius in this?" or "Of course, of course, but have you heard what Tiberius Pomponius is up to?" Then comes that brief awkward moment when they look at you, trying to place you, trying to figure out who you are talking about. The trick is to keep their chain of thought away from yourself and on the subject. Pretty soon they were happy to explain to me that I know nothing, that the man in question was now posted to Capiricia and could not possibly affect matters in Hellica. When I pretended I meant another man of the same name only to confuse the *cognomen*, there came a detailed description of the genealogy and achievements of the man and his family for five generations back. My identity forgotten, the original subject of the conversation put aside, the chinwaggers and gossips of the Forum take glee in tracing lineages — and their associated fortunes and misfortunes — above all else.

In the beginning of the case, when I had come to the Forum

without a clear idea, without a name to follow or a subject to gossip, I had gotten nowhere. Now that I had specific names to drop, I got much relevant information. A bit too much, in fact. It seems like there were a few possible persons, with differing *cognomina*, of each of the names I was after. Going between groups of gossips, crossing information, comparing notes, doing the mental calculations of age, descriptions, current postings, I got two things by evening — a headache, and a much shorter list.

Now to make the list even shorter, and nighttime was the perfect time for it. I had two Tiberius of the Pomponii of a likely background on the list, the backbencher senator that Corpio knew and a slave merchant. However, since I knew not if the name was of one of the cabal or not I decided to leave them aside for now.

Next were the Gaius of the Marcii. I found the analysis by Corpio quite good as well. Of those who were *Viri Militares* — career military men — one was too old and one posted abroad. Others of the same name were two merchants and a senator. None possessed the military background, though, which my gut insisted the man at the cabal must have. With the absence of further evidence, I trusted my feeling.

That left me with Quintus Fufidius the *incantator*, the man Corpio could offer me the least amount of information about. I heard of two *incantatores* bearing the name, both rather obscure and so came accompanied with little information from the gossips. The first was *cognominated* Calvus, balding, and the second *cognominated* Verres, swine.

First order of business was to find their addresses. Off I went to the Collegium Incantatorum at the eastern end of the Forum, to skulk by side entries. It was not long before a young messenger slave made his way out, looking busy and important beyond his years. Such boys, I knew from my short time at the Collegium, knew everyone. Running errands all day long, delivering messages and summoning people to *contiones*. Of course the smarter the boy the more self-important he would be, but what kind of a Fox would I be if could not bribe a ten-year-old?

* * *

Considering the man I had seen at the cabal meeting had a bad comb-over and that his house was closer, I went after Calvus first. I walked past his house, a small *domus* up from the Forum towards the Clivi Inferior. A modest private residence with the outside walls washed in pale blue, the shutters in the high windows painted green. I kept walking past and ducked into an alley. The hour was late, the last light still lingering in the west behind the dark mass of Vergu, torches and lamps now lit inside houses, families sitting down for dinner.

Most people would be home by now, with slaves attending to night duties. I had no idea what kind of man Fufidius was, whether he had family, whether he had business this night elsewhere. The lights inside could mean anything. I considered my options as I stood in shadows. I needed to ascertain the man's identity, see if I recognised his face, without him recognising me in turn.

I moved further down the side streets until I saw a passing citizen hurrying home. I put on my best country accent and stepped well into the middle of the street with a bewildered expression. "Excuse me, my good man! Would you be able to help a lost fellow Egretian?"

"Push off, *citocacia!*" he said as he shoved past me and sped up his pace walking away from me.

"*Fellator asini,*" I muttered at his back.

The next citizen to pass was a kinder soul. "I am looking for my city friend, Fufidius Calvus, who I was told lives nearby. Perhaps you know him?"

"Fufidius the *incantator*? He lives one street up, I think," said the man.

I cast a look at the steep street. "Only, I have been chasing around the town all afternoon, as there seem to be a number of that *gens* who have taken the title of *incantator*. My friend was older than me, and fonder of sweet pies. His thinning hair back in our youth earned him his *cognomen.*"

"Then I am afraid you are out of luck, my friend," said the man, "for the man I know to live there got his *cognomen* from his father but his hair from his mother."

I tried a few more passing men just to be certain; by the time I pieced together a description of the Fufidius Calvus who lived in that house I was convinced he was not the one I was after.

By the time I found the place where Fufidius Verres lived, the stars were out in all their numbers across the heavens. It was an *insula*, but not the large tenements of the Subvales. This one was an upmarket affair, only three stories high, and I knew the apartments would be bigger and better appointed.

I was faced with the same problem again — how to see without being seen — however, luckily, *insulae* have many more open stairways and access points than a private *domus*. Another thing that the better *insulae* possess are the guardians at the doors. While private domiciles mostly keep their street doors barred and employ a door slave on the inside, the apartment buildings mostly have open hallways and employ burly slaves or freedmen to stand guard.

I found the man sitting on a stool next to the doorway, sipping watered wine. A quick appraisal of his clothes and the state of the foyer, and I measured a few *sestertii* into his hands. It turned out that the *incantator* Quintus Fufidius Verres who lived on the second floor was my man. The guard was altogether too happy to gossip, the man apparently never tipping him properly and treating him as a slave even though he was a free man. I learnt much from the guard, confirming Fufidius' identity from his description, his habits, the slaves he kept, the friends he entertained. I learnt that he mistreated his two slaves, though not as badly as some masters; and that he had recently been forced to sell his third slave to pay for his rent. I learnt that he had few friends come over and spent many nights away. I even learnt about his favourite brothel. Very importantly, I learnt that one of his regular visitors matched the description of the Hellican foreigner I'd seen at the cabal.

I also learnt that he was not at home tonight. I decided to stop at his favourite drinking and whoring place, as it was but a short detour on my way home. The place was quite easy to find, on the slopes above the Forum, just off the Via Crispa that leads towards the Porta Alta. Down an alley between two temples on the side of the road, I found a door over which hung a bronze *fascinum*. The image of the winged phallus has long been considered a protective charm amongst our people, an ancient *numen* power that wards off the evil eye. The proprietor must have tried to make it appear a more up-class establishment and assure his patrons that no harm should come to those who visit. Still, hanging a penis over a door is an international sign of what to expect inside.

Nor was I mistaken. The interior was lit by many oil lamps, though the numerous gauze sheets in saffron, orange and red hung from the ceiling gave a diffuse quality to the light as well as obscuring the view of what happened further in. The door slave who showed me in indicated a couch and turned to fetch his master, but I put my hand on his arm and held him back.

"Tell me," I said and pressed a silver *denarius* into his hand, "Does the name Quintus Fufidius Verres mean much to you? An *incantator*, aged around fifty, with bad hair and bad manners?"

The man palmed the coin quickly and nodded.

"And does he have a favourite girl?"

"Helvia," the man replied.

I let go of his arm and sat down as he disappeared inside. I did not have long to wait. A young man entered from a back room and made his way to me with a smarmy smile. A pretty slave girl with bare breasts followed him in bearing a bronze tray and laid a wine cup next to me.

"Ah, my good man. Your first time with us? I assure you, you will not be disappointed. We provide the best quality and cater to all requirements," said the man. "What services can I arrange for you?"

"The usual comforts," I replied. "Though I have heard good things about a woman called Helvia in your employ."

"Ah yes, a most talented girl. Busy now, unfortunately, yet I am sure I can offer you her equals." He clapped his hands twice and three women entered in single file, then stood to face me. Their ages ranged from mid- to late-twenties, I estimated, and all had an air of experience. I guessed he first estimated his clients' desires before summoning a selection of girls or boys.

"I really would rather wait until she is free," I said.

He tried to dissuade me and have me take another, but eventually just shrugged and said, "I will send her here when she finishes."

I sat there for a while, sipping my wine, listening to the moans and screams, the banging of beds against walls and other sounds of pleasure that were coming from inside the house. Fortuna must have been smiling at me — or perhaps grinning maliciously — for not long after in stepped Quintus Fufidius himself. I sat very quietly as he adjusted the belt of his tunic and made his way to the door, hardly sparing me a glance. Then he stopped, turned around and gazed at me for a long moment.

"I know you," he said. Definitely grinning, Fortuna.

"I think we met, although perhaps in circumstances that are best discussed elsewhere."

"What brings you here, then?"

I waved my hand at the decor. "The usual business. I heard good things about this place, and thought to visit it."

He stared at me a moment longer. Helvia must have provided exceptional service, for he said, "Come, let us share a drink." He was definitely in a better mood than the last and only time I had seen him. He looked at me now more curious than disparaging.

"I know a place nearby," he said, "where we will be guaranteed privacy." He led me towards the lower slopes of the Clivi Ulterior, above the Porticus Aemilia. "The clientele here tends to be of senatorial rank, or other people of influence. Discussions of import are carried on there almost daily, yet none leak beyond the walls. Ah, there it is!"

The place was certainly upmarket. Three steps led up from the street to a wide doorway, a well-groomed slave standing to attention just inside. The interior was lit by many bronze lamps of various designs, set above individual tables arranged spaciously around the room. Towards the walls and the back, private booths were arranged with couches and partitioned with wooden screens. Rather interestingly, the ceiling was decorated with paintings of bouquets of roses. I felt a slight tingle in my hair, telling me that perhaps the implications of *sub rosa* were not enforced merely by convention.

We settled down at a table of polished wood. A slave appeared almost immediately and placed before us pitchers of spiced wine and

water, and bowls of olives and salted nuts. The place exuded high quality, the likes of which I was not used to. I became aware of the noise
around us, yet the quiet murmur of people talking at other tables quite
near to us was somehow always unintelligible.

Quintus Fufidius settled down in his chair and turned to me
"How did you find us? I think you are the first to come without being
invited first."

"Word does travel around. Even the best kept secret leaves
traces for those who know where to look."

"And where did you look?" he asked.

"I deal with supplies of exotic paraphernalia. From locally grown
herbs to imported components of rare high quality. When certain
things come into demand, I hear about them."

"And how did that lead you to us?"

"My turn, I think," I said. "Tell me what brought you to Zymaxis."

He paused for a moment, eyes narrowed, and I read on his face
a conflict between haughtiness and curiosity.

Haughtiness won. "You will need my vote, if you want in," he
said. "So you had better answer my questions truthfully and in full.
Otherwise, you will end up on the street. Or worse."

I was too tired to be subjected to an investigation. "This will be
your loss then," I said. "Just think. If I found you out, and have returned
bearing gifts to impress the cabal, there would be others. And not all
might be as kindly disposed as me."

We stared at each other for a while, locked in a battle of wills. I
wondered if I was taking the wrong approach, if fawning and scraping
would have bought me an easier ticket to the cabal. As I was only
looking to infiltrate them to learn of Caeso's death, a position of power
was not a strict necessity. Then again, I had never liked him from the
moment I'd first laid eyes on him.

He blinked first. "Oh, very well. I shall play your little game. You
would do well to remember, though, that satisfying my curiosity now
does not guarantee you my vote, or even a prolonged life. I joined for
the same reason everybody did — personal advancement. The ruling
circles in the collegia and the Senate are nearly impossible to break

into. The Fufidii are an ancient and respected family, but in recent centuries we have not had a single consul or even a *praetor*, and hardly any of us has risen to the rank of *rhone* in the various collegia. The *cunni* at the top all come from a few families and keep a strangle-hold, squeezing everyone else from attaining position. The elections are a joke, you must know. Oh sure, every so often a *novus homo* makes it in, just enough for them to keep up appearances that the posts are open to the public. In reality these *homines novi* are always singularly rich, which is how they get in. Unless you are born to a family of power or somehow manage to ransack a whole province, you will never get elected. Well, I will see this changed."

He paused to drink from his wine. "My turn again," he said. "How and why did you track us? Why do you seek to join us? And make your story a good one."

"My father was a dealer in exotic goods, a supplier of necessary materials for many *incantatores*. I was the first of my family to have joined the Collegium Incantatorum. I did not dream of attaining the rank of *rhone* and becoming a true *novus homo*, but I still dreamt I would make my mark. However, my father was cheated out of his business, and I was thrown out of the Collegium. I, too, would see things change and money matter less than ability. I took up my father's old line of trade, and when in recent months certain items became in demand I made enquiries and followed the source of the demand. I saw my chance for a change." I sipped my wine and looked sidelong at Fufidius. He seemed satisfied with the answer, as so often people are when you simply echo them back to themselves. I asked my next question. "And how do you see Zymaxis affecting such a change?"

"I will not discuss matters of the cabal with you," he said flatly. "When — and if! — you are accepted as a member, only then will we be free to discuss this."

"Tell me at least what you make of Zymaxis' chances, then."

"A pretty good chance, of course, or I would not have associated myself with him," Fufidius replied. "Tell me which materials have so caught your attention?"

I decided to bait him. "Ferret's bile to make ink for power tattoos, uncommon herbs and minerals from Mitzrana for the preservation of bodies, slivers of star-stones, lilies and orchids harvested under starlight. Unusual, though perhaps none too impressive. Yet tracked to the same source, and one might conclude you had ideas to attempt something long forbidden."

"You are insane if you think that. We want to change the order of things at the top, not burn the whole city down." He drained the last of his wine, rose, and said, "I grow weary of this game. I got your measure. Meet us three nights hence, three nights before the *Ides* at the same place, and pray that your offering is suitable and you are accepted. We do not take kindly to miserable gifts and failed attempts."

He turned and left. I sipped the rest of my wine in silence, and then followed his example and made my way home.

CHAPTER XXII

I started the next day with an overdue errand. After a comforting breakfast of home-cooked farina porridge sweetened with dates, I went to visit my friend Sosius again. I owed him a report about the library in Ephemezica. He would have already gotten one from his agent Baebius, but I owed him the courtesy. And, of course, I was still holding onto the scroll with the Rite of Pelegrinus.

I made my way to his shop at the Basilica Antonia. Once seated in his office, I recounted my review of the library and the haggling Baebius and I had carried out with Epphelipos. By now Sosius had received a detailed report from Baebius as well as a summarised index of the important works. He was quite happy with the result, his calculations indicating that he would be able to turn a nice profit over this.

"I wanted to thank you again for the service you rendered me," he said. "Baebius makes a good agent, but his knowledge is of a broader nature, not as specific as yours. I slept better knowing that Spurius Vulpius' son had given his approval for the deal."

"Think nothing of it," I said. "It helped me tremendously in my current case. I did keep a few scrolls with me for closer review. Most of the arcane material turned out rubbish, yet a few have promise of real value. One, however, was exactly what I was hoping to find."

"I am glad to have helped, then!"

"It does present a dilemma, however…" I said. "You see, the contents are strictly forbidden. The majority of the scrolls are borderline legal, can be classified as research into — rather than instructions on how to perform — the *nefastum scientiam*. This particular scroll, however… well, it's about as far over the border as a Mitzrani camel herder in a fishing expedition to Kebros. You might be able to find a buyer, but you run the risk of being reported to the Collegium Incantatorum. And if that happens, your business — and possibly your life — are forfeit. So my question is, do you wish to keep this scroll? I have gotten what I need out of it. While I have not been open about the matter, I still needed to consult a few other experts on some parts of the text. I would suggest we burn it before anyone official comes to suspect we possessed it or that indeed it ever existed."

"Now you wouldn't have found a buyer for it, would you?" Sosius asked me, half smiling. I guess the look on my face answered him plainly enough, as he continued, "Very well. I abhor burning knowledge, so will treat it with the respect and secrecy it deserves. Bring it to me. I think I have an idea of a good way to dispose of it that shall not put me or you at risk yet might still take advantage of its value."

I was a bit sceptical of his ability to do this, but it was his business after all.

"Tell me about the rest of your travels," he changed the subject, and I was happy to oblige. I told him of the pearl diving and pirate attack, of my travels around the Kebric Isles, and finished with the magnificent roast gryphon feast of Aulus Paulinus. A connoisseur of adventure stories, he made the right faces, gasps and exclamations at all the right times. When I got to the *fugum fellis*, he was snorting with glee at my hoodwinking the governor.

"You know," he said, wiping a tear from his eye, "I think I met this Aemilia of yours. I had a young girl walk in not two days ago, asking for the original edition of Liberalis. It was the first time I had heard about it, of course, and told her so. I think she didn't quite like the answer, though she acquiesced to my expertise. Now that I understand where this was coming from, I find it even more amusing."

I had a chuckle myself. Apparently, I had left quite an impression on young Aemilia, and she was determined to prove me wrong.

***

Next on my list was trying to learn about Gaius Marcius. I knew Corpio was doing the same, but wanted to see if I could find information from a different perspective. Between Corpio's analysis and what I had learnt from the Forum gossips the day before, I was certain that the man I was looking for was the one called Gaius Marcius Gaetanicus.

According to Corpio, he had been co-opted to be part of the *fetiales*. Officially priests of Iovis Pater of good faith, they were responsible for Egretia's declarations of war and peace as well as confirmation of treaties. In effect, they represent Egretia as diplomats. The *fetiales* are traditionally chosen from amongst leading military men. Most military men are not in possession of a keen diplomatic mind, and often view international relations as something that belongs on the end of a spear. Those who do show intellectual promise are selected, trained and assigned duties usually relating to a particular province or region. They are entrusted to advise the Senate about foreign matters, and in times of trouble are sent to negotiate treaties or even declare wars upon our enemies. That is common knowledge, as any boy in the street will tell you.

There is another side to their training, however, one less publicised. Not all the *fetiales* are sent as diplomatic envoys. Some are sent to travel their assigned regions without the official banner of Egretia, to learn about foreign army movements, and occasionally to sow dissent amongst the populace and sabotage enemy war efforts.

Spies, in short.

Sometimes advancing Egretian interests is better served not with sword and spear, but with the encouragement of local coups or a quiet assassination. The *fetiales* have the men ready, both to advise on matters of policy and to see it carried out.

Such men tend to be fanatically loyal to Egretia, though. The founders of our colleges were smart, and to build a lasting and effective order they implemented rigorous screening of the members from those who would be easily bent or bribed.

From my own queries with the forum gossips I learnt that Gaius Marcius was the great grandson of the famous Sextus Marcius

Gaetanicus, conqueror of the Gaetanii and establisher of our first foothold on the continent on the far side of the Mare Saepiae almost a hundred years ago. Gaetanicus' grand-uncle, eldest son of the great Sextus Gaetanicus, had been consul some seventy years ago. His father has served as the Primus Rhonus of the Collegium Militum.

This was one of the families in power that Fufidius had been railing against last night. Why would such a man be interested in a change of the social order? What might drive him to join Zymaxis' revolutionary cabal?

Only one way to find out. It didn't take me long to enquire after the family's lodging, talking to neighbours and slaves at back doors to locate the right house. He was living in a good-sized *domus* up on the Clivi Ulterior, as befitting a man of his background. I didn't need the man himself, however, just his slaves and neighbours. I wanted to learn when he has been seen, what parties he had attended, what comments about the political status quo he had made. This took a while, as I had to choose my cover stories carefully. Men of rank do not just open up to random strangers and tell intimate stories involving their friends.

Unhappy slaves do.

Between a fast-talking sly tongue and a few coins donated to self-liberation funds, I learnt quite a bit. He was the eldest son and had inherited the family house after his father's death three years before. He had a wife by the name of Aurelia, married about ten years ago. No children. Arbarica seemed to be his usual posting. Served as legate to Decius Corvinus in his three-year campaign and as a provincial *quaestor* before that. He had failed to return as one of the five *rhones* of the Collegium Militum in the elections the year before but was planning on running again in the elections this year, sticking to the *cursus honorum* within his college.

What I did not learn, however, was anything of less than impeccable record. No whispers, no conniving, no dissatisfaction. Was Gaius Marcius so paranoid that he was forever wary in every moment, even of the invisible people who move our society along? Likely it was a combination of a habit from his time with the *fetiales* and the small circle of the cabal. He would be a man used to relying on himself, and might not have his servants all around at all times. Well, at least not the ones I had managed to bribe.

After tracking down the house slaves and buying them drinks, learning of his favourite taverns and spending coins on the serving girls and taverners, and walking the hot pavements of our fair city from one end to the next, most of the daylight hours had been spent.

The last of my investigations was in the Campus Civicus, close to the training fields of the army and cavalry. I followed a lead, chasing a tribune who had served under Gaius Marcius in the last campaign. I pretended to be about to join a legion under Gaetanicus as an *evocatus*, and wanted to know the gossip about the commanders. A young man on the start of his career, he was happy to get a drink from a grizzled centurion on leave. In return I learnt he had been in the command tent with Gaetanicus a few times, privy to some discussions.

After sufficient drinks — I made his far less watered that mine — and a promise of dinner, he told me of events during the campaign against the Tigumani. Corvinus was a hard-headed general of the old style, believing in the old war trifecta of fire, rape and slavery, preferably in that order. Gaetanicus was of the opinion that more can be accomplished with targeted strikes than pitched battles. They had gotten into a few arguments about this.

The campaign had proceeded as they often do, with a series of skirmishes and minor sieges. Our legions had eventually faced a considerable force of the Tigumani and were preparing to do battle on the plain the next morning. Gaetanicus had maintained that the balance of power was not in our favour, the lay of the land was too muddy for our heavy infantry while the enemy's archers and light cavalry could manoeuvre around our legions with more ease. Corvinus had been of the opinion that our men would be able to hold the line and our auxiliary cavalry able to charge around and keep the enemy horses and archers occupied. Gaetanicus' analysis that our cavalry would face a more difficult route due to the low hills and that the enemy could use their archers to pick them off before then had been met with a dismissal that they were barbarians and would never do anything short of charging blindly forward. Corvinus had insisted that our legions would be able to just hold the line and march forward until they had obliterated the enemy.

Rather than see good men die in what he deemed a stupid strategy, Gaetanicus had ventured out that night without official sanction. Wearing no armour and with his face painted black with charcoal, he had managed to circle around and sneak into the enemy camp. He had left their commander with a slit throat and an Egretian dagger buried in his chest, and taken his winged helmet.

In the morning as our legions had prepared for battle, the enemy had mustered against them. Their commanders had tried to hide the death of their general, and had believed in their superior numbers and favourable conditions. Without permission, Gaetanicus had ridden out in front of the lines and yelled to the enemy to bring their general forward so that they could speak. When they had obviously delayed, he had produced the stolen helmet from his saddle bag and thrown it at the front lines of the enemy. "Know that today you fight headless," he had yelled at them and ridden back. What had followed was a complete rout, and a major turning point in the campaign against the Tigumani.

Corvinus, however, had been less than impressed. While he could not openly chastise Gaetanicus, he had withheld the due honours and completely ignored this incident in his report to the Senate, taking full credit for the defeat for himself.

My informant was under the impression that Gaetanicus had not put much value on it, used to the antics of inept generals. The men in the ranks had known what had happened and understood the importance, and appreciated Gaetanicus significantly more than their official commander, though they had been constrained in what they could do to show it. Gaetanicus had officially maintained that the truth would reach the Senate in time.

Could this incident, and probably a few others like it, have been a driving force for Gaetanicus to join Zymaxis' cabal? Turn him to the point of wishing a change in the social order of the city he was sworn to serve?

* * *

By the time I headed back home the sun was setting behind Vergu and the streets were cooling down. On my way from the Campus Civicus to the city I planned to stop for a bath and a shave at the Baths of Mauritius next to the Pons Orientalem. As I walked towards the cluster of buildings surrounding the baths I saw that a throng had gathered around there. I neared the crowd cautiously until I heard the sounds of a street-play in progress, and behind it I could see a cloth tent mounted with a pennant bearing the image of the sphinx. I was in luck — I had found Mahatixa's troupe again.

I waited at the back of the crowd till the end of the performance, hoping that Mahatixa would not hold our last conversation against me. I caught glimpses of her dancing and acting as the troupe performed their skits. From what I saw she was as graceful as ever, her lithe brown body captivating the watching men.

The cast finished their show to much applause and started to collect coins from the audience. I dropped a couple of small bronze coins into the bowl of the actor who passed me. Once the crowd dispersed and the troupe were packing up, I made my way closer and touched Mahatixa on the arm.

I was surprised by the response. She turned around and shoved me, yelling something in the guttural Mitzrani language. Harkhuf materialised swiftly between us before I even finished stumbling back, his teeth bared and muscular arms ready for a fight.

"Oh, it's not him," said Mahatixa.

"Him who?" I asked. Harkhuf remained between us, still glaring down at me.

"That pest Gnaeus Drusus. Nothing good came of this whole affair. Yourself included."

"I had hoped I left you on better terms. But Drusus? I thought neither of you cared for the other?"

"I certainly never did, though he seemed to have developed a taste. The toad was here a few days ago, tried to convince me to come with him. He began with a sweet talk about how he'd shower me with gifts, and when I refused he attempted to drag me in force. I gave him a black eye and the bastard tried to hit me back, but Harkhuf here had learnt his lesson since you tricked me and was quick to scare him away.

One shove from him, and the little *cunnus* ran like a coward with a dirty loincloth."

"Now, what would Drusus want with you?" I mused aloud.

"I do not know and I do not care," Mahatixa replied. "Having Caeso infatuated with me was a novel experience, and I enjoyed the attentions of one far above my station. He had a kind heart, that of a poet. We spent many hours walking and talking, looking out to the sea from his favourite secluded spot on the Insula Laridae. He knew this small cave in the cliffs of the isle, not normally visible when standing at the base of the Pharos. We made love there…" She paused, then shook herself. "This is all gone now, and the world has kindly reminded me of the realities of station and fortune. Drusus was a toad, and I care not what he wanted. And you are no better. I am done with the lot of you."

She turned away from me, and Harkhuf stepped to stand in front of me with arms clasped across his chest and a dangerous look in his eyes. I smiled up at him and departed quickly.

CHAPTER XXIII

The next day I set out across town again. A messenger had delivered an invitation the day before from Typheus to meet Corpio at his mansion on the Septentrionali, to discuss the information he had found out for me about the members of the cabal.

This being four days before the *Ides* of *Maius*, the weather was getting hot. The first scorching winds out of the south made their way to our fair city, drying everything in their path. The side effect of the weather was that I could no longer wear long-sleeved tunics and strap my dagger to my left forearm as I liked, and had instead to hide it inside my tunic, attached to a loop made especially for it.

I walked down the hill and passed behind the Forum Bovarium, already alive with the bleating and lowing of animals, the cries of haggling and smells of freshly butchered meat. I joined the Via Recta at the state wharves and walked up that straight avenue to the Forum. The Forum was already busy, men about their business seeking bankers and attorneys across the many imposing porticos, temples and buildings that surround the open spaces. I made my way to the Vicus Caprificus and started the climb up toward the northern cliffs. At the intersection with the Via Caeca I stopped for a drink of water and refreshed myself at the fountain with the statue of Nikoleon slaying the Gorgon. The water was fresh and cool, fed directly from the Aqua Sextiae that ran above me on its tiered arches. I dropped a small coin to a legless beggar sitting beside the crossroads shrine and continued up to the Septentrionali towards the house of Corpio.

By the time I reached my destination, most of Corpio's clients had already been dealt with, their patron dispensing his advice, promises, or money, and delegating tasks in return. When his atrium finally cleared of the last of his clients, Typheus admitted me to Corpio's study.

"This matter has been dragging," said Corpio as I seated myself. "I never expected it to take this long. Are you sure about this cabal of yours? Do you really think my little Caeso was involved with them?"

"You remember the heart of cold ruby I extracted from his chest," I reminded him, and saw him shift uncomfortably in his chair. "The best information I have to date points to this cabal, whose members are attempting to overthrow the lawful government of Egretia. Using forbidden ceremonies would no doubt give them the power to achieve their aims. I do believe that your son fell victim to such a ceremony, albeit botched and with disastrous results."

"Well, I do not know whether to hope you are right or wrong on this, but I do wish this matter to be laid to rest already. Quietly." He paused and then waved at his secretary. "Typheus, would you summarise what we found about the names Felix gave us?"

Typheus cleared his throat and started. "First the *incantator* Fufidius. The Fufidii are a rural family from the town of Ausculum on the Erratus. Two of their members reside in Egretia and have been trained as *incantatores*. The first is Fufidius Calvus–"

"Who is not our man," I interrupted.

Typheus cast a quick glance at me, then continued reading from his notes. "The second is Fufidius Verres. He completed his studies some thirty years ago, tried specialising in *magia inanitas* but ended up as an *elementor*. Served as a minor *officius* at the Collegium, tried to get elected a *quaestor* a couple of times and failed. Apparently, he was not well liked by his superiors or colleagues. Has been making his living in the city, hiring out for odd jobs or as tutor to younger aspirants to the Collegium." Typheus looked up at me.

"I managed to track him down, hence I know he is definitely the man I saw at the cabal. Your information matches what I have learnt about him. *Magia inanitas,* you say.... Well, those who manage to understand it are never well in the head afterwards. He is either inept or unbalanced, and my impression is of the former. Please continue."

"Next is Gaius Marcius. Based on your assessment of the person's age and the military background, and considering who was present in the city at the time, we believe this to be Gaius Marcius Gaetanicus." I nodded. "Son of Gaius Marcius Gaetanicus who served as *Primus Rhonus* of the Collegium Militum fifteen years ago, great grandson of the famous Gaetanicus. His branch of the Marcii goes back to the founding of Egretia, with several consuls and *rhones*. He was up for election for the post of Rhone of Soldiers last year, but failed. It seems like his failure is due to Corvinus, who holds a grudge over something that happened during their campaigns. He omitted him from official reports, and has been lobbying against Gaetanicus. His official complaint appears to be that Gaetanicus disobeyed orders, and had been sabotaging his command. He circulated rumours about some siege of a Tigumani fort, where Gaetanicus disobeyed direct orders and risked lives of the legion's *incantatores* in what Corvinus called a "mad scheme" to open up the city. Nothing provable of course, and Corvinus knows better than to try and take Gaetanicus to court. The prevalent opinion in the Senate is that Decius Corvinus is simply somewhere between jealous and incompetent, yet as a proconsul he had enough clout and clients to ensure Gaius Marcius will not be elected. There is talk of Gaetanicus running again in a year or two, with some rumours that he might run for *praetor* in the Senate instead of *rhone* within the Collegium Militum."

Typheus paused for a drink of water. His report gave me a more complete view, complementing the gossip I had learnt on the streets with gossip from the Senate. It also gave deeper motives for Gaetanicus to want to lash out against the establishment holding him back. His family had a long list of illustrious ancestors, while Corvinus' family was relatively new to the high echelons of power. However, the Decii Corvini were far richer, and their star was currently in ascendancy.

Corpio echoed my thoughts as he said, "He wouldn't be the first *vir militaris* to become impatient with the pace of civilian life and disillusioned upon his return. I have seen this many times before. Military Men used to having their orders obeyed without question, who suddenly need to engage in oratory to win debates. To be denied the election to *rhone* at the right age, a thing he must view as his birthright, would surely sit sorely with him."

"Last we have Tiberius Pomponius Pulvilus," said Typheus. "A *pedarius* — backbencher senator. It seems that he studied in the Collegium Mercatorum and then served as a minor *quaestor* there a while back. However, when opportunity presented itself about four years ago, he elected to join the Senate instead of continuing the *cursus honorum* within his collegium, although his chances of rising in the Senate are slimmer. He runs a slave trading company, specialising in niche markets rather than volume supply. The company is quite profitable, and his customers mostly belong to the rich elites, who can afford the best. It is rumoured that he sold the *Princeps Senatus* a Hellican tutor for his young boys for the astronomical sum of four talents of silver. The more malicious tongues say that only three were for the tutor, and one talent was for a young woman, quietly installed in a cosy apartment."

"Leaving aside the rumours about our *Princeps Senatus*," interjected Corpio, "Pomponius' decision to become a *pedarius* in the Senate rather than continue within the Collegium was puzzling. Normally, those who embark on the *cursus honorum* do not switch from the collegia to the Senate. While technically a position of *quaestor* would allow him to run for *aedile* or *praetor* when his time comes, the restrictions placed upon *pedarii* senators in terms of allowed business practises would mean his income would suffer."

"I was also not able to ascertain who his patron is," added Typheus. "So far, he has not been publicly accepted and recognised as a client of anyone of note. It does not mean that he hasn't been registered, only that we cannot know his ultimate allegiance."

"Will this information shed any light on the death of my son?" asked Corpio.

"It helps me understand the men I will be meeting tomorrow," I replied. "And it might give me the key to anticipate their actions. I know now more about the ceremony and about the provisions that were needed to carry it out, though I fear I still miss some key pieces to this puzzle. I cannot yet bring you hard evidence against the cabal in the death of your son, or on any other matter, but I am sure I will soon."

"I have given some thought to what I might do with such evidence," said Corpio. "Public prosecution in the courts is out of the question. I would keep my family's name out of this business. However, if you cannot deal with them directly, if you can give me solid evidence — good enough to take to the *rhones* of the Collegium Incantatorum — I can ensure that they will be dealt with effectively and permanently."

* * *

After my interview with Corpio, I decided on a hunch to go to the Insula Laridae and see if I could find Caeso's secret lovers' hideaway that Mahatixa had mentioned the night before. I made my way to the Pharos, walking along the Vicus Caprificus to the east, catching glimpses of the cliffs and sea to my left and the sloping hill and the bay to my right. I reached the point where the Septentrionali ends in a steep slope, and wound my way down to the Pons Ignis.

Across the bridge, rather than take the beaten path up to the base of the Pharos I started to look for tracks. I grew up in the city walking the pavements, and my stint with the legions was short and mostly involved just trudging along behind the man in front of me. My wilderness skills were lacking, but luckily this wasn't a real wilderness. I wandered around the base of the small island, looking for rocky steps one could take with a woman friend to find a secluded corner for a tryst.

The first such spot I found was indeed occupied by a pair of lovers. I was deep in thought, and my surprise at stumbling upon them was almost as big as theirs. I recovered quicker though, and as they were just a couple of young teenagers escaping their chaperones I shooed them away. They hastened away, giggling and slipping into their clothes, and I had no doubt they would meet here again soon enough.

The spot they occupied proved unremarkable, though. A narrow rock shelf in a shallow alcove the wind had carved into the overhanging cliffs. No features or signs of humans, besides some discarded shards of portable clay *amphorae* on a rock below.

I continued to search. I had learnt to trust my instincts a long time ago, and they were telling me that meeting Mahatixa last night and hearing her comment about her and Caeso's love trysts here was not by chance. But when the sun was high in the sky and almost two hours of searching yielded nothing, I was ready to announce to the world that I knew nothing on chance comments.

I sat on the latest of the small rock shelves I had discovered, dangling my feet over the edge. The cliff behind me provided shade, and I enjoyed the cool breeze drying my sweat. I was past the tip of the isle, and I looked out across the opening of the Bay of Egretia and gazed at the many ships making their way in and out of the bay.

A wave crashed below me, and the wind carried a spray of ocean water to my face, hinting it was time to go back. As I stood up and faced the cliff again, I noticed a shallow step in the stone beyond a vine climbing down from a rock outcrop, where I had thought the path ended. I grabbed onto the vine for support and stepped around the outcrop and onto the cramped space behind it. The foothold was precarious, but beyond it I could see a narrow crack in the cliff face. I put my hand around the edge of the crack and swung my leg around it. It found purchase, and as I edged around the crack I found myself in a low and narrow cave.

Remembering the time I had retraced Caeso into a cave on top of Mons Krodus, I proceeded with caution. I could feel a soft tingling on my skin, but it was not the kind of feeling I get when in the presence of a place occupied by a *numen*. This felt more like the traces of *magia elementorum*, which I attributed to the Pharos above me. I had had the same feeling from the moment I had stepped off the Pons Ignis onto the isle, yet somehow inside this little cave it had intensified.

As the cave mouth was facing away from the sun, the interior was dark. I stepped outside and around the edge of the opening, and with my knife managed to cut a length of green vine. I climbed back to the cave, sat down near the opening and started to work on the vine.

I stripped the leaves, and then with a bit of muttered incantations and incessant rubbing, I had it dried and twisted into a tight cord within a few minutes. It was a handy trick I had learnt many years ago from a woodsman, when we had been stuck in a mountain cave waiting for a storm to pass. Another household charm to create a spark without a flint, and I soon held an improvised burning wick that gave me enough light to see inside the small cave. The ambient *magia* from the Pharos made this whole process easy and quick.

The cave was not large, only a few paces deep. The space was narrow and low, and rather empty. At the back was a little alcove, hidden from view from the front of the cave. I carried my burning wick and saw the remains of a small fire and some clay jars heaped in the corner. I started to carefully sort the pile of jars and inspect their contents. There were also a few utensils strewn between them, a bronze mortar and pestle, measuring spoons, utility knives and needles. Everything was covered with dust. Most of the pots and jugs were empty, but a few held traces of herbs and other supplies that I recognised from the ingredients list I had been researching for the Rite of Pelegrinus.

A couple of narrow-necked and stoppered jars contained thick liquids. Carried to the sunlight near the entrance, one liquid was red and the other a dark blue. Both smelled like ink, though not the usual kind made from squid.

I went back inside to look around some more. As I moved, I disturbed the ashes from the small fire and noticed that in between them were a few scraps of burnt paper scrolls. I knelt and put my wick down away from the ashes, and started to carefully extract all the burnt bits of paper I could find. I kept those that had remains of writings and drawings, and put them in one of the empty jars that seemed cleanest and driest.

I found nothing else of note, so picked up the two ink jars and the one containing the scraps of paper, and made my way back. It would be a long walk around the base of the Insula Laridae, across the bridge, and all the way along the shores of the bay to the south side. I elected instead to hire a boat and charge the expense later to Corpio. The advantages of working for a rich customer, with well-negotiated terms.

* * *

I reached home by mid-afternoon. I went straight into my study to place the jars I had retrieved from the cave on the table, and then stepped back out to the garden to wash my face in the fountain. The horribly leering faun dispensing the water from his engorged phallus seemed almost to wink at me, in a way that would make even jaded whores uncomfortable.

I was about to head back to my study when Dascha ambled into the garden. "A man was here to see you earlier, *domine*."

"What did he want?"

"He would not say. Insisted on speaking only with you. Was waiting outside, skulking behind the tree, until I emptied a chamber pot over the wall at him."

"You did what? Why would you do such a thing? He could have been a customer!"

"He wasn't," Dascha said with extreme self-assurance. "I saw him this morning, following me around. He was talking to the neighbours, too, before he came knocking at our door. Young men take the old for slow and stupid, but my mind is just as good as it ever was, *dominillus*. That man was asking far too many questions about you."

My indignation cooled down. Dascha always used the diminutive of 'master' when she wanted to remind me that she had been with my family for longer than I had been alive, and that she knew her business. A subtle way for a slave to put a young master in his place.

"Dinner will be ready shortly," continued Dascha. "Will you eat in the *triclinium* or your study?"

"In my study, please," I said and went there myself.

So someone was making enquiries after me. It could be unrelated to my current case, of course, a prospective client, perhaps — but I do not believe in coincidences. I wondered what had taken the cabal so long to start asking around. I had barged in on their meeting uninvited and unannounced over a month ago. I would have expected their curiosity to be piqued and for them to start asking about me sooner. Perhaps they had, and I had missed it when I'd been away. I would have to be careful when I next met them, although my cover story was sufficiently close to the truth that their investigations were unlikely to uncover anything beyond my generally disreputable background.

First, I opened the jars containing the coloured liquids. In full light they looked quite sludgy. I poured a sample out into a clay bowl and mixed it with water. It appeared and felt like ink. I mixed samples of the two and created a shade of purple, and when droplets stained my hand the colours reminded me of Caeso's tattoos.

I made sure to wash my hands thoroughly.

Next I pored over the burnt pieces of paper. I laid them out carefully before me, like a puzzle with most of its pieces missing. I deciphered one by one, and made notes. That it was the text for the Rite of Pelegrinus I had no doubt. The snippets I had found read remarkably like the scroll I had retrieved from the library in Ephemezica. There were mentions of ink and *stigmas*, of chants and rituals.

I got my final confirmation when I found a largish snippet containing the symbol for *Aten* — that crazy unity of the multitude that Akhirabus had talked about. I compared it to the place in the text from Ephemezica, and found some differences in the surrounding text. I would have to take it to Akhirabus for final analysis. Rather than take the full scroll, I prepared a wax tablet with a few paragraphs of context from the two versions for Akhirabus, and then retired for the night.

CHAPTER XXIV

The next day was the day Fufidius had told me to meet with the cabal, and I had to prepare myself for the night. I started at the Pickled Eel with a very hungover Crassitius. His tirade of invective at me and my ancestors was highly descriptive and punctuated by miserable groans. In the end he did promise to send Borax to accompany me later.

My next stop was not far from there on the street of the embalmers. I soon sat with Akhirabus in his back office, watching him hum and haw at the wax tablet in front of him.

"There are subtle differences between the two versions," he said. "You say this one is the one actually used?" He tapped on the side of the wax tablet where I had copied the burnt fragments I'd found in the cave. "As I told you before, there are many ways to interpret — or misinterpret! — the *Aten* symbol. This fragment is not big enough for proper context, yet from what I can piece together I would say that the implications are that the ritual must all come together and be completed between sundown and sunrise. Understand that *Aten* also rather simplistically represents the sun, for the religiously minded at least.

"However, in the source you first found and brought me, the interpretation is quite different. Here, the *Aten* is taken to be the celestial unity as I have mentioned before. It would not mean the meeting of sun and stars at dusk, but rather, during an eclipse! A solar eclipse, to be precise, when the sun, moon and earth are in alignment and the stars are visible."

I knew enough of incantations and rituals to understand the implications. "This would explain why the ceremony failed," I said, "assuming that the Ephemezican copy is correct and this one is but a poor mistranslation."

"It is hard to tell," said Akhirabus. "These rituals are complex and practised rarely, practised successfully rarer still. It could be this, or any of a number of other errors in understanding and execution. You cannot be certain which one is the right one, and failed attempts do not encourage a repeat."

"Do not worry." I said, "I plan to destroy all evidence of this rite, together with the men who performed it."

My last stop that morning was in Brewyn's shop. I showed him the ink and needles I had found in the cave, and he confirmed that they could be used to inscribe tattoos, and would indeed create the same marks he had seen on Caeso's corpse.

"Still, there is nothing of power inherent in them," he said to me as he rubbed a bit of the ink between his fingers. "Of the many ways to create *stigmas*, an ink such as this is merely a conduit, not a carrier of power itself. And as a conduit, there are still many ways to draw the power in. Most will do so gradually, the *stigma* being built together with the tattoo. The ones I saw, though, I tell you, were like a lightning rod. The power rushed in at full force, all at once."

* * *

I made my way back home, planning on a meal of leftovers and some rest before that night. I felt I was missing something crucial. The pieces of the puzzle in my mind just did not fall into place properly: their edges — the evidence and testimonies I had gathered — just did not match.

Deep in thought about the revelations of the last two days, I wasn't paying nearly as much attention as I should have. Thus it was that when I opened my front door and stepped in, I was taken completely by surprise when the man shoved me roughly from behind and stepped in after me.

I managed to break my fall with my hands and roll over to face my assailant. He didn't waste much time and was on top of me even as I fell, pinning me to the floor with his weight. I tried reaching inside my tunic for my dagger, but he grabbed me by the front of my tunic with his left hand and slapped me hard across my jaw with his right.

"Where is it, *matris futuor*? Where are the scrolls?" he demanded. Behind him I saw another man standing in the doorway.

I wasn't going to answer, and concentrated on pushing him off. I gripped his arms, but before I could throw him off he jumped up and landed with both knees into my midsection. By the time I managed to draw a breath, he held a knife to my throat.

"The scrolls, *cacator*, the scrolls you got in Ephemezica. Where are they?" He spat on my face.

"Gone," I said, "memorised and burnt."

"Even better," he gave me an evil grin, "I get to torture y —" He was interrupted by a loud clang and a shout. The clang was made by Dascha as she came suddenly around the corner and struck his head with a heavy iron skillet, caving his skull in and sending bits of bone and brain splattering on my face. The shout was from the other man at the door, taken by surprise as well. I struggled to free myself from the weight of the man on top of me as the other man lunged forward with his sword to strike at Dascha.

He almost got to her, but was jerked back with a half strangled grunt. He stopped and looked dumbly down to his midsection where a bloody metal point was sticking out. He fell forward to his knees with a sickening squelching sound as he slid down along the blade stuck into him. Behind him stood Borax, his left hand still holding the man's cloak he had used to yank him, and his right holding his long, bloodied dagger.

The man was wheezing his last, though, and thanks would have to wait. I got up, kicked the knife away from the man's hand. Still breathing hard, I knelt down next to him and said, "You are dying. You can die quickly and receive the funeral rites if you tell me who sent you, or you can be assured that I will desecrate your body before feeding it to the dogs." I pressed onto his wound to stress the point, and he gasped in pain. "Your shade will never know rest. Who sent you?!"

He coughed and spat blood. "Philokrates." He coughed again. "That's the only name I heard from our leader." He coughed up more blood and his eyes started to glaze over.

I slapped his face and raised my voice, "Who is your leader? What sodality do you belong to?"

"The cr…" he coughed, "the crossroad college at…" he coughed again, his whole body wracked with pain. He spasmed, blood gushing out of his mouth, and lay still.

I rose up and turned to face Borax. He had sensibly closed the door behind him and was cleaning his dagger on a piece of cloth. "Thank you," I said. "I owe my life to your timely arrival."

"Marcus Crassitius said you needed me tonight, and told me to go wake you up from your afternoon nap," he said with a smile.

"I'd have you stay by my side, tonight and for the next few days. I'll pay Crassitius later — right now I have a feeling I will need you again soon. Now help me with this one."

The name Philokrates meant nothing to me, but it sounded Hellican. Was this the Hellican I had seen at Zymaxis' cabal? The man there was not a citizen of Egretia. He seemed affluent, but that did not preclude connections with the Egretian underworld.

For those less familiar with the Egretian approach to divinity, we see our *numina* — the presence of godly powers — everywhere. They are in the open skies, the fertile grounds, the burial places of the dead — and in crossroads. Every crossroad has a guardian presence, one of the *lares* — the gods of homes and human domains. Every home has a shrine to the family's *lar* and the *di penates*, the gods of the pantry and food. Outside the house, we have *lares* everywhere — houses, fields, boundaries — even public ones for Egretia itself.

Crossroads are special. Minor alleys might have just a sign set in the wall, a place for the locals to pour libations for the local *lar*. Major crossroads have guardian colleges. These are tasked with keeping the *lar* of the crossroad happy by maintaining the streets, fountains and sewers in clean and working order, and by throwing the annual *Compitalia* in their honour. Members are drafted from the local community. Usually, a simple religious association.

The *lares* and their associated worship go back a long way in our history. Longer than the city, and much longer than the three collegia ruling our daily life. These dedicated institutions are sometimes charitable confraternities, caring for those in need, and sometimes little more than criminal organisations. The religiously minded say that the colleges are affected by the particular temperament of the *lares* of the crossroads and indeed of the roads themselves. The cynics say that these colleges are nothing more than taverns for the lowlifes with nothing better to do, getting official sanction for organised crime.

Whatever your view of them, I was obviously dealing with one of the shadier branches. That usually meant one of the shadier neighbourhoods as well. My only way to find which one was to go knocking on dingy doors and ask if perchance they had been paid for my head and would they kindly stop.

Considering that the dead man mentioned his leader fixing the contract on me with this Philokrates, there might be other members on task. I wanted Borax at my side the whole time until this case was resolved.

We searched both bodies, but found no mark or anything of interest. The men were citizens, by their iron rings, yet besides small pouches of coins and their knives, they carried nothing else. We wrapped them in rags, and I sent Borax to hire a donkey from the markets while I helped Dascha clean up the blood and gore. When Borax got back we loaded the bodies on the donkey and carried them through the streets like rolled up carpets. We made our way out of the Porta Fulvia to the temple of Libitina in the Egretian necropolis on the hills across the river Fulvius.

"Don't know who they were, and don't care," I told the clerk and gave him the men's money pouches. "See that they get as proper rites as this will buy."

I kept my promise. I am not usually afflicted by bouts of honour and disposing of the bodies in the nearest sewer would have been quicker, but I have seen enough vengeful shades of the dead not to want one associated with my home.

* * *

When we finally left home that evening on our way to the Dented Skull, we had hardly ventured out of the alley that leads to my house from the main street when a figure stepped in front of me to block my way. Before I could even react Borax interposed himself between us, grabbed the man by his ragged tunic and lifted him clear off his feet.

"Stop!" I said as I recognised the face. "I know him, Borax, he's a friend."

"So we're back to friends now?" asked Araxus.

"Don't push it," I said as Borax put him back down. He still glowered at Araxus, which was fine by me.

"You seem extra jumpy," said Araxus.

"We had some unwelcome guests earlier. You have something for me?" I asked.

"In a way. There is a lot of buzz in the circles of those sensitive to the flow. Better we talk inside, though."

We went back to my house and I knocked on the door loudly — in the wake of this afternoon's attack I had left Dascha with instructions to barricade the door as soon as we left.

Once seated in my study with wine and olives, Araxus began his report. "There is something going on, some subtle but fundamental shift in the flow of *magia* around. I trust you remember the basics from our years in the Collegium, so I won't bore you with unnecessary explanations. It's not tangible, not quite visible yet. Not something so glaringly obvious that even the useless *pederes* at the Collegium couldn't just ignore, you know what they're like. This time… it's almost as if the *numina* are restless. As if Vulcanus shifts in his sleep under Vergu."

226

"I thought you didn't believe in sentient *numina*."

"I don't," he said, "but the people I speak with are not from the Collegium. They have an older understanding of our world."

"And do the rumours offer any reason that might cause Vulcanus to shift in his sleep?" I asked.

"None yet," Araxus replied. "And it is definitely new. There are always shifts in the streams, yet this time it's different. It has an air of expectation to it. They say something is coming, and that it will come very soon. I don't hold much with the *Augurs* at the Collegium, but even they should start seeing the signs."

"Well, it has been going on for at least six weeks," I said, "Since the ceremony that caused Caeso's death at the very latest, and probably much earlier if you factor in the preparations."

"That's just it — it hasn't. This is a new thing. A matter of days," said Araxus. "It might not even be related. You know how it goes — the old believers say the *numina*, and the cynics prescribe it to natural phenomena; the a*ugurs* will look for signs of deeper meaning, and the *elementori* will try to control it."

"Somehow I don't believe in coincidences any more," I said.

"It's an all-or-nothing proposition," said Araxus in a philosophical tone. "Either it's all coincidence or nothing is. Right now, though, we don't have time for philosophy or other *tauri stercus*."

"No, we don't," I said. "Either the *augurs* did not notice, as you say, or they noticed, yet did not make it public. They rarely do. I was on my way to meet with the cabal when you jumped us. If they have anything to do with the shift of power, with the *numen* of Vergu, as you say, I might find out about it tonight. I wonder...." Araxus looked at me to provide more details, but I was thinking about something else. Thinking very hard, considering our shared past.

In the end I knew I had no choice. If this was real, I would need his help. "Do you remember our old signal?" I asked.

"You mean...? Yes, of course I remember," he replied.

"Good. Borax is very large and very good at what he does, but I might need you, as well. If this comes to pass, it will be an ugly business. Will you render me your help?" I looked into his disparate eyes, searching.

"Gladly," he replied. And I believed him. I don't know why, but the look in his one green eye made me believe that this time he would make good on his word.

"Give me a strand of your hair, then," I said. He plucked a long hair from his head, and I did the same. I got a slim wooden toothpick and wrapped both strands together around it. We each pricked our left thumbs on the sharps ends, and spoke the incantation. I placed the *res magiae* on my desk, then picked it up and put it in my dagger's sheath. I wanted it on hand at all times.

CHAPTER XXV

I sat with Borax at the Dented Skull, sipping watered wine and chewing on olives and bread. I had little to go on about the identity of the would-be assassin. The only man who would know I possessed the scroll was Sosius, but his shop had closed for the day when I had called at his office on the way.

As we waited, I saw the men of the cabal arrive one by one and make their way downstairs. Only five men arrived this evening before Zymaxis. Gaetanicus first, coming alone and making his way straight down; then the freedman a few minutes later; Fufidius and the other young *incantator* turned up together in deep conversation, and barely nodded at Septimius the proprietor on their way; the last one I saw walk downstairs was wearing a hood, and I could not tell who he was.

Finally, I saw Zymaxis arrive at the tavern. As he walked past me I hailed him. He turned to me, and in an instant I saw the recognition on his face. "Felix, you're back. Finished with your task? Ready to impress us?"

I took out the sealed clay jar from my satchel. "I think you will be suitably impressed."

"Not here," he said. He indicated for me to follow and walked to the back and down the dark stairs.

When we reached the room under the tavern, it was set as before, lamps lighting the obscene frescoes, furniture pushed against the walls apart from two tripod side-tables covered in black cloth. As we entered, the men ceased their conversations and gathered in a circle. The man who wore the hood now had his head uncovered — the Hellican foreigner.

"We are not in full attendance tonight," started Zymaxis. "However, before we discuss each member's progress, we shall address Felix's petition to join us. We charged Felix with bringing us something to further our cause, as all of you have done in the past. What that thing might be we have left open, given his self-proclaimed profession." He looked around at the gathered men as he spoke, then turned back to face me. "Show us what you have brought, Felix."

I walked to one of the stacked tripod tables and carried it to the centre of the room, took out the clay jar again from my satchel and presented it to the group. "Here, my dear fellows, is the culmination of a month of research and daring. You are all men of the world." I looked from the soldier to the freedman to the *incantatores*. "You would have travelled, you would have heard legends, you would have learnt the importance of the right ingredients when attempting great feats of *magia*. You might have been privileged to see such being used, and witness one of the great incantations." I took a small knife from the side table and started to cut carefully around the wax seal. "But how many of you can claim to have accessed some of the rarest, most precious of such arcane materials? I am certain that what I bring to you today will be found of use, either directly or through the vast sums of money it will command from the right buyer." All eyes were on me as I removed the lid and let the air fill out with the aroma of bloody organs pickled in vinegar. "Fellow men," I said, and wished I had a wooden ladle as I dipped my hand inside the jar and closed it on something soft and slippery. "Allow me to present you with the recently preserved eyes and organs of a gryphon!" I drew out my hand and held it aloft, and in it were two wobbly, dripping, milky-yellow eyes, staring vacantly into the room.

* * *

The gathered men were suitably impressed. The soldier's face was hard to read but I thought him surprised, as gryphons were common only to the desert mountain ranges far to the east; the freedman seemed a bit queasy at the sight and smell of the organs in vinegar; Fufidius looked on greedily, whilst his companion's younger eyes were gleaming at the potential of spells he had probably only read about; a puzzled expression crossed the face of the Hellican, before it reset itself and became inscrutable again. Most importantly, I saw a look of great greed and excitement on Zymaxis before he recomposed himself.

"That is, indeed, a truly valuable contribution. I shall have to verify the quality of the product, of course. Why don't you tell us how you got ahold of such precious items?"

I decided to go with the truth. Well, most of it. Embellished a little. By the end of my story they got the right impression, that I was an audacious rascal, not afraid to put one over on the slow-witted elite. I got them laughing at the right points and clapping me on the back by the end of it.

An exaggeration, perhaps, though they did nod their appreciation at the results. Zymaxis also voiced his approval and addressed the cabal. "Men, I think this meets the criteria we set. Objections?"

None were offered. "Excellent," said Zymaxis. "All that remains is for you to swear the oath. Two of our members are away tonight, so we shall do this on the night of the full moon together with the other business. There is another initiate due to take his oath that night, and you can both then attend the following ceremonies. It will be good for you to witness true power.

"In the meantime, allow me to introduce our current members. This is Lucius Duronius," he indicated the young *incantator*, "a rising star within the Collegium Incantatorum, who feels he's being held back. His colleague is Quintus Fufidius Verres, an established *incantator* of great experience, snubbed by the oligarchy of the Collegium. Of Gaius Marcius Gaetanicus," he indicated the soldier, "you may already have heard. He was instrumental in the campaigns of Marcus Decius Corvinus south of the Montes Mauretanii, yet feels cheated of the glory that should have been his by right. Gaius Rabirius Capilanus, a freedman of Gaius Rabirius Silanus, is looking to increase his standing in our society and restore some justice. And lastly, Philokrates, a Hellican that made Egretia his home, yet found many doors closed because he was not born here." I was half-expecting that name, so hoped my face did not register any surprise. We both exchanged blank looks, staring into each other's eyes.

Zymaxis continued. "All of us have achievements behind us and still in front of us, yet we are all united by the feeling that we are prevented from achieving our full potential by a stale and stagnant oligarchy. Indeed, we do all that we do for the glory of Egretia. Yet are our efforts recognised? No! We are rewarded with mere pittance, crumbs; held back from achieving even more by men who feel threatened that the past eminence of their families will no longer mask their current ineptitude and decrepitude." He continued in this vein for a while longer, working himself — and us — into a fervour. I participated by nodding and grunting my agreement with the rest of them.

Eventually, Zymaxis' diatribe slowed down. "You will now have to excuse us, Felix. The next business is for blood members only. Remember though! You must meet us at the top of Vergu on midnight of the full moon. You will take your blood oath then, and become one of us, a true member of our cabal."

* * *

The disadvantage of hoods is that they block one's peripheral vision. They are also highly conspicuous on a warm summer night. Thus Borax and I had no trouble in identifying Philokrates as he emerged from the Dented Skull and follow him around town.

I didn't know where he lived, though, so we had to act fast. At the first opportunity — an alley far enough from the Dented Skull, and dark enough for our needs — I called out his name.

He turned instinctively towards me, his face highlighted by the moonlight. "Philokrates," I said again, "How glad I am to have caught up with you. I have something I need to tell you, it's really important! I found something that I am sure you will find interesting. It's a rather unique scroll…"

We approached him calmly as I spoke, all smiles and visible hands. When we got within a couple of paces from Philokrates I stopped walking, but Borax very nonchalantly took another two steps and threw a hard jab at Philokrates' jaw. I caught his arms as he staggered and kneed him between his legs. He sank down, Borax grabbed his hood and covered his head with it completely, and I delivered another knee to his covered head, just for good measure.

Borax hoisted the unconscious body on his shoulder and followed me to the nearest entry to the Cloaca Maxima. I lifted the grill covering the entrance with some effort, climbed down, and received the body of Philokrates as Borax lowered it to me before jumping in himself. As soon as we were out of sight, I cut strips from Philokrates' cloak, bound his feet and his hands, and then gagged him. I didn't think we were observed, but even so we kept walking down the sewer, away from the grill. The air was thick and heavy, the smell suffocating.

With the light filtering through the sewer entries almost too dim, I tore another piece of Philokrates' cloak, and using the incantation as I had in Caeso's cave, I got it to light up. This being a damp environment and far away from the locus of *magia ignis* under the Pharos, it took me considerably longer before I managed. I wrapped the strip of cloth around a stray stick, and with this makeshift torch we made our way further down the line of the sewer, toward the egress point in the cliffs.

Our ancestors, balancing hygiene and paranoia, have built many offshoots to the Cloaca Maxima. Wherever possible, these branches head to the sea cliffs on the north side of the city, spilling their foul contents into the sea rather than the bay. At the point of egress, all openings are protected by sturdy metal bars, spaced so that nothing larger than the bodies of dead rats will be able to pass through. The city keeps public slaves to clean the sewers, and make sure that the openings never get blocked up with detritus.

We walked for a while in silence. At one point Philokrates woke up and started to groan through the gag, but we ignored him; Borax had no trouble keeping him tightly on his shoulder.

Luckily, we were not too far from the cliffs, and made it to the opening before we succumbed to the horrid smell. Borax dropped

Philokrates next to the grill, where the light from the almost-full moon was sufficiently bright that we did not need to rely on the clumsy torch.

Safe in the knowledge that we were close enough to the base of the cliffs that the sounds of the surf would drown any screaming, I still took out my dagger and pressed it to Philokrates' neck before taking the gag off. "Scream and it will be your last," I said. "I have some questions, and if you want to see the sun rise, you will answer them promptly. Am I understood?"

He nodded, and I removed his gag.

"I only have two questions, really," I said, "First, why did you send those men after me?"

"So it *was* you," he said with a slight note of surprise. "I wasn't sure until now. I… We…" he started and stopped a few times. "I can't discuss matters of the cabal with anyone who did not take the blood oath."

"Do try," I said and drew my dagger along his shin, leaving behind it a glistening dark line. To his credit he only drew in breath sharply.

"You misunderstand," he retorted, "I really cannot. The oath is not mere words, there is power in it. It binds us to secrecy and to Zymaxis' will."

"I have been accepted by your cabal, you've seen it tonight. Zymaxis gave his approval. The rest is only formality. Now — why did you send the men after me?"

"I can tell you as much as I told them," he replied. "We have heard that there was a library of — shall we say, eclectic and esoteric material — for sale in Ephemezica. Zymaxis commissioned me to acquire it, as I have procured similar material for him in the past. But by the time I got there it had been sold and shipped. I sent agents to track it. The agents finally reported that the contents were in Egretia and for sale, and when I enquired after it, I found out the scrolls we were interested in were not with the rest. I dispatched men to track those scrolls and retrieve them. My agents told me today only that they found the identity of the man who possessed them and promised I would have them tonight. When they told me the name Felix, I had completely forgotten about you until the meeting earlier. When you…" he stopped and paused. "Tonight at…" he paused again, and I rested the point of my knife on his shin again. "Let's just say I was expecting you to bring something other than what you did."

"Good enough for now. Second question, how did you manage the ceremony on Caeso without notice?"

A look of surprise crossed his face. "What? No! We…There was never…" He paused and shrugged. "I can't talk about any of this."

"This blood oath of yours is really getting on my nerves," I said. "Last chance to answer before I forcibly break its bonds. It will not be pleasant for you." I gave him my most evil grin.

"I doubt what's in store for me is pleasant either way," he replied stoically. "I know you will not leave me alive. If I thought my admission would buy me a quick death I would cooperate, but I really can't."

"Come now," I said. "I am not a cold-blooded killer. I have made a reputation for myself by keeping my word. And I do give you mine now, that should you tell me everything I need to know, I will do what I can to see you exiled rather than crucified. It may be so far from Egretia that you will have to go to the land of the Hyperboreans, but you will still have your life."

"Then kill me quickly, because I will not be able to tell you anything," he said sadly.

"Borax, hold him tightly, please." I sheathed my dagger and then unscrewed its pommel and extracted the pouch of herbs. I selected one of the fine razors I keep in a special compartment along its sheath. "You see," I explained while doing this, "I have analysed the herbs Zymaxis uses, I know his supplier, and I know about oaths, too. This time I came prepared with antidotes in case he makes me drink anything again. Yet for one who claims the oath is already blood-binding, well… we'll just have to get the antidote into your blood."

I sat on Philokrates' feet as Borax came behind him and held his torso in a bear hug. I pulled up his tunic to reveal his muscular thighs. "This will hurt," I said, and started to work with the razor. I drew the blade in intersecting lines along his skin, to form a sigil I knew.

"Please, you don't understand," cried Philokrates, "I really don't have any options. I would tell you all if I could."

"Oh, I do believe you," I said. "This is why I am doing this now.

You can prove me wrong by answering my question — how did you manage to do the ceremony on Caeso?" He only shook his head.

"Very well, we shall have to proceed." I tore a piece of his tunic, wrapped the seeds and herbs I had, and singed it with the torch. Starting my incantation now, I took the smouldering pack and started to rub it into the bloody sigil on his skin. I kept muttering the chant, ignoring the strangled cries from Philokrates, his twitching and spasming.

When I deemed it enough, I repeated my question, still holding the smouldering pack to his cuts.

"Stop this, man, please stop!" cried Philokrates. "I can feel it burning in my veins! I can't speak, it hurts!"

"Tell me how you did Caeso in!"

"I can't! I swear to you I can't!" His spasms were increasing now, but Borax still held him tightly.

I burst the burnt cloth and rubbed the hot seeds and burning herbs directly into his cuts. The sigil itself started to glow faintly, the blood now visibly pulsing in a bright red that had nothing to do with the moonlight. "Tell me about Caeso!"

"We never — *aargh!* — we never touched him!" he spat and screamed, then his whole body convulsed and shook. A spasm in his leg threw me off and even Borax had difficulty holding him down.

Philokrates cried out wordlessly again, a scream of anguish. Blood started to trickle from his nose and ears, and his red-shot eyes looked like they were about to pop out.

Which they then did, with a squishy plop, and hung by the strands of nerves on his cheeks. His next scream was cut short by a gushing of bloody vomit coming out of his mouth and nose. He jerked one last time and then just lay there, dead, with the sigil burning angrily on his thigh.

Well, one thing I was certain of, as I looked at the dead body lying in a pool of sewage, blood and vomit at my feet. Whatever other precaution I might take, I absolutely must avoid the blood oath.

CHAPTER XXVI

When I got up the next morning, I had no idea of the twists Fortuna had in store for me that day. Not having foreknowledge of things to come, I woke up late and ate lunch at home together with Borax, who had slept in one of the unused rooms in my house.

The night before, Borax and I had walked back further than the entry by which we had climbed down to the Cloaca Maxima, all the way to the major intersection of sewage lines under the Forum Egretium. We had emerged covered in blood and human effluence, looking like the public slaves who keep the Cloaca free from blockages. I had made a small offering at the temple of Cloacina, joining the line of sewage workers rather than that of the married men. I had also bought us both a long wash at the Baths of Sestropius. By the time we had made it home the eastern sky had begun to pink.

I started my business for the day rather predictably. I had three new names from the cabal meeting, one of whom I knew to be dead. Planning my options, I deemed the Forum to be unproductive. The young *incantator* — Duronius — was too young to attract the attentions of the gossips yet, and Rabirius the freedman was not a public figure. The criminal element was out for the moment, less I stumble on those who had been hired to get my head.

I therefore decided to try Sosius again, as the most likely to advance my investigation. Philokrates had proved a poor source of information, but from his assassins I knew he was after a scroll. No doubt this was the Rite of Pelegrinus I had retrieved from Ephemezica. I needed to know if the cabal had managed to get their hands on any other such scrolls, and if Sosius had any information at all about Philokrates or what he was in the market for. I also wanted to find out how Philokrates had found out about my being Sosius' agent.

When I ventured out that morning, I was accompanied by the ever watchful Borax. We stopped at his apartment so he could get a change of clothes — the tunic I had given him as replacement for the one he had worn to the sewers was far too tight for his size — and then made our way to the Basilica Antonia.

I was in luck; Sosius was in. "Are you planning on going into the *lanista* business, or is there another reason for that large specimen that follows you?" Sosius asked as we settled down in his office.

"It appears someone is really interested in the scrolls from Ephemezica, and in particular the ones I kept with me. Let's say that I now have a deadly interest in your customer list."

Sosius paled. "I trust you are unharmed, though? I assure you I had nothing to do with this."

"Oh, I trust you," I said, "But someone did find out I hold the interesting bits from the collection. I need to determine everything you know about who and why."

It turned out that Sosius had received some interest in the library I had acquired for him in Ephemezica. The description of the man he gave me matched Philokrates. It seems like the enquiry had come while I had been on Kebros. Sosius had not attached a special meaning to the encounter, as the man had not expressed a specific curiosity about the esoteric material in the library. One of his assistants, trying to be helpful, had given Philokrates the master index to the collection as soon as they had gotten the shipment from Baebius. It had seemed an innocent move on his part, a way to earn some coins on the side by promising Philokrates a first selection of the contents before they were fully reviewed by Sosius. When Philokrates had asked about the scrolls of *magia*, the assistant had mentioned that he had overheard Sosius and me talking about it.

So while this confirmed what I had known, it unfortunately got me no further. I tried another tack, questioning Sosius and his assistant whether they knew how Philokrates had found out about the library in the first place, and if they had sold them any other esoteric material in the past. The assistant, now quite distraught at having been caught accepting bribes and causing his master embarrassment, tried his best to please us by digging through old sales records and questioning the other junior clerks mercilessly. It turned out that Philokrates had made quiet enquiries after such items in the past. He had trodden carefully and bribed Sosius' employees with some shrewd sense — he had given them just enough to make sure they would report the interesting scrolls to him, but not enough to make them worry that he was after the *nefastum scientiam* scrolls and report his overtures to Sosius or the Collegium Incantatorum.

Going over the scrolls he had managed to buy in the past, we saw that he had definitely been interested in the unsavoury aspects of *nefastum scientiam*. This is of course highly regulated by the Collegium, and yet it has never stopped the black market from thriving. Sosius was a reputable dealer, and the scrolls he dealt with were borderline material, not enough to get him in real trouble. Well, not unless he thought he could get away with it.

The material that Philokrates had acquired from Sosius included treatises on the movement of stars, codices of translated terms and gods, and a dissertation of the nature of virgins. That last was of the *magia vita* kind, not the kind with Hellican drawings of what shepherds and shepherdesses do when they are not shepherding sheep.

None of that information was controlled or forbidden, but with the assumption that they had other sources and taken together and with what I knew of the cabal, these scrolls could spell some very disturbing rites.

* * *

I made Sosius agree to let me burn the scroll with the Rite of Pelegrinus. Some would say that destroying knowledge is a horrible thing, a crime. They would argue that all knowledge has its place in the world, that natural philosophies — no matter how horrid — have their role in increasing our understanding of the world around us.

Much as I dislike it, however, I am with the Collegium Incantatorum on this. If I had left the scroll with Sosius, it would eventually have made its way to some other *mentula* who would attempt to perform the rite. If I had surrendered the scroll to the Collegium, they would have turned on me and start asking uncomfortable questions. And besides, as Caeso had demonstrated, it would not really prevent some hapless idiot from attempting to perform the rite. And there was always the chance that my scroll contained the correct version, and that said hapless idiot might actually succeed. Not even the great Iovis Pater would protect us then.

No, better burn the thing and be done with it.

I made my way back to my house, wanting to be rid of the scroll as soon as possible. I wasn't too worried about Dascha; as she had demonstrated the day before, she was quite capable of dealing with those who persisted past her evil looks in gaining entry. Yet the thing weighed heavy in my mind, and I wanted to be free of it.

Dascha took Borax with her to the kitchen. He looked worried at first, her smile with its crooked and missing teeth not instilling confidence, but she promised to bake him special garlic bread rolls — guaranteed to increase a man's virility.

Once back in my study, I took out the scrolls I had kept from Sosius and set a heavy brazier burning. I read the scrolls again, my heart heavy with the task of destroying the centuries of knowledge enclosed in them. When I was sure I had learnt and understood as much as I could of the important aspects, there was no more use in delaying.

I started by ripping the scrolls carefully into strips and bits. I tried to tear across words and symbols, destroying the ink lines as much as I could. Some of these old scrolls were written much like *stigmas* are, with power in the ink itself.

After a while I had a large pile of paper and parchment scraps on my desk. I started feeding them carefully into the brazier, not wishing for the same mistake Caeso had made by leaving recognisable fragments behind. I gazed at the pieces of parchment crackling with strange colours, the smoke rising thickly. I decided to try an old augury trick. It was probably my least favourite subject in the Collegium — an irony, considering the profession I had ended up in — but along the way I had picked up other knowledge. There is power in signs and symbols, in patterns of natural phenomena. The power itself is usually easy to locate, yet even centuries' worth of books and rules about its interpretation cannot make it anything less than a highly subjective art.

And right now I was burning materials imbued with years of power, and the question on my mind was directly related to their content. I stared and stared into the flames, examining the way the fragments burst into flame and were consumed, tracing the patterns of smoke as it rose to the ceiling. And whether it was a real augury, or inhaling the smoke of the burnt ink, or my mind simply tricking me into seeing the things that I wanted to see, eventually I was transported....

Walking through the dense wood, I could hardly see the ground, for the faint moonlight did not penetrate the canopy of trees and a thick white mist was curling around my legs, obscuring roots. I tripped and fell, got up, walked on. Vague glimpses in rare breaks amidst branches offered me faint stars that were not enough to show me direction. Before me, around me, behind me, between the trees, all I saw was the fog. I kept walking, avoiding branches and roots, drawn inexorably towards my unwanted destination.

The clearing.

I took careful steps across the moonlit grass, but when I reached the other end I saw it was not a clearing, rather the edge of the forest on the side of a mountain. As I walked around the boulders at the clearing's edge, I found myself on a steep path, high up on the side of the mountain.

I kept walking along the path, climbing up, going ever higher and following Caeso, whom I knew to be ahead of me.

I reached the very top, where the path levelled and passed in a narrow gap between two huge slabs of granite.

It opened up to a wide ledge, overlooking the crater at the top of the mountain.

A faint red-orange glow was coming from it, and I could see in front of me the silhouettes of the two people I had followed here. One was Caeso, I was sure, though I have never seen him alive. The other I had seen in life, only a long time ago. When she turned to glance back, the silvery moonlight illuminated the high cheekbones, the clear skin and perfect eyes of my Helena.

Only, her skin was not clear and smooth, but marked with faint lines glowing in blue and red.

Just like Caeso's torso.

He grabbed her and lifted her and jumped, and I ran towards them, towards her outstretched hand reaching to me as the ground was crumbling under my feet, and we were all tumbling down to the fiery lake of Vulcanus, with the mountain collapsing in on us, and the hot air was singing my skin….

I cursed and withdrew my hand from the brazier, immersing my singed fingers in a cup of cold water.

So much for visions.

* * *

The vision, or perhaps just the smoke, left me with an incapacitating headache. I was debating with myself about the best course of action. While I was fairly certain of what had happened by now, that Caeso had been the chosen recipient of the Rite of Pelegrinus for the cabal, I still had no conclusive proof. I needed a way to entice a confession out of one of them — which, as last night's confrontation with Philokrates demonstrated, would be hard to get.

Being the recipient of the Rite, Caeso would have been granted tremendous power. Even without the training of an *incantator*, the sheer immensity of raw power at his fingertips would have made him the most powerful being alive. The price would have been a loss of humanity and sanity, although obviously he had paid a much higher price for the attempt.

Zymaxis had not chosen himself to be the recipient. He was probably aware of the risks involved. And yet he must have trusted in his ability to control Caeso after the completion of the ceremony. To grant someone else such power, he must have possessed compelling means to bend him to his will.

Means like the blood oath. Here again Philokrates had demonstrated, in a very unfortunate way for him, just how much control was Zymaxis able to exert on the members of the cabal. They were not puppets, as they were still imbued with some free will, but they did not possess full free choice for their actions.

Assuming that Philokrates' colleagues would be bound in a similar manner, and assuming that Zymaxis had made the choice for Caeso to receive the Rite of Pelegrinus, it seemed to me that the obvious way to both get a confession and deal with the cabal was to go after its head.

One slight problem stood in my way — I had never managed to track down Zymaxis' whereabouts outside of the cabal meeting.

And thus, proud of my cogitation despite my headache, having finally devised a clear path forward and about to set forth and see it implemented, I was caught unprepared for the bucket of piss that Fortuna dumped on my head.

The time was early evening, the last traces of blue still visible in the west while the first stars showed in the east, the gibbous moon yet to rise. I sat together with Dascha and Borax for an informal meal in the kitchen, a quicker and simpler arrangement than having Dascha wait on me in the *triclinium* while Borax ate with her in the kitchen. No proper Egretian master would dare be caught eating together with the slaves like that, but I wasn't a proper master and was eager to get on with tonight's business.

In appreciation of Borax's gladiatorial past, and no doubt in an attempt to entice him to come again, Dascha cooked everything with garlic. Lettuce salad with anchovy and garlic dressing, baked garlic bread buns, squid stuffed with pine nuts and garlic, and snails in coriander and garlic wine sauce — I did not ask where she'd gotten that last expensive delicacy on such short notice. While we were polishing off the last of the snails and getting ready for the sesame honey cakes — without garlic, I hoped — there came frantic knocking on the front door.

Borax and I looked at each other, and then made our way to the vestibule. We both held our daggers in our hands, and Borax carefully opened the little slit window in the door to peer outside.

"Finally! Is this the house of Felix the Fox?" I heard a reedy voice.

"Who wants to know?" asked Borax.

"I have a message for him from Cornelia!" said the voice.

Borax looked at me. "Only one," he said, "and looks harmless."

"Let him in."

Borax lifted the bar from the door and stepped aside for the man to enter. In stepped a dishevelled-looking man whom I recognised as one of Cornelia's slaves who had accompanied us on the voyage back from Kebros. He saw me and looked relieved. "Felix, please! Cornelia asks you come at once. It's Aemilia — she's been missing since last night!"

CHAPTER XXVII

Cornelia's house was situated high up on the Clivi Ulterior, as befitting her illustrious ancestry. This was the most exclusive district of Egretia, where the richest families kept their mansion-sized city houses. There are a few arterial streets radiating from the Forum and snaking their way up the sharp inclines of Vergu. From these, many smaller alleys branch off, running between blank walls to modest doors. The rich live their lives facing inward, with an austere facade to the street.

We marched up almost at a run, the distraught slave leading us first along the Vicus Petrosa of the Meridionali and then up from the intersection with the Via Crispa through the Clivus Incudis, going behind the Porticus Aemilia, up past the Aqua Sextiae and into the highest reaches of the Clivi Ulterior. At these heights, waters were not supplied by our main aqueduct, but by springs from Mons Vergu itself. The ultra-rich got clean water, clear air and unobstructed view, and were separated by an hour of strenuous uphill climb from the rest of the populace.

The slave got us inside and straight into Cornelia's study. This was the first time I had seen her without total self-composure. The woman who had flaunted social convention on the Kebric Isles was hardly recognisable in the one in front of me, pacing back and forth, hugging herself, hair dishevelled. She lifted her eyes to me when the slave showed us in, and I saw tears well up in her eyes. She drew a deep breath and composed herself by sheer force of will; the woman was not used to appearing vulnerable.

"Felix, I am glad you could come so quickly," she said. "It's Aemilia — she's disappeared and I fear for her life."

"Tell me everything from the beginning. Don't rush, try to remember every detail."

"She was unimpressed with you during our voyage back, as you might recall. One of her first acts when we returned was to search for that first edition of Liberalis you talked about. Once she got laughed out of the respectable book merchants, she came home absolutely fuming. Well, you've met her, that just made her even more determined. She started out to prove that you were a complete fraud. I learnt that she was aiming to solve Caeso's death and prove to her uncle that you are cheating him. When I found out, we had an argument over it. It was not proper behaviour for a young woman of her age, and far too dangerous, besides. Eventually, I forbade her to do anything about it." As Cornelia spoke the tempo of her speech increased, and story came gushing out without break.

"Then yesterday we got an invitation from my friend Caecilia Metella. Their son Quintus Aquilius won a prominent case in the extortion court, and the daughter Aquilia is the same age as Aemilia and a good friend to her. I was hoping that this would provide her with a distraction. Caecilia Metella and I have been thinking of young Quintus as a possible prospective husband for her. We wanted to see them together to know the match would be a good one, before Caecilia would get her husband to think it was his own idea. Last night was to be the perfect opportunity for this.

"We got there by the tenth hour of the day. It is not far from here, but we took the litter as I thought we might be coming back rather late. The party was a big affair, as young Quintus will be standing for election as a *quaestor* this year. I instructed Aemilia to catch Quintus Aquilius' eye and speak with him. I knew she was not enamoured with him, yet none of us ever are when we marry. It would be a good match if they get along, better than some other alternatives, and she understood this and cooperated.

"I must have lost track of her during the party. As celebrations finally wound down, after the desserts were served and the entertainment program finished, I went out to look for her. I could not find her, and when I found Aquilia she told me that Aemilia had complained about a headache rather early in the evening and had herself taken home in our litter.

"I spoke with the master of my litter bearers, and he told me he had carried her back by sunset. When I got home I knocked on her door, wishing to speak with her about the prospect of marrying Quintus Aquilius. She didn't answer, but I thought nothing of it at the time — it was rather late, and I assumed she was asleep.

"Then this morning she did not come for breakfast. I queried her slave girl, and it turned out that Aemilia did not spend the night here. She sent all her slaves away when she came, and left instructions not to be disturbed. When the slave girl came to check on her in the morning, her bed had not been slept in!" Cornelia finally paused for breath, the story having come gushing out without break.

"It seems that Aemilia made some other arrangements for last night, an assignation from which she never came back. The young fool is always getting herself in too much trouble! I fear that she was trying to show you up, started to investigate the dark business Caeso got himself tangled with, and managed to get herself drawn in. At first, I spoke with all the slaves in the house, tried myself to figure out where she might have gone to. I set out with a few of my more intelligent and trusted slaves to make enquires, but got nowhere.

"I know Aemilia had a low opinion of you, though I think she was wrong in that. She just does not handle being mocked well. You strike me as a different man. Honest may not be the right word, but I do not believe you are a charlatan. You have been looking into Caeso's death. If anyone can find out who she went to meet and what trouble she got into, it's you. Please, Felix, please get my daughter back to me!"

* * *

I asked Cornelia more questions about who Aemilia had

mentioned, who might she have gone to meet, but learnt little as the girl had not spoken on the matter with her mother after their row. Questioning the slaves and servants of the house revealed more information. They were quite eager to help, as distraught by the young mistress' disappearance as any member of the family would be.

Aemilia was usually accompanied by her body slave, an Assyrican girl named Naama, and one of the family's pool of guards. However, while the slaves had walked with her and could describe to me the places and some of the people she had met with, they were not privy to her conversations. By piecing together those descriptions, I gathered she had met with Caeso's friends and had only done preliminary investigations into other sources. I knew already that she had met with Sosius, and could now add Porcius and Lutatius. I also got vague descriptions of other people I did not recognise, although from the general description of the places where they had met and Aemilia's attitudes, I gathered she was taking a social approach. Not having the background in *magia*, nor indeed the details of his death, Aemilia would not know what to look for. Her angle was Caeso's friends, trying to find out how he'd gotten involved in this business in the first place. The girl was shrewd, if not particularly wise.

I do not believe in coincidences, as I have mentioned. I discounted that this was one of the many random acts of violence that plague our city at night. That left the obvious conclusion — she had met someone who did not appreciate her poking her nose into their business. What and whom did she uncover, that would lead to her disappearance?

I started with the most direct course of action. "Could you bring me some personal items of Aemilia's?" I asked Cornelia. "Four things she uses or wears daily, like a favourite hair-pin or garment. I will also need access to your kitchen, cleared of slaves."

She knotted her brows and paused for a moment, then gave instructions to the slaves to bring me some of Aemilia's belongings. Soon I was alone in the *domus'* very large kitchen, with only Cornelia watching me from the doorway. I cleared the large wooden table which the cook used as a work bench, and spread Aemilia's effects on it. There was an exquisite bone hair-comb, a short sleeping tunic that still had her smell on it, a polished silver mirror and her favourite wax tablet and stylus on which she drafted her poetry.

I took a small bronze spoon, and with a nod of apology to Cornelia, hammered it flat with an iron skillet. I filled the skillet with wine next, and heated up a mixture of sharp spices in it and some blood from a cut of meat I found, chanting under my breath all the time. The major disadvantage of not having studied properly at the Collegium was that I was not privy to the proper methods of augury. I did, however, have enough of an understanding to be able to pick up a lot of folk practises and incantations during my travels and years in the business, remove the superstitions, enhance them with proper procedures, and distil them to working essentials.

When the blood-wine mix was properly ready, I rubbed each of the four items against the flattened spoon and placed it on the table, marking the corners of a square. I dipped the spoon in the mix and traced a circle with it, enclosing the arrangement. I climbed on top of the table and tied the spoon with a piece of long string to one of the rafters. It hung down as a pendulum, and I tried to get it as close as I could to the middle of the circle made up by Aemilia's possessions and red goo.

"You might want to step back," I said to Cornelia. Still standing on the table, I started the main part of the incantation. As the tempo of the chanting increased the spoon began to swing on its string, pow-ered by the flow of *magia* coursing through it. When the makeshift pendulum was in full swing and without stopping my chant, I lifted the heavy skillet and started to drip the gooey wine and blood mixture down the string.

The idea with such ceremonies is that the pattern traced by the dripping red goo will indicate the location of the desired object. When looking for people, using their personal effects and the right inflection can give quite detailed information. I have done these ceremonies a fair number of times in the past with much success. I was sure of my methods, unconventional as they may have been; once, when looking for a stolen set of precious citrus-wood bowls, the resulting pattern had such an uncanny resemblance to the profile of the house's steward that he collapsed into tears immediately and confessed to the theft.

Not tonight. The spoon started to spin erratically, as if the string was held by a spasming man with the falling disease; it emitted a keening noise that set my teeth on edge. It splattered the red mixture all over the kitchen, slapped my right knee once painfully, and then broke the string and flew straight into the silver mirror. The force of impact was so great that it skewered the mirror and impaled itself into the thick wooden table.

I cursed profusely as I climbed down, only stopping the stream of invective when I saw Cornelia's face. "I do apologise," I said. "This ceremony is usually infallible in locating the missing. However, it seems that Aemilia is now being shielded from scrying. If we needed any more proof that this was not a random disappearance but connected to Caeso's dark death, this is it."

The hour was getting very late by the time I left Cornelia's *domus*, and there was no point in attempting to track down the people Aemilia had met with. Places of business were closed for the day, and the people ensconced in their homes with instructions to the door slaves not to admit anyone unknown.

I would have to set out early tomorrow. I decided I would not waste time with Corpio, even though I knew Aemilia had gone to meet with him and his steward; I believed they had already told me all they knew. Instead, I would have to track down the other people she had met; those I already had spoken with and the others for whom I just had descriptions, partial names and a few addresses, mostly for private residences. She had kept her meetings to socially acceptable establishments and circumstances — which would make it harder for me, as I was not part of those circles.

There was just very little I could do for Aemilia this night. But as much as I needed sleep in preparation for the day to come, I got almost none of it, plagued by heavy dreams of her fate.

* * *

The next day we set out before dawn as planned, and visited the people on my short list of suspects. I tracked a few of those Aemilia had met, though far from all. I spoke with them, some pleasantly and some more forcibly, yet learnt little new. Yes, Aemilia has been asking questions about Caeso; but most of them did not know what he had been involved with in the first instance, so had not been able to provide her with anything relevant. Some tried to brush me off, some tried helpful suggestions of where I should look, suggestions that I dismissed as useless or unlikely.

As the day wore on, my heart sank further and further. A dreadful shadow in the back of my mind crept ever forward, eclipsing every other thought, though I tried my best to ignore it. One person who should have been on the list I got from Aemilia's slaves, but wasn't, one man I could not find anywhere in the city. And tonight was the night I was to confront the cabal, with the blood oath and initiation I felt ill prepared for.

We got back to my home at dusk to prepare for the night ahead. We were dead tired, yet could not stop to rest. In order to keep going, I made us a special brew, one I had learnt in the legions. It involved boiling of certain herbs — leaves, stems, berries and dirty roots — together with some minor incantations. The result is a drink that looks and tastes like boiled mud, bitter and nasty like a mule's kick to the gut, but it does keep a man alert for hours. Borax sniffed at it and made a face, unimpressed. When he saw me laugh and swig the foul concoction, he had no other option to preserve his manly image except to gulp it all down.

We left after sunset. Centuries ago, our ancestors had built a proper road leading up from the Forum to the very peak of Vergu. The road leaves our city walls at the Porta Alta and snakes around the mountain in a full circle. We used to hold state funerals at the very top. These days, funerals — like that of Caeso — are held a short distance outside of the walls, in a place where the ground presents a wide ledge with good views inland. Beyond that ledge the climbing gets rough, and the road is poorly maintained. To climb to the very top would take a healthy man almost four hours. In daylight. We were going by torchlight, any traces of light having long crept out of the sky by the time we left the walls. We would make it just on time for midnight, although I suspected most of the cabal would already be there. Ready and waiting for me.

CHAPTER XXVIII

When the full moon rose, we snuffed our torches. The light was sufficiently bright for us to see the path, and I did not wish to advertise our approach. I left Borax with instructions to hang back, stick to the shadows and wait for my call. There were no signs of torches behind us, as we were probably the last to arrive. I wanted to keep Borax as a surprise. He was clearly not used to this kind of sneakery and his huge bulk was conspicuous, but I felt I needed all the help I could get tonight.

We were on the north face of Vergu now, getting close to the final ascent. The moon was shining brightly, illuminating the badly maintained track. Years of neglect and disuse, exposure to the elements, storms and the occasional shifting of Vulcanus sleeping under the mountain had eroded the path down to a very narrow strip of uneven white stones, set between overhanging and dropping cliffs.

We made the turn that led to the last stretch of winding, slippery stairs carved into the mountain rock. The climb was just like in my vision of yesterday, which was unsurprising, as I had made this ascent in years past.

We reached the last step leading to the deep ledge at the top. This open space faces east, overlooking our great city. At the sides were the massive slabs of hard granite, so sheer they could be climbed no further. At the back I saw the narrow gap that leads to the crater at the centre of the peak. There was a fiery glow coming from within, though thankfully it looked as if coming from braziers and not from down the bowels of the crater.

I stood for a moment, catching my breath, looking out on the dark sea mirroring the silvery moon and the many small dots of fires down in Egretia. I gave the last instructions to Borax.

I put my hand inside my long tunic sleeve, found the sheath of my dagger strapped to my forearm, and extracted the *res magiae* — the wooden toothpick wrapped in the two strands of hair and sealed with blood. I held it in between thumb and forefinger for a moment, then broke it and dropped the broken pieces, ground them into the rock them with my heel.

I turned to face the narrow gap, and walked in.

* * *

I emerged on the other side to see the members of the cabal. Seven figures next to two tripod-mounted braziers turned to look at me as I stepped out of the other side of the narrow passage.

"Ah, Felix, right on time," said Zymaxis. Standing around him in a semi-circle I saw Gaetanicus and Fufidius, Duronius, Rabirius Capilanus, and two of the men I had seen in the first meeting but not in the second — the fat merchant and the seaman.

"You'll be glad to know we have formally approved your application, and will not need to kill you." He said this with a smile, and I took it as an attempt at humour. "We were quite impressed with the offering you made — we already have some ideas about how to utilise it! But, to business. I believe you have met everybody here, with the exception of Tiberius Pomponius" — he indicated the merchant — "and Numerius Otacilius" — the captain. We exchanged nods and taut smiles.

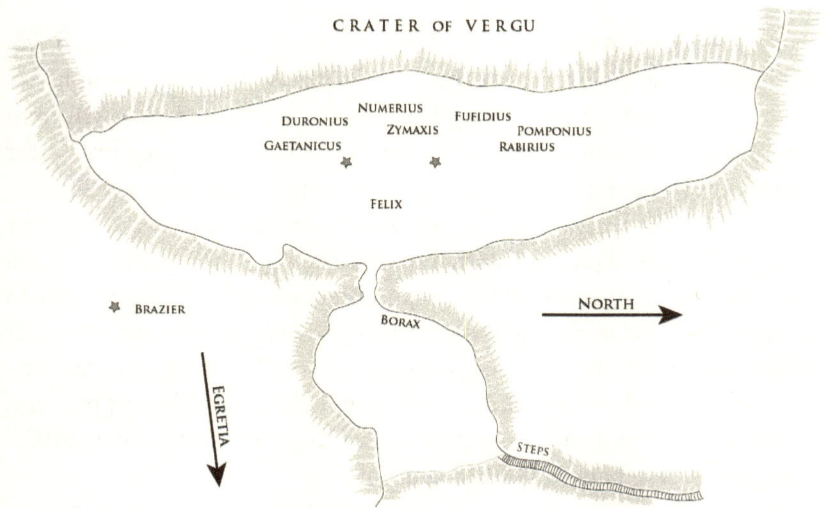

Zymaxis resumed. "Men! We are now prepared to finally embark on the next major step of our vision for a new Egretia. We are moving at last, not just hanging back in the shadows with silent preparations. Initiates! Approach, and make ready to take the blood oath."

I was standing where I had come in, a few steps into the ledge between the narrow entry and the edge of the crater. The seven men were arranged in front of me, their faces lit by the moonlight and the burning braziers, and behind them gaped the open crater. Then from behind me to the left I heard footsteps. I turned to look, and saw a man approaching from the dark recesses of the stone walls to stand next to me, his face half-anticipated and recognised in an instant.

Drusus.

The man who had been missing from the list of leads Aemilia had visited, yet the one most expected.

And behind him, walking as if in a trance, was the muffled figure of Aemilia with her hands tied, led by him with a length of rope.

Drusus gave me a curious look, then nodded at me and came to stand next to me. Only then did I realise how tense my muscles were. If he would have tried to expose me as the investigator of Caeso's death — well, it was not like I had a cunning plan in coming here tonight. Thinking about my idiotic lack of proper preparations, I just hoped that my *cognomen* of *felix* would hold true.

"You two are our newest initiates. Our cabal is still small, yet our power is growing. With the contributions you have brought us, you have guaranteed yourself a place at the new Egretia that will soon rise. Tonight is a new beginning for you, and a new beginning for everybody, us here and those sleeping unaware in the city below.

"Tonight we attempt to awaken Vulcanus. The ceremony has been well researched, and with Luna above us in this month sacred to Maia, we shall fulfil all the requirements carefully. We are set to harness the power that lies under this mountain, and use it to our advantage in forcing the new order. This will be the spearhead, the fulcrum with which we shall bring down the strangling oppression of the collegia and open the path to a future unfettered by artificial constraints." He paused before continuing.

"Sadly, we are missing one member of our group," said Zymaxis, "but we shall have to start the ceremony without him. You see, it appears that our dear colleague Philokrates gave his life to our cause." I tensed as he paused again for effect. "He gave his life instead of betraying us. I know that through the power of the blood oath that binds us. I also know something about the circumstances in which he died — and that it is now time to deal with the traitor amongst us!"

* * *

'Cack!' was the only thing that went through my mind as I reached inside the sleeve of my tunic to grasp my dagger and hoped that Borax was paying attention before I leaped… But I stopped.

Zymaxis turned his back on us. Beyond him I saw Duronius, who was standing at the edge of the semi-circle behind Gaetanicus, raise his right arm and clench his fingers in a complex pattern into a fist. Gaetanicus stiffened, then his arms and legs spread out as if pulled by invisible chains in four different directions as he floated gently upwards off the rough floor of the ledge, matching the hand motions of Duronius.

"Look and understand!" Zymaxis said over his shoulder to Drusus and me. "Our group is not child's play, but deadly serious. We have even attracted the attention of the *Fetiales*," he spat. He turned back to the floating Gaetanicus, "Isn't that so, traitor? Did you think I would not find out? Did you really believe you could hide your true motives from me? I knew from the moment you joined us that your loyalties to Egretia never wavered. I knew all along that you sought to bring us down, and that you would need to be disposed of before we made any real moves. I only wish I would have done it sooner, and saved Philokrates' life. *He* was a true follower! *He* gladly gave his life for our cause! You… wretched worm! You only thought to destroy us, destroy the bright future we plan for Egretia! I would have sacrificed you tonight, except that the ritual requires virgin blood. We will keep you like this, for you to witness the culminations of our long preparations, the rise of the new dawn. We will leave you as nothing more than the dog that you are." Zymaxis spat at the ground in front of Gaetanicus, having exhausted his diatribe.

As Zymaxis was speaking I was doing quick mental calculations. When I had come in, it was myself against eight members, with Borax ready to jump in. Assuming I could move first in total surprise, we'd still be facing three or four each. However, if Zymaxis really thought Gaetanicus a traitor, he was the enemy of my enemy and potentially a grateful ally. If he was as quick of mind and body as his training suggested, I could make it a well-trained three against a very surprised six. Much better odds. And besides, Zymaxis was really getting on my nerves.

So while everyone's attention was on Zymaxis and Gaetanicus, I drew my knife and stabbed Drusus in the guts, withdrew the blade, and hurled it at Duronius before Drusus even began to scream. The throw was an awkward one and I only clipped Duronius with my dagger; it did not embed itself cleanly in his flesh. Still, it was enough to break his concentration, and Gaetanicus fell to the ground.

I rushed past Drusus, who sank to his knees, to retrieve my knife from where it fell at Duronius' feet, as Borax, observing hidden from the opening, rushed in. I slammed into Duronius and pushed him away so that he stumbled and fell, then bent down to pick up my dagger.

I looked up at the scene before me and saw a snapshot of the cabal regaining its senses. Zymaxis drew a curved knife and was yelling at them to get me, Numerius had a nasty look and a nastier-looking long dagger, Fufidius was gathering the energies for an incantation, Pomponius was still a bit bewildered but was reaching inside his tunic for a knife, while Rabirius Capilanus held his out in a shaking hand.

"I hope I didn't make a mistake," I said to Gaetanicus as I helped him to his feet.

"Idiot, I had it under control," he said, though as he looked at me I could see the same quick calculation and resolution behind his eyes. He drew his dagger and stood next to me facing the others.

By now Duronius was scrambling back to his feet and preparing an incantation, and I saw Borax rushing in with his blade at the ready.

"*Viri! Impetus!*" Gaetanicus yelled next to me and nearly made me jump. I thought it was a bit over-enthusiastic of him to give the two of us the same attack command one would give a legion, when my gaze was drawn to the cliffs behind the men of the cabal, where what looked like solid rock suddenly moved aside, and from a hidden niche jumped out four men in full military mail armour and swords.

What followed next was utterly chaotic in a way only those who have experienced battle can appreciate. Gaetanicus clashed with Numerius Otacilius, but was being beaten back as Zymaxis leapt upon him as well, yelling wildly in a language I did not know; the four soldiers were repulsed by Fufidius whose hands streamed sticky fire at the first of them, sending him screaming to his death as he stumbled over the ledge; Borax was beset upon by Pomponius and Rabirius, more because he was in their way to escape than any undue bravery.

Duronius seemed to have developed a sudden grudge against me. He sent a gust of wind that knocked me flat on my back, then picked a handful of gravel and threw the pebbles at me one by one, speeding them like small *ballista* missiles that exploded almost like those of full-scale military equipment.

Dodging and rolling, I looked for an opening, and when one of the braziers was knocked down and sparks flew between us and made him recoil, I jumped forward, too close now for his missiles, ignoring the tiny burns on my skin, I plunged my dagger deep, deep into his shoulder. He sank to his knees with a cry as I pulled my knife back, and might have cried for mercy if I had not cut with my dagger again, and this time with better aim I slit his throat, feeling the spray of his hot blood on my arms.

I looked around. Gaetanicus was still battling both Numerius and Zymaxis, who both turned out to be vicious knife fighters, and were managing with concerted efforts to push him towards the precipice. Beyond him I could see Borax stepping over the recumbent body of Rabirius and thrusting at Pomponius; his gladiatorial skill left no doubt about the expected length of that engagement. Further along I saw Fufidius, whom I had thought to be a third rate *incantator*, holding his own against the trained legionaries. His fingers streamed trails of fire like whips, and where they touched the fire seemed to stick and ignite the rock itself. The men could not close with him, their shields no match to his sticky flames. As I watched, he caught another with a sudden spurt, his screams horrifying even as they turned into gurgles as the flesh melted from his face, his bones crackling; the stench of burnt human body mixed with the acrid smell of *magia* is something I do not ever want to experience again.

I turned and thought to aid Gaetanicus when I heard behind me a voice breaking as it cried, "Stop!" and then again, cutting through the noise, "STOP!"

I turned and felt a chill as I saw Drusus, tottering on his feet, the side of his tunic soaked with blood, holding Aemilia with a knife to her throat, dangerously close to the edge.

His cry worked, as everyone's attention was momentarily on him. The fighting stopped, everybody frozen in momentary indecisiveness.

"Don't do this, Gnaeus Drusus," I said, "there is still a chance for you–"

"Shut up!" he yelled back. "Just shut up! All of you stop or I throw the bitch down!" I saw Aemilia's eyes, saw the trance that had bound her before was now replaced with fear.

I dropped my dagger and spread my arms at my sides, took a slow step towards him, "I'll make sure you walk, Drusus, if you just let her go–"

"Don't come closer! You stay right there!" he screamed and waved the knife at me.

Aemilia took advantage of his moment of distraction when the knife was no longer at her throat, elbowed him in the wound at his side and jumped forward. But Drusus with his left hand managed to claw at her long hair and yank her back so hard she fell down at his feet.

"*Stultus fellator*," I heard Fufidius behind me. I cast a glance back, heard him utter words of power, saw him raise his leg and stamp his foot down. A crack in the stone ledge leapt from his foot and sped towards us, forked as it neared the edge. I turned and saw the stone shelf on which we stood crumble, slide back into the gaping mouth of the crater. I saw Aemilia cry out and reach for me even as I stumbled and reached for her hand, too late. She reached out to me, arms outstretched beyond my reach just like in my vision at the sibyl of Kebros. I saw the stones of the ledge tumble beyond the cliffs into the crater, and Drusus with them.

But not Aemilia.

Frozen in space, I stretched and reached out, clasped her hand, drew her to me. I saw the stones under me crumble and fall, yet I stood with Aemilia in my arms on air, even as Drusus' body crashed on the jagged rocks below.

I turned and saw Araxus hovering above the ledge. I walked, without looking down, without thinking of the nothing I was stepping on, back onto the wide ledge.

Fufidius recovered quickly, and with a snarl went to reassert his dominance. Two streams of liquid fire again erupted from his hands, this time far longer, thicker and brighter than before. He poured all his might into them, swinging them like whips to envelop Araxus.

Araxus caught them in his hands, let them envelop his arms, drew them up like snakes spiralling up to his shoulders. He flexed his arms, and the whiplash made Fufidius stumble forward. I saw the look of consternation on Fufidius' face, the beads of sweat on his forehead, and still he tried, pouring everything he had into a fire that was strong enough to melt granite.

He gave it everything, until he had nothing left. And Araxus, both his eyes now jet black, laughed, and with his laughter came gushing forth all the flames he had drawn from Fufidius, spewing forth from his mouth to envelop their poor originator till all that was left was a pool of molten slag where Fufidius had stood.

Gaetanicus was also one to recover quickly, and while we stood stupefied looking at the battle of *incantatores*, he took the chance to knock both Numerius and Zymaxis down.

* * *

We stood together, breathing hard, looking at the corpses and beaten men around us. More soldiers poured onto the ledge from the same opening we had come through, bound and gagged the men of the cabal who were still alive, attended to the wounded and the dead. They had been waiting hidden along the path leading up, with orders to let anyone come up unhindered and allow no one to go down.

I held Aemilia until her shock passed, turned to crying, stopped. I left her with the medic to ensure her health. I found Araxus — his right eye now back to green, his left as black as ever — and thanked him. His face was grey, his brow covered with perspiration and his muscles shaking from the exertion of the powerful magics he had performed.

"Next time," he told me, "let me know you plan to be so far out of the city when you activate the signal. I could have come with you. I like a dramatic entrance, but the time and effort to get here nearly cost you your stupid life."

I left him and stood at the edge again, looking at the broken body of Drusus on the rocks far below me. I heard a man come stand next to me.

"I must say I did not expect what you did," Gaetanicus said. "I had infiltrated this cabal months ago, getting ready to expose all their recruits. Zymaxis kept his secrets tightly, always tasking us individually, rarely letting us share our progress all together. I had to wait till he gathered us all, finally ready to act, to be sure I got everyone. When you came asking to join us, I thought you were just another conspirator. When I found out you were asking questions about me, I thought you might need to be silenced. I am glad it turned out this way, though I still don't understand why you came to us in the first place."

"I was asked by Marcus Quinctius Corpio, the Rhone of Fish, to look at the death of his son Caeso. A cabal performed an ancient forbidden rite on him. That's how I found out about Zymaxis and his followers."

Gaetanicus looked at me blankly. "Caeso who?"

CHAPTER XXIX

It was midday of the *Ides* of *Maius* by the time I collapsed on my bed, utterly exhausted. So tired, I fell right into a dreamless sleep even though I was left with more questions than answers.

I had spoken long with Gaetanicus the previous night, and had even been allowed to question the surviving members of the cabal in his presence. I had described Caeso to him, and he recalled the youth in passing. 'A boy,' he said, 'accompanied Drusus once, then was gone and never seen again.'

Pomponius had been severely wounded, and had died without waking up. I had questioned Rabirius next, but he had not remembered Caeso. Numerius had refused to answer any questions, and although he had been wounded I was too tired to try anything with him.

Zymaxis had survived, as well, and relatively unharmed, as Gaetanicus managed to subdue him in the final fight. He had been lying trussed and gagged when I had approached him, a baleful look in his eyes. Two soldiers had been stationed over him, swords drawn and ready to strike should he only twitch the wrong way.

I had removed his gag and he had spat at my face. "I should have realised you were naught but a worm, a spineless lackey!"

"Not a lackey, just a sensible citizen of Egretia. I have seen enough of crazy *incantatores* and have no wish to blow my home up in a volcanic eruption."

"You understand nothing! You see nothing!" he had shot back at me. "A small man with a small mind, no sense of possibilities. Why I even allowed you to live in the first place I do not know; I should have realised no one like you would have the courage, the smarts to approach us–"

"I am only here to talk about Caeso and what you did to him," I had interrupted.

He had paused in blank surprise. "Who?"

"Caeso, the young friend of Drusus. You know, the one you performed the Rite of Pelegrinus on."

He had looked at me for a moment with knotted brows. "You must be deluded, mad as well as an idiot. Why would I perform that rite on anyone?"

"You wanted a way to bring down Egretia, did you not? A man under your control whose life force had been replaced with the raw power of the six elements would have given you a way to achieve this, no less than awakening Vulcanus."

He had shaken his head sadly. "Well, perhaps I did see something appropriately devious in you…. If only you applied your mind to our cause instead of betraying us for petty cash…. But no. We never tried that path."

"And Caeso?"

"A young man, friend of Drusus?" I had nodded and he had continued. "He came once with Gnaeus Drusus, when I was less discriminate about recruiting. He showed an interest in joining but I thought him a dilettante, and was confirmed when he showed the next time with his girlfriend. I told him never to bother showing his face again. It was evident that he lacked the force of character to commit himself; he was after excitement, entertainment, and would not — could not — stay true to our cause. We dismissed him promptly, and without cause for regret. If someone performed the Rite of Pelegrinus upon him, it was not us."

It had been the eighth hour of the night when I had finished questioning the survivors. Though Aemilia had recovered quickly and wanted to go home immediately, we had all been too tired and sore after the battle. It had been too dark to climb down the treacherous path along the Verguvian cliffs in our sorry state. The soldiers had kindly given us blankets, and we had huddled in a corner. Araxus had sat down with legs crossed and a straight back, watching over us. Something profound had changed in him, or perhaps I had just been too tired and had wanted to believe this. Aemilia, Borax and I had slept fitfully on the hard rocks for the remaining five short hours of the summer night.

By the first light of morning we had started down the mountain, escorted by armed soldiers sent by Gaetanicus. It had been a long way down, which after the eventful night had felt not much easier than the climb up. We had made our way to Cornelia's house on the Clivi Ulterior, and I had insisted on bringing Aemilia to her mother personally, despite the armed guard. They had fallen into each other's arms in tears of relief, and I had excused myself.

Araxus and Borax had accompanied me to my home. We had walked in silence. Araxus had bade me goodbye when we neared my house, turned and continued on his way. I had dismissed Borax, wishing nothing but a long sleep.

* * *

I woke up an hour before sunset and went to the Baths of Mauritius in the Campus Civicus. Sore and still dirty, I hired a slave to oil and scrape me thoroughly with a *strigil*, and then spent a long time in the warm and hot plunges. Once I felt sufficiently clean and relaxed, I paid for a deep and relaxing massage.

Body restored, I let my mind roam free. Last night had put me right back at the beginning. I had been so certain I had figured out what had happened to Caeso, how the cabal had tried to perform the Rite of Pelegrinus, and the cause of their failure through the misinterpretation of the *Aten*. I had really just gone for a confirmation, a confession.

And yet I had been wrong.

I might have doubted Zymaxis' account. I had no way to force the truth from him, no time for either incantations or simple torture. But I didn't. My gut feeling, after having questioned many a man, said that Zymaxis was not lying in Caeso's account, at least not then at the top of Vergu when he faced his defeat. He really never had paid the youth much attention.

The other members of the cabal could not have spoken, either, as evidenced by Philokrates. Gaetanicus, having access to the full backing and resources of the *Fetiales*, had managed to avoid being bound by the blood oath. He was left as a free agent. By the time Zymaxis had realised this, he had thought he would be able to use him. When Philokrates had disappeared, and Zymaxis must have had a connection through the blood-bond to know he was dead, he had assumed Gaetanicus had been the traitor responsible.

Gaetanicus, free of the bond and satisfied with the turn of events, had no reason to lie to me about Caeso. He had plans and resources to deal with the cabal that night, and while my involvement had been an unexpected turn of events, it seemed like he had under-estimated Fufidius. Araxus and I may have changed the course of the show-down, but in the end he had reached his desired goal. When I asked him to keep the Corpio family name and mine out of it, he was happy to oblige. More glory for him.

So I had no reason to think he would lie about Caeso, or sup-port Zymaxis on that one point. Not that I would normally trust our master-spies, but I was not asking about state secrets. And he struck me as an honourable man.

And yet... I had amassed a volume of evidence. Caeso had been tattooed with all the right markings for the Rite of Pelegrinus. I had found out from Famnius that he had access to the library of the Collegium Incantatorum. I had found traces of the scrolls and inks in the cave under the Pharos, a cave I'd learnt from Mahatixa that he had frequented.

So how? And who?

Absent a cabal, how had Caeso been murdered?

It was dark by the time I left the baths, and I was ravenous. I made my way back home, to a warm stew cooked by Dascha. A full stomach and a good night's sleep would get my thinking out of its circuitous rut.

I woke up the next day refreshed in mind and body. I always think better when I walk, so I took a wax tablet and stylus for scribbling and set out. I wrote down pieces of the puzzle, moved them around, drew arrows and lines. I reviewed everything I had found, took a critical look at what I knew, what I assumed to be connected. I ran my mind back over every meeting, every detail I'd gotten about Caeso. His behaviour last year, his voyage to Kebros, the sibyl and what he might have experienced on top of Mons Krodus. I now knew Drusus had hidden information from me, told me only such details as he had thought I would find out regardless, but was he connected to Caeso's death?

I reflected on the testimony of Mahatixa, the street mime with whom Caeso had been in love, the one who had rejected him. I thought of Porcius and Lutatius, his friends who had seen his health deteriorate, physically and mentally. I recalled what Corfidius and Opimius, Publius Corpio's men on Kebros, had told me. I speculated about Famnius, who seemed at first to have been keen to work with an enthusiastic youth and then had felt betrayed.

I tried to put up a picture of Caeso, a sequence of events for the last few months of his life. I did this while pounding the pavements of our city, resting occasionally in the shade of a tree near a public fountain, or stopping to get a bite of food or drink from a street vendor. By afternoon I found myself on the wharves of the Campus Civicus. I was sitting with my feet dangling over the edge of the walled shoreline, the wax tablet lying open next to me, the scribbles by now a complete mess.

My mind was running in circles. I had a dead body, absent a killer. I had a necromantic rite, absent a cabal to perform it. I had many pieces of the puzzle, but was absent the picture connecting them. I was missing some key insight that would make everything fall into place.

I gazed out across the waters of the bay. A warm summer day, the dazzling brilliance of the sky reflected in the calm surface. Many boats and ships were out, rhythmic drumming setting the pace for the rowers and echoing all the way to the shore. Beyond them, the opening to the wide oceans where ships put up their large, square sails. Those fortunate enough to have an on-board *incantator* filled their sails immediately, but most had to work and tack with oars until they picked up wind and speed.

And towering above them, on its own small rocky island, the Pharos, the lighthouse marking the entry to the Bay of Egretia. It was the tallest structure in our city, raised as a solid block of marble by Iunius Brutus in a feat of incomparable control of *magia*. Its light was so bright it could be seen for miles even in broad daylight. Such was its power that lasted through the ages, that I could feel the tingling on my skin even from where I was sitting on the other side of the bay.

And suddenly I understood.

* * *

We were sitting in Corpio's mansion on the Septentrionali, comfortably reclining on the couches of the *triclinium*. It was the evening of the second day after the *Ides* of *Maius*. I had sent word early to the key people affected, and was satisfied to see that all the important individuals of this case had gathered here tonight.

Corpio was reclining on the central couch, with Gnaeus Drusus Scaevola, the father of Caeso's friend, in the *locus consularis* — the place of honour — next to him. Typheus was allowed to stand at the back behind his master. Cornelia and Aemilia were sitting on the left hand couch next to Corpio, and I reclined together with Gaetanicus on the right-hand couch, sipping my *mulsum* while they all looked expectantly at me.

"It all started last summer, when Caeso fell in love with a street mime," I began. "He was immature and foolish, perhaps, but that is how the hearts of young people work. He knew there was no future in it, which perhaps made him all the more attracted to her. She rejected him at first, as she was just as aware as he was about the futility of such a relationship. Eventually, she succumbed to his charms. You must have suspected something," I addressed Corpio, "when you sent him away to Kebros."

Corpio nodded. "I thought it was something of the sort. I thought of him as a spoiled child with his toys taken away, wanted him to grow up. Now I wish I never did."

"These things have a way of finding their course," I said gently, "even when we try to circumvent the Fates. You also sent the son of your friend Gnaeus Drusus together with him. He was a man full of life, with a bright future ahead of him, and I imagine you both believed it would be a good influence."

"He was very ambitious," said Drusus' father, looking haggard. The realisations that had come with his son's recent death weighed heavily upon him.

"The two boys toured around the Kebric Isles. From the accounts I gathered, it seemed at first that Caeso was inconsolable, a young man with a flair for the dramatic, pining for his lost love. And then something changed. This was the time you were there, too, you must have seen it," I looked at Cornelia and Aemilia.

"Indeed, although I attributed it just to his heart healing," said Cornelia.

"I always thought my cousin was soppy," from Aemilia. "Even as a child he would get excited over many things, only to lose interest quickly."

"Well, it seemed he found a new thing to occupy his mind, a new outlet for his excitement. Young Marcus Corpio, Publius' son, told Caeso and Drusus about a mysterious *lamia* on one of the isles. The two of them went there, although the old woman turned out to be no monster. She was a sibyl, a prophetess sitting on an ancient spring of power, and they found her and received their visions. While we can never know what each young man saw in his vision, we know that both climbed the Mons Krodus a few short days later." I stopped to take another sip of wine and organise my thoughts. I had the big mosaic of events clear in my mind, yet I knew some pieces to be forever missing.

"Our people have always been worshipping the *numina*, the faceless gods and presences that rule our world. Our religious orders are charged with worshipping and placating them, and our *incantatores* study the energies that seep from them into our world. Some say that these *numina* are nothing but the energies of *magia*, with no sentience behind them. Some say the *incantatores* are only the pawns of the *numina*, blindly acting out their parts to the amusement of the gods. Be that as it may, just like our city is nestled in the arms of Vergu under which Vulcanus sleeps, the top of Kebros is open to the vastness of sky and air, a stormy place where the presence of Iovis Pater can be felt. I believe both young men climbed the mountain following their vision at the sibyl's, and both found the shrine on top. What they experienced of the *numina* there… awakened a new life in them. The two youths came down that mountain charged with a clear purpose, in search of true power." Another sip to ease my parched throat.

"They started to seek power upon their return to Egretia. Drusus must have stumbled on Zymaxis' cabal, although I do not know how. I do know he tried to get Caeso involved as well, but Caeso showed no real interest in joining the cabal and was never admitted to it." I looked at Gaetanicus, who nodded.

"I followed that tenuous link to the cabal because of the way he died, you see. I recognised the signs of the Rite of Pelegrinus when I inspected his body. They are unmistakable. There was a tracery of tattoos above his heart and on his chest, and when I cut under his skin I found his heart had turned into a large stone ruby." I saw Corpio shudder at the memory, and the rest shudder at the sacrilege of desecrating a dead body. "The tale of Pelegrinus is one told to aspiring *incantatores*, a tale of caution about attempting the *magia vita terminalis*. By now it is mostly legend, and the Heart of Ruby — its most famous characteristic — bordering on myth. Caeso, perhaps, was in a way seeking to heal and fortify his own broken heart.

"I had, almost by chance, managed to get a copy of the Rite of Pelegrinus. It was in the same library Zymaxis had sent Philokrates to retrieve from Ephemezica. It has been thoroughly destroyed," I added to calm Gaetanicus, who perked up at this. "It confirmed that the markings and tattoos could only mean the Rite of Pelegrinus. But this rite, you see, requires a cabal of eleven initiates to perform. And Zymaxis' group never numbered eleven *incantatores*, am I right?"

"You are correct," said Gaetanicus.

"Back to Caeso. At the time I did not know this, of course, I only saw a rite that had to be performed by a cabal. That linked him to

Zymaxis in my mind. Drusus, I presumed, was merely his fair-weather friend, and not involved in any of this. So on I went, and attempted to infiltrate the cabal in an attempt to expose those who killed Caeso." Another sip, and time to organise my thoughts. This was still exposition, the hard part would come later.

"In order to gain acceptance, I was asked to retrieve an item of magical value to further their cause. Exactly what, was left up to me. I had in my possession the scrolls from Ephemezica; however, while on Kebros I saw another opportunity for something that will bring great value on the markets for incantation supplies. When Aulus Paulinus the governor chose to entertain his province with games and finish off with a spectacular beast hunt for a gryphon, he saw only his future elections. Unaware of the value of organs of such mythological beasts, he had it cooked and served to his guests. Without much difficulty, I managed to put some doubts into Aulus Paulinus' mind about the edible nature of the beast, and thus got access to the carcass. I extracted a few of its valuable organs and returned to the party.

"But Aemilia here nearly exposed me. I didn't count on someone who had read the classics of natural philosophy. I was forced to deceive you," I addressed her, "for which I am very sorry. Both for being dishonest, and for how it almost led to your death." She gave me back a look I could not quite read, not hostile but with layers of meaning we men will never fathom.

"However, I am digressing in my story about Caeso. When we got back I had already missed the cabal meeting on the *Nones*, and that was perhaps for the best. It gave me time to continue my investigations here in Egretia. Now with exact knowledge of the Rite of Pelegrinus, I was able to chase down the specific ingredients that were required to complete it. Information I never shared in its entirety, not with anyone. There are special inks and ointments for the rite, you see, and they had to be purchased and prepared. Such things always leave a trail, if one knows but where to look. And indeed I managed to find this trail, amongst the less reputable merchants of supplies for incantations. It took some digging, but I found out who sold the supplies to a young man matching Caeso's description. I also managed to find Zymaxis' supplier, although what he sold Zymaxis had nothing to do with the rite. I even, after talking to the street mime again, found out about the cave at the base of the Pharos which Caeso used to create those inks and preparations for the ceremony." Another pause, to see that all present were riveted. I was presenting facts, but there were enough gaps that the ultimate conclusions could be subtly different.

"I should have realised then what was happening, yet the implications were just too hard to accept. During this time, Aemilia, as I mentioned, had been going around trying to solve the death of Caeso and prove me wrong. Being an intelligent and educated young woman, though lacking any education in *magia* nor having intimate knowledge of the circumstances of his death, she began the same route I took, by asking his friends and acquaintances and trying to piece together the last few weeks and months of Caeso's life. This was a very logical approach, but one that ultimately proved very dangerous, because as we now know, Caeso was never part of the cabal. Drusus was. Being a prospective initiate he was charged like me with providing them with a special gift. His, however, was not an open ended but a specific request. He was to supply them with a virgin sacrifice for the ceremony on the night before the *Ides*. He made an attempt on Mahatixa, the street mime whom Caeso had fallen in love with, but was foiled by her friends. Getting desperate, he was approached by Aemilia asking about Caeso's death. Thinking to deal with two problems at once, he abducted her, drugged her and brought her as his price of admission to the cabal." I saw Cornelia shuddering at the thought.

"From there we know what transpired. Cornelia asked me to help locate Aemilia, which I could not as she was shielded from magical scrying by Fufidius. I made my way to the top of Vergu, where Gaetanicus was preparing to trap all members of the cabal in the act and put an end to them. But before the ceremony or our initiation could start, Zymaxis turned on Gaetanicus, believing him the killer of Philokrates. In the ensuing battle, the cabal was destroyed.

"Drusus died that night, as did Duronius and Fufidius the *incantatores*. Zymaxis, not being a citizen, was flogged and crucified this morning. Numerius Otacilius and Rabirius the freedman will be tried for *perduellio* — high treason — and very fittingly thrown off the cliffs of Vergu to their deaths. All as it should be, yet still it does not tell us what happened to Caeso." By now I was the only one sipping his wine, the rest barely making a sound.

"My biggest problem was always how the Rite of Pelegrinus was performed without attracting attention. The rite is a lengthy process, five days and nights of chanting and channelling the energies. There are many *incantatores* in our city, almost all of whom have the *visus verum* — the true sight. Any *incantator* with his eyes open would have seen the ripples immediately, would have felt the rite being performed. I had no answer for that, even though from the details of the ceremony and his death I knew it had to have been performed here in Egretia.

"I should have picked up on this earlier. From Caeso's deteriorating physical health in the weeks before his death, from how he was the one who bought the ingredients for the inks and the rite, from how Zymaxis was always saying that the ceremony on the *Ides* was their first big move, and from how Caeso had no training in any of the branches of the *magia*. The sibyl even told me so, in as plain words as she could. I should have seen it earlier…

"Here is what happened. Last year Caeso was heartbroken over Mahatixa as only a young man can be. He stumbled upon the sibyl of the Kebric isles, or was led there by the Fates, which set him on a new path. He climbed the Mons Krodus, and the *numen* there awakened something new in him. I believe it gave him guidance and insights on how to attempt that rite all by himself. I would not hazard to guess the reasons of the forces behind such events, though I think he was shown a path which he followed closely." And therein lay my greatest issue, though none of the others saw it yet.

"When he got back to Egretia he spoke with a friend of a friend, an *incantator* at the collegium. This *incantator* was a young man who liked having the boy look up to him. They started to discuss *magia*, and by his testimony Caeso picked it up as if possessed with a great natural gift. Caeso managed to trick him, got his new friend to show him into the archives of the Collegium's library, and there he managed to abscond with a scroll for the rite. I believe that by then he knew exactly what he was looking for." I looked for a moment from Corpio to Aemilia and back, then continued with my chosen interpretation of events.

"He proceeded according to the instructions in the scroll, with modifications to enable him to achieve it all by himself. He crafted the inks and tattooed himself. This was the cause of his pale and drawn looks, what was thought to be his deteriorating health before his death, as it took him a while to complete. He then, somehow with the understanding awakened in him by the *numina*, managed to complete the ritual by himself. He used an ingenious source of power. Whereas the rite normally requires eleven initiates to channel and complete, he managed to draw it in all by himself, onto himself. This source of power was also the reason why it went unnoticed. You see, the *visus verum* lets those who have it notice the flow of energies around our world. But some spots have so much energy and are so bright, that looking at them with the sight is like looking into the sun, blinding and painful. We have such a source right here in Egretia. Caeso did his ceremony in his little cave under the Pharos, drawing on that ancient raw power to fuel it. All the *incantatores* of the Collegium, well-trained and ever-watchful, are so used to never looking directly at the Pharos with the *visus verum* lest their eyes be burnt, that the surge went unnoticed. Even if someone did observe it at that point, it would have looked like a freak lightning strike, I imagine, nothing that triggered any of the standing alarms for incantations of such power.

"And thus Caeso, seeking to heal his broken heart, was caught in the machinations of the gods. Given direction by his vision at the sibyl's, invested with the raw talent by the *numina,* acting ingeniously, he performed what no one has managed to successfully complete in centuries. Yet for all the ability and insight he was given, he was still uneducated in the traditions of magic. All his new gifts did not stack up to the years of study, and left him with a fatal flaw. He misinterpreted one of the sigils in the rite. Lacking the finer understanding, he fell for the simpler interpretation and performed his rite on the boundary between night and day, instead of performing it on a night of a lunar eclipse. So while he managed to execute one of the most complex and demanding rituals known to man, this fatal flaw of understanding spelled his end."

What remained after that was the catharsis. Corpio was wrought with tears, at the son who could not find approval for his love, and died in seeking a magical means to turn his broken heart to stone. I consoled him that as far as I could tell, Caeso was a bright lad who got caught in the power plays of the *numina*, and had no evil intentions for himself.

Cornelia and Aemilia looked relieved that it was truly over. Gnaeus Drusus *pater* was still shocked at his own son's activities. Gaetanicus, I think, was satisfied with the neat wrapping of all the loose ends.

I left them there to deal with their emotions, the closure for their loss of a son, cousin, friend. I saved them the simpler explanation for Caeso's final failure, that Corpio, by forcing Caeso to go abroad, had caused his son to hurry through the completion of the rite and he simply stumbled and executed badly one of the shortcuts and modifications that enabled him to perform it by himself — even guided by Iovis Pater himself. We could never be sure exactly what went on during his last months, so why not choose a version that would let his father heal in time, rather than break completely?

Typheus came out after me while I was getting ready to leave and handed me a heavy purse. "I trust you will find everything in order. In addition to the agreed price for your services, Cornelia has included something by way of personal thanks." He left me there, and when I looked into the purse I saw on top of the silver and gold coins the single black pearl we had found on the ship with Margaritus.

I put the sack on the loop inside my tunic and was about to leave, when Aemilia came in. We were standing alone in the atrium, next to the shimmering pool. The reflected light danced in her eyes as she said, "Thank you for giving solace to my uncle. I also never got to thank you for rescuing me." She stepped closer to me, stood on her toes and kissed my cheek. "But don't let that make you think I like you," she added with a smile, turned, and walked back inside.

And suddenly, very unexpectedly, my heart felt something I had thought lost since that night I found Helena's mutilated body in the well.

~ Finis ~

I hope that you have enjoyed this book. If you have, please consider supporting the author by leaving a review on Amazon.com and Goodreads.

There is nothing more important to an author, than reviews!

Join Felix and the others in the next instalment of his adventures, In Numina, or visit egretia.com for short stories and news.

AUTHOR'S NOTES

Following are some notes about the culture of Egretia and the adaptations I have made to the Roman world.

While the Egretian society borrows heavily from that of ancient Rome, please remember that this is primarily a fantasy novel and do not take it as an accurate reflection of historical reality. I have conflated many aspects from over a millennium of Kings, Republic and Empire. The calendar and gods, for example, reflect the earliest known versions, while the legions and circus games are definitely from the imperial period.

For example, an aspect I twisted to fit my needs are the *fetiales*. The real *fetiales* were priests of Jupiter as the patron of good faith, and acted on foreign affairs. They were not spies or special forces, however; I mixed the old religious institution of the *fetiales* with the late empire's *areani* and *frumentarii*. Similarly, the *augurs* were a priestly college devoted to the interpretation of the will of the gods, not magicians specialising in divination. All this is tied together with some atrocious pig Latin. Except the swear words — those are mostly authentic.

In fact, more information about the origins of the concepts and words in this book can be found with a web search. There is only one made-up term, the title of Rhone. I just could not find an appropriate word that sounded good in both Latin and English, and would have the appearance of high rank. When making up the word, I actually went with a more Greek-sounding word, rather than a Latin-sounding one. That is an allusion to the mix of many elements of Alexandria into Egretia.

I have also used the names of some real-world ancient authors — Antoninus Liberalis, Nikander, Plautus. And as with the other Latin terms, I have twisted their writings from mythological tales to actual monsters. Praxiteles is, of course, an historical Greek sculptor; art is eternal.

One topic I was careful to avoid in this book was the age-old struggle between the Patricians and Plebeians. This subject is alluded to in the way Zymaxis and his cabal rail against the "old guard". This may come up in future books, but I felt it was not needed for the plot here.

The Collegia and the Senate

Rome had many colleges. These were sodalities — fraternities and associations of various kinds. When integrating the magical aspect of Egretia into the Roman-like society, I took a similar approach. The *incantatores* are organised into five main schools, according to their speciality.

I did, however, take this organisation further. Training to be an *incantator* requires a lot of instruction. That led to the colleges taking on a teaching aspect, something that wasn't a part of the ancient Roman colleges. And, of course, if the magicians can do it, why can't the military? That led to a profound change in the social structure of Egretia over Roman culture.

There are four main colleges in Egretia: that of magicians (*incantatores*), that of the military (*militum* — soldiers), that of merchants (*mercatorum*) and that of priests (*sacrorum*). The college of merchants was needed to balance the military and magic ones, and the college of priests, relegated to a minor position, is there to collect all the many and varied priesthoods under an easy umbrella.

Each of the main colleges is divided into five main branches, and teaches aspirants as cadets. In some cases (soldiers, merchants) this is training for the elite — foot-soldiers just get basic training to go about their business, and small merchants can operate anywhere.

In the case of the *incantatores*, however, this is primarily where they learn their craft. Other cultures around Nuremata (the continent on which Egretia is located) have differing ideas about how to approach the *magia*. This is alluded to in Felix's talks with Akhirabus; nothing about magic is ever concrete or absolute.

These colleges are professional organisations. There is still the Senate, which controls Egretia in terms of legislation. In this novel I have glossed over many aspects of the complex political structure of the Roman republic, with its various assemblies and who-got-what-powers in regards to passing laws and controlling the courts throughout the years. The main point here is that the Senate is a political body, its members restricted in their other activities. To create some more tension and social mobility, I have extended the *cursus honorum* to include postings within the collegia. More on that in future novels.

Gods and Numina

The gods of Egretia are modelled after the ancient Roman *numina* — the faceless divinities. This corresponds to the older Roman view, before Hellenisation became popular and gods appeared in more human form.

Ancient Romans were notoriously superstitious. Their view of religion was that it was contractual — they performed the rites, and the gods fulfilled their part. Instead, I mixed in some Greek philosophy about the nature and existence of gods. I felt that the advent of controllable magic in the world would make the learned adopt a more atheistic outlook, leading to a different kind of clash between the educated and the masses.

Of the *numina* mentioned in this book, I have also used the ancient Roman names rather than the later renditions.

To aid in understanding, the triad of three main gods:
- Iovis Pater — the old name for what later became Jupiter; the main patron god of Egretia
- Mars Pater — Father Mars, god of war, but also the protec-

tor of fields and agriculture
- Quirinus — god of the people of Egretia (*Quirites*); In Rome, originally a Sabine entity that came to represent the people of Rome. Of a military nature, in Rome he later became an aspect of Mars; in Egretia, they are still separate deities.

Other important *numina* mentioned in the book:
- Fortuna — goddess of luck and fortune
- Neptunus — Neptune, god of the seas
- Vesta — goddess of the hearth
- Vulcan — god of earth and metals
- Dis — god of the underworld, and also the place where the shades of the dead go
- Lares — many gods of homes, places, families, crossroads
- Di Penates — gods of the pantry
- Anna Perenna — goddess of the year

As can be seen, the Egretians have every bit as many gods and superstitions as the Romans had, and see gods and presences that control their life everywhere. The difference is that Egretians live in a fantasy world, where these presences might be real — a matter hotly debated between the common folks and the *incantatores*.

Calendar

The Egretian calendar is based on the old (pre-Romulan) Roman calendar. There were ten months, of 30 or 31 days, and a period of unassigned days between years called Intercalaris. The first five months were named after important gods, while the rest were named positionally.

The month names are:
- Martius — 31 days — named after the *numen* Mars
- Avrilis — 30 days — named after the *numen* Fortuna Virilis
- Maius — 31 days — named after the *numen* Maia
- Iunius — 30 days — named after the *numen* Iuno (Juno)

- Quirinalis — 31 days — named after the *numen* Quirinus (In Rome it was positional — Quinctilis)
- Sextilis — 30 days — sixth month
- September — 30 days — seventh month
- October — 31 days — eighth month
- November — 30 days — ninth month
- December — 30 days — tenth month
- Intercalaris — 61 days, variable due to leap years

The Egretian year, like the Roman year, is solar-based, while the months are lunar. The year starts with Martius on the first new moon before the spring equinox and finishes on the last day of the moon after the winter solstice. Intercalaris then falls in the "mid-winter" period between the winter solstice and the following spring equinox.

Like the Romans, Egretians count back from specific days of the months.
- *Kalends* is the first of the month
- *Nones* — ninth day before the *Ides* — is either on the 7th of the month (Martius, Maius, Quirinalis and October) or the 5th on "short" months
- *Ides* is either on the 15th on long months or on the 13th on short months

The Egretians do not have the concept of a week, but have a similar rhythm with market days held every eight days.

Our story thus begins on the day after the *Kalends* of *Avrilis*, or the second of April by modern counting. Felix leaves for Ephemezica five days before the *Ides* of *Avrilis* (April 9), and returns from Kebros on the *Nones* of *Maius* (May 7).

The day is divided into twelve daylight hours and twelve night hours. Because the division is the same year round, the length of the hour changes with the seasons. On the winter solstice (shortest day) a daylight hour is only about 45 modern minutes, while on the summer solstice (longest day) a daylight hour is about one hour and fifteen modern minutes. The sixth hour is always midday or midnight.

Obscure References

There are a few homages strewn throughout the book. They deserve a special mention, with my sincere thanks to their originators.

The firm of Gordius et Falconius
Refers to my two favourite detectives from ancient Rome: Gordianus the Finder by Steven Saylor, and Marcus Didius Falco by Lindsey Davis. Both are series of books, telling the stories of hardboiled private detectives in ancient Rome.

Gordianus lives in the first century BCE, and watches the major events in the decline of the Roman Republic.

Falco operates in the time of Vespasian, and Davis does a wonderful job of exploring many aspects of life in the early empire.

Aulus Paulinus and the quote about shepherds and shepherdesses
These come from the British sitcom *Chelmsford 123*. I still watch re-runs every few years, and it still makes me laugh every time. If you can find a copy, do yourself a favour and watch it.

Scenes on the Pharos and Cloacina
The scenes depicted on the Pharos in Chapter II are the Egretian version of some early Roman history. For example, Junius Brutus was the founder of the republic (having thrown out the last of the kings — not by being a magician), and Servilius Ahala killed Maelius who wanted to become king of Rome again, not Athanasios ("un-dying") the necromancer.

As for Cloacina — yes, she was the Roman goddess of the sewers, and yes, she was also the protector of marital sexual relations. I could not make this stuff up!

Larks' Tongues in Aspic
One of my favourite King Crimson albums. With dishes like that, who wouldn't want to sample the Egretian cooking? The rest of the dishes and food in the book are mostly authentic Roman cuisine,

with the exception of the sunflower seeds, which were not known in Rome at the time. *Garum* was an important Roman condiment, though *liquamen* is just a term used later and not a different grade of sauce.

Shakespeare, Star Trek and other pop-culture icons
One reference each, but if they didn't make you groan when you read the book I won't point them out now.

More of Felix
Felix and the others return in the next novel in the series, In Numina. Please visit **www.egretia.com** for more information, including short stories, news, an expanded glossary and high resolution maps.

GLOSSARY

Aedile one of the civil servant posts in the Senate (as opposed to the *collegia*). Aediles were responsible for maintenance of public buildings, regulation of public festivals, and enforcing public order.

Anna Perenna goddess of the cyclical year. Her festival was held on the *Ides* (15th) of March.

Aqua an aqueduct (literally, water).

Aqua Sextiae the main aqueduct of Egretia, bringing fresh water from six sacred springs in the foothills on the mountains to the west and cascading the waters throughout the city.

Augur an *incantator* specialising in augury, the branch of *magia* concerned with divination, prognostication and clairvoyance.

Aureus a gold coin, worth 25 *denarii*.

Avrilis the second month of the Egretian year.

Bestiarius a gladiator trained to fight wild beasts.

Bireme a war galley with two banks of oars.

Cack shit. Not proper Latin (which would be *cacat*), but I like the four-letter expletive nature of the word.

Campus (pl. *Campi)* a flat expanse of ground.

Canicula female dog.

Capsa (pl. *Capsae)* a special box or large bucket used to hold scrolls.

Century the smallest unit in the legions, 80 fighting men and 20 non-combatants. Six centuries make a cohort, and ten cohorts make a legion. Each group of eight soldiers in a century tent and mess together, and have a mule cart and non-combatants assigned to them.

Centurion the commander of a century. The most senior and able soldier. Their ranks do not correspond to the modern non-commissioned officers. Rather, centurions were the effective field commanders, while the general with his legates and tribunes were the strategic and administrative leadership. There were some 60 *centoriones* in a legion, ranked by seniority within each cohort and across the legion.

Cestus a gladiator trained to use his fists. In fights they usually wore spiked brass gloves.

Circus the arena where games and races were held.

Citocacia stink-weed, a mild insult.

Client in the Egretian social order, a client pledged himself to a patron. His oath was to serve the interests and wishes of his patron, and is return he was granted favours and assistance. The obligations could be to vote according to the patron's wishes or fulfil other tasks, and the favours could be money or assistance in being elected to public office, as examples.

Clivus (pl. *Clivi)* a slope of a hill or mountain. Often used as part of a street name, for streets on a steep incline.

Cloaca (pl. *Cloacae*) sewer drains. The Cloaca Maxima are the main sewage lines that run under Egretia.

Cloacina the divinity of the sewers, and also the protector of sexual intercourse in marriage. Her shrine was next to the Forum, close to an intersection of the major sewage lines.

Cognomen the third name of a person, often a nickname but also inherited to distinguish branches of the same *gens* (see below). For example, in the case of Spurius Vulpius Felix, the *cognomen Felix* means 'lucky' and was given to him; with Marcus Quinctius Corpio, the Corpio *cognomen* is inherited from father to son in the ancient *gens Quinctia,* and their branch would be known (in plural) as the *Quinctii Corpiones.*

Cohort the main tactical unit of a legion, composed of six centuries, or about 480 fighting men and 120 non-combatants at full strength.

Collegium (pl. *Collegia*) a college, an association.

Collegium Incantatorum college of sorcerers.

Collegium Mercatorum college of merchants.

Collegium Militum college of soldiers.

Compitalia the annual festival in honour of the *lares*, those of the home, of the crossroads and the public *lares* of Egretia.

Cunnus (pl. *Cunni*) cunt.

Consul the highest-ranking elected public official. They were the executives of the Senate. Two consuls were elected yearly, and served from one Martius to the next.

Contio (pl. *Contiones*) an assembly, often of a political nature.

Convivium a banquet or feast.

Curia an assembly hall, usually in reference to the Senate.

Cursus Honorum the "course of offices", a sequential order of public offices held by aspiring politicians. In Egretia it includes public offices within the Senate and within the colleges. One could be a *quaestor* in a particular college and use it as an admission for the Senate, rather than stand election as a public *quaestor*, however that was not common due to the business restrictions imposed on senators.

Denarius (pl. *Denarii*). A silver coin, worth four *sestertii*.

Dimachaerus (pl. *Dimachaeri*) a gladiator wielding two short, curved swords, one held in each hand. They wore only metal greaves on both arms and light helmets, and were quite mobile. They were thus pitted against heavier opponents such as *myrmillones*.

Dis god of the underworld, both richness of soil and minerals and of the dead. Also the name of the place where the shades of the dead go.

Dominus master. Female: *domina*. When talking to a person, the case **'domine'** is used.

Domus a private house or home, usually in the city. Country houses are usually referred to as villas.

Elementor an *incantator* who specialised in manipulating the six elements of *magia*.

Ephemezica a large city-state in Hellica. Refer to the maps in the beginning of the book or online.

Evocatus (pl. *Evocati*) a soldier who had served out his time and obtained a discharge but then voluntarily enlisted again at the invitation of the consul or other commander.

Fascinum the embodiment of the divine phallus. Charms made in the image of a winged penis and testicles were used to ward off the 'evil eye'.

Fellator one who performs oral sex; used as verbal abuse. Felix's favourite curse, *fellator assini*, is one who performs oral sex on donkeys.

Felix lucky.

Forum a public open space. Most *fora* (plural) would have had many public structures associated with them — from small buildings to large temples on the edges, with altars, fountains and plinths for statues in their midst.

Forum Bovarium meat markets.

Forum Egretium the heart of Egretia, where the main buildings and administrative centres lie, and where the population gathers to hear and discuss news and laws.

Forum Frumentarium grain markets. In Egretia it also doubles as the Forum Holitorium — the vegetable and oil markets. This is where the public grain is stored; private merchants might have other stores and shops throughout the city.

Forum Piscarium fish markets. Considering the maritime nature of the Egretian culture, fish and fish products (like *garum*) were a significant staple.

Garum fermented fish sauce. In Rome this was done with fish meat and guts fermented with salt. The addition of cuttlefish and the distinction of grades based on it is a purely Egretian thing.

Gens (pl. *Gentes*) a family or clan, all the members sharing the same *nomen gentilucum* (second name). For example, Marcus Quinctius Corpio belongs to the gens Quinctia.

Gladiator a combatant who fights for the entertainment of the crowds. Mostly men (though there were women gladiatrices and other curiosities), mostly slaves or criminals given this as an alternative to exile or death. Because of the high training costs, a gladiator had to want to become one, and fights were rarely to the death. Traditionally, gladiatorial games were part of funeral rites, but in recent years as their popularity has grown, any excuse will do to display a good match.

Some gladiators achieve celebrity status and are used for more private entertainment. Those who survive five years or thirty matches are usually given their freedom, though they suffer from social stigmas (as well as any other debilitating injuries they may have sustained).

Gladius the short straight sword favoured by the Egretians.

Gryphon a legendary creature with the body, tail, and back legs of a lion; the head and wings of an eagle; and an eagle's talons as its front feet.

Hellica a region to the East of Egretia known for its high art, philosophical predilections, and almost constant warring between its city-states. Named after the river Helios and the largest city-state of the region.

Heraclion a large city-state in Hellica, sitting on a promontory on the eastern gate to the Bay of Euxis. It is the on the border between the primarily Egretian regions to the west and Hellican regions to the east.

Hoplomachus (pl. *Hoplomachi*) a type of gladiator, armed with a small round shield, a spear and a dagger, and wearing padded greaves on his legs and right arm. As the *hoplomachi* are lightly armoured and more mobile, they are commonly pitted against the heavier but slower *myrmillones*.

Hyperboreans mythological people who live far to the north, beyond the home of Boreas, the north wind.

Ides the middle of the month, either the 13th or the 15th depending on the number of days in the month. See notes.

Insula (pl. *Insulae*) literally an island, the term is used also for the large tenement houses. These houses are single structures with lanes all around them separating them from other buildings, hence "islands".

Irrumator the receiver of oral sex. Used as verbal abuse less offensive than 'Fellator' (q.v.).

Intercalaris the period between the last month of the year, December, and the first month of the new year, Martius. It was of variable length, 60 or 61 days. See author's notes about the calendar.

Kalends the first day of the month. See notes.

Lamia (pl. *Lamiae*) a monster, sometimes depicted with the lower body of a snake, reputed to eat children.

Lanista the owner and trainer of gladiators.

Legion the smallest independent army unit that can wage a war. Made up of 10 cohorts, or about 4,800 fighting men and 1,200 non-combatants. The non-combatants included engineers, artillery operators, and — in Egretia — military incantatores.

Libitina the Egretian goddess of funeral and burial. Her temple is outside the city walls in a sacred grove. Undertakers have their offices there (or in the street of the embalmers), and are known as *libitinarii*. Her temple holds records of all funerals in the city.

Loggia a covered exterior gallery or corridor, usually on an upper level, with the outer wall open to the elements and the roof supported by a series of columns.

Ludi games or festivals. Traditionally, games include chariot races and wrestling or boxing matches — not gladiatorial games. The gladiatorial games are reserved for funeral rites, but in recent years they have started to make it into general games under the flimsiest of excuses, as a way for politicians to attract the crowds.

Ludi Florae known also as the Floralia, these games are dedicated to the goddess Flora. The festival has a licentious, pleasure-seeking atmosphere, and features many theatrical performances.

Ludi Megalenses see *Megalenses Ludi*.

Magia the magical energy that permeates the world of Egretia. Its nature is a topic much debated amongst the philosophers.

Magia Elementi elemental magic, according to the classification of the Collegium Incantatorum. There were six recognised elements.

Magia Inanitas magic of the empty spaces. The most mind-bending of all branches.

Magia Vita life magic, pertaining to living things.

Magia Vita Terminalis magic of the end of life, a proscribed branch of the *magia vita.*

Magister (pl. *Magistri)* expert.

Magistri Carneum literally "masters of the flesh" — physicians and healers, but with education in *magia vita.*

Maior greater; when applied to siblings it means the elder.

Martius the first month of the Egretian year. Begins on the first new moon before the spring equinox. Named after Mars, the god of war and an agricultural guardian, for the beginning of the agricultural and military campaign year).

Megalenses Ludi the Megalensian games, dedicated to the great mother. These were not the usual circus games, but contained many theatre plays and much dining and carousing in good nature. The great mother herself was an import to Egretian culture from the far east. Her priests were eunuchs and her main worshippers were women.

Mentula (pl. *Mentulae*) the primary word for a penis. Used as an insult, it would translate to prick, dick.

Mentulam caco a common form of verbal abuse. Literally, "I shit on your dick".

Minor lesser; when applied to siblings it means the younger.

Moecha a slut.

Mons a tall hill or a mountain.

Montes a mountain range.

Mulsum wine sweetened with honey; often spiced as well.

Myrmillo (pl. *Myrmillones*) a heavily armed gladiator, bearing a large square shield in the left hand, a metal sleeve and *gladius* (short sword) in the right, and a metal greave on the left leg. Their biggest distinction is the heavy helmet stylised as a fish head.

Nefas religiously forbidden, against divine law.

Nefastum scientiam forbidden or dangerous knowledge.

Nobilitas "the known", those people and families who have achieved a public standing. Even though this is the root for English 'nobility', the term is not quite the same and does not equate with modern perception of aristocracy. A family would be considered part of the nobilitas when a member achieved fame, became a *nobilis*. Usually, this meant by attaining a consulship, although other cases are known. Contrast to *Novus Homo* below.

Nones the fifth or seventh of the month. See notes.

Novus Homo (pl. *Homines Novi*) a "new man". The first of a family to be elected into the Senate and attain a high position (properly a consul, but colloquially also applies to praetors and rhones).

Officius the first (lowest) grade of public official within the colleges. It was not part of the *cursus honorum*.

Parilia a spring festival, dedicated to preserving the purity of sheep and shepherds.

Pedere fart.

Pharos a lighthouse. It usually refers to the great lighthouse of Egretia.

Phrylia an important Hellican city-state.

Pons a bridge.

Porta a gate in the city walls.

Praenomen the first name of a person, e.g. Gaius, Marcus etc. Note that women do not have a praenomen, but are named after the *gens* (family name). There were only about thirty-odd names, of which about half accounted for the vast majority of the population.

In this book, I went with the later spelling of G in Gaius, Gnaeus etc., rather than C (Caius, Cnaeus), and Caeso instead of Kaeso, as there is some debate about the truly old forms, and they are less familiar. I did use 'I' instead of 'J' for Iunius (Junius), Iovis (Jove) etc. These spellings reflect the Roman world of the late Republic.

Praetor a high-ranking public official, second to the consuls. There are normally six praetors elected each year.

Princeps Senatus the first senator, the leader of the house.

Perduellio high treason, punishable by death.

Pyxis (pl. *Pyxidae*) a small box with a close-fitting lid, often used to store women's cosmetics or other creams and unguents.

Quadran a very small copper coin, worth 1/40th of a *denarius* (or 1/10 of a *sestertius*).

Quaestor a low-ranking official. The first rung in the *cursus honorum*.

Quirite the language of the people of Egretia.

Quirites (plural) the citizens of Egretia. Based on the old word for spear (*quiris*), and was used in Rome as well to refer to citizens.

Res magiae literally, "a thing of magic".

Retiarius a gladiator trained to fight with a weighted net and a trident. His only armour is a padded greave on the left arm. The *reiarii* are highly mobile warriors, and thus often pitted against the heavily armed but slower gladiators. At first it seems like they were under-classed, but the development of the *secutor* as an enhanced *myrmillo* shows that they needed to be better balanced.

Rhone a made-up word. In Egretian, *rhonus*. Equivalent to a Roman *aedile*, with the senior rhone of each collegium — the *primus rhonus* — equal to a praetor in terms of rank, if not civil authority. As mentioned in the notes, the word has a Greek — rather than Latin — feel to it, as a way to allude to the Alexandrian influences on Egretia.

Rudis the referee in gladiator games, named after his staff.

Secutor a variation of the *myrmillo*, this gladiator was developed specifically to fight against *retiarii*. Wearing essentially the same armour and weapons, a *secutor*'s helmet is smooth to prevent the net from catching on it, and provides full coverage except for two round holes for the eyes, to protect against the prongs of the trident.

Semi a small bronze coin, worth half a *sestertius* (or 1/8th of a *denarius*).

Sestertius (pl. *Sestertii*) a common bronze coin. One quarter of a *denarius*. The price of a meal.

Stadium (pl. *Stadia*) 600 feet, or about 180 meters.

Stercus shit.

Stigma originally (in Latin) a hot mark tattooed (branded) on runaway slaves. In Egretia it means a tattoo of magical power.

Strigil a curved tool, often made of metal, used to scrape dirt and sweat off the body during Egretian baths. A person would have his body rubbed with oil, and then scraped with the strigil to remove the oil and the dirt. Only then would the person move to the hot baths to soak.

Stola the female equivalent of the toga, it was the traditional garment for women. Made from linen.

Stultus stupid person, idiot.

Sub Rosa literally, 'under the rose', a symbol of sworn secrecy.

Tablinum the office of the master of the house, usually connecting the atrium at the front with the peristyle garden at the back of the house.

Talent a measurement based on how much a man can carry, roughly 30 kg (66 lbs). Often used to measure large sums of money or bullion. A talent of silver *denarii* contains 6,250 coins (equivalent to 25,000 *sestertii*) and would be enough to pay the salaries of a cohort of soldiers for a month.

Triclinium a formal dining room, with three long couches arranged in a U shape. The men reclined, while women sat on chairs facing them. Long low tables in front of each couch were set to hold the food and drinks. In recent times and with looser company, women have started to recline together with the men.

Veneficitor an *incantator* who specialises in the Veneficium branch of the Collegium Incantatorum.

Veneficium the study of herbs and poisons and the properties and methods thereof. Part of the classification of magic according to the Collegium Incantatorum.

Via a main road.

Vicus a main street.

Vigiles the watchmen in Egretia, tasked with firefighting and basic police work.

Vinalia a festival dedicated to wine gardens and vintage, held on April 23. Another Vinalia, the Vinalia Rustica, was held on August 19 for the grape pressing.

Visus verum true sight.